THE DEAD LORD

Had there been less light, Christopher would not have been able to identify the corpse draped across the back of the wagon. But when he saw the cross-bow bolt, still buried in the blue neck . . .

"A hunting party found him deep in the wood," the wagon driver said. "Do you know who this is?"

Christopher stiffened. *Know him? I served him!*

"This is Lord Woodward! One of Arthur's own battle knights! Sir Lancelot wants me to take the body to the king himself."

And the king will think I killed him. . . .

BOOKS BY PETER TELEP

SPACE: ABOVE AND BEYOND

SQUIRE TRILOGY:

SQUIRE
SQUIRE'S BLOOD
SQUIRE'S HONOR

Published by HarperPaperbacks

SQUIRE'S HONOR

BOOK THREE OF THE SQUIRE TRILOGY

PETER TELEP

HarperPrism
An Imprint of HarperPaperbacks

HarperPaperbacks   *A Division of* HarperCollins*Publishers*
10 East 53rd Street, New York, N.Y. 10022

Cover illustration by Jim Burns

First printing: January 1996

Printed in the United States of America

HarperPrism is an imprint of HarperPaperbacks. HarperPaperbacks, HarperPrism, and colophon are trademarks of HarperCollins*Publishers.*

❖ 10 9 8 7 6 5 4 3 2 1

SQUIRE'S HONOR
is for Nancy

ACKNOWLEDGMENTS

I am particularly indebted to Eyal Goldshmid, Georgia Howorth-Fair, Peter Ives, Christopher McClelland, Kip McGuire, Herb Middlemass, and Jim Poppino for their work on the prologue and first chapter of this novel.

My editor, Christopher Schelling, my agent, Robert Drake, and my best reader (and wonderful writer herself) Joan Vander Putten, were there for me on this one—as they were on the first and second volumes. I know of no more comforting feeling in the world than to have the guidance and support of friends such as these.

Associate editor Caitlin Deinard Blasdell had patient answers to my sometimes naive questions and was never too busy to talk to me. She's a rare find in our world of answering machings and voice mail.

Though I know Sara Schwager only through her blue copyeditor's pencil, I would be deeply remiss if I did not thank her for the excellent work she did on all three volumes of the *Squire* series. She forced me to look at etymologies and ironed the wrinkles out of my prose, much to the betterment of the manuscripts.

Rose and Vincent Palladino provided me with a roof over my head so that I would not have to write this novel in the rain. That helped! They have been much more than in-laws, and they have my love and deepest respect.

AUTHOR'S NOTE

The Arthurian legend contains many anachronisms and contradictions that are maddening to writers who wish to be technically and historically accurate. While the military strategy, accoutrements, and politics were carefully researched, some were borrowed from other time periods for dramatic effect. The sailing vessels known as *cogs* in this novel are actually late twelfth century German merchantmen used by a group of traders known as the Hansa League. I chose the Hansa League's cogs because they not only suited the plot well, but I had a plethora of photos on which to base my descriptions. The port of Blytheheart, probably my favorite locale in the world of *Squire*, is purely fictional and only loosely based on several British ports of the period. With these details aside, lean back, quibble if you must, but most of all, I hope you enjoy this third volume of the *Squire Trilogy*.

Peter Telep

PROLOGUE

Christopher weaved into the dense maze of tree trunks. The early evening storm had birthed in the wood a rank scent that reminded him of a foul well. He knew he should not complain about the smell of the forest, for if the forest had a nose, he knew he wouldn't smell very good to it, either.

He forged on, and despite his rustling and the millionscore sounds of the droplets wrestling through leaf and limb, an unsettling silence pervaded. It was a silence within him, a feeling that someone was near. He came upon a fallen beech tree that lay in his path. He lowered his gaze, stepped over it, then heard the approach of someone or something come from ahead.

"Ho! Squire!" Though Christopher recognized the voice, there was something odd about it, a peculiarity he could not identify. He moved forward, then shifted around a tree.

The forest opened up into a wide clearing, and Lord Woodward stood on the opposite side of it, facing him. Christopher moved uneasily toward his new master.

Woodward's gray hair was wet and disheveled, and his beard looked as if it had not been trimmed in a moon or two. The knight fingered the hem of his blue-and-white surcoat, which he wore over a linen shirt. He pulled the garment down in an effort to remove the wrinkles from it. Christopher judged the act as futile. The removal of the wrinkles in his surcoat did little to better Woodward's appearance. A burst of lightning picked out the knight's eyes, which were narrowed by what might be anger. Darkness gathered around Woodward, but Christopher dismissed the image. It was only in his mind. It had to be.

Christopher reached the edge of the clearing, then took cover under a nearby tree limb. "Lord, I've come as ordered." He gestured with a hand to their surroundings, then, with a frown, added, "But wouldn't a tent near the ramparts have been drier?"

Woodward rested his palms on the balled hilts of the spathas sheathed at his sides, then he stepped away from the pair of overhanging limbs buffering him from the storm. He moved into the center of the clearing. He ignored the rain that washed over him. "A tent back there would not have been as private for our conversation."

"What is it, my lord?" Christopher swallowed, then breathed deeply.

"Come here. Into the clearing."

While biting the inside of his cheek, Christopher felt his heart beat a stroke much harder than it had before. The rain stung his head as he moved into the open. Water dribbled into his eyes. A chill wreaked havoc with his spine, then fanned out across his shoulders. He stopped an arm's length away from the knight.

"That's better, boy," Woodward said. "Men talk this way."

Christopher could smell Woodward's breath; it was soured by ale. Now it was evident why they stood like dolts in the rain. Drunk men talk this way.

"It's cold," Christopher blurted out.

With an uncoordinated wave of his hand, and the volume of his voice a notch too loud, Woodward said, "Pay nature no heed. Heed *me*. He belched. "The rumors about you that have pierced my ears make it impossible for me to sleep." The banner knight took a step forward, putting his face only a finger's length away from Christopher's. "Are the rumors true, boy?"

I am a true servant, to my heart, to my mind, and to God. It is my destiny. And my fate.

He fought to keep his gaze on Woodward as a muscle in his neck twitched. He wanted to look away, to run away from everything. But he kept on looking, and Woodward's stare gored him with the efficiency of a well-honed glaive.

"I want an answer, boy! I demand one!" Thunder had clapped during Woodward's shout, but even the unsettled heavens had not stifled the knight's words.

Christopher found it hard to breathe, hard to stand. The moment threatened to choke the life out of him. What could he say? What could he do? He feigned innocence. "I don't know what it is —"

"How does a saddlemaker's son like yourself become a squire to banner knights? How does filth like you get loose among us? Do you know that the word had traveled with a courser's speed? How long did you think it would take until it reached me? All of those moons you had been lying to me! And to think at one time I had asked you to watch over Marigween! My God, boy. I had been betrothed to her. How could you have done it? Knowingly? How could you have had a child with her? And out of wedlock, no less? And all of it behind my back!"

He knew that this moment was a part of his punishment for disobeying the king. He had saved his friend Doyle from the hands of Seaver, but in order to do that he had betrayed Arthur's trust. Thus, Arthur had stripped him of his duty as squire of the body, squire to the king, and had given him to Woodward. Christopher

had suspected that Arthur had done it to teach him a
lesson, and to give him ample opportunity to confess his
sin to Woodward.

Where did those opportunities go?

Christopher stood, armed only with an apology on the
tip of his tongue. Death was a heartbeat into the future.

Woodward took a few steps back, then clumsily withdrew both spathas from their scabbards at his side.

"My lord, this cannot happen. I beseech you. I ask for
mercy and forgiveness. There is another way!"

"No! Fight!" Woodward tossed the sword in his right
hand.

Christopher stepped out of the sword's path and let it
splash into a puddle behind him.

"Pick it up!"

"I will not." Christopher had known from the first
time he had kissed Marigween that a confrontation with
Woodward would come. He had invented a millionscore
ways to blanket the fact, and had justified what he had
done an equal number of times.

But now he knew bedding Marigween had been
wrong. It had been against the church. It had been
against the codes of knight- and squirehood. It had
been lust. And then it had been love. And now they had
a son, a son that Woodward probably felt should be his
own. The relationship had been founded on deception.
And Christopher had not only betrayed Arthur and
Woodward, but his first love, Brenna. He had cast her
aside for Marigween, and now felt as if he had betrayed
himself. The great error he had made by courting
Marigween now stood before him, six feet of sword-
clenching fury.

I have forsaken the truth.

"Everyone knows what you've done, Christopher!
And now your cry for mercy is a confession to me,"
Woodward screamed. "I doubt even the king would

blame me for slaying you. Pick up the spatha. And let God be the judge of what you've done."

"My lord, God has already judged me. I have since suffered the loss of my rank, the loss of one of my friends, and the loss of someone else close to me. I pray now for your mercy."

"Thanks to Saint George you will not be my squire! You've a yellow belly! And you've one last thing to lose."

He refused to let Woodward's words goad him into combat. He leveled his gaze on the banner knight and tightened his lips. He listened to the drone of the rain, to the sound of Woodward's panting, to his own ragged breath. Then a crack of thunder startled him.

"Nothing to say? Well then, you *are* a coward. A boy of evil. And you deserve to die." Woodward pulled back his arm, then lowered his spatha until it was horizontal and ready to run Christopher through. Then Woodward closed the gap.

Christopher shot a look to the other spatha lying in the puddle. Even if the weapon was within reach, he figured he wouldn't have put it to much use against a knight of Woodward's skill. A voice inside told him to turn and run; another one argued to stay and die, to meet the fate he had brought upon himself. Was it fear or guilt or a growing sense of hopelessness that tingled within him? Or was it a sickening blend of all of those things? His world would end soon. But was there atonement in death?

He wasn't going to find out. He turned, dug his right boot into the earth, about to —

Fwit!

"AHHHHHH —"

Christopher stopped, then cocked his head.

Woodward lay supine on the forest floor, an unmarked crossbow bolt half-buried in his neck. His arms and legs writhed spasmodically. His eyes were wide, locked open in the blank stare Christopher had seen all too many times on the faces of dead men.

Fearing he might be the bowman's next target, Christopher dropped to the slimy earth. His chest reverberated from the impact. He looked up, focused his gaze on the low-lying brambles from where he sensed the bolt had come. No movement. Not a single rustle.

Christopher's breath slowed and grew even. He called out to the bushes several times. As moments passed, he grew cold and stiff and frustrated. Then he made the decision that whoever had fired the bolt was gone. He rose, his gaze on the brambles, but there was still no movement from within them. He wiped his muddy hands on his shirt, then flipped his hair off his forehead. He moved to Woodward, then paused to stare grimly at the dead knight. Once again, he looked to the brambles; then it dawned on him. He would be blamed. He closed his eyes as tight as he could, tossed his head back, clenched his teeth, then prepared to scream, a cry he knew would rise above the din of the storm.

PART ONE

HEIR TO MURDER

1

Above the eastern wood, the gray sky conceded to the deeper hue of night. Below, windswept tree limbs and shadows of branches mingled into one, making it hard for Christopher to see as he ran through the forest. He slipped on a bed of acorns and strayed into a bramble. His linen leggings tore open, and the tiny thorns of the bramble found his damp skin below. He paused to inspect the wound. There were a few thin cuts across his calf. He swore off the damage and moved on.

Have to keep moving. Have to.

He could not stop asking himself who had killed Woodward and why? Had it been someone out to save him from Woodward's blade, or someone trying to see him hang from the gallows tree for Woodward's murder? If the murderer was a friend trying to help, he had inadvertently become a foe. If the murderer was an enemy, then who? There were many senior squires who had despised Christopher because of his swift ascension to the rank of squire of the body, and they had rejoiced when he had lost that rank. Could one of them have wanted to see him suffer further? Who? There were more than a score of senior squires.

Then there was the question of what to tell Arthur. But what was he doing now? Was he running from the place of a crime or running to get help?

Christopher hadn't decided that yet. It depended on how guilty he felt he was, or rather, how guilty he felt

the others would think he was. He reached up, bent a
wiry limb out of his way, ducked under it a bit, and continued.

He thought about the murder, about his part in it,
about his defense. Christopher did not own a crossbow,
but that meant nothing. The bolt was unmarked and the
murder weapon would never be positively identified.
His accusers would say he borrowed or stole a bow,
then hid it after he shot Woodward.

The person who killed Woodward obviously had known
about the meeting. That person had killed the banner
knight out of hatred for Christopher, or out of love.

Which of his friends knew?

There was Neil. The stubby archer had become a
trusted friend after Doyle had been banished.
Christopher had not believed he would ever get as close
to another friend as he had been to Doyle, but Neil's
warmth and consideration, along with his admiration,
had made Christopher think otherwise. Yes, Neil was a
longbowman, and probably as handy with a crossbow,
but if Neil had killed Woodward, why hadn't he come
into the clearing? Had he been too scared?

Orvin knew about the meeting. Yes, the old knight
was at his camp on the ramparts near the castle of
Shores. Orvin had warned Christopher to temper his
distrust of Woodward. He had urged Christopher to listen to the battle lord, and to confess his crime to the
man. Despite his eccentricities, Orvin was a wise man.
Could he have killed Woodward? His hand was not too
wizened to squeeze the trigger of a crossbow. He would
have done it to help Christopher, of course. Yet he
would have come into the clearing and admitted his
wrongdoing; Christopher was certain of that.

Who had Woodward told about the meeting?
Christopher could only guess. Perhaps the murderer had
followed Woodward into the forest, had waited for the

right moment, then had seized the opportunity. But the
bolt had been fired at a moment when Christopher's life
had been threatened. If the murderer was not a friend
trying to help, hadn't he waited too long? Why hadn't
he simply shot Woodward before Woodward and
Christopher had even had words? And after shooting
Woodward, why hadn't he shot Christopher? The more
he thought about it, the more it seemed like a friend had
been trying to help him. Once the friend realized what
he had done, he had fled the scene. That could be true.

Or not.

Christopher reached the edge of the wood. He discovered he was a score of yards north of the tree where he
had tied his courser. He jogged toward the silhouette of
the horse, kicking up mud and blinking the rain from
his eyes.

Why did this have to happen?

The courser whinnied as he untied its reins, crossed
around it, and stuck a muddy boot into a stirrup. He
slapped a damp hand onto the pommel of his saddle and
swung up onto his mount. He wheeled the courser
around just as the sky thundered so loudly that
Christopher swore he felt the earth shake under him.
His courser reared and threatened to throw him.
Christopher tightened his grip on the reins and leaned
forward.

"Easy. Easy now!"

The horse came down onto all fours, bucked a bit
more, then grew calm.

Thunder rumbled again, far off this time, a distant
relative of the first crack. Christopher dug his heels into
the flanks of his mount. In the unrelenting deluge, he
started for home.

The ruins of the village of Shores were on Christopher's
southern horizon, and lay in a shallow valley encom-

passed by a very thin dotting of trees. The rain had finally given way to a mist. It was only a short ride north to the castle, and soon he'd be riding by the infantry and peasant levy laying siege to the fortress. And then — perhaps — he would report to the king what had happened. He craned his neck and took one last, longing glance at the village behind him, the village where he had been born, the village that had been pillaged and burned by the Saxons twice in his lifetime. Instead of the even-shaped silhouettes of the gabled roofs along Leatherdressers' Row, the place where his father had once built their home, he now saw the jagged black teeth of destruction. A traveler did not have to get any closer than this to know that Shores was no more. But Christopher knew in his heart it would be rebuilt. This time, however, the Saxons wouldn't destroy it. The invaders would either be living peacefully among the Celts or they would be driven from the land. Christopher hoped he lived long enough to see either one of those futures. He turned his thoughts from the moons to come to the pending hours. He knew one thing. He needed to tell someone what had happened. The cage of his mind was not strong enough to contain the knowledge. His own guilt, he knew, would free the news.

As he reached the crest of a long, lazy hill, the castle came into view, bathed in the liquid silver light of a first quarter moon. The old Roman fortress stood atop the limestone ramparts, and every time Christopher saw it from this distance he felt like a little boy again. He saw the castle as a stone-piled path to the heavens, brimming with magic, miracles, and excitement. But the too-brief second of bliss faded. The reality of the present struck hard. The torches burning in the watchtowers of the castle had been lit by Saxon hands. The tiny specks moving about the wall-walks were the foolish Saxon archers, made vulnerable by their own light. Within the solar of the castle was a Saxon named Kenric. Christopher ground his teeth in anger. The castle belonged to the Celts. *They* had inherited it from the Romans. How could it have fallen into the hands of the barbarians? Someone should have intervened. Nature should have intervened.

God must have a plan. Tell me, Lord, what is my future and the future of my home?

He let the question float to heaven, but knew better than to wait for a reply. God kept his own sundial.

As Christopher drew closer to the castle, he saw a great line of men and siege machines arise out of the distance. They marched along the eastern horizon toward the castle. He could hear the jubilant shouts of Arthur's watchmen posted in the perimeter forest.

Christopher counted at least a score of mangonels; the giant rock launchers' huge wooden wheels created a cacophony that rivaled the booming of a cavalry. There were an equal number of trebuchets, their swinging arms used for rock throwing now tied down for travel. Pulling up the rear were the spear-throwing ballistas.

Besides the siege machines were, of course, the fresh men. Reinforcements from Gore, no doubt. Yes, Arthur would take the castle back from the Saxons. Nothing would be able to stop his mighty efforts.

This was great news for the Celts. And especially welcome news for Christopher. In all the commotion of the new arrivals, Woodward would probably not be missed. At least not for a day or two.

Why am I thinking that? I have to talk to the king!

He needed guidance more than ever, and there was no question of where to find it.

When Christopher arrived at Orvin's tent, what he found surprised him. A blazing cookfire threw bright, flickering light upon Orvin, who stood choking Merlin outside the tent. Orvin's face was tightened into a knot. Merlin's multicolored eyes were wide and pleading. The druid gripped Orvin's wrists in a vain effort to free himself.

"There is no one in the realm more foolish than you, magician!" Orvin screamed as he shook the wizard by the neck.

Merlin's reply, if he had one, did not make it past Orvin's grip.

Christopher swung off of his courser, dropped to the ground, then ran to the codgers.

Orvin was so intent on squeezing the life out of Merlin that he did not see Christopher's approach. Christopher seized Orvin's wrists, then wrested him from the druid.

Merlin gasped for breath, then slid a hand under his beard to rub his neck.

Orvin lurched forward for another attack, but Christopher wrapped his arms around the old knight, effectively pinning the man where he stood. Orvin's long, thin white hair whipped into Christopher's face, and Christopher blew the strands away.

"No. Let me finish him. Let me finish him before he destroys all of Britain." Orvin cocked his head toward Christopher; the old sky watcher's eyes were wide and burning. He shifted forward, tried to break free, then added, "He's just about ruined your life, young saint!"

"What are you talking about?"

Merlin cleared his throat. "It was *not* my fault, Orvin. She insisted. I told her not to go, but she left while I slept!" With his hand still lost under the snow of his beard, Merlin took a step toward Orvin. "Why can you not think before you act? Is it not a fool who lets his anger become the order of the day?"

Orvin huffed. "Is it not a fool who sleeps while left with the charge of a woman and child?"

Christopher released his grip on Orvin, crossed in front of the man, and placed his hands on the knight's shoulders, should he try to get at Merlin again. Urgently, he asked, "What's happened? What's happened to Marigween and Baines?"

"Ask the *great* Merlin," Orvin said with a smirk, then gestured with his head toward the druid behind Christopher.

Christopher turned, then stepped toward Merlin. "All right. What?"

Merlin took a step back. "She left a note three days ago. May I say her Latin is beautiful. She's bound for the port of Blytheheart, on the southwest side of the Bristol channel. There's a small monastery there." The druid rolled his eyes. "Ignorant monks. How I do despise them."

"Why did she leave?" Christopher asked.

Merlin sighed. "The whys of women."

"I want to know why she left the safety of your cave. Now tell me!" Christopher felt his hands tremble. For a moment he realized his tone had been more than a little disrespectful, yet this was not the time to sit politely and chat while his wife-to-be and son were who knew where.

"She was bored, I believe," Merlin answered, his gaze finding Christopher's. "In your absence she had done nothing but complain. Oh, she had been a princess, daughter of Lord Devin, and had been used to being surrounded by chambermaids, used to bathing more, used to sitting at a dais table and partaking of the finest food of the realm. And there she had been, poor Marigween, confined as a prisoner to those stone walls. And all because of the Saxons. 'Well,' she said, 'they are *not* going to be my captors.'"

Christopher sensed Orvin coming up from behind. The old knight dropped a palm onto his shoulder, then spoke into his ear. "A convincing story, yes, young saint. But a lie. He had to come here to Shores to aid Arthur. He could no longer guard Marigween. I'm sure he encouraged her to leave."

"Strike that from your mind, Christopher," Merlin said. "If Arthur needed me, he would've sent word by carrier pigeon. He did not. I've come here simply to bring this news and extend an apology. Ask yourself, why is it that Orvin did not remain at the cave to guard your son and Marigween?"

"It is your fault I could not stay there!" Orvin shouted back. "No one could live with such a cackling fraud!"

Orvin's mouth was too close to Christopher's ear; Christopher flinched under the volume of the reply, then pulled away from Orvin and turned to face him. "Why can't both of you let go of your anger? Look what has happened!"

Orvin drew in a long breath, appeared about to say something, but then held his words behind pursed lips.

Christopher regarded Merlin. "Had she really been that unhappy at the cave? We had brought her so many luxuries. She never expressed her unhappiness to me."

Merlin nodded. "She hid it from you, as some women are wont to do, squire. You've experienced only a handful of feminine emotions in your day. You've a firkin full yet to learn about."

Christopher sighed. Life was now a two-edged sword, with Woodward's murder honing one edge and Marigween's flight sharpening the other.

"What does he know of women, young saint?" Orvin asked, back to his verbal foray.

Merlin began, "What I have observed —"

"Please. Your feud has become infamous, and it is not helping at all. I am in trouble. I do not wish to be an arbitrator in your millionscore disputes." Christopher caught his breath. He listened to the crackle of the cook-fire. No one spoke. Then, he bowed his head. "I'm sorry."

His elders continued to hold their tongues.

Christopher closed his eyes and tried to gather his thoughts. He wished his life would slow down so that he could catch up with it. There were too many unanswered questions. He still didn't know why Marigween had chosen a monastery in Blytheheart as her destination. Yes, the monastery would provide her with relative safety, but to get there she would have to travel west through the central part of the realm. She would be forced to ride over the Quantock foothills, which might be occupied by the Saxons. Hadn't she considered the dangers involved in such a journey? And how could she have been foolish enough to ride unescorted with their baby son? The more he thought about what she had done, the more furious he became.

He opened his eyes and looked to the druid. "Merlin," he said, in a softer, more reasonable tone, "why did Marigween set out for Blytheheart? She could've gone to Gore, or so many other places."

The druid's cottony brow narrowed in puzzlement. "I thought you already knew the answer to that question. Her uncle resides in Blytheheart."

"Her uncle? I didn't know Lord Devin —"

"No, he is her mother's brother, Robert. He is a monk."

Marigween's mother was dead and Marigween, when asked about the woman, fell into long periods of silence. What Christopher had gathered from Orvin was that the woman was of exceptional beauty and had died perhaps a half dozen years earlier. Naturally, Merlin did not know of Marigween's reticence concerning her mother. And now, with her father dead, she would not talk about him, either. It was as if she thought the silence would cleanse away the pain, or make their deaths part of some other reality, not this one. Christopher knew that silence only fueled sorrow. They lived in a fragile age, and grieving was a common and necessary part of life, a part Marigween denied herself. He'd let himself cry when his own parents had been slaughtered by the Saxons.

"She never talked about her mother," Christopher explained. "A painful subject. But now you've shed some light on her rebellion." He shifted his gaze to Orvin. "She's about a day west from here. You must try to catch up with her or get to that monastery and make sure she arrived safely."

Orvin's expression soured.

Merlin pointed a bony finger at Orvin. "Do you love the boy?"

"Yes, I love the boy. What has that —"

"Will you go?" Christopher interjected. "I-I want to go, but I have to stay."

Orvin answered, "I know you begin service to Woodward on the morrow." Then, as if struck by a thought, his face lit up. His lips curled in a smile. "I'll go after Marigween. And Merlin's coming with me."

"I'm not sure if that's a wise —" Christopher started.

"I will go," Merlin said as he crossed to a warped cider barrel outside the tent, then sat upon it with a sigh. "Perhaps during the ride Orvin and I will reach a truce, or perhaps we shall do better and kill each other. In any event, it would be my pleasure."

"Another lie, druid. You simply refuse to let me get to you. But I know I will," Orvin said. "And at least I'll be keeping you away from Arthur."

Christopher felt a night breeze rustle his still-damp shirt. He moved closer to the cookfire and rubbed his palms together. "It's settled then. You'll both leave this eve, but not before you hear some horrible news."

"I don't think I can hear any more," Orvin complained.

Christopher bit his lower lip as he considered whether he should tell them about Woodward. They were, after all, going to leave anyway. How could they help him while they were on a journey to Blytheheart? What advice could they impart to him? They would both tell him what he already knew: that concealing anything from Arthur would point more guilty fingers at him. Then again, maybe they'd have some ideas. He should at least tell Orvin. Holding back something this grave from his mentor would in the least sense be an insult. If nothing else, it might be interesting to see how the old sky watcher would react to the news of Woodward's murder; Woodward had always been a constant source of irritation to Orvin.

"You did not come here by accident, Christopher," Merlin said. "You sought Orvin for something. Advice on the eve you return to the army?"

"In a way," Christopher answered.

"What then can I do for you, young saint? Turn your eyes away from that tired one."

Christopher frowned and shook his head; Orvin's assaults on Merlin would never cease. He flipped his gaze from the druid to the old knight. "What if I told you Lord Woodward is dead, shot in the neck by a crossbow? What if I told you I am the only person to witness this act?"

"Is this to be a hypothetical exercise, or has this really happened?" Orvin asked, joining Christopher at the cookfire. The old one held his palms out to the flames.

"He was drunk. He was going to kill me."

"You killed him?" Orvin asked, his jaw falling slack as he leapt to a conclusion.

"Someone fired a shot from behind a tree or behind a thicket. Woodward fell. He's still out there."

Orvin closed his eyes and lolled his head back. "Oh, dear St. George and St. Michael, you've taken a foul wretch from this earth, but what have you done to this young man in return? Seek God for me and ask for His mercy upon this young saint."

Christopher eyed Merlin. "What should I, I mean what do I do now, Lord Merlin?"

The druid scratched the rim of his nostril with a long, sharp fingernail, then smoothed out his mustache before answering. "You will tell Arthur everything that has happened. You will include every detail, everything you can remember. Close your eyes when speaking to him. Live the moment once again."

"Arthur's council of battle lords will get to him," Orvin argued. "He will be on a pyre by the time we return from Blytheheart. And if Arthur protects the lad, then one of Woodward's men will find and finish him." Orvin put a finger to his lips. He stared into nowhere. "Or, perhaps, Woodward's murderer was really trying to execute the boy."

Merlin shook his head in disagreement. "Postulate nothing. There are facts. They are real, and he must act upon them. We could spend an entire summer speculating on what really happened. A knight has been murdered, and it appears this young squire has committed the crime."

Orvin moved uncomfortably close to Christopher, then fixed him with a penetrating stare. "Christopher," he said gravely, "did you kill him? Were you defending yourself?"

"Orvin, it was you who taught me that every man is a true servant, to his heart, to his mind, and to God. Under this sky, in this forest, before this fire, I speak to you only the purest truths. What I said is what happened. I speak of life, and of death, and I've never spoken of them more honestly."

"Arthur was wise to want you near him," Merlin observed. "He is an understanding king, and he values the truth as highly as you do, Christopher. You should already know that."

Christopher nodded. "I do, Merlin. I do." He turned away, then let his gaze fall to the ground. "But I'm still afraid."

2   Seaver shifted to the alcove window of his chamber in the castle keep. He reached up and tried to lift open the latch that held the wooden shutters closed.

I am not a dwarf! I am a short man. My limbs are normally proportioned!

It didn't matter that he was a normal, but short man. He suspected that every Saxon within the walls of the castle thought of him as a dwarf.

A dwarf cannot reach this latch either!

Shut up! You are not *a dwarf!*

In past moons he had told Ware to open the window for him so that he could scoff at Arthur's feeble army below. Now and again he would fire off an epithet in Celtic. But Ware was dead, and the rumor was that the feeble Celt army now grew. Seaver wanted to see for himself.

But damn the height of that latch.

He dragged the livery trunk at the foot of his bed over to the stone sill. He stepped onto the trunk, then onto the sill, lifted the latch, and pushed open the wooden doors —

— to view a nightmare.

"It is over," he murmured to himself. "Kenric is done. I am done."

Celt siege machines rolled into place along the moat on this, the east side of the castle. It was reasonable to assume the Celts had more machines on every side of the fortress. Seaver had feared this would happen. The firepower the Celts had amassed in Gore was well-known by his people; Seaver had warned Kenric about it and told his master that there was nothing to stop the Celts from bringing their rock and spear throwers down from that not-too-distant land.

Now, as the archers posted along the wall-walks pulled back their bowstrings and released their arrows, Seaver wished Kenric were beside him — so that he could see the distraught look on his leader's face.

True, Kenric was his master, and it was *he* who had promoted Seaver to second-in-command of this army. Kenric had permitted him to soar for a brilliant but brief time. It was over now. He had failed. Christopher of Shores and his two friends had escaped from the castle, carrying with them information on Saxon supplies and troop numbers. The three young Celts had been Seaver's responsibility and they had slipped through his grip — along with his command. His demotion had been the result of only one mistake. There were no second chances in Kenric's army.

He gazed solemnly at the scene below. Moon- and torchlight revealed an inevitable defeat. He turned back to the dim, empty box of his chamber.

I don't belong here anymore. Kenric will come through my door in a few moments and officially strip me of my command, as he promised he would. His delay in doing so is only the first step in his torture of me.

It didn't help matters that there were fellow Saxon battle lords that hated Seaver, that wanted him dead, that wanted Renfred appointed to his position. Seaver had not forgotten how Darrick the mangonel operator had come to him on the wall-walk one night and had threatened him. He remembered how he and Kenric had tortured then killed the man. As he looked back in his mind, Seaver grew more disgusted. Men should not have been questioning his authority in the first place. And though he still feared Kenric, he didn't completely agree with his master's plan. They waited for help from the north that might never come. Kenric would sit in the castle and die here. And if Seaver stayed, he would die along with his master.

The night wind towed along a bit of icy air, yes, but it was a cold, hard idea that sent gooseflesh fanning across Seaver's chest.

He still possessed a fleeting authority, an influence that would lift him out of despair. There wasn't much time to exploit his power. He hopped down from the alcove sill, not bothering to close the shutters. As the shouts of archers grew noticeably louder, Seaver ticked off a short mental list of things to do and acquire. He swung open his chamber door and strode into the torch-lit hall. There was an excited rhythm in his step, reminiscent of the day he had first been promoted.

Seaver stepped from the spiral staircase and emerged outside onto the north wall-walk of the keep. The archers here shouted to each other as they frantically adjusted their positions. Down below, past the curtain walls, Celt archers along the moat played hide and seek behind their wooden mantlets; they fired and ducked, ducked and fired. Celt arrows rained down on the wall-walk like too much deadly hail, and one Saxon archer close to Seaver wailed as he took an arrow in his chest then back-slammed to his death. Seaver dropped to his hands and knees and enlisted the stone parapet for cover.

"Shoral!" he shouted. "Lieutenant!"

A middle-aged man with a forestful of gray and

brown hair shifted around the hunkered bodies of several archers and crawled his way to Seaver. His beefy face glistened with perspiration and his bloodshot eyes mirrored his frustration and lack of sleep. "They've brought in their siege engines, sir. Have you seen?"

"Shift every archer to the south side of the keep. Pass the word. I want them shoulder to shoulder there. And tell the Greek fire bearers to move their cauldrons of pitch as well." Seaver listened to himself as he spoke, heard his words come out like verbal iron; only once before had he been this intent on giving an order — the day he'd ordered the death of Christopher of Shores.

The order *had* to come out forceful —

For the order was insane.

And the lieutenant's reaction reflected that. "Sir, if we do that, we leave three sides of the castle vulnerable!"

Seaver felt no remorse as he answered, "Trust me. You will see the merit of my strategy before the night is over. Obey. You know the consequences."

Before Shoral could protest further, Seaver turned away and crawled toward the entrance to the staircase. Bowstrings *twinged!* and crossbows *fwitted!* He heard men swear and fall behind him.

Once inside the alcove of the stairs he stood and, without a second look, descended quickly.

His breath was ragged by the time he reached the dungeon. The young jailer there flicked him a quizzical look from his key desk as Seaver ordered the man to unlock the gate and let him pass. Seaver marched down the hall, eyeing cell after cell, until he came upon the sleeping form of a short, Celt armorer who had refused to cooperate with his captors. He knew that the man was scheduled to be executed and Kenric had just forgotten to give the order. Seaver called to the jailer, told him to open the cell. The jailer obeyed, and as he found the right key and jammed it into the lock, Seaver noticed a sheathed dagger bound to the young man's belt. Without asking, Seaver slipped the dagger from its holder, then rushed into the cell. He went to the armorer and slashed open the man's throat. Then Seaver realized his mistake as he watched blood erupt from the writhing man's neck.

"Get in here!" he shouted to the confused jailer. "We have to get his clothes off before he gets them bloody!"

The armorer did not die quickly, and it took some wrestling before they were able to begin removing the man's livery. Fortunately, the man was on his back, and most of the blood ran down onto the mattress.

"My lord, why are we stripping him?" the jailer asked.

"Kenric's orders. Now, help me into these, and cease with your questions."

"Yes, my lord."

Dressed in the frayed tunic, leggings, and light boots of a Celt armorer, Seaver left the cell. He ordered the jailer to fall in close behind. They headed for the last cell on the left side of the block. There, Seaver gestured with his head for the jailer to open it.

The jailer paused, winced with apprehension. "Lord Kenric ordered this cell never to be opened."

"I know, jailer. New orders. Open it!"

With a half-stifled sigh, the jailer heeded the command.

Seaver pulled the barred door open the second he heard the tumbler on the lock fall. He nearly knocked over the jailer in the process. Seaver's gaze came to rest upon a stone in the far wall, one with an iron manacle loop set into its face. The edge where this stone met the others was clean and betrayed the fact that the stone had recently been moved.

Seaver knelt, grasped the loop and pulled. The stone budged a little, but it was too heavy for him. "Get down here and help me pull this out."

"My lord?"

"You heard me!"

"These are Kenric's orders?"

"They'll find you like that armorer if you don't help me now."

Seaver saw the guard's Adam's apple work. The young man crouched next to Seaver. Together, they tugged, and finally the stone came free from the wall. Before the dust settled to reveal what lay beyond the stone, Seaver moved into the rectangular hole. For once it was good to be small.

"My lord. What shall I do now?"

"Return to your desk and wait," Seaver called back.

The smell of stagnant water polluted the air. He fanned it out of his face and stood. Light from the hole revealed a stone floor identical to the cell's, save for the fact it ended a few yards ahead, giving way to a trench-like pool. The hall was narrow, even by a small man's standards. He was *within* the north side curtain wall of the castle. He looked up, saw that the ashlar walls extended up past several different sets of loopholes to a stone ceiling which was, in effect, the floor of the wall-walks. Torchlight drifted down from a few of the loop-holes and drew long, yellow-edged shadows across the gridwork of piled stones. He listened. Faint cries from the distance. Nothing from the loopholes immediately above.

Good. They've all moved to the south wall. It will only be a few more moments before the real noise begins.

A few trace remnants of the flint and rubble that once filled this wall trailed under his boots as he stepped toward the pool. The water came into focus, and Seaver saw that it looked as bad as it smelled, near-black, a sludgy goo. He felt his stomach heave, his cheeks sink.

A tiny sound registered from behind the wall that

faced outside. Seaver stepped to the wall, pressed his ear against it. The stone vibrated.

Then he heard the shouts. The shouts of Celts who stormed this side of the castle. He shifted away from the wall to the pool, slid off his boots, tightened his lips, and drew a deep breath. With a brief, silent prayer to Woden, he let himself fall into the warm slime.

Seaver swam forward, then closed his eyes and ducked at the point where the water disappeared under the wall. He felt his way into a narrow tunnel, the walls of which were slick and made pushing off difficult. He kicked desperately with his feet and wondered how long this blind journey was going to last. He had to give Christopher a small measure of credit. The squire had slipped into the castle this way and it was, to say the least, unnerving to swim through the muck of this tunnel. Seaver hadn't even finished tipping his mental hat to the boy when he found his hands abruptly free of the walls. He reached out, probed for more of the ceiling; it was gone. He wanted to open his eyes and orient himself, but remembered the murk of the water. He instinctively swam upward, and in a few strokes his head popped above the surface.

A thunder of battle cries met his ears. He snapped open his eyes, then resumed his kicking to stay afloat. Struggling through the water-induced disorientation, Seaver's vision finally focused on the north curtain wall. He cocked his head sharply toward the encroaching roar, saw what he had hoped for: a human wall of ladder-carrying Celts that splashed into the moat. They would swim across the water, dig their ladders into the muddy berm, and attempt to scale the curtain walls.

The first wave of men swam toward him, and Seaver shouted, "Thanks be to St. George. I'm free. Free!" His Celt was a bit awkward, but he knew it was convincing enough to fool this peasant levy.

"Out of the way, man!" one of the ladder-carriers growled.

"Ho! We're coming through!" another cried.

"To victory!" Seaver yelled back, then ducked his head under the water. He paddled out of the way of the Celts and toward the shoreline.

There were scores and scores of men in the water with Seaver; he was one of the many, nondescript. Soon, the moat became shallow, and Seaver rose. He dragged himself toward the shoreline, and once there he collapsed, partly for the benefit of the archers and siege machine operators watching, partly for himself. He hadn't been swimming in many, many moons.

He hoped being wet, covered in mire, and wearing the garb of a Celt armorer was enough to conceal him from the levy. He heard a gruff voice shout, "Get that man up and behind cover."

Hands were suddenly upon Seaver's arms and legs. He shut his eyes and let them take him. He marveled at how he calmly surrendered to the enemy; if they discovered who he really was, they would castrate and kill him—in that order, of course. He chanced a peek and saw that they were taking him behind a bulwark of mantlets. He was placed upon the back of a two-rounsey wagon driven by a portly old Celt. He turned his head, feigned a dizzy spell. Already draped across the flatbed were two archers, one bleeding from a wound in his neck, the other gripping his left side, the linen shirt around his hand darkened by blood. Seaver closed his eyes.

"Where'd that one come from?" he heard the fat wagon driver ask.

"I think he was trampled near the shoreline," someone to the right of Seaver answered. "Poor little man. Get him and these other two down to Hallam's tent."

The driver cracked his reins, and the pair of rounseys hitched to the cart started forward, away from the

castle. The path ahead would take them through a
dense wood.

After only a few moments of travel, Seaver could no
longer shackle his emotions. He laughed out loud, so
hard that he felt his ribs grow sore. The archers and the
driver must have thought he was mad, but he didn't
care. He was, after all, truly free. Free of Kenric's rule,
free of fighting a now-hopeless battle against the Celts,
free of both a certain loss of command and certain
death.

He sat up, threw the first archer off the wagon even
as the other shouted his question. A second later, the
other tumbled onto the dirt path. Seaver moved to the
front of the wagon. He tore the reins from the driver's
grip and wrapped them around the fat man's neck. He
choked the life out of the driver, pleased that it took less
time than usual. The driver joined his human cargo on
the road, not as lucky as they.

Wagon driver Seaver steered the cart along the path,
now passing row after row of abandoned cookfires and
empty Celt tents. Every peasant and soldier now
stormed the castle walls. He flipped a glance back to the
fortress, considered how he had just recently ruled over
the scores of Saxon men there, thought of the honor and
prestige of it all.

He felt the leathery reins in his hands and the sensation put it all into perspective for him.

Seaver had already lost everything. Oh, he would love
to run a pike through Christopher's head, to exact a
revenge so potent anyone who witnessed it would fear
him forever. But he wouldn't let his thirst for revenge
keep him here and turn him into a fool. It was time to
go back to Caledonia, to Ivory Point. Home. He would
hop on a Saxon cog at the port of Blytheheart and sail
up the Irish Sea to a new life, founded on one he had
left too many moons ago.

3

"What happened to your hand? Come now, tell me the story, laddie."

Doyle would be asked that question for the rest of his life. Seventeen was, in his estimation, too young for one to wear the scars of battle. If he were older, he might actually take pride in his deformity, boast of it to younger men, use it to prove that he'd once been captured and tortured by the Saxons. He would be a proud warrior. He could say he was *there*.

But he was seventeen. And deformed. And he had yet to find a true love. No woman would want him now. He would be the tall, lean boy with "the hand."

"It's nothing," he answered Montague.

The fat brigand threw his head back and pressed the nozzle of his flagon to his lips. After a few gulps of ale he exhaled in delight, adjusted one of the many gemstone rings on his thick, soiled fingers, and answered, "If I lost my thumb and forefinger, laddie, I wouldn't call it nothing. He chuckled, his breath coming with a force that would bend the flames of the cookfire, were he close enough. "Will you ever tell the tale?"

Doyle turned his head away, tried to tuck the memory of how Seaver had butchered off his fingers back into the farthest, deepest crease of his mind.

"I believe you won't," Montague added.

Doyle remembered his scream of agony, heard his own voice now, shrill, piercing, accompanied by the pain that shot up his arm. He stiffened away a chill, tried to repress all thought, and eyed the landscape.

The forest where they had spent the night was just south of the River Cam; it stood atop a slope about one thousand yards from the water. From this vantage point Doyle could see Queen's Camel Abbey to the far north,

flagged by a line of smoke that rose above it. To the east
lay the headwaters of the River Cale, and to the southwest he could barely make out the highest tower of the
castle of Rain. A large banner flew from that tower, but
he could not see if it bore Lord Nolan's coat of arms.
The castle was probably still under Saxon rule. He
turned his gaze to the Cam, saw the morning mist unroll
from the shoreline reeds. As his eyes continued their
sweep, he spotted a pair of Saxon scouts. The soldiers
were dismounted and conversed as they watered their
horses. They were probably on their way to the castle.

"What are you looking at, laddie?" Montague asked.

Doyle uncrossed his legs and pushed himself up. He
put a hand to his forehead, squinted. "Two Saxon
scouts. They've got a pair of rounseys."

"Splendid," Montague said, his tone lifting in light of
the news. "I'm tired of walking. Help me up, will you?"

Doyle turned from the Saxons and eyed Montague,
the huge hill of flesh with the long, filthy, slick hair and
matted beard.

*How did I ever wind up with this whoreson round
man?*

This was the price paid for murder: banishment. King
Arthur had been merciful. By law, Doyle should have
ornamented the gallows tree for what he had done. He
considered whether that might have been better; at least
death was a destination. Now, with the village of Falls
and the castle of Rain in the hands of the Saxons, there
weren't too many places in this part of Britain to go.

Doyle had hoped he would join a jewelry merchant in
Falls and start a trade with him, a trade that would
extend to Glastonbury, to Brent Knoll, and to the ports
on the south side of the Bristol channel. Everyone here
knew Weylin, the man who had raised Doyle, and everyone knew that Weylin had taught Doyle to be an expert
merchant of jewels. Doyle had developed a keen eye for

quality gems and settings. The problem was, those who could employ Doyle's talent were either captured or dead. Besides that, jewelry wasn't very important when one's home and family were threatened. Banishment was worse now than it would have been had the Saxons not invaded. Doyle had two skills: archery and the buying and selling of jewelry. With his fingers gone, the only thing he'd be shooting was a crossbow — and not in any Celt army. The demand for jewelry had dropped off to nothing. If he was, however, an armorer or bow maker, then perhaps there would be some way for him to make a living. But what master craftsman would take a deformed boy as an apprentice? Besides, he was already too old for that.

He could go back to Gore and seek the aid of his parents, though that would violate his banishment. Besides, they had never been real parents to him. The only parent he'd ever really had was Weylin. Even after he had discovered that Weylin had kidnapped him as an infant and had raised him as his own, Doyle had still loved the man. He was glad to have lived his young life with the merchant. Weylin was intelligent and kind, and he could not get the man's soft gaze and tiny smile out of his mind — nor would he ever forget that fateful day when Shores came under siege and the Saxons had murdered the man before his eyes. Doyle had had to run. It wasn't his fault that Weylin had died. But it hurt, it hurt badly. He could *never* forget.

Many moons later, his parents wanted to resume their roles, and worse, control his life. It was far too late for that. Doyle would never be so desperate as to need them— even now, when desperation was the dominant feeling.

If he would not forget Weylin, then he would forget his parents. Ale was a friend he had hired to help. But ale had become a foe that had driven him to murder. He could guzzle firkin after firkin and never be able to drown away what he had done. Christopher had tried to stop him. He should have listened to his blood brother. Instead Doyle's anger had taken the lives of two young Celts. It was not Innis's murder that bothered him, for that wretch deserved to die. No, Leslie's death clung to his shoulder and whispered black words in his ear. Such a little boy. Only thirteen. And he died. . . pathetically. He could still see the vivid picture in his mind, how the arrow had caught the squire just under the earlobe.

Doyle heard Christopher's cry in his mind: "WHAT ARE YOU DOING? WHO ARE YOU? YOU KILLED THEM! YOU KILLED BOTH OF THEM!"

Leslie, you shouldn't have threatened to turn me in! In your heart, you wanted to see Innis killed as well! Why did you have to be so honest!

Because he was, as Christopher told me, a true servant, the embodiment of a great knight-to-be. And I am nothing but a murderer. A drunk. A freak. And I am wanted by no one, no one except someone just like me.

Montague.

So that is how I've come to be with this villain.

Doyle circled around the cookfire to Montague, proffered his good hand to the brigand. Montague's sweaty palm made contact with his own and, with the usual repulsion, Doyle hoisted the pot-bellied bull calf to his feet.

"My thanks, laddie," Montague said. He tried in vain to smooth out his stained silk shirt. He tucked the shirt deeper into the bulging waist of his threadbare breeches, then went on, "And if I can offer you two bits of advice: never eat as much nor grow as old as I." There was no one in the realm who appreciated Montague's humor more than the man himself. He was the happiest woolsack Doyle would ever know.

"I'll never be like you," Doyle said, wanting fervently to believe that, but sensing in his heart that it was not true.

Montague lifted an index finger. "But you already are. And we need each other." As he lowered the finger, his lips tightened and the whimsy vanished from his eyes. "They cut up my three faithful lads and left me alone to die, just as you were left out here by Arthur, alone to die. Fate's tossed us together, and together, laddie, we'll forge a new life. And I'm full of new ideas this morning."

"Such as —"

"Such as what we're going to do. We're going up to the Bristol channel. That's where the deniers are to be made. This war has raised the port trade. We can slip back into the merchant world. I have a friend at the port of Blytheheart who might be able to help."

"That port is five or six days away," Doyle informed him, "and that's not walking. And we'll have to cross over the Parret River, and the foothills of the Quantocks. Have you ever been up there?"

"Montague has been on top of every mountain, in every hole, sailed every river, and explored every wood in all of Britain. There is no place that can hold me down, laddie."

Doyle seriously doubted that. "If we do manage to start a trade in Blytheheart, it will be an *honest* one. From the beginning. I will not rob my way into a business."

Montague batted off Doyle's implication with a quick wave of his hand. "No need to remind me of that. It's high time I settled down to something honest. I'm weary of the road. And with the Saxons buzzing about like bees, it's far too dangerous to drift. The blood of my boys taught me that."

With no ideas of his own, traveling to Blytheheart was as good as any, and Montague did make it sound worth their while, yet he wondered about Montague's "friend." Surely trade boomed in the channel ports, but they were so far away. If only the village of Falls had not fallen; it was once the inland trading mecca of south central Britain. They had to travel all the way to the coast to find a decent marketplace now.

Doyle had stressed to Montague that if he was successful in starting a trade, it would be honest. But in order to get to Blytheheart they would have to brigand their way there. Would he be successful if his future was established on such behavior? Was it all right if he stole from Saxons, since they were the enemy and would do the same if they had to? He remembered something that Weylin had told him, that two wrongs do not make a right.

But what did he really have to lose? He'd been stripped of his duty as an archer in Arthur's army, stripped of the means even to fire a longbow, and stripped of the place he had decided to call home, the castle of Shores. If there was a time to take chances, it was now.

Doyle returned his gaze to the Saxon scouts standing at the river's edge. "All right then, Monte. Get out my crossbow. I will show you what a good shot I still am — even with this hand. And I won't even have to kill them."

4 Little Baines, bundled in linen and nestled tightly in a riding bag strapped across Marigween's chest, used his tiny arms to pull himself higher in the bag to expose his shoulders to the sun. There was something about the morning light that the baby enjoyed. The rounsey's bouncy trot had given him a case of the hiccups, and Marigween found the sound more annoying

than amusing. Everything annoyed her now, most particularly the fact that she was lost.

"Where are the five guards, Baines?"

She scanned the low, sun-browned hills that formed a meandering line on the western horizon. The five tallest peaks, nicknamed "the guards," were nowhere in sight. If that half circle of small mountains was visible, it would point the way south to Glastonbury, where at least she could find a place indoors to sleep.

After leaving the cave, she had spent the first night in the stone forest. Too excited to sleep, she had listened to the owls all night. Baines had been remarkably quiet. The second, third, and fourth nights had been spent in the various woods that dappled the landscape of Shores. Only a pair of woolen blankets had stood between them and the creatures of the night. She had feared being discovered by some nocturnal beast, but had been even more wary of the watchmen or hunters that might have roamed the wood. Saxon or Celt, both would have meant an end to her journey.

Now Shores was behind her. She was in open territory. The minor thrill of adventuring to Blytheheart was gone. She couldn't find the guards. She might wander into a Saxon army or camp or something even worse. What would the barbarians do to her? To her baby? She clenched her reins, then snapped them, snapped away the horrors in her mind. Those images would only make her too frightened to continue. She was headed west; that was correct. The guards would probably appear sometime today. She shouldn't worry herself; that was foolish.

She felt Baines continue to be jolted by the hiccups. As she grew calm, she allowed herself a smile. "You drunk little baby. Been lifting a tankard too many, have you? Wait until your father hears of this . . ."

Christopher. She mouthed his name. He should have

been her husband by now, but the wretched war had always come in the way. She could not deny him his duty; he had to serve. But what kind of life could he really give her? Everything was still frozen because of the war, and on top of that, many more questions would have to be answered. How would they explain their son? What about Lord Woodward? He was bound to learn of her relationship with Christopher. What if the abbot condemned them? What if . . . ? More doltish fretting. She knew it was wrong to worry, but why was it so hard to stop?

Flies buzzed about her rounsey's ears. She had given up trying to swat them away to ease the animal. The horse's ears flinched the way Baines did under his hiccups. Her rounsey would have to comfort itself, as would she.

Marigween sighed deeply over her life. But at least now she took action; she did not rot in Merlin's damp cave. The old man would never understand her. Yes, she had been spoiled, but she was not one to demand luxuries. Christopher had tried to make it comfortable for her, and relatively speaking it had been, but he could do nothing to busy her mind. She really didn't need a four-poster bed with a thick mattress to sleep on; didn't need a cushioned seat at a dais table to eat from; didn't need a large tub to bathe in or sweet-smelling shifts to put on afterward. She could live without all of the physical amenities of being a noblewoman. But she could not live without the stimulation of her mind.

Merlin had been interesting to a point. But he had never spoken plainly or directly, and she had tired of riddling through conversations with him. And he had never taken her to the place where he had retired nightly. She had tried following him more than once, but he had somehow disappeared down one of the many tunnels that began in the rear of the main cave, and

Marigween had always found herself back where she had started, having walked in a perpetual circle. Merlin had a special place back there, but he wouldn't share it with her — probably because she was a woman. She despised his secrets.

Ah, she missed her chambermaids. She missed their conversations over the nature of men, the nature of the realm, the nature of what it is to be a woman, a noblewoman. Philosophy had been as absent as Christopher from her life. Her mind was now shriveling into the workaday pea of peasant. Her Latin went unpracticed, save for a few notes to Uncle Robert and her good-bye note to Merlin. She had run out of things to read in Merlin's cave. She had run out of ways to enlighten herself. That had been what she had missed most about living in a castle, about being a noblewoman: the light of knowledge, of discovery. At least in Blytheheart she could practice her Latin with Uncle Robert, could read the many scrolls they had at the monastery, could converse with the many, many people that traded and lived at the port. Blytheheart was alive, and its life might renew her spirits.

If there was one person who had kept Marigween going thus far, it had been Baines. Mothering took up a good part of her day, and she loved tending to little Baines, making him smile whenever she could. But she wanted mothering to be only a part of her life, not all of it. She loved Baines to the core of her being, but she would not be happy if she sacrificed everything for him. It was not being selfish. It was being human.

"I remember, Mother, I remember when I asked you if you liked taking care of me."

It had been a cool, quiet night in the manor house. Marigween had crept into her mother's bed. Father had been off fighting a war as usual, and she lay there staring at the faint, moon-cast shadows on the splintery rafters.

Mother wrapped an arm around her and said, "When you are a good girl, I love taking care of you. When you are a bad girl, I love taking care of you. Do you know why?"

Marigween shook her head.

"Because you are my flesh, my blood, and there is nothing you can do that will ever stop me from loving you. My love has no bounds. You are a part of my life. The most important part."

"How come I'm only a part of your life?"

Mother held her tighter. "Because I am me and you are you. And one day you will have a child. And that baby will be the most important part of your life. But you will still be you and that baby will still have its own life. One day I'll have to say good-bye to you. And that will be more painful than anything. A large part of my life will go away. If you were all of my life, then when you grow up and leave, I would die."

"I don't want you to die. Don't. Please don't . . ."

Marigween's cheeks and neck were cooled by the many tears that suddenly flowed over them. She barely noticed the horse under her. She was consumed by a new remembrance, the day Mother had died. Father wouldn't let her go into the room, but the door was slightly ajar and she had caught a glimpse of Mother. She was shocked at how pale Mother looked. Her hair looked too red, her skin too white. Doctors and monks surrounded her. Near the window, Father cried.

"I was too young, Mother! I needed you. I need you now! Don't you know Father's gone and I'm alone?"

The tears of orphans. Marigween felt the world could be flooded with them. Hers alone might engulf Britain. She was terribly lonely. She hungered for a shoulder to rest her head on, someone to assure her everything would be all right.

Marigween looked ahead. The five guards remained

hidden. She wished she could lift the horizon with the force of her teary stare, fold it back toward her, and view what lay on the other side.

5

"How goes it now?"

"My lord, some have breached the walls."

"And from you, sir?"

"I do not understand their tactics."

"None of us do."

"Aye, they shifted all of their archers to one side!"

"Indeed, they're mad!"

"Your report?"

"They've dispersed from the south side."

"Tell me, what of those who reached the wall-walk?"

"They struck down a few."

"Aye, they did, but too few made it."

Christopher shifted his weight from one leg to the other, standing next to a pair of guards just inside the entrance to Arthur's tent. At the back of the tent, the king was on his feet, his gaze trained on a recently drawn map of the castle in his hands. A group of battle lords created a curtain wall of armor and muscle between Christopher and his lord.

An audience is exactly what I do not need.

He could not deliver the news of Woodward's death to Arthur with a group of battle lords standing around to pass swift judgment on him.

I should have told him last night. It wasn't too late. A night's rest has not made it any easier. Now my delay has made things even worse.

"What about you, Lancelot? What do you have to report from the castle of Rain?"

The blond knight spoke through clenched teeth. "Those foul, greasy boars still infest the fortress. I conveyed your message to Lord Nolan, and he asks that we solve our conflict here with all expediency so that we may lend him a few of our brothers-in-arms."

"Ha, were it only that simple! But we will do it. Now. I've a new plan to undermine the walls." Arthur set the parchment map down across a hastily assembled desk: a sheet of wood atop a pair of barrels. Then he looked up and studied the faces of the half dozen men before him. A question narrowed his brow. "We're missing someone. Sir Woodward, I believe, yes? Has anyone seen him?"

As a few of the battle lords voiced their "no's," and one muttered that he had not seen him since last night, Christopher turned away from the group and began to slip past the two guards toward the tent flaps.

"Christopher?"

An epithet fired in Christopher's mind, though he lacked the time and privacy to voice it. He stopped, turned around. "I see you are very busy, my lord. My business with you can wait."

"Woodward knew about this council, did he not?" Arthur was insulted by Woodward's lack of attendance and he made no effort to hide the fact in his voice.

"Yes, my lord."

"Then where is he?" The king's brow was now high in demand.

The other battle lords turned to face Christopher. He noticed them, their hard eyes, but none harder than the king's. He wanted to dissolve into the wind, or, at the very least, slip out of the tent.

Christopher knew he *looked* guilty, knew there wasn't much blood in his face, knew he exhibited all of the things he always did when nervous, all of the things most people did when under this kind of pressure. First, he put an end to his rocking back and forth. Then he moved on to his hands, let them hang limp. Next he opened his mouth slightly and breathed. He did not swallow; he just breathed. He could do nothing to calm the nerves in his eyelids, which twitched violently, but he doubted anyone in the tent would notice them. All right. Whether he looked a little more calm was arguable. He did feel a tinge less nervous.

One decision was final: he would only confess the truth to Arthur in private. He would have to delay things now. But in the face of Arthur's question, he would have to lie. Would he be able to explain the lie away later? He remembered what Merlin had told him: to close his eyes and be honest. He remembered how Orvin had worried about the other battle lords; the old knight had said that one of them might find and finish him.

Moons ago Christopher had disobeyed Arthur's orders and had rescued Doyle from the castle. For that he was no longer squire of the body, squire to King Arthur, squire of all of Britain. He was now squire to a dead man. Christopher had been dishonored when he had been relieved of his duty to the king. He had not upheld the codes of knight and squirehood. He had betrayed Arthur's trust in him. He had started down a path filled with potholes of deception, holes he kept tripping over. It seemed he had been more a true servant *before* he ever became Arthur's squire; once he was the king's servant the lying began, and now, no longer Arthur's squire, the lying piled up and threatened to block out the sky. He had a relationship with Marigween that was founded on lies and lust. That fact had caused him and Woodward to meet in the forest. That fact had caused Woodward to die. In one respect, Woodward's death had been his fault. Woodward would never have challenged him if he had left Marigween

alone. If Woodward were still alive, Christopher might
be able to prove his worth by excellent service to the
man and earn back his title. Christopher might be able
to serve the king again. But not now. Perhaps not ever.

Is it really too late for me?

He wondered if he was caught too tightly in his web.
Had he chanced his way too close to the gallows tree?
He tried to see himself through Arthur's eyes. Here was
a misguided youth who let his heart rule his mind. So it
was with young men. Age brought the balance of mind
and heart. Christopher could see that far, but he could
not imagine what Arthur would think of him after hearing about Woodward's death — compounded by the
fact that he had lied about it.

The lies got easier the more he told them. The journey
to evil, Orvin had once said, is as quick and easy as trac-
ing it on a map; in a blink you're there. It had been only
a blink ago that Christopher had been thirteen and innocent and practicing with Baines in the eastern wood.
Full of truth and honor and dreams galore, the world
had been untamed and unexplored and ripe for
Christopher of Shores.

In a blink, years had passed. A blink ago, Arthur had
asked him where Woodward was. In a blink further,
Christopher would take a fork in his life's path; either
stall the inevitable or let it all come out and damn the
suspicions of the battle lords to hell.

*Those eyes. Look at them. They'll kill me. I know
they will. Orvin was right.*

"My lord, I do not know where Woodward is. I have
not seen nor heard from him since yesterday."

As he had by his courting of Marigween, Christopher
knew he had once again abandoned what he held so
high. Suddenly he knew he had made a grave error,
knew it was the coward's way out of the situation, knew
it was not the course of a true servant. He had to stop

the lies; only then would he be at peace. But just as suddenly it was too late to pull the words back.

The king frowned, twirled a finger in his beard. "It's *his* castle we're trying to win back. You'd think he would like to know about our progress and future efforts."

"I wager he romanced a bottle last night," Lancelot said, cocking an eyebrow.

The battle lords responded with chuckles, some teasing each other over their own flirtations with the same.

The king lowered his gaze to the map. "We'll not wait for him. And you gentlemen should find seats. Have your squires bring in some trunks or stools or something to sit on. We're going to be here for a while."

"By your leave?" Christopher asked.

Arthur tipped his head in agreement. "And if you see your master, Christopher, send him directly here. Tell him his tardiness will cost him." Arthur smiled at Lancelot, a smile that seemed some private joke between them.

Christopher withdrew from the tent, five breaths away from fainting.

Outside, the midday air was fresher and thinner than the damp, mildew-tinged atmosphere of the tent; it struck a hard blow to his lungs and made the weight of his head sink back onto his neck. The August sky, once sunny, had clouded over in the brief time he had been inside the tent. He closed his eyes and rubbed them.

I'm slowly ruining my life.

But it's not my fault Woodward died! I didn't kill him!

Yes, but you drove him toward vengeance — and that is what got him killed!

"I heard him ask you about Woodward," Neil said.

Christopher lowered his hand, opened his eyes. Neil had taken an arrow from the quiver slung over his shoulder and now absently adjusted its fletching. Since

returning to Shores, Christopher found it harder and
harder to recognize Neil. The barbarian was just as
stubby, just as chubby, and just as hairy as he was the
day Christopher had first met him in Doyle's tent back
on the Quantock hills. It wasn't Neil's appearance that
had changed; it was his attitude. To others, the change
would be perceived as only minor, but it bothered
Christopher very much.

In reply to Neil's remark, he only sighed.

"So why did you lie to the king?" Neil asked.

Christopher's tone went offensive. "What are you
talking about?"

Neil *tsk*ed. "I know you too well, Christopher. Your
plans, your scheming. You know something about
Woodward."

"Maybe I do," Christopher said, honing his voice further with each word. "But these days, I'm not sure I
would even tell you. You'd probably turn me in."
Christopher stalked past Neil and started down the
muddy path that led away from the king's tent, a path
lined on one side by more tents, the other by reeds that
fenced off a view of the Cam.

He heard Neil's boots behind him, then felt Neil's
hand on his shoulder. "What do you mean by that?"

"You know," Christopher grunted, then pulled out of
Neil's grasp and continued marching.

Neil jogged up beside him and kept pace, though his
body was taxed far more than Christopher's. Between
heavy breaths, he managed, "Is it because I'm friends
with *him*?"

Christopher stopped dead. Neil nearly tripped over
him. "You can be friends with whomever you want."

"That's it, I knew it." Neil shook his head, his lips
pursed in disgust. "You'd probably like him if you got to
know him. If you'd give him a second look. We're all in
the same army, Christopher."

"You and I, we share something, we've both lost our best friends. Phelan's dead. Doyle's banished. It is you and I now, Neil. I trusted you to be loyal to me."

For a moment, the irony struck Christopher. Neil had betrayed his trust, the way Christopher had betrayed Woodward's and now Arthur's trust. The way he felt now was the way Arthur would feel when he discovered the lie. The feeling was ugly, and it unearthed a rage.

Neil puffed air. "I'm friends with Robert of Queen's Camel, the squire who replaced you, and that's being *disloyal* to you? I'm thrilled we're finally having this conversation. Now I know why you've been brooding."

"I have *not* been brooding!" Christopher stomped forward.

Neil fell in close behind, then called after him. "It is not as if we're great friends! He's simply interested in improving his skill at the longbow and asked me to help. I was flattered."

Christopher dug his right heel into the ground, stopped abruptly. This time Neil ran into him. "Watch it!"

"Ouch! If you would just listen."

"All right. Explain to me your . . . *friendship*." Christopher felt his back teeth come together, and he bit down hard.

"It is mainly instructor to student, but occasionally he talks about home, or about his journeys up to the Savernake forest, or fishing in the Thames. He's a very good storyteller. You would be amazed."

I'm amazed you're his friend.

Christopher folded his arms over his chest. "But is he a good squire?"

Neil's nod was reluctant, but positive. "I could make you feel better and say he is not."

"You've seen more of him than I have. Do you think he's better than me?"

Neil shrugged. "I'm an archer. I don't know."

"Come now, you can tell. You've seen enough squiring in your day."

"He has a lot of experience."

"In combat?"

This time it was Neil who turned away and started off, leaving Christopher standing in the path. "You're jealous, and you're taking it out on me. Think about that."

It was hard to look into the mirror created by Neil's words. The truth was difficult to tell, perhaps more difficult to face.

Am I really jealous of Robert? I've avoided him, but does that really mean . . .

Who wouldn't be jealous? I want what he has! What he doesn't deserve! He didn't earn the title! I fought on the Mendips with Hasdale. I fought on the Quantocks with Arthur, and I'll fight again. Just because he shows some skill and is of noble blood does not mean he deserves squire of the body!

Maybe he doesn't. But neither do I right now.

I am jealous, so jealous that it's killing me.

Christopher watched Neil storm away. Was it right to be mad at the archer for befriending Robert? Was it Neil's attitude that had changed — or his own?

"Neil?" he shouted. "Wait. You're right."

Neil didn't stop walking. "I know. Let's go back to my tent and talk about it. I have some fruit there."

The tent was cool and private. The old linen blankets they sat on offered reasonable comfort. Neil finished two apples before Christopher had taken a bite out of his first. He was too engrossed in telling Neil what had happened in the forest with Woodward. Neil chewed loudly, listened earnestly, and his mouth opened in surprise like a jester's when Christopher told him about the murder.

"I even wondered if you had done it," Christopher said. "But I couldn't figure out why you wouldn't come into the clearing."

"I wouldn't come into the clearing because I wasn't there," Neil said forcefully. "If I had shot Woodward, I would've done it with my longbow."

"Not if you were hiding in those brambles. There wasn't enough room."

Neil conceded the fact. "I guess I might have used a crossbow. But that doesn't matter. What are you going to do now?"

"I don't know. I know I should tell Arthur the truth. And soon."

"I think you're right about the battle lords. They'll probably want Arthur to at least slap you into a pillory. Were I you, I'd talk to the king in private."

Christopher pulled his knees into his chest, wrapped his arms around them. "I'm scared. Someone wanted to save my life or ruin it. Or someone wanted to kill me and shot Woodward by mistake." A new thought sparked another guess. "Or perhaps someone wanted to make sure I would never become squire of the body again!"

Neil shook his head. "Robert of Queen's Camel did not kill Woodward." His tone left little room for argument.

Christopher swore under his breath, then challenged, "How do you know?"

"He could not hit a mantlet from fifty yards."

"That's with a longbow."

"Longbow or crossbow. I can close my eyes and shoot better than he."

"Perhaps it's all an act for your sake. He knows we're friends."

"There goes your imagination again." Neil plucked his third apple from a burlap bag lying beside him, shined it on his shirtsleeve, took a loud bite, then chewed as he spoke. "One thing's certain."

"What's that?"

"That I'm glad I'm not you." He swallowed, then said, "Well, at least you won't have to worry about Woodward finding out about you and Marigween, or your son. That's one less burden to shoulder."

"You fool. Now I've got a problem a score times worse. Not only that, Marigween's left Merlin's cave and is taking our son to Blytheheart."

Neil paused in the middle of taking another bite, then lowered the apple from his lips. His expression turned ominous. "Why?"

"I'm not sure. She was bored, I guess. I asked Orvin to go after her. He took Merlin with him."

"Christopher, haven't you heard?" There was no mistaking Neil's urgency.

"Heard what?"

"The Saxons are amassing a large army in the Parret River valley. Arthur believes that army will advance east then divide at the Cam, some coming to aid the Saxons here in Shores, the others going to fight Lord Nolan's army in Rain."

"The Saxons are in the Parret River valley?"

"Aye," Neil answered, "and —"

"Marigween has to cross that valley —"

"To get to Blytheheart. She'll ride —"

"Directly into their hands," Christopher finished.

"And so will Merlin and Orvin."

Christopher saw his baby son, resting atop the crimsoned blade of a Saxon halberd; saw the hairy buttocks of a fat barbarian as he silenced a screaming Marigween with the choking length of his manhood; saw the snowy heads of Merlin and Orvin floating in the river, their bodies lying decapitated on the shoreline. The visions were accompanied by a chill so icy it seemed to freeze his heart for a moment. As in combat, his body abruptly detached from his mind. His feet wanted to work. They wanted to carry him to a horse, get him moving, get him out of the tent. He rose, bounded for the tent flaps and the sunlight beyond.

"Where are you going? Christopher you can't —"

Without looking, he plowed outside — directly into someone headed inside. "I'm sorry, I —" He looked up.

As if by command a breeze fluttered over her, lifted her dark mane away from her face. It appeared as if she had just combed her hair, and the sun ignited some of the even lines, turned them red. Every curve, every glimmer of beauty struck pain in Christopher. If he allowed himself even the tiniest moment of desire, he knew the guilt would come. He buckled his thoughts down to Merlin, Orvin, Marigween, and his son.

Her lips opened, but she said nothing. Neither did he. Even hello was awkward. Was there even time for it?

He began to move around her. "Brenna, you look like you want to talk. I wish I had time, but —"

She stepped in his way. "I want to be friends," she blurted out. "I don't want to avoid you."

"I'm sorry. I have to go. It's important. We can be friends. And we'll talk some other time."

He shuffled around her, felt his shirt lift from his chest as he jogged away. There was a burning sensation across his shoulders as he expected her to call after him, and after a few yards he thought he heard her cry, but wasn't sure if it was real or not. He did not turn back to find out.

6   Brenna closed her eyes, then drew in a deep breath. Christopher had left her many times, and she had always called after him; she would not replay the

scene again. She balled one hand into a fist and held
back the urge to shout his name.

The sun was in her face, its warmth a consoling
touch. She exhaled, loosened her hand, craned her head
back to let the heat spread over her. The chirping of the
pipits and wrens in the nearby beech trees faded and
were replaced by a voice within her, his voice.

*"Lady Marigween, daughter of the late Lord Devin, is
the mother of my child. We have a son. I courted her at
the same time I courted you — before I even left for the
Mendip hills. I returned from battle to find I was a
father."*

She remembered rising after Christopher had delivered
the news. She had trembled, hadn't known what to say.
She had felt foolish, betrayed, angry, and had wanted to
die. Tears had fallen as she had attacked him with words,
told him *she* would have to pay for his mistake. She had
questioned whom he loved more, and he hadn't been able
to answer, but she knew — even now — that she still
dwelt in his heart.

The more Brenna remembered their last good-bye, the
less it seemed to hurt. She had come to terms with it,
even made friends with it, let it come and go as it
pleased, occasionally talked to it and let it fill her mind
before she closed her eyes at night. A moon had passed,
and one day she had simply realized that her relationship with him was over. If it ever did resume, it would
be something very different. They would never have the
innocent love they had first shared when Christopher
had been a squire-in-training. It was time for a new
beginning. She wanted to be his friend. He would be living in Arthur's camp, as she was, and that meant she
would frequently run into him. It would be too painful
and awkward to turn her head away every time she saw
him.

He had just said he would be her friend. But he didn't

have time for her now. She had surprised him. Why did he have to rush off?

He must still care! Didn't you see how nervous he was?

Fool! Do you want to be hurt again? Be his friend. Don't love him. Don't be weak. Be a woman!

She had reassured herself that she would be all right without him. And she was. Life went on without Christopher.

But seeing him again. It hurts.

She opened her eyes, let her gaze adjust to the daylight, then turned her head toward the rustle made by someone coming out of the tent. Her lips formed a wan smile of recognition. "Hello, Neil."

He looked past her toward the line of Christopher's departure. "Sorry about that, it's just —"

"Don't apologize for him. It's not going to be easy with Christopher back."

"You won't have to worry about him." She looked her question. He read her face, then explained, "Christopher will be out of Shores by nightfall, maybe sooner." His gaze lowered to her cream-colored shift which was spattered a bit with blood. "I heard you're helping Hallam treat the wounded. A friend of mine told me you bandaged one of his wounds. He said you did an excellent job."

She shook her head clear of the business of helping the wounded and focused on Neil's earlier statement. "Why is Christopher leaving Shores?"

Brenna shared a tent with Hallam's daughter, Kate, an unmarried maid twice her age who was obsessively neat. Kate would explode if she saw the current condition of their quarters. Brenna tore through four different clothing trunks, throwing garments everywhere, stuffing things she needed into two riding bags she stole from

Hallam's wagon driver. The black rounsey used by Hallam's messenger was left unattended while the man ate supper. She had to hurry before he returned, had to hurry to catch up with Christopher, who Neil had said might be gone already. There was little guilt over stealing a horse; she'd probably treat the animal better than the messenger did, and besides, there would be too many questions if she tried to borrow a mount, questions that would delay her, and she had no time to waste.

With the bags finally full, Brenna hurried out of the tent, then stopped, realizing she had forgotten one of the most important things. She dropped the bags, spun around, and knifed through the tent flaps. She kicked through the abandoned clothing toward a crossbow and full quiver that rested upright in the far left corner. The weapon had been given to her as a token of thanks by Peter, an archer she had nursed for half a moon. He even showed her how to fire it one cloudy morning.

She emerged from the tent with the quiver, its strap slung over her shoulder, and the crossbow in her hands. She had traveled from Gore to Shores unarmed, and was nearly raped by that fat Montague and his boys, but this time she would be traveling with firepower — and she would not hesitate to use it.

"Where are you going with the bow, Brenna?"

Kate's flimsy shift did absolutely nothing to hide the volcano of flesh that was her belly. As she stepped closer, the belly seemed to erupt here and there, pushing the shift up and down, turning it into the veil for a lava pool of lard.

For a moment, Kate turned her attention away from Brenna. One of the tent flaps was caught open and she was able to steal a glimpse of the tent's interior. "All the saints! What happened to our tent? Did *you* do this?"

Brenna hoisted the riding bags in one hand, rested the T of the crossbow over her shoulder next to the quiver's strap. "Sorry about the mess, Kate. I have to go." She started away from the tent toward the opening of a thin trail in the wood.

"What are you talking about? Wait!" Kate came from behind and seized the neckline of Brenna's shift, pulled back, and brought Brenna to a choking halt.

Brenna pushed forward and broke free, but Kate reached out again and caught the shift in nearly the same place.

Brenna raged aloud as she tried to twirl out of Kate's grasp. Her shift tore, leaving Brenna free and Kate with only a piece of the dress in her hand. With all her might Brenna wound back with the pair of riding bags. She felt the wind rush as she brought them forward and smashed them into Kate's face.

The big woman collapsed onto her buttocks with a thud that could have come from a downed oak. The momentum of the riding bags nearly knocked Brenna off-balance; she let go of them just in time to steady herself.

Kate began to cry. She reached up and attended her cheek. Between wails and whimpers, she exclaimed, "You're mad! The devil is in you!"

Kate could have let her go, could have stayed out of Brenna's way. This was her fate for interfering. All of the criticism she had foisted on Brenna for being even the slightest bit sloppy had now landed Kate on her rump. It was unfortunate that Brenna released all of her pent-up anger in one blow. Maybe Kate didn't deserve to be hurt this badly.

"I'm sorry, Kate. Really, I am. I just have to help someone." She fetched the riding bags, then crossed to the entrance of the trail. Before venturing into the wood, she added, "I'll explain it all to you if I return."

"You won't be welcome back here!" Kate shouted. "My cheek! It's on fire. Look what you've done to me!"

Kate's cries were promptly lost in the soughs and flutterings of the forest, and in the sound of Brenna's sandals as they crushed the dry, fallen leaves that mottled the reddish brown trail.

Her shoulders were about to cave in by the time she reached the hitching post of the messenger's rounsey. She patted the horse's breast a few times, then moved around him and slung her riding bags over its back. She fastened them to the sides of the saddle, then let the crossbow fall into an extra leather loop on one of the bags, suited for the purpose. The quiver would remain on her shoulder. She crossed to the post and untied the rounsey's reins, threw them over his head, then slipped one foot into a stirrup.

Hold a moment. What am I doing? Why do I think I can help Christopher, anyway? I've helped him before, but this is something far more dangerous.

Why don't I just stay and forget about the whole thing. Helping the wounded men is rewarding. My life here is not all that bad, why should I jeopardize it?

Brenna could question her actions all she wanted; it did nothing to change the fact that she was governed by the overwhelming desire to go after him. She didn't know why or when or how, but she felt, she *knew*, he would come to need her. Christopher had told her about how Orvin would read the sky, that there was a strange art up there, that one with a faithful gaze could see what would be. Brenna didn't need to study the sky to know she had to go. As Kate was ruled by her need for things to be neat and orderly, so was Brenna possessed by her duty to help Christopher. She was probably being as irrational as he, but the feeling had nothing to do with logic and everything to do with — she hated to admit it — love. She might never have him again. The odds were truly against

it. But he was all alone in the world and everyone he
cared about was out there and he had no one to help him
but her. Neil said he would not go to Blytheheart with
Christopher, that he was tired of Christopher getting him
into trouble. Brenna was Christopher's only ally. How
could she bandage wounded men at Shores when he
might be suffering out there?

*What am I doing? Am I admitting I still love him and
can't bear the thought that he might die?*

*I don't have a choice. I might still love him — no
matter how many mistakes he's made.*

She had surrendered to her heart, and might hate herself for that later. What was it about Christopher that
made her want him? Why could she not find another to
replace him? She had tried once, and that mistake with
Innis made her realize how special Christopher really
was. Born on Easter day, born on the day that Arthur
drew the sword from the stone, born into the humble,
simple world of a saddlemaker and his wife, Christopher
had risen with extraordinary courage and speed to per-
sonally serve the king. He defied all social borders and
carved himself a throne of the highest order for one so
young. He was not meant to live an ordinary life, and
Brenna felt she was meant to share that life with him.
She, too, had come from humble beginnings, and since
leaving Gore moons ago she had done things that made
her feel alive, like a woman. The two of them together
might reach goals that spread far beyond the confines of
Britain. It was a glorious dream she had cast away when
they had last said good-bye. But no matter how many
times she had let it go, it always surfaced in her mind.
No matter what Christopher did, and no matter what
she did, for that matter, they somehow belonged
together. Even the child he had with Marigween did not
repress the dream. She could not help the way she felt.
In this respect, she was too weak to fight. She might be

her own worst enemy, but she would not ignore her heart. If she did, she knew she would be miserable for the rest of her life.

Still tingling with apprehension, she mounted the rounsey, reined the horse around, and heeled him into a trot. She would take the southernmost trail around the ramparts of the castle; that course was the swiftest and probably the one Christopher had chosen.

7

"I repeat, why is it you carry your bow and sword? They are just extra weight."

The setting sun cut wide bands of light and shadow across the western hills, and one irreverent row of radiance found its way directly into Orvin's eyes. At least he didn't have to see Merlin to insult him. "How do you propose to ward off brigands? With the dragon that is your face?" Orvin chuckled, then added, "Get rid of the extra weight you say? I should get rid of you!"

"You would not do that, Orvin. You take too much pleasure in chiding me." It was a miracle: for once Merlin was right.

Orvin adjusted himself in his saddle. His legs had grown sore and this burro was too slow, nothing like his old Cara, the best mule he had ever owned. What did he expect from a druid? It seemed not a one of them knew anything about the qualities of a good mule.

Merlin rode just behind him, unfortunately within earshot. Why couldn't he shut up and ride farther away and give up on trying to talk Orvin into abandoning his crossbow and broadsword? They'd be dolts to ride unarmed; then again, one of them could already be described as such.

"If we had better mounts," Orvin informed the other, "you wouldn't be worrying about the extra weight."

"It is not so much the weight of the weapons that distresses me, but rather, your lack of skill with them."

"Ha!" Orvin reached a thumb under his crossbow's strap, slid the weapon off his shoulder. "I've been firing this very bow since I was a boy," he began.

"And the bow's trigger, I suspect, is as laden with rust as your aim." It was an odd sound, Merlin's laugh, somewhere between the whine of a dog dying and the squeal of a piglet.

"I've kept this weapon oiled and waxed over the years. And I replaced the bowstring just before we left. It is in perfect condition. As for rust in my aim, perhaps you would like to provide me a moving target and I'll give you a demonstration of my skill. In fact, why don't *you* be the target." Orvin knew this last would rouse some kind of retort from Merlin, but strangely, the druid kept his mouth closed. "What's the matter, magician, no barbs to bounce my way?" He squinted back at Merlin. The other's gaze was captured by something ahead of them.

Orvin looked to the hills, observed that the five guards rose slowly on the horizon and would soon thankfully eclipse the sun. And then he just barely picked out a thin ribbon of gray smoke. He blinked, made sure his eyes weren't deceiving him; they did that now and again. No, he'd made no mistake. The wisps of smoke were there, created, more than likely, by a lone cookfire. Whoever built the fire was clever enough to know that the telltale smoke would be hidden by the five guards in the west, and hard to see through the setting sun from a vantage point in the east. The flatlands to the north of the guards, and the Yeo River to the very far south were part of a north–south course that was not the common line of travel in this part of the realm. The

chances of someone approaching the guards from either
of those directions were small.

"That smoke," Merlin said, standing in his stirrups, a
hand screening the glare from his eyes, "sets our
course."

"Oh it does?" Orvin asked. "I'm glad we've established who's leading this party. Are you going to ride us
to ruin, the way you are with Britain?"

Merlin dropped back into his saddle, heeled his burro
so that he moved up next to Orvin. "I had hoped — *to
suggest to you* — that we could ride south and around
Glastonbury." He cleared his throat. "But we shall have
to head north."

Orvin flipped the druid a grimace. "Go north *around*
the guards?"

Merlin studied the distance. "Indeed. And west of
Glastonbury through a mountain pass, one which will
take us down to the Parret River."

The druid could not see the incredulity that now
waxed Orvin's face, so Orvin would have to let him
hear it. "You don't mean for us to cross the Mendips
and the Quantocks?"

"We will not exactly have to cross —"

"Forget your plan," Orvin said, hatcheting off
Merlin's words — and enjoying the act. "We go to the
smoke to find out who it is. I do not want someone trailing us all the way to Blytheheart. And from now on,
druid, don't think so much."

Merlin made no reply, as if deaf. Then he quietly
stated, "You invite danger."

Orvin pushed one of his riding bags aside and dug for
the windlass hanging beside it. As he unlatched the bow-
loading instrument, his gaze still narrowed on the druid,
he answered, "No, old man. I don't invite danger. I've read
my skies. Have you read yours? Danger not only invited
herself to this banquet, but she was first to arrive."

8 The leveret was truly a gift from Woden. Seaver could not explain the baby rabbit any other way. Here it was, late August, in the bleached grass valley of the five guards, and among all of this lifelessness he had been able to find game. The rabbit had come out of a wiry, near-leafless bush, hopped once, twice, then paused, twitching its nose. Seaver had thrown his small frame into the air and had caught the beast with his bare hands. As he'd choked the life out of the lev-eret, tears had gathered in his eyes.

When he'd first arrived, Seaver had resigned himself to a meal of dried, salted beef. The meat, along with a flint stone, double-woolen sleeping blanket, fresh linen breeches and shirt, and a small, fairly sharp skinning knife had been given to him for the wagon and one of the rounseys he had stolen from Shores. The farmer he'd traded with was wise not to ask questions, for too many of those might have cost the simple man his life. Before even doing business with the man, Seaver had been ready to kill him and take everything. For once in the land called Britain, he had made a trade that didn't end in a double cross. Perhaps Woden looked favorably on his sparing the man, and that was why he gifted Seaver with the leveret? It was possible.

The dance of the cookfire's flames tired Seaver. He sat and sucked the remaining marrow from the last of the rabbit's bones, threw it into the swaying ribbons of orange, yellow, and red, then yawned. The heat tingled his cheeks. He crinkled his nose, then drew in another deep breath, smelling the semisweet mixture of charred wood, animal fat, and bone. He laced his fingers together behind his head, then lowered himself slowly onto his back. Embers whirled up through the smoke, tiny red stars quickly lost in the low-angled light of the sun. He thought for a moment how he was like those tiny bits of fired wood, alive among the bright flames for a short time and then hurled in circles, up into the unknown. He wondered if he would be able to accept his new life in Ivory Point, accept going back to the old and inglorious familiar. But Ivory Point could have changed. The little over a score of tofts might not even be there when he returned. The way the Saxons had burned so many villages in Britain, perhaps the Celts had made it up that far and done the same to his village. Or a rogue group of Picts might have taken control. He had better not count on finding his home the same way he had left it; he might be in for a grim surprise.

It would be difficult going back, he knew. The journey so far had not been easy, but the idea of returning might soon pose a bigger problem. He hadn't seriously thought about what he was giving up when he had left the castle. He had simply reacted to the situation, thinking he had no choice. He didn't think he could have stood up to Kenric. Riding away from Shores, the first doubts had hit home. He realized now that descending would be as hard as ascending. He had risen from being one of half a dozen scouts all the way up to Kenric's second-in-command. Now, within a few moons, he would fall all the way down to the life of a farmer. He knew no one back home would understand what he had lost — or even be impressed with his tales of battle; they all thought him an ass for leaving in the first place. They said abandoning his mother was cruel and selfish. But she had supported his desire to join in the quest for land. And he had promised her he would take her to Britain when they had won the territory.

Instead, he would return home to a dying land and try to rekindle a bit of life that barely existed in the first place.

Scores of men had stiffened when he approached, had
snapped at his every command. Parading in front of
them was, as he had once thought of it, like having
wings, like looking down on the world from a point all
had to look up to. As Kenric's second, he was far from
the earth, much closer to the clouds, clouds he nibbled
on like sweet pastries. Back on his mother's toft, he
would not only be close to the earth, he'd be working it.
And the only thing snapping at his commands would be
the ox pulling his plow. War had its horrors, but its
heights were unmatched. The battle for Britain had
transformed him into a giant. He perceived himself as
someone far greater than a farmer. Could he slip back
into his old peasant garb and obliterate the thoughts of
what he had once obtained and thrown away? Was he
denying who he really was? Farmer? Warrior?

Father, what would you do?

Father had never existed for Seaver in the physical
world. There were only his mother's tender eyes, calming touch, and soft voice. If she had told him more
about the man, he wouldn't always have to imagine him.
Sometimes, though, Seaver thought it was better the
way it was. Father sat with him now before the cookfire.
The man had no peers. The only flaw he had was his
mortality.

Father, what would you do?

The man rose without answering, then stepped into
the cookfire. The flames danced over his armor, and
soon the flames *were* his armor. He shrank into a tiny
ember that twirled up into the smoke and then winked
out.

Seaver pulled himself upright, then stood. He lifted
his gaze to the sky. "Woden, it was you who allowed me
to escape from Shores, you who allows me to eat so
well. Thank you. Guide my journey and my life. Your
watchful eye does not go unappreciated."

As he lowered his gaze from the heavens he noticed two dots on the horizon, and then a shimmer from one: reflected light. Something metal. He studied the dots another moment, then concluded the travelers had probably spotted his cookfire and were headed his way. If they were hostile, his little dagger wouldn't help him much.

Seaver repeatedly kicked dirt into his cookfire; the flames hissed, spat smoke, then finally died. He crossed to his sleeping blanket, cursed the fact that he had already unrolled it. He gathered the blanket along with his food pouch and dagger, then went to his horse and jammed them into his riding bag. Packed, he swung himself up and into his saddle. His horse reacted weakly to the crack of the reins, so he spurred it hard, aiming for a steep, rocky hill on the northwest side of the valley. He cocked his head over his shoulder to check on the proximity of the travelers. Judging from their distance, he should have ample time to find cover before being spotted. Once in the mountains, he'd employ every trick he knew as a scout to cover his tracks. They'd never find him.

9

Doyle had delivered on his boast of being an excellent marksman. He'd been able to hit one Saxon in the arm, the other in the leg. Though he had been successful, he still loathed the time it had taken to load the crossbow, for he used to get off seven arrows from his longbow in the time it took to windlass a crossbow bowstring in preparation to fire just one bolt. The crossbow also lacked the penetrative power of his old longbow. Had the Saxons been wearing more armor, there would have been problems. But, if all that mattered were end results, there was no use in complaining over a victory because it was too slow, or because the projectiles didn't quite make it all the way down to the victims' bones.

While both Saxons had dropped in agony to the shoreline of the Cam, he and Montague had stolen their rounseys. Naturally, Montague had had a few cocky remarks to utter to the enemy soldiers, but Doyle had reminded him that they didn't understand him anyway. Montague had argued that the Saxons still got the gist of his taunt. Maybe they had, maybe they hadn't. They had seemed awful busy trying to remove the bolts from their writhing appendages.

Doyle had been glad to find that his horse's pack contained a hefty supply of dried fruit, fish, and pork. Montague's riding bag had also contained food, a hammer, shoe nails, and half a dozen horseshoes. Judging from the Saxons' packs, they had not been on their way to the castle of Rain, but were headed somewhere much farther. Maybe, Doyle had speculated with irony, to Blytheheart.

The two would-be merchants had trekked around the five guards, past Glastonbury, and into the foothills of the Mendips. They had eaten well, slept well, and traveled swiftly. During the ride, they had seen no one, save for a small caravan of wool traders heading north to Bath on the horizon. Blytheheart was only a finger's snap away, Montague had told Doyle. Doyle's mind had blossomed with visions of his new life, and his heart had throbbed with excitement.

Then they had reached the crest of a foothill of the Mendips. They had looked down into the Parret River valley, and Doyle's spirits had dropped all the way to Lucifer's dungeon.

Three Saxon armies had combined in the valley, each

numbering roughly five hundred men. Now, from his vantage point in a thin stand of trees, Doyle once again surveyed the entire scene, familiarized himself with the new positions of the sentries that fanned out in a half circle from the river. The watchmen had adjusted their locations four times since nightfall. There was no way to hide an army of that size down in that low-lying grass-land; hence, the Saxons remained ever vigilant of their perimeter. They knew their cookfires blatantly dotted the valley, turning it into a shadowy whirlpool swarming with fireflies that could be spotted from nearly a league away if one approached from the south. Doyle saw how they placed double the number of sentries at that cardinal point.

He felt Montague's thick, hot breath on his neck, then heard the brigand emit a low whine, like the turn of a rusty axle in his throat. "My stomach's still not settled, laddie. Aye, I think just looking at them is what's doing it."

Doyle gazed over his shoulder at the portly personage, the gobs of hairy flesh on one side of his face unfortunately illuminated in starlight. "I'm sorry this army's souring your stomach — truly I am," he hissed between clenched teeth.

Montague sighed, and before he even spoke, Doyle knew a plea was forming. "I doubt they'll see it, let's spark up a fire. I've got to get some warm drink in me to settle this burn."

Doyle turned fully toward the highwayman, then slowly shook his head. "No, Monte. We're going back up this hill and staying undercover with the horses this evening. Those sentries down there will be moving farther and farther out, maybe even into these foothills. I don't want your cure for an upset stomach turning into an invitation for them. I still have a lot of cider left. Drink it cold. And stop moaning."

Montague's pout was so immature that Doyle trembled with the desire to smack it off his cherubic face. He huffed away his anger and strode past Montague, sidestepping over the large spine of an oak root that rose above the earth.

All he wanted to do was get to Blytheheart and put his life back into some kind of remote order. Why did they have to run into a Saxon army? Wasn't being banished penance enough? Wasn't having Montague as a companion punishment enough?

Doyle paused, hitting a mental roadblock in the path of their future. He turned back to the fat man. "What if the Saxons control the port?"

Montague belched, sighed, groaned softly, caught his breath, then began to trace Doyle's path back up the hill. His gait was carefully measured in an obvious attempt to keep his delicate, fat belly from being jarred by the rocks, weeds, and roots that littered the ground. He walked as if barefoot on broken glass. "If you'll show a little compassion for me, I'll tell you."

"All right. All right," Doyle said, "I'm, oh well, I guess I'm sorry for, for that."

Montague smiled, the hairs of his mustache curling. "That's my laddie. Now, don't you know the Saxons don't need control of Blytheheart?"

Still waiting for the mountain of a man to catch up, Doyle dropped his weight to one leg in disgust. "Will you move?"

"Patience, laddie, please! Oh, there it goes again." He stopped, palmed his too-swollen abdomen. "Lord, strike me down dead now — or cease this pain."

Doyle swore aloud, went to the man, slung a giant arm over his shoulder, and began dragging the other up the foothill.

"Easy now, lad, easy. Yes, that's it. That's good. Here we go now. Here we go."

"Take your mind off the pain," Doyle ordered him,

"and tell me why the Saxons don't need control of Blytheheart."

"Well," Montague started between pants, "they're already trading freely there under the condition that they will not use the port for military purposes."

"What?" Doyle asked, even before the disbelief caused one side of his mouth to twitch.

"Aye. The abbot of Blytheheart negotiated an agreement with the Saxons moons ago." Montague chuckled a bit. "He's even allowed Pict cogs to dock and fill their holds with grain, and perhaps by now, even more."

"Celts are trading with Saxons and Picts?"

"Not only trading, but secretly supplying their armies. The Jutes'll be next." He cocked a thumb back over his shoulder. "Those Saxons down there in the valley are probably dressed in wool and armor made by Celts, are riding horses bought from Celt hostlers, and are eating food grown, shipped, and sold by Celts. Doubt me? Take a look at one of the horseshoes in my pack. It bears the stamp of a Celt guild. True, the horses could've been stolen, but I wager they weren't."

Doyle stopped, and in a fierce, fluid motion whipped Montague's arm off his shoulder. He backed away from the man as the newly formed, tight ball of anger bounced a few times within the pit of his stomach. "Those merchants . . . they're traitors! — all of them."

Montague pursed his lips, one of his chins lifting. His gaze dropped to a patch of sun-yellowed grass now gray in the half moonlight. "You call them traitors. I call them gifted." He lifted his eyes to regard Doyle with an emphatic stare. "The Saxons, Picts, and others first came here because their lands were poor. We called them barbarians, but they learned our ways. Now they've employed our land better than we ever have. They've brought ideas from the Orient and from those strange holy lands, and now they have capital and a burgeoning trade. They're not going anywhere. They won't be driven out. And when the war ends, it won't be Arthur or that Kenric you spoke of who's victorious. The merchants gifted with foresight will be the ones wearing the crowns." He paused for effect. "Us."

Doyle widened his eyes and stiffened. "If we're going to do business with the Saxons, then I don't want any part of it." His right hand tingled with that accursed feeling, the feeling like he still had a right index finger and thumb.

Montague stepped toward Doyle, reached out to reassure him. "No, no, no," he said as Doyle retreated a step, "this abbot of Blytheheart — he's a very agreeable old man. I've been thinking about this during our ride. Listen. I want to propose a long-term contract with him, say seven years. He'll pay us a cash sum in advance and a fixed annual payment. For that, we will purchase and or commission all of the articles and artwork for his abbey as well as the monastery, some to be on loan for the various feasts, some to become permanent fixtures. I know he'll pay handsomely for our expertise. We'll acquire merchandise for him from as far away as Wales, or maybe even sail like the Saxons to the Orient. He'll pay our travel expenses and all the rest. I think that friend I told you about can get us a meeting with him."

The idea softened Doyle's temper a hair. They wouldn't be trading with Saxons. Yet the abbot of Blytheheart seemed bound not by God and his laws, but by correct numbers. He had named his price, and the Saxons and Picts had paid it. As his port flourished, so did he. Doyle guessed the abbot would have to confess his sins hourly to be truly forgiven. His transgressions probably piled as high as the greatest peak in the Quantocks.

"So," Montague said, finally close enough to rest his palm on Doyle's shoulder. "What do you think?"

Doyle considered the question, realized it didn't matter what he thought. They should figure out what to do once they reached Blytheheart. If they got there at all. He told Montague, "I think we should take turns sleeping tonight. When you're awake, concentrate on a route around the army. And we're going to have to cross that river. We'll probably have to swim for it."

Montague drew back his head, repulsed by the idea. "I haven't been —"

"Don't worry about swimming. You'll float, as much as that's hard to believe. Now let's go. I want to move before sunrise."

"No," Montague complained, "not before sunrise. And why is it hard to believe that —" he cut himself off.

Doyle directed his attention to the top of the foothill and put his legs in motion for that destination, leaving Montague behind. "Live or die. Your choice," he called back.

"Live or die, live or die," he heard the fat man repeat under his breath. "If I were ten years younger and ten pounds lighter . . ."

"Make that one hundred pounds!" Doyle corrected.

"Hey. Watch it, laddie. Just watch it. You need me to get that meeting with the abbot."

"And you need me," Doyle pointed out, "to get there at all."

10

The knight lay on his back, his face exposed through his open bascinet. A javelin sprouted from his breastplate, and a gauntleted hand still clung to the pole. Marigween could see how the man's skin had rotted to the bone. The knight's beard seemed

attached to his jaw without the aid of flesh to hold it
there. With his lips gone he smiled forever, a per-
verted, toothy grin that sent shivers through her. Grass
sprouted up around the knight, covered his legs almost
completely. Had she been riding any faster, her horse
would have tripped over the corpse; the fact that she
hadn't was the only thing to be thankful for right now.
She finally knew where she was, all right, and the news
was dreadful.

Five years had passed since she had gone with father
to Bristol, and she remembered they had taken the
northernmost route through the Mendip hills, a route
that looked very much like the one before her. Then
there was the knight. Christopher had told her of his trek
into the Mendips with Hasdale's army. He had told her
of a dead knight they had encountered. Marigween even
remembered his name: Wells. He had betrayed Hasdale
and was banished. All of this really meant that somehow
she had steered north of the five guards and wound up
here, on ground Christopher had once trodden.

She was south of Bath, only a day's ride away from
the town. The temptation to rest there was strong, but a
diversion would only mean delay and questions from
curious innkeepers. If this dead knight was an omen, so
be it. She would not stop now.

Marigween expected the temperature to drop at night,
but she had not figured the elevation or the harsh,
northern wind into her expectations. She knew that
even in August the Mendips were cold — but would
they get colder than this?

After pulling the hood of her cloak over her head, she
slid Baines's blanket over his shoulders. She wished she
had a little woolen cap the child could wear, but wishes
did nothing to fight the cold. How much farther would
she ride until settling for the night? The present landscape seemed dangerous and offered no respite from the

elements. The only thing she could do was look for an oasis of timber somewhere, get out of this vulnerable grassland. Even the smallest stand of trees would break the wind and provide a bit of cover. She had to decide whether to head north or southwest in search of a camp, for each of those directions represented a different course to Blytheheart.

She could go north over the route she was slightly familiar with, arrive at the coastline, and follow it down to Blytheheart.

If she chose the southwestern path, she would traverse the foothills of the Mendips, parallel the main hills until she got to the Parret River. Once across the water she would ride the northern ridge of the Quantocks into Blytheheart.

The second route was shorter, the terrain easier. But she was unfamiliar with the landscape, and could get lost again. However, she wouldn't have to cross a river.

If she rode north she would have to contend with the cold, sometimes rocky hills of the Mendips.

Baines coughed, followed it with a soft gurgle. Marigween reached down and felt his nose; it was very cold and running. The child was bound to get sick from subjection to the extremes of heat and cold. She had to get him to Blytheheart, to steady warmth, as soon as possible.

She would ride southwest. It was the shortest route. Surely there was a toll crossing over the Parret River.

The moon was low on the horizon and the silhouette of a mountain peak shaved off the bottom of the half disk. She turned her horse away from it and kept the hills to her right, the northern wind at her back.

Less than a score of yards away from the fallen knight, she heard barks from what sounded like a pair of wolves. Her rounsey neighed, bucked, and snorted in alarm. She stopped the horse, reined him around, and

cantered back to the knight. There, she twisted and
tugged the javelin free from the knight's chest, tightened
her grip on the cold, sanded wood of the shaft. She
coaxed the rounsey into a trot; he bucked again as more
wolves announced their presence.

Marigween could not pinpoint the location of the
wolves, but even as her gaze fought into the gloom to
catch a glimpse of them, her mind had already placed
her in the chilling center of a small pack of the snarling,
drooling, beasts, gleams firing in their yellow and gray
eyes as they caught the scent of the tender child
strapped to her chest.

11

When Christopher returned to his tent he
learned that Clive, the junior squire under him, had
loaned Christopher's courser to Sir Bors, whose horse
was ill. Bors needed Christopher's mount to lead a
lance of scouts north to the Cotswold hills. A Pict
army was said to be gathering there.

Christopher threw Clive to the ground, leapt on him,
and then pinned him. "You fool!"

"I'm sorry, Christopher. I thought, I-I thought it
would be all right."

After catching his breath, Christopher swallowed the
drool that had gathered in his mouth. He held the
scared, blond twelve-year-old another moment, let out a
sigh of disgust, then released him. "Clive, I do not . . .
it's just . . . I apologize. I acted with my heart — not my
head."

Clive sat up and brushed the dirt from his shoulders.
"No, it was my mistake, Christopher. You need not
apologize."

He explained to Clive why he needed his horse so badly, and while the junior squire set about hunting down a replacement mount, Christopher packed for his journey. In about an hour his preparations were complete, and he stood tapping a boot restlessly outside his tent. Riding bags, leather backpack, and two new sheathed spathas lay on the ground next to him. He was successful in acquiring some apples, raisins, and pears, cider, pork, and a small sack of oatmeal. The pork was fresh and would have to be eaten within the next two days. After that, he'd be living on the fruit and oatmeal and whatever game he could acquire.

Despite being ready for the trip, there were two things he lacked. First, the broadsword Baines had given him. When he had fallen off the wall-walk and plunged with Ware into the moat, he had lost the sword. The siege on the castle made it impossible for him to retrieve the weapon from the bottom of the moat. Once he had taken Baines with him to fight the Saxons; then Baines had died and he had taken the boy's sword with him, for strength and luck; now all he had was a longing for the sword and a clouded vision of the boy in his mind. He had named his son after the youth who had inspired him to become a squire, and that was where the memory of Baines was reborn and would live on.

Christopher also lacked the spirit of another friend. The longbow and quiver that had been given to him by Doyle were not packed for the journey. The bow was too large and cumbersome, and meant to be fired while standing, not mounted. Christopher wished there was some way to get around the bow's size, for he longed to carry it with him. The weapon represented Doyle's past life, and his relationship with Christopher. Doyle gave up the bow, releasing a life, a relationship, a past. Christopher did not feel worthy of possessing the bow; loading an arrow was somehow an unholy or desecrating act. To fire it would seal Doyle's fate forever, and, since receiving the weapon, Christopher had never done so. Perhaps it was for the best that the bow remain in his tent. Yet he couldn't help feeling he should have both Baines' broadsword *and* Doyle's longbow with him. In that way he would not be journeying alone. The spathas he had were freshly forged and quite functional, but they were dead metal. They lacked life, spirit, history. There was no sweat of past engagements settled into their grips, no battle scars across their shafts. They were ordinary and somehow not ready for battle. They were untried, untested, and chancy. Yet his reluctance over the weapons would never be strong enough to stop him. It would take a far greater force to hold him back from saving Marigween, Orvin, Merlin, and Baines.

He stood outside his tent for eternity and a day, or at least it felt so. Twilight was long forgotten by the time Clive returned. The boy led, no — it couldn't be.

"Christopher! I found you this mare." Clive's excitement was matched only by his naïveté. "Look at how white she is, like a cloud, and judge her gaskins. Perfect, aren't they?"

He grabbed Clive by his shirt collar and yanked him close. A familiar pale mask instantly gripped the boy's face. "Do you know whose mare this is?"

"I'm sorry," Clive squeaked back. "I thought you wouldn't know."

Christopher unhanded the squire. "I may not be serving King Arthur anymore, but I still know his stable of mounts." He regarded the horse. "This is Llamrei, the new mare that Lord Uryens had been holding for him in Gore. She came with the men who brought the siege machines." He cocked his brow. "I suppose you didn't ask the king if you could take her, did you?"

Clive's reluctance spanned a trio of heartbeats, then he ever-so-slightly shook his head, no.

Christopher tightened his brow. "How did you get by the hostlers?"

Clive's self-satisfied grin had a strange, feline quality to it, and the faint mustache of his pubescent upper lip added to the effect. "They're not very watchful. They didn't even see me kick open the corral. And while they were chasing down the other horses, I led Llamrei out."

In truth, Christopher was not the one who had stolen Arthur's horse. He had not told Clive to steal a mount to replace his rounsey. Christopher was, however, responsible for Clive, and if Clive committed a crime, then it was Christopher's fault. Thus, in truth, he *was* guilty. The situation reminded him of a quip an old gravedigger had once told him: the first rule of holes — when you're in one, stop digging.

Accepting this mount would bury Christopher a little deeper, but there wasn't time for Clive to find another horse.

Christopher put some fire into his gaze and prepared to speak the way his old squire trainer Sloan had moons ago, when the scarred battle lord wanted to reinforce a point. "Clive, what you did was wrong. *Never* do it again. I have to take this horse. It's wrong for me to do so, but the people I love most need me now."

The boy lowered his head. "I understand."

"If I can flee before anyone notices," Christopher said as he began to stroke the mare, "they'll think she ran away."

Clive brightened. "Yes. You're right." Clive apparently liked that idea better than Christopher did.

"But that's not the truth, correct?"

"If they ask, I will not tell them anything," Clive assured him. "I'll say I don't know where you are and haven't seen you."

"If they ask, you tell them the truth. You tell them everything," Christopher corrected. "Don't worry about me." He looked to his gear. "Now help me pack her up."

Llamrei was, by far, the most amazing mount Christopher had ever ridden. She took turns effortlessly, leapt with only the slightest bit of goading. He was able to take the south trail around the ramparts at full gallop. Though his journey had barely begun, the horse was already well lathered; he couldn't push her this hard for too long.

Trunks and limbs whirred by. A brown squirrel darted across the path, but Llamrei charged on, undaunted. Christopher wished he had taken a torch, but then again, the wind created by the horse's speed would have blown it out. The half moonlight was come-and-go, and he didn't see the other, slower-moving rider in the path until he was nearly on top of him.

"Whoa! Whoa!"

Christopher yanked hard on the reins. He began to slip out of his saddle and thrust his legs downward, locking his boots tighter into the stirrups. A cloud of dust rose at his back and drifted around him as he arrived to trot at the other rider's side. The trail was barely wide enough to accommodate two mounts.

The other rider coughed, waved dust from his face, then shouted, "You could've killed me!"

The voice was high. Too high. The other rider was not a man. Another look proved him right.

Her countenance softened as she recognized the man who had nearly killed her.

His countenance hardened as he recognized the woman in his way. "Brenna, what are you doing out here? And where did you get that horse? And why do you have riding bags, and that bow and quiver?"

A crossbow. Could she . . .

"I talked to Neil. I'm going —"

"Now wait —"

"I know what you're going to —"

"Then why don't you listen —"

"Because you need me and —

"I need you to stay here. It's too —"

"Dangerous for *you* to ride out there alone and —"

"You've been thinking too much. Remember —"

"I know what you did to me. And what I did —"

"This is truly mad. Truly —"

"Could I finish speaking. Please!"

Her scream raced all the way back to the elbows of limestone that jutted from the ramparts, and they listened to its echo and the hoofing of their horses for a score of breaths before talking again.

Staring at the easy lines of her profile, Christopher finally said, "I *will* talk you out of coming." If nothing else, she was too beautiful to come. He would never allow her to be scarred.

Don't think of her that way!

"It's getting a little cold," she started coyly. "You need to keep all that warm air inside you — instead of wasting it."

"That's something new," he said, smiling to himself.

He saw her regard him from the corner of his eye. "What?" she asked.

"You're . . . I don't know how to put it. Have you been spending time with Orvin?"

"I've been busy working with Hallam."

"Hmmm." He glanced at her crossbow and quiver. "Can you fire that bow?"

"Yes, I can. You'd be surprised."

"Did Innis teach you?"

"An archer named Peter."

Christopher shrugged. "I don't know him."

His suspicion had been triggered the first time he had seen her with the crossbow, but he had dismissed the idea in an instant. Brenna could have been the one who had shot Woodward. She did not know how to fire a crossbow. She had probably managed to get her hands

on one and had it with her for show, a visual threat with
no action behind it.

But now she confessed she could fire it. She didn't
know about Woodward's death, unless she was the murderer. If she wasn't, then he couldn't ask her if she had
killed the knight; by asking he would be leaking the
news of the murder. He did trust Brenna, but the fewer
people who knew what had happened, the better. If she
was the killer, then perhaps he could lead her into a
confession.

"Watch out!" Brenna screamed.

Christopher's introspection had veiled his vision. He
failed to see the horse-drawn wagon rumbling up the
trail, headed directly for them. There was no room to let
the wagon pass.

He and Brenna braked and steered toward the wood
on the right side of the path. Their horses plowed
through yellow, spiny gorse. Then Christopher felt the
ground abruptly drop; it was a slope of sorts, short but
very steep. The mare struggled for footing, but her
hooves slid wildly over a bed of fallen leaves. The earth
leveled off, but the momentum created by the slope kept
his horse moving out of control.

Christopher knew he had to slam his chest forward
onto his saddle, as Brenna did beside him, but he impul-
sively reached up to push a particularly low-hanging
limb out of his way.

And hidden behind that limb was another one, as
thick around as one of his hips. His arm slid up and
over the limb and became snagged on it. As his mount
moved forward, he felt himself being torn out of the
saddle. He yanked his boots back out of his stirrups as
the mare finally vanished beneath him. The weight of
his entire body rested from his arms. With an almost
inaudible groan he reached up with his free hand,
vised it around the limb, and lifted his body up to dig

out his arm. The mare came to a halt a few yards
ahead.

"Are you all right?" Brenna called from somewhere
beneath him.

With his arm finally over the limb, Christopher let
himself drop, and acorns crunched beneath his boots.
Brenna was off her horse and caught him by the shoulders as he was about to fall back on his rump. She
steadied him, then shifted to face him.

It was odd, the pain under his arm, a combination of
pleasant and unpleasant sensations, similar to that spot
near his elbow that he had once hit. His eyes were sore
with tears of pain, and his lips strangely fought back a
giggle.

"Thank St. Michael you had the good sense to get out
of your stirrups," Brenna noted. "Otherwise —"

"Otherwise half of me would still be in the stirrups
and the other half hanging up there. Either that, or I'd
be a yard taller." Christopher rubbed the ribs under his
arm, then his shoulder. Oh, it was a sweetly horrible
pain.

"You down there? Are you all right?" The shout came
from above the slope, from the trail. Through the fence
of tree limbs, Christopher saw that the wagon which
had driven them off the road had stopped, and the
driver now stood at its side, staring down into the wood.

"We're alive — if that's what you mean!" he shouted
back.

They gathered their horses, pushed off a few tree
trunks, and made it to the top of the slope. They broke
free of the gorse enclosing the wood, and, in a few
moments, emerged onto the trail a few yards away from
the driver.

"They ought to widen this path," the driver said, then
brushed a bead of sweat from his wrinkled forehead.
"That was close."

"Oh . . . my lord," Brenna said in shock.

At the moment the moon was right, unfettered by
clouds. Had there been less light, Christopher would
not, from his angle, have been able to identify the rot-
ting corpse draped across the back of the wagon, but
as it was, the image of the crossbow bolt still buried
in Lord Woodward's blue neck was perfectly clear.

"Uh, my apologies for that, my dear. Wish I had a
blanket to cover him up," the driver said grimly.

Christopher stiffened. "You found him?"

"No, a hunting party did. They just hired me to go
back and fetch him. He was deep in the eastern wood.
Had to drag him all the way out of it." He huffed in
disgust. "This job was worth a lot more than two
deniers."

"Where are you taking him?" Christopher asked,
somehow growing even more stiff than he already was.

"Do you know who this is? This is Lord Woodward.
He's one of the king's battle lords. Sir Lancelot wants
me to take the body to the king himself."

Brenna took a step back from Christopher.

He looked at her. "I didn't —" he began urgently.

"You didn't what?" the driver asked.

He drew in a long, slow breath. "I didn't mean to ask
so many questions."

A dark thought consumed Christopher. If he could
stop this driver from delivering his cargo . . . but how?
Beat or tie up or kill the man? Add another evil to his
growing list? Woodward's body would eventually be
discovered no matter how hard he tried to hide it. And
there wasn't time to do that. No, it was better just to
leave. He had to keep his mind fixed on the journey. But
the situation here was a wound that would not heal but
grow steadily worse.

"Well, I'm glad you are both all right. I'm off, then.
I've money to earn. Good evening to you both," the

driver said, turning away. "They really ought to widen this path."

Christopher led his mare away from the cart, then paused to mount the horse. Brenna climbed atop her own mount, then looked at him, studied him.

As they started off, he said, "I didn't kill him, Brenna. You have to believe that."

"You didn't seem surprised that he was dead," she said accusingly. But could she be acting, when, in fact, she had done the killing?

"I'll tell you everything," he said. "Woodward wanted to meet me . . ."

Before he continued, Christopher closed his eyes and tried to clear his thoughts. He wanted to remember exactly what had happened. He wanted to fill her in on all of the details, and perhaps while telling the story, see if he could get her to reveal something she might be hiding. Yes, he closed his eyes to clear his thoughts, but all he could see was Woodward lying on the back of the cart. Suddenly, Woodward sat up, tore the crossbow bolt out of his neck, and, as black blood gushed from his wound, he screamed, "Squire! You will pay for this!"

Part
Two

Line Dancing

PART TWO

THE PORT OF BLYTHEHEART

1   The Saxon army gathering in the Parret River valley finally finished its organizing and dividing into respective ranks, and, with only a few hours of night left, its newly formed Vaward Battle headed directly toward the foothill where Doyle and Montague were camped.

Thank St. Christopher that Doyle had decided to stay on watch all night. While Montague snored and repeatedly broke wind, Doyle kept his gaze trained on the army. Now, as battle horns resounded, he jogged back up the foothill to where Montague lay sprawled at the base of an oak and kicked the highwayman in the thigh.

Montague jolted awake. "Yaowww!" He scowled at Doyle and rubbed the fire in his leg.

"Get up. They're coming."

Doyle crossed to his mount, fetched his riding bag, then once again regarded his companion. "I think you had it wrong back there, Monte. I think you need me a lot more than I need you. My idea to move before sunrise was a good one." He slid his riding bag up over his rounsey's croup and positioned it behind his saddle.

"Luck," Montague said groggily.

Doyle fastened his bag to his mount, then smiled over the pleasure of having thrown Montague's foolish argument about moving before sunrise back into the brigand's face. To Doyle's continual disbelief, the fat man invariably put his own physical comfort over the much larger concern of survival. You had to make sacrifices to stay alive; the concept seemed *too* obvious. But Montague refused to put himself out. Doyle was near-positive that it was only through his goading that the gaudy grain sack had made it this far.

Montague knuckled sleep grit from the corners of his eyes, stretched as he sighed through his nose, then replied, "All right, laddie. You're the young smart one. I give you that. But once we're in Blytheheart your charge is over." He lifted a thumb, tapped it on one of his sagging breasts. "I run things there."

"We'll see," Doyle said, then tugged at the leather cords binding his bag to be sure they were tight.

Montague licked his dry lips. "Yes we will."

It was too early to begin an argument, and their current situation made one even less desirable. Doyle swallowed back the retort in his throat, threw Montague a hard look, and finally said, "Just get up and get ready."

In the predawn gloom they trotted to the west side of their foothill, and, camouflaged by an adequately thick stand of trees, paused as the Saxons' Main and Rearward formations clustered into flanking positions of the Vaward. All three groups began their march, each containing a torch-bearing cavalry of crossbowmen and armored swordsmen in front, followed by longbowmen on foot and a rear guard of more mounted crossbowmen protecting at least a half score of supply wagons. It was a rare spectacle — and it was just Doyle's luck that he had the opportunity to see the massive groups of ascending men; to feel the ground quiver under their weight; to smell the torches, horse dung, and smoldering cookfires that rose and all but choked the air.

He hoped it would all be over soon, and once the Saxons were gone, crossing the river might be as simple as paying the flatboat master his denier toll. Then again, the Saxons could have killed the flatboat master on this side of the Parret and sent his vessel to the muddy bottom, in which case Doyle would find out whether Montague had really forgotten how to swim. But even if he did remember, maybe Doyle was wrong: perhaps the fat man would not float. Suffice it to say that it would be nice if the flatboat master was still alive.

The Saxons advanced through the copses and knee-high grass at the base of the foothill. As they did, Doyle and Montague eased forward in the opposite direction toward the river. They steered as far west as their tree cover would permit. The Saxon cavalry created a thunderous cacophony that multiplied and reverberated across the hills, a sound Doyle had not heard since his battle days on the Quantocks. The clatter triggered memories of his murdering of Innis and Leslie. There was a sour taste in his mouth from not eating since yesterday, and he forced saliva over his tongue to wash it out. He wished he could wash away the memories as easily. He was sure to hear the roar of hooves in the future, and could not avoid the sound and its accompanying recollections. He must live with them. Live with everything. Were it as easy as thinking it . . .

"Doyle!" Montague stage-whispered, "We can make it to the toll cross now. I think that's a flatboat down there at that quay. And I think someone's on it."

Montague, who was ahead of Doyle, paused at the edge of the last stand of trees between them and the river. It was some two hundred yards to the shoreline. Two hundred wide open yards. All that was needed was for a curious rear guardsman to flip his gaze in their direction. To anyone else, the silhouettes of two horsemen moving toward the river might be regarded with apathy. But to a Saxon the dark shapes might be Celt scouts on their way to report the movement of the army; they would have to be pursued, captured, and killed.

"Wait another moment for the guard to get a little farther up the hills." Doyle closed his eyes; he hadn't realized how tired they were. The lids argued against rising again. He felt his mouth hang open a bit, his body fall slightly forward in the saddle. His arms were weights almost too heavy to bear.

Then, struck by the lightning of the moment, he snapped open his eyelids, jerked up his head.

Stay awake. Stay alert. Can't sleep. Don't.

Montague's rounsey whinnied, then nuzzled up to the foot of a beech tree to look for something to eat. "I know, I know, dear," he told his horse, "I feel the same."

Again, Doyle felt the hand of sleep press hard on the back of his head. He felt fingers reach around and attempt to force his eyelids closed. He cleared his throat, breathed deeply, and tightened his hands on his reins. "Let's go."

He let Montague lead as they began a trot toward the shoreline, a trot which quickly shifted into a canter but held back from a gallop. Montague was smart enough to realize that the footing grew more unstable the closer they got to the river. Reeds and hollow-stemmed rushes grew as far away as one hundred yards from the water, which meant the ground even that far out was precariously soft. Add to that the ruts and dangerous potholes left by the Saxons' horses and supply carts, and this course was about as dangerous as the practice field that stretched below the castle of Shores. Few riders ever made it across that acreage at full gallop.

Montague's large buttocks bounced in the saddle, two large jelly sacks of flesh bursting over the seat's wood and leather rim. Doyle lifted his gaze to a more pleasant sight.

The clouds were thin, small, and numerous, spread out evenly above him, haloed in orange and brushed delicately over the slowly fading stars. Like guards changing, the moon would soon bed down in the Quantocks, relieved by the sun. He dropped his gaze slightly to the mountains, only shadows really, but the familiar outline was enough. This was the first time he had been back to the Quantocks since the killings. This was not getting bucked off a rounsey and remounting; this was venturing into a part of himself that he would rather not go. The mountains were mirrors and he did not want to look into them. He would play a little game to cross them. The land was not a place of evil, but a happy stepping-stone to Blytheheart. His gaze would leap over the past and anchor itself in the future. He would develop a new picture of himself: Doyle, the well-paid merchant with admirable taste; Doyle, dressed in the height of fashion, eating the most expensive meals; Doyle, living in a grand manor in the center of Blytheheart. And the women would swoon as he strolled by them, overcome by his grandeur. Yes, they would swoon! The loss of his fingers would be regarded as the smallest of scars on a man very large in prestige.

"Ho, man, ho," Montague cried.

The flatboat master stood on the rickety wooden quay, the dark, blue-green waters of the Parret rushing beneath him. His long, wintry hair was pulled into a ponytail, his shaggy beard pulled into the same. Except for his beard, there was nothing particularly notable about him.

Until he opened his mouth.

"What did he say?" Montague asked as he dismounted. He clenched his rounsey's bridle and started forward.

Doyle stopped his horse where the quay met the muddy shore, then lifted himself out of his saddle. "I didn't quite hear him," he said, hitting the earth with a faint thud. He stepped onto the quay, its timbers tracking his steps with baritone creaks, and then accosted the master. "I'm surprised you're here. The Saxons let you live I guess, huh?" The master frowned as he paused before him. "How much for passage across?"

The master shook his head, a query crinkling his sun-browned face.

"What's wrong?" Doyle asked.

And then the master fired off a volley of sentences that were about as understandable to Doyle and Montague as the barking of a hound.

But Doyle caught something in the way the man stressed certain words. It hit him. He turned to Montague, and, with a grimace forming, reported, "He's a Saxon."

Montague shrugged off the fact as completely unimportant. "Show him our money. He'll understand that." He looked to the master. "Money. Deniers, yes?"

"Denier, yes," the master answered in broken Celt, "one denier," he pointed to the opposite shoreline some thousand yards away, "to go ac-ross." He thrust his palm toward Doyle.

Doyle looked back to Montague. The brigand nodded and gestured with a hand to pay the man. With a trace of reluctance, Doyle turned back, then untied the leather change purse strapped to his waist. He fished out a denier and handed the coin to the master. The Saxon licked one side of it, rolled the taste around in his mouth, then smiled, his teeth remarkably white.

"Our money's good," Montague said behind him, then guided his horse onto the quay. "Let's not waste any more time."

As the master helped both of them transfer their rounseys across a short, weather-beaten gangplank and onto the splintered and slightly warped rectangular deck of the flatboat, Doyle puzzled over the master's testing of the coin. Could he really tell a slug from a denier by its taste?

If the master was indeed a skilled money taster, he was an even better flatboat skipper. He deftly guided the craft with his long stick in the strong current and brought them downstream toward a quay on the opposite shore. During the ride, Doyle chewed heartily on some smoked whiting from his pack. The fish was a little tough, but any food was good now. He washed the whiting down with some cider, while Montague tore greedily into his riding bag. The fat man stuffed everything he could into the beard-framed abyss that was his mouth.

They reached the quay, and, with speed born of experience, the master tied the flatboat to two of the pier's thick wooden piles. He dropped the gangplank into place, then, with uncalled for courtesy, proceeded to help them guide their nervous rounseys over the board.

Once on solid ground, Doyle and Montague mounted their horses. The master waved and uttered something, a good-bye perhaps, then turned back to his ropes and prepared to shove off.

Shading the rising sun from his eyes, Montague said, "Now, that wasn't so bad, eh laddie?"

Doyle shook his head, no. It was, in fact, the first time he had ever used a toll cross, though he had certainly heard about them.

"Aye, but I am," Montague continued with a slight chuckle, "a little disappointed in you."

Doyle delayed his reply as he reined his horse toward the Quantocks and started toward the rolling hills. Montague came up on his side. Without looking at the man, he asked, "What are you talking about?"

"You just did business with a Saxon."

Doyle looked down at his three-fingered hand. *Damn!* He'd forgotten what he'd told Montague about wanting no part in dealings with Saxons. Yet trade with the master seemed so natural, and he doubted he and Montague would have been able to swim across the Parret in that current, or, had they bound the flatboat master and stolen his vessel, they probably would not have been able to pilot it to the opposite shore. They would have been swept downriver and leagues out of their way. They needed that Saxon and he needed their patronage. He appeared the average merchant. Did he have a family somewhere? How different was he? Was he one of the butchers Doyle had faced on the Quantocks or that particular devil who had robbed him of his fingers? No. He was just a man. Just a man trying to get by. Just a man like Doyle. This was not a startling revelation, for he and Christopher had talked politics occasionally, and Christopher had always argued that one day Saxons and Celts would coexist peacefully, that Saxons weren't any different than Celts. Both peoples harbored the ugly talent for war; both possessed the wisdom to put an end to the bloodshed.

It was ignorant and unfair to blame the entire Saxon people for what had happened to him. They were all victims, in one form or another, of the war. He hated the Saxons because they had taken Weylin away from him. But they hadn't stopped there. They had maimed him, had stripped him of who he had been, a fine archer.

But who's really to blame?

He had thrown himself to the Saxons because he had wanted to die; he had wanted to end the guilt over killing Leslie and Innis. But instead they had disfigured him, had kept him alive, and now the torture continued, torture brought on . . . by himself.

Perhaps it was time to let go of his hatred, let go of blaming the Saxons. It wasn't going to be easy, and it wasn't going to happen overnight. But maybe one day he'd be able to look upon the Saxons without prejudice. Then he might feel better about himself.

Doyle slid his boots deeper into his stirrups, pulled down the drawstring on his shirt to close the neckline. The wind of his momentum cut across his face, and for a moment he looked at Montague.

The old robber caught him looking and half shouted, "It's all right, laddie. The Saxons killed my boys. I don't feel any better about dealing with them than you do. But we have to live. And she's changing, this realm. She really is."

By late afternoon, Doyle and Montague reached the end of the northwest side of the Quantock hills. Here, the hills became a series of wooded bluffs that overlooked the port of Blytheheart. The two marveled at the harbor as they reached the summit of a considerable wide cliff. A dirt trail snaked away from them to the east and led to the outskirts of the port. Before venturing down, Montague wanted to dismount, rest a spell, and exploit their God's-eye view by giving Doyle a verbal jaunt of the seaport.

There were four main cobblestone streets, each running north to a connecting road that paralleled the Bristol channel. There were at least a half dozen side roads that linked the streets, and they, too, were of the most expensive stone.

To the west, Montague pointed out the stocks and pillory of the punishment mound, and farther inland, the elaborate roof of the monastery; the building and adjoining grounds took up an entire block. Still farther south was a passage Montague called Plower Street, the grain market, and there were a great number of shanties set up there, around which merchants bustled like so many colorless specks.

At the base of the ramparts in the west was an enormous cathedral, supported by literally fivescore buttresses. Stained glass, lancet-shaped windows of intricate design were set into every stone wall. An immense bell tower rose above the great church and now tolled Vespers in unison with the monastery's bell. The cathedral was encompassed by a curtain wall of indeterminate height from this angle, but Montague said it thwarted thieves, or at least slowed them down a whole lot.

Farther west, and on the same street as the cathedral, a tiny inn stood in its shadow. Montague reported that the boardinghouse had been relegated to Saxon merchants since there had been a few Celt-Saxon clashes at the Bove Street Inn, which stood on the northeast side of Blytheheart. Bove Street itself, besides being home to the inn, its stables, and, Montague added with a gleam in his eye, its brothel, was also where Blytheheart's summer fair was in progress. Peddlers' tents were shoulder to shoulder and created a miniature trading city that was bordered by St. Thomas Lane and the bluffs in the south. But the peddlers' tents were nothing compared to Merchant Row, one of Blytheheart's main north–south streets on the east side of the port. This, Montague said, was the home of the real action. It was, Doyle thought, the marketplace of Falls ten times over. There had to be at least one hundred stalls down there, and he could not believe the number of people swarming the street, even more than in the grain market. And strangely, the people in both markets ignored the Vespers bell.

Montague must have sensed his question coming, and he informed him with a knowing grin that the people down there in the markets were predominantly Saxons and Picts; they had come from the two merchant cogs docked at Blytheheart. Doyle looked to where Montague suggested, saw the four huge wharves that jutted out into the channel, two empty, two the temporary stop for the cogs. There was a lot of activity on the gangplanks of both ships. Barrels and crates came off and went onto the vessels, all under the auspices of a vast number of herring gulls and terns that squawked at sailors as they traced circles overhead.

On the opposite side of the street that faced the

wharves was a string of gable-roofed homes. Doyle
guessed that the richest of Blytheheart's merchants
resided there, but he was only half-right. Montague said
that the abbot's chancellor lived in the largest house on
the west side, next to the Customs House. The chancellor was responsible for monitoring all financial matters
in Blytheheart for the abbot. He had one of the port's
largest private residences, either to discourage him from
corruption or as a product of it. It was like offering free
food to a scullion; the boy would steal less food from
the kitchen that way. Give the man who handles all the
money everything and he *may* not want more.
According to Montague, you can never have enough
money, and he'd wager a score of deniers that the chancellor was so deep into the abbot's till that he would
need someone to grab him by the ankles to pull him out.
Doyle chuckled over that, then turned his gaze to the
center of town.

The abbot of Blytheheart, the port's most powerful
man, lived in the most complex and elaborate abbey
Doyle had ever seen. Queen's Camel Abbey was a peasant's toft compared to it.

Montague noted with a touch of irony that it was
Lord Street that divided Blytheheart neatly in half and
led to its center, where stood the abbey's seven-foot-
high circular curtain wall. There were perhaps two full
acres of land within the circle, and on that land stood a
barn, stable, two wells, at least three separate gardens,
and the rectangular abbey house itself, rivaling the
cathedral in its ornate design. A cloister court broke the
center of the abbey, and Doyle saw several persons
walking across its many-fountained landscape.

On the other side of the abbey's curtain wall were
cultivated parcels, and on them, loosely grouped clusters
of timber-framed peasant houses, their roofs thatched
with wheat straw. Two mills stood out among the struc-

tures, their patched-hemp sails turned steadily by the
sea breeze. Grain sacks were being carried away from
one of the mills by a line of workers, one tiny bit of
activity among a sea of movement.

Doyle took one final sweeping gaze of the port. He
took a deep breath, awed.

Montague rested a hand on his shoulder, squeezed
him twice. "Welcome home, laddie."

2 *It's only a dream.*

The wolf pack tightened its circle around Marigween
and Baines. A frigid wind lashed over mother and child,
and rustled the fur of the growling animals.

One leapt in the air.

Marigween's rounsey bucked as she pointed the dead
knight's javelin in the direction of the beast and closed
her eyes.

She heard the wolf bark and wince, and felt the
beast's weight on the end of the javelin, a force that
threatened to pry the weapon from her grip.

She opened her eyes —

As another wolf took to the air. There wasn't time to
yank the javelin from the breast of the first wolf. She
released the weapon as the carnivore crashed down on
top of her; its yellow-eyed gaze bore into her own.

She fell from her horse. Baines let out a cry. The
wolf's hot breath reeked and his gummy spittle leaked
onto her cheek as they plunged toward the ground. Her
rounsey made a human-sounding cry as the other wolves
attacked it.

She hit the earth and was thrown onto her side.

The wolf fell away, rolled over, and righted itself.

She sat up, her back ablaze with pure, raw pain. She thrust her legs forward and dug her heels into the grass in a gasping effort to retreat. She wrapped a protective arm around her child. She tried to use the other hand to boost herself up to stand.

But he came. He lowered his gray-black head and his jaw fell open. The beast's black lips curled back. Ivory-white canine teeth that would tear her flesh into small, digestible chunks were slick with drool.

She was game. She knew that. The wolf could not know the sadness of what it was about to do.

"Stay away!"

He leapt and landed, and his heavy, long-nailed paws knocked her onto her back. She lifted her head and looked to her chest.

The wolf wrapped its jaws around Baines's head. He growled as he bit down, then tore the baby from the bag and off her chest. The animal shook its head violently with the baby in its mouth, as if it enjoyed the way the child writhed and instinctively lifted its arms and clenched its hands at the fiery pain in its head. Marigween wailed and felt the wolf's needling teeth as if they were in her own head.

After another round of prancing with the baby, the wolf dropped the child to the ground.

Slick with gore, Baines did not cry. He did not move.

"No. NO. *NO!*"

Another wolf trotted onto the scene and began a barking, scratching fight with the wolf who'd killed Baines, a fight obviously over the child's sweet flesh.

Still another wolf wandered into Marigween's line of sight. This one stayed out of the fight and turned on her.

The wolf pried its way past her flailing hands and sank its teeth into her neck.

And now her neck should feel warm from her blood, but it was cold.

Her ears should detect the snorting of the wolf, but they only registered her own labored breath.

Her nose should crinkle under the musty, sweaty scent of the wolf's coat, but it remained smooth with no odor to tighten it.

Her mouth should be sandy and dry with perhaps a bit of salty-sweet blood seeping into it, but it hung limp and numb.

In the heavens, the stars swirled together into a single, white-hot disk that burned for a heartbeat, then slowly flooded crimson from top to bottom.

Marigween could remember the details of the dream with excruciating ease — two nights spent dying in the dream and two mornings waking up soaked had been ample reinforcement. Strangely, Baines had not cried out for his nightly feeding. Had he, too, been dreaming?

The wolves had not appeared on the Mendips. But those sounds had broken mental locks and had loosed some of her carefully hidden fears. Her apprehension lived freely in the dream.

But it's only a dream.

Reality was around her, safe, comfortable reality, a reality that held the promise of reaching Blytheheart before sundown. Already she could smell the brine in the air. Twice she breathed it in, breathed in the promise.

It hadn't been *that* hard to reach the Quantocks, she reflected. Things had gone fairly smoothly. She had noted something that could have happened, though.

When she had arrived in the river valley, she had observed that some massive group of people, an army perhaps, had recently been there. The earth had been torn up and the remains of cookfires had been scattered all along the shoreline.

The Lord had indeed been watching over her; He had moved a possible threat out of her path.

She had crossed the Parret River by way of a silent flatboat master who, when he had been asked, would tell her nothing about the group that had been in the valley. He had only smiled and said it would be one denier to go across. His Celtic was broken and strangely accented.

Now as she guided her rounsey in a steady, gracious trot, she tried to remember what Uncle Robert looked like. It had been so long. She knew he still wore the traditional shaved-center pate of a monk; his hair would not have changed. He might have gained weight. She remembered him as being very big, but to a little girl all adults are big. The one thing that had stood out about uncle was his laugh, his *hee, hee, hee, hee, hee*. Always five *hee*s, as if he'd practiced it.

She remembered when he had held her in his arms. He had laughed his laugh and she had touched his lips, curious about how he produced that strange, silly noise. She longed to hear it now. His letters received by carrier pigeon during the weeks she had been in Merlin's cave had only mimicked the cadences of his voice, but they had reminded Marigween of his warm sense of humor, and had clearly conveyed his excitement over her coming to Blytheheart. He had already arranged quarters for her just outside the monastery, on a farmer friend's toft, and she'd be allowed to stay as long as she liked.

The memory of that ancient man and his ancient cave she had lived in seemed just as ancient in her mind. Marigween's future lay just beyond the Quantock hills.

She could see the tiny lights of the monastery on the west side of Blytheheart, but there was only one trail down into the port, and it led off to the east. The sun had set, and Vespers services were probably over for at least an hour already. The air was thin and near-wintry here in the bluffs. The wind swept over the channel and

arrived with a temper. She'd thought her nights on the
Mendips had been cold; they were balmy compared to
the cliffs. She made sure Baines was bundled as tightly
as he could be, and, ignoring a chill that probed her
shoulders and chest, she descended the dirt trail toward
Blytheheart.

The wind did not feel as strong by the time she
reached the point where the dirt stopped and a long,
cobblestoned lane began. Buildings on either side of the
lane thankfully dispersed the brunt of the seaborn
breeze. As her rounsey stepped onto the stone,
Marigween realized he had thrown a shoe, the suspect
hoof *click-clock*ing differently from the others. At least
she was here and could easily get him reshod.
Marigween pulled her cloak tighter to fully conceal her
sleeping child, then heeled her slowing mount.

To her right she could see at least twoscore tents, but
there were probably even more obscured from her view.
No doubt, Blytheheart's summer fair was in progress.
Nearly every tent was illuminated from within. The
flickering light of torches and candles threw shadows
upon the canvases. She could hear chatter, faint wisps
of music, and smell what had to be cauldrons that surely
contained steamed meat and vegetables. A pang hit her
stomach. It had been nearly a week since she'd had a
warm meal. That would be the first thing she would
request of her uncle. The second would be an equally
warm bath.

Marigween reached an intersection, but continued
straight along her northern course. She knew this road
would take her to Pier Street and that road would lead
her across Blytheheart in an east–west path toward the
monastery. Now she neared a rather large inn with
dozens of merchant carts lined up in its front yard.
There was a stable and hostler's permanent lodge
behind the inn, and another, long, rectangular, three-

story building off to inn's right. The place's front door
swung repeatedly open as traders came and went. She
heard two of them chuckle from the stoop, then saw
one, a young clean-shaven lad, look her way. She
averted her gaze. He called out to her. She heeled her
rounsey and the horse complied with speed, but his bare
hoof now gave him more trouble.

Three merchants walked past her on her left. They all
shouldered a long pile of even-cut timber and all wore
tired, blank gazes. Only the rear one gave her a second
look.

At the end of the lane, she turned left onto Pier
Street. With dismay, she saw that about a thousand
yards uproad people crammed the path. Though the
waxing gibbous moon was cloaked by a fairly thick layer
of clouds, Marigween could still make out the well-
rigged mastheads and partial outline of the keels of two
ships docked at the wharves to her right. The crate-lined
street led to the quays, which in turn led to those vessels. She wished there was a side road to get by the
crowd. On her left was an unbroken line of ship-related
storefronts that stretched all the way off to what was
assumedly the Customs House opposite the ships. There
was only rocky shoreline to her far right and the unseen
channel beyond. With no other course but straight, she
resignedly continued forward.

Once she was a member of the crowd an illusion took
hold, and the knots of people did not seem as tight as
they had from the other end of the road — or had the
illusion been back there? Either way, passage was not as
difficult as it had looked.

Marigween received several offers from rough-
skinned men who swore they could shoe her rounsey
quickly and cheaply, though their words implied payment would not necessarily have to be made in deniers,
and one suggested a "favor," which Marigween knew

would somehow include the removal of her clothing. She politely smiled and shook her head, no. They called after her with warnings about how she was ruining a good mount.

Sack, crate, and barrel handlers jostled to avoid her as she came opposite the first ship. Men carrying packed goods went up the vessel's gangplank, disappeared into the hold, then came out empty-handed. One loader's gaze was obscured by the stuffed burlap sack on his shoulder, and he wandered into Marigween's path. The loader did, however, hear the clatter of Marigween's rounsey and hastened his pace — just in time to avoid being bumped. He shouted back to Marigween, his words foreign, his voice understandably burred with anger. Marigween swallowed the tiny lump in her throat, steeled her head, and stared forward.

After a few moments, the normal hum and buzz of pedestrian traffic resumed behind her, and she felt the muscles in her shoulders loosen a bit. She approached the Customs House on her left. Its front door was open, and its interior glowed from candlelight. She could see perhaps a half dozen officially clad customs officers inside, each seated behind desks at the rear of the office. Merchants formed lines that neared the doorway to pay their tariffs. The whole affair was kept honest and civil by a half score of guards in tunics of link-mail, their hands at ready rest on the balled ends of the swords at their sides.

She passed the Customs House and saw that for the first time on Pier Street the buildings did not abut each other. There was an alley perhaps two yards wide between the Customs House and the next two-story structure. With no windows on either building to face the alley, it was cast in shadows so dense they obscured its true length and what lay at its rear. At its foot, the passage was littered with pieces of stone and gabled roof that had weathered off the buildings.

Marigween felt something sweep over her, a feeling, a tremor, something that told her to move and move quickly. It was much more than the old warnings about dark passages and women traveling alone. The feeling was not entirely based on the visual impact of the alley; she reasoned it would have come on her even if she were someplace else. She never ignored her intuition. She shot a look behind her.

Merchants entered and left the Customs House, and there was no one apparently following her. In fact, there was no one even close to her.

But in that second, there was a scuffle of feet in front of her, and by the time she swung her head around, three men, their faces masked by black cowls, blocked her path. The tallest one went immediately for her rounsey's bridle and brought the horse to a jarring halt.

"What do you want?" Marigween asked, summoning force into her tone, but feeling the fear well up and drown any further attempts at bravery.

Another of the men went to her right side and yanked her boot out of the stirrup.

"Hold! What are you doing!" That same feeling she'd had during the wolf dream returned, the one that left her dry-throated and her ribs sore from the punching of her heart.

The cowl on her left seized her arm and began to tear her out of her saddle. She fought back, but the cowl on her right now utilized her foot to force her leg up, and the momentum he created was too much to battle. She fell into the arms of the cowl on her left, and one of her boots hung from its stirrup a moment, then was wrested free by unseen hands.

She cried out for help, but in the time she had to take another breath, her arms were pinned by the wrists to the cobblestone. One of the cowls stuffed a rag into her mouth.

Baines began to cry, and suddenly there was talk among the cowls. The one on top of her said nothing, but the other two exchanged argumentative words. The tongue was foreign, slightly familiar, probably Saxon. It sounded like they hadn't counted on her baby. She'd hidden Baines extremely well under her cloak.

Movement. The pressure lifted from her wrists as the cowl rose and fell back onto his haunches. She sat up, lifted one arm, hand balled to strike him, the other hand going to the gag in her mouth, but both arms were caught in wrist holds by the other two cowls.

As the two began to drag her into the alley, the other ran after, leaned over, and dug Baines out of the bag strapped onto her chest.

Marigween grew stiff and tried to pull down her arms. Tears filled her eyes. She bit down on the gag and screamed. No one would hear the muffled plea. Her gaze stayed with Baines. Now, she didn't just want to save herself and her baby. She wanted to kill all three of these devils for their violation; for having gone just this far they deserved to die. But this wasn't over yet.

The cowl that carried Baines moved in front of her, out of sight.

Marigween screamed again and felt her gag soak with saliva. All that was her, muscle and mind — all that was woman — fought to get free. The strain sent her to the peak of a mental mountain, then she plunged back into a black lake of futility. The men were too strong.

The alley's walls blurred by, and the image of the street and wharf at the end of the alley was lost in tears and gloom. The images were dreamy, and ironically she wished she were back in the wolf dream now. Even though it horrified her, she'd been able to hang on to the inner sense and comfort that it wasn't real and morning would soon come. Reality, once the safe comfort, now wore the black cowl of death.

She listened to more gibberish from her attackers. The alleyway ended, and she glimpsed the rear of the Customs House. The Customs House, with all its armed guards — and no way to alert them.

She was thrown onto her belly. Her chin slammed onto the stone. The stinging in her breasts competed with the multitude of sudden aches that awoke in her legs. Presently her hands were wrenched to the small of her back, and some kind of cord was spooled around them. Another pair of hands was at her ankles doing the same. Her gaze tracked straight along the bumpy cobblestone to the bottom edge of a wooden fence. Through a broken picket she could see movement. Someone was watching from behind that fence.

It didn't matter. They had her. And whoever viewed the scene was probably too afraid to interfere.

An absence dawned. She no longer heard Baines's whimpering.

Marigween scraped her swelling chin over the cobblestone as she craned her neck. All she could see were the boots of the cowls. A second later she was rolled, spun into a woolen blanket, and her gaze was reduced to a scope of cloth at one end. Dizzy, she gazed through the hole, then sensed hands on her. Then her view rose to a pair of peasant tofts behind the Customs House, then that was swept away to a view of stone as they turned her. She fought weakly against her restraints for a few moments as they carried her, but, as before, she fell limp in defeat.

Had they killed her child? If so, she hoped their plans for her included death. To lose Baines was to lose the most important part of her life. She would never be whole again.

Lord . . .

My baby . . .

                  *   *   *

Tania had seen them before, these impressment gangs. They kidnapped men and forced them to serve on ships. They also took women who acted as concubines for the ships' officers.

What was that young woman doing riding around the port alone? Tania knew few women who were as foolish or as unlucky.

She stepped to the edge of her fence, opened the gate, and crossed to the rear of the Chancellor's House. She glided along the stone wall until she reached the corner of the house where it bordered on the alley. She peeked furtively into the dark passage, then she noted with satisfaction that the gang was gone. She prayed the bundle they'd left behind was still all right.

There it was, on the ground where cobblestone met the foundation of the Customs House, bound tight in its own linen blanket, face covered for suffocation.

With her heart leaping, she crossed the alley, ran to the bundle, and lifted the baby into her arms. She folded away the blanket to reveal the tiny, pink face. Gently, she shook the infant a bit and blew air into his face.

And then the child coughed.

"Praise be to His name, little one. You're all right."

An instantaneous future, a wonderfully new future birthed in Tania's imagination.

Already she knew she could love this child. It would take no effort. She could raise the baby as her own. But what would Hayes say? First her husband would tell her that they were both too old to raise another child, that four had been enough. Then he would throw her illness back into her face; he would say that she wasn't capable of being a good mother because of it. But what of the baby? The child deserved them, deserved their love. She wouldn't think of the baby's parents anymore. They were gone. She'd saved this little one's life. She deserved to raise the baby. Why not?

She fully unwrapped the child and held his naked form up to the stars. "You're coming home with me. I want your father to meet his new son."

With a joy she had not felt in only God knew how many moons, Tania rebundled the boy, nestled him in the crook of her arm and hurried off toward her toft.

3

Seaver walked down Pier Street toward the wharves. The sunlit Bristol channel dazzled in a way the murky, green waters around Caledonia never had. He allowed himself a moment to consider staying, and his gaze at the legendary port was almost wistful.

But what would he do here? There were only a few deniers in his pocket from the sale of the rounsey. How far would they get him? He would have to become a laborer in the grain market and carry sacks on his back all day. If he decided to do that, he might as well become the farmer who produced those sacks — and that he could do back home. As far as passage was concerned, he knew he had certain talents a ship's captain could use that would earn him a free ride.

He shuffled by the loaders and ship's crew, then crossed onto the wharf where the Saxon cog was docked. He asked around, and in a few moments found the captain. To Seaver's delight, the man turned out to be the same skipper who had taken him to Britain in the first place, though Jobark had commanded a warship back then. The hale, ponytailed sailor was happy to see Seaver — that is, after having his memory nudged.

They stood before the barnacled keel of the cog, and Seaver eyed the man's cinnamon-colored beard. "And what's this?" he asked, swiping a finger across the hair.

"The sand of the seas, true enough," Jobark explained with a glimmer in his eye. "And perhaps one of the reasons I left the *Trowgel* in the first place." He wiped a sweaty palm on his short-sleeved tunic, then scratched an itch on his right bicep. The tanned muscle bulged, and a blue vein split it neatly in two.

"Ah," Seaver said with a knowing smile. "A bit more freedom as captain of a merchant cog, eh?"

"Yes and no," Jobark said, his tone lifting in the singsong way Seaver remembered. "Kenric once told me the beard makes me look weak. He *suggested* I take it off."

Seaver shook his head, hearing the suggestion — an order — in his head; it was the type of obscure and frivolous command that Kenric was wont to make. Were Seaver capable, Kenric would probably have ordered him to grow. "Don't have to worry about him now," Seaver assured him, "whether you're on a warship or a merchant cog."

Jobark nodded. "So you say. But the army you saw moving east, they're going to help him, no?"

It was probably true. The help that Kenric had been waiting for *was* on its way. Had Seaver made a grave error by fleeing the castle? Would Kenric be victorious now? And if he was, would he send assassins out to find and kill Seaver for desertion? And would they go as far away as Caledonia and Ivory Point to find him? Fears. Fears. All of them as yet unjustified. He blinked them off and frowned. "That army has to divide, and besides that, from what I could tell, they're inexperienced conscripts. Whoever is leading them cannot be anyone special. Most of the capable Saxon leaders have been in Britain quite some time now. He's probably some new promote."

Jobark stepped in close, lowered his voice, and his gaze searched the wharf for overhearers. "Rumor has it

that his name's Cerdic. He's with his son Cynric. And
are you fitted for this? They're Jutes."

The question narrowed Seaver's brow. "Who placed
Jutes in charge of a Saxon army?"

Jobark made a half shrug. "It's odd. I don't know. But
I will say this: It's a glass that reflects the times." He
stepped back, then waved a hand. "Look around. Look
at the Picts, the Jutes, the Saxons, the Angles, they're all
here. And even those from the East with those thin eyes
o' theirs."

Jutes in charge of Saxons? It was a Jute who'd murdered his father. That fact spurred a prejudice he would
never overcome. Never would he take an order from a
Jute. He would slit his own throat first. He didn't care
how irrational it was to hate the entire Jute people based
on one incident. Blood ties were blood ties, and the
Jutes had broken his.

He had looked at the port, as Jobark had prompted,
but, too lost in thought, the landscape glazed into a
mottled blur. He faced Jobark. "I'm going back home. I
offer service to you for passage."

Jobark bit his lower lip. "I guessed that already. But,
if I recall, you'll be of no help to us with the rigging. I'll
have to use you as —"

"Are you running a few gangs?" Seaver asked, cutting off Jobark's resigned decision to make Seaver a
mindless loader before the captain got it out of his
mouth.

Jobark's brow rose. "I am, true enough," he said, and
his voice hinted at some irony Seaver had stumbled
upon. "I just sent one out last night. They fetched me a
red-haired, soft-skinned lady — and I mean *lady*, not a
minx — that's going to make sailing back to Caledonia
like a boat ride in Woden's realm." His newly formed
smile lowered a notch with more thought. He puffed air,
then continued. "But they had some trouble. They got

her onto the wharf but wound up in a fist and slash with
a few of the marshal's guards. I lost one to the pillory.
He's up there now."

Seaver looked to the west, saw the punishment
mound and the heat-wavered tops of the pillory and
stocks. "Though I'm not much for a dial, I've been
known to track the sun rather accurately — which is to
say that my time to come is good, eh? You need someone? Someone who speaks Celt?" That last would cinch
it for him, he knew.

"Good sailors are hard to come by," Jobark said.

Seaver smiled. "I know where to look."

"Yes," Jobark said, his nod indicating that he had
already made his decision, "I think you do."

4   "Brigands! Devils!"

In the torch of midday, Orvin watched as their mules
and all their supplies were led away by the four young,
filthy-faced highwaymen.

It had taken three of the boys to knock Orvin to the
ground. Merlin, old fool that he was, had simply dismounted while the others had worked on Orvin.

Orvin had not even had the chance to draw his sword
or fire his crossbow, for the brigands must have been
watching them for a while and had timed their ambush
perfectly. They had appeared from nowhere.

He swore under his breath, swore again, then looked
at Merlin, who sniffed curiously at the air. He shouted
to the druid, "I've gone hand to hand with Saxons! Beat
them down to their knees! I rescued the young saint's
Marigween from my burning stables, killing a Saxon to
do so!"

"Then how is it we stand here with no mounts, no weapons, and no food?" Merlin asked, still sniffing the air.

Orvin snorted. "*You* could've helped! Three of them on me, the other about to engage you — and what do you do? — just hand him your mule. In the name of ALL the saints, where was your *cunning*, your *brilliance*, your . . . *magic*?" Orvin still had one weapon: his mouth, and he would continue to feint, riposte, parry, and stab with it.

But if Orvin was a verbal swordsman, Merlin was a chess player, finger-combing his beard and studying his board, oblivious to the blade poised over his head. "The illusory and the real often blend into a borderland. But we are far from that realm. Here in Britain, magic is in the mind, in the earth, in . . ." he sniffed again, "the senses."

"Rhetoric," Orvin spat. "Is that the kind of nonsense you feed to Arthur? No wonder we've all such a belly-ache!" He turned away from the druid, stared at the spot where the brigands were last seen: a hill to their southeast. "I loved that bow and sword. And we had food. And my back . . . and what are you sniffing at?" He faced the white-haired menace.

"The sea," Merlin answered. "We're not far."

"You're wrong," Orvin said grimly. "We're still at least a day or two away — three or four on foot. But if you'd listened to me, we could've stayed with that Saxon army back there. Maybe we didn't *see* Marigween with them, but she could've been bundled up and stuffed onto the back of one of their supply carts — or hadn't *that* crossed your mind? And stop sniffing! It's annoying!"

"Magic is in the mind, in the earth, in the senses. Let's return to the mind, and more precisely to mathe-matics. Calculating the army's movements and the esti-

mated time Marigween left the cave, the odds of her
encountering the Saxons lessen the slower she rides."

Orvin shook his head negatively. "You're speculating
on the army's original position and how fast Marigween
is traveling. The product of your calculations is as good
to us as —" he paused again, this time watching Merlin
as the druid bent over and drew something from the
short, yellowed grass. "What have you got?"

Merlin held it up between his thumb and forefinger:
the dark brown, rotten core of an apple. "She was here.
She made it past the army."

Why was it that Merlin had to continually prove what
a nincompoop he was? Why couldn't the old man just
retire into his cave to a life of private insanity? But the
better question, Orvin realized, was why God was punishing him. Why Orvin? "You're telling me that apple
core belonged to Marigween?"

"Indeed. She took it from my cave. It's a special vari-
ety from the East. A dozen of them were given to me by
Leondegrance. Here."

Merlin tossed the core; it fell into Orvin's palm but
bounced out and dropped to the grass. Orvin made the
mistake of bending over to retrieve the core. Pain shot
from the muscles flanking his lower spine. He gave up
and straightened. "Forget this game, Merlin."

The druid started toward him, waving a finger, and
his beard was a snowy scarf whipped over his shoulder
by a sudden gust. "If you'd look down at the stem,
which is still attached, you'd see how thick it is. I
noticed it the very first time I received the apples. I
repeat, Marigween is in Blytheheart. And we'll be there
before nightfall."

Orvin wanted to believe Merlin, but everything that
made sense in the realm told him the druid was straining to prove himself and was wrong on both counts. He
lifted his head, let the wind play over him, then closed

his eyes. "We've reduced ourselves to rotten apple cores, druid." He opened his eyes. "Strike that. It's you who is —" Orvin abandoned his reproach, since Merlin was already walking away from him. Even from the back Orvin could sense the old man's gait had purpose, definite purpose.

He didn't want to resignedly follow the druid because there wasn't anywhere else to go; Orvin wanted to have a plan of his own. But even if Merlin was wrong about Marigween and she was back with that Saxon army, it would be suicide to go after her now — with no food or mounts. And even if Merlin was wrong about the proximity of Blytheheart and it was, indeed, three days away on foot, the chances of making it there were far greater than those of getting anywhere else. So, even though it had appeared to make no sense at all, the druid's argument now burned with an ember of credence.

If Orvin needed a plan of his own, it would be to go along with Merlin — for the time being. Once in Blytheheart, if they discovered Marigween had not made it to the monastery, then he would find a way to get a mount and supplies and go after that Saxon army himself. He would leave Merlin at the monastery, for he knew how much the druid loved the monks. It would be Merlin's time for penance.

With the crack of an ankle, Orvin took a step forward, then paused to guide his booted foot onto the apple core; he heeled it into the grass and soft earth.

5   The Yeo River wandered across southwest Britain like a serpent in search of a mate; it found two brides in the forms of the Parret and Forves rivers.

Their union created the swift current that formed the southern and eastern lowlands of the Quantock hills.

Christopher stood staring at the sight where the three rivers converged. White water sparkled in star and moonlight. Brenna was on the bank at his side. Neither of them spoke, their silence born in a small part from the long ride, but predominantly of Christopher's relentless insistence that she return to Shores. She shouldn't be with him.

"We'll camp up past the reeds," he finally said. "Is that all right?" His voice was weak, unenthusiastic.

She looked at him. "I think you're doing the right thing and I want to help. I'm sorry about Woodward."

He threw her a wide-eyed, scolding look. "Stop saying that." He softened a bit, swung his head back to gaze at the rivers. "It's difficult for me right now. It's hard to battle all of the different things going on. Marigween running off, Woodward murdered, you wanting to come along." He realized his breath was labored, and his agitation dug furrows into his heart; it was through those channels that all of it rose to the surface. "I lied to the king, Brenna. To the *king.*"

She shifted closer to him, and from the corner of his eye he saw her lift an arm to wrap it around him; but she stopped and instead drew back to scratch an itch under her ear. "I keep telling you I'm sorry and you keep telling me how you lied to the king, and I keep wanting to tell you I'm sorry — and you keep telling me to stop saying that."

She'd done the impossible: raised a faint smile from him. "I'm sorry," he said. "Let's not talk anymore." He yawned, turned, and crossed in front of her, then headed up shore toward their grazing horses.

"It will be all right," she said.

"No one really knows what will be," he muttered.

*   *   *

Christopher awoke in the middle of the night. Restlessness was something he had grown used to, not that he liked it any.

The Saxon spy Kenneth had come in the wee hours to bury his dagger in Christopher's throat.

He had seen his first master, Hasdale, talk in his sleep the night before he had been killed. And Hasdale had spoken in a voice that was his father's — Orvin's.

Then there had been the dream in the stone forest, the dream about Orvin and Arthur, the dream in which they had given him advice.

Dreams, nightmares, murder attempts. Was a quiet night too much to ask?

Christopher knew he wasn't meant to live a normal life, and Orvin had reminded him of that on more than one occasion. But couldn't the extraordinary happen during the day?

The night was full of humidity and rhythm that had earlier put him to sleep. He sat up from the blanket that served as his mattress, and the other blanket on top of him fell away. He swatted at a mosquito that buzzed at his bare shoulder, then listened: rushing water and crickets. Both there. Both soothing. No noise had awakened him. What was it?

He drew in a long breath, let it go in a yawn, then stretched his arms and arched his back, sensing the bones of his spine crackle as he did so. He yawned again, then turned to look at Brenna. She slept soundlessly on her back, one arm at her side, the other crossed over her chest. Her blanket was tucked neatly under both arms, picture-perfect. Her long, black hair was an ebony halo of restless curls. Ah, the raven maid. There was a time when he would have leaned over and kissed her.

The thought was shattered by a sigh; the noise had not come from Brenna, but from over his shoulder. He turned around —

And there beside him, sleeping faceup on her own blanket was Marigween. Her eyelids fluttered open, and, as her gaze focused on him, she pursed her lips and smiled.

Christopher shot a look to Brenna on his left, then another one back to Marigween on his right.

He reached out and grabbed Marigween's hand; it was warm. Jolted by the sensation, he dropped the hand as though it had burned him.

"What is it?" she asked.

Christopher shushed her, then stole a glance back at Brenna to make sure she still slept.

But now he could see her neck move as she swallowed, then saw her tongue swipe across her lips. Her eyes opened. "Christopher?"

He crawled to Brenna and seized her hand. Flesh and blood, healthy, real, warm.

"What is it?" This time the question from Brenna. She sat up and looked to Marigween. "What's wrong with him?"

Christopher whipped his head to Marigween.

The former princess narrowed her thin brow as she looked at Brenna. "I don't know. He looks like he's seen Lucifer himself." She shifted her gaze to him. "Are you all right?"

He just stared at her, then looked to Brenna, who wore the same look as Marigween.

"He must be having a dream," he heard Marigween speculate.

"But how?" Brenna asked. "His eyes are open."

There was nothing as bizarre as hearing Marigween and Brenna talk about him in such a casual manner. They were puzzled by his expression, and behaving in a very uncatlike way. They should be clawing each other's eyes out.

"Marigween," Christopher began, and he heard the tremor in his voice. "How did you get here?"

She looked at Brenna, rolled her eyes, then looked to him. "On a horse."

"No, I mean have you been with us?"

"Yes. You asked me to come along."

"And me as well," Brenna chipped in.

He gazed at the raven maid, felt the incredulity once again warp his countenance. "I asked both of you along? Brenna, are we not going after Marigween?"

If Christopher wore a look of puzzlement, Brenna's was even more questioning. "No. We're all going to Blytheheart to be married."

A hand warmed his shoulder. He craned his neck a bit to find Marigween kneeling next to him. "You love both of us," she purred, "don't you?"

He drew back a bit from Marigween and studied her face, her wonderful eyes set into her smooth, fair skin, her red hair pulled back into a neat tail for sleeping. Then his gaze moved to Brenna, and her equally alluring appearance. But there was more to both of these women, much more, and Christopher had explored the deeper beauty of both of them. He had wandered within both of their hearts.

If only he knew his own heart half as well.

He did love both of them, each in a unique and incredible way. It seemed his life would not be complete if he did not have both of them.

But the laws of God, knight, squire, and man were too ingrained in him. To desire such a union was evil and absurd. Why then did he crave it? Why did they tempt him with it?

"You both want to marry me?"

"Yes," they answered in unison.

Two wives. Where had he heard of such a practice? Was it the Romans who had taken many brides? The Saxons? He'd forgotten. What did it matter? It wasn't for him.

But wait. He'd admitted something. He loved both of them. No, he didn't. He'd said good-bye to Brenna.

And there it was. He'd said good-bye, but he'd never stopped loving her — even in the face of Marigween and his son. Was it cruel and horrible that he still held feelings for Brenna? He'd tried to submerge them, but her presence now stirred them all back up. If she only had stayed in Shores.

He stood, pulled the drawstring at the waist of his breeches and knotted it, then walked away from the women toward the shoreline, hearing them talk behind him.

Christopher waded into the river until his feet were covered. He looked down and studied the bubbles created by the minnows, noted the way they blossomed into larger and larger ringlets. It was a hot night, and his upper lip itched with sweat. He reached down and caused the minnows to scatter. He cupped a bit of water, splashed it over his face, then groaned.

Christopher heard the sound of grass being crunched and turned toward it.

Brenna rubbed an eye as she approached. "Couldn't sleep?"

"Is Marigween still back there?" he asked.

Brenna blinked a few more times to clear her gaze. "What?"

"Do you want to get married?" he asked.

Her gaze averted to the mud and weeds. "I . . . don't understand. What about —"

"Wait. Where are we going?"

"Are you all right?"

He grabbed her by the shoulders. "We're looking for Marigween and my son and Orvin and Merlin, yes?"

She looked at a ghost, or at least her expression said so. "Yes."

Christopher released her, closed his eyes, then breathed a shuddery sigh.

When he was young, he had usually been able to sense when a dream began and when it ended. Since becoming a squire, that minor luxury had evaporated into the thin air of his imagination. Sometimes reality did not seem as real as the dreams.

Brenna added something about being worried about him, that he needed sleep, that he had too much on his mind and had to relax if they were to find Marigween.

Though he agreed with her words, he knew he could not heed them. "I cannot sleep anymore. Let's go," he said, then turned abruptly from the water. "We have an army to find."

If Brenna had any complaints about riding in the middle of the night, she kept them to herself as they packed.

Moments later, mounted and about to leave, Christopher gazed one last time at the convergence of the three rivers, a marriage as natural and God-inspired as any he had witnessed.

They arrived in the Parret River valley at sunrise.

Christopher reined Llamrei to a halt and inspected the ground. "They were here, all right."

"Do you think they got Marigween?" Brenna asked.

Christopher ground his teeth and spoke through them. "If they did, she's three or four days west of us now — if she and Baines are still alive."

"You named your son after —"

"Yes," Christopher confirmed before she went on with it. He scanned the orange-hued horizon with the serendipitous hope that he'd see a cookfire somewhere, the fire of Orvin and Merlin, or even Marigween. Then he spotted the quay, a flatboat docked at it, and a figure that stood on the pier. The figure waved an arm at them.

"I guess he wants to take us across," Brenna said. "What do we do? Do we head back, or hope they're all in Blytheheart?"

"This is a shot from a thousand yards, but I've an idea. Come on." He heeled his mare toward the river.

In a few moments, Christopher's hunch was borne out. Indeed, the flatboat master had taken a young woman and child across the river — as well as two old men. He was happy to tell Christopher all about it as they floated downstream, even happier it seemed that the young man on the white mare could, to his surprise, speak rather fluent Saxon. The words came back to Christopher with relative ease. Were it not for his time spent with Garrett's Saxon army, he and Brenna might have wandered for moons in the wrong direction.

Christopher gave the master an extra denier for his trouble, then he and Brenna coaxed their mounts into a canter over the foothills of the Quantocks. It took the rest of the day and a good part of the early evening for them to reach the bluffs just south of Blytheheart.

Christopher followed Brenna, and the two wound their way west through the broad wood atop the bluffs. Over the raven maid's shoulder, Christopher thought he saw the port's lights past the last stand of trees. Something shimmered in the sunken distance.

He leaned over and tried to peer around a trunk blocking his line of sight when something fluttered past his ear, something that sounded like a bird. He smacked his ear but connected only with his own flesh. He cocked his head, searching for whatever it was that had buzzed him.

Brenna had heard it too. She stopped and turned. "What was that?" Her attention went to the air above him.

"Bird?" Christopher hazarded. His eyes rolled up, and he lifted his head to scrutinize the shadowy tree canopy for a definitive answer. Sensing that something was not right, he swung himself out of his saddle and dropped to the ground.

A winged silhouette swam silently out of the darkness and dipped to career into the back of Brenna's head. She screamed as she frantically reached up to grasp the unseen demon. The thing shot away before her fingers touched it.

She shivered aloud.

"Dismount. Now," Christopher ordered her.

It wasn't a bird. It was black, its wings membranous, its head that of a rodent. Christopher had seen them before in Merlin's cave, and as he probed the darkness overhead, he slowly discovered many, *many* more of them.

The bats seemed to claw the air by the elongated fingers attached to their wings rather than glide through it as a bird would. Their legs worked in unison with their wings, causing a strange swimming action. Whether they clawed or glided through the air didn't matter; the fact that he knew they had razor-sharp teeth did.

He covered the back of his head with his hands and ducked for cover under Llamrei. He watched Brenna drop down and move under her mount.

"What are they?" she asked

"They're bats," Christopher told her, feeling the hairs rise on the back of his neck.

"What do we do? How do we get rid of them?"

Before Christopher could reply, Llamrei bucked and neighed and threatened to step on him. Christopher slipped out from under the horse, chanced a glance above the mount's back and saw two or three or yes, four bats dart just over the animal.

Then the white mare bucked and suddenly charged north through the trees. She was headed for —

"No!" Christopher bounded after the horse.

"Stop her, Christopher!" Brenna's shout was all but lost in the clatter of hooves and the mounting thump of his pulse.

Ignoring the moment and all feeling, he ran. He caught a flash of white through the brown and green: the mare's rump vanishing behind a trunk. He leapt over a fallen limb and felt locked into the pursuit.

The bluffs came up too fast. He sensed more fluttering at his ears. His skin crawled. He slapped the air above him, hit a bat, knocked it sideways, hit another with a lucky strike that brought the flying rat to the ground ahead of him, but it sprang into the air before he could step on it.

Llamrei neighed again, but he couldn't see her. He reached the edge of the wood, then heard the sound of pebbles and rock being rolled together, then another call from the horse, one which came from below him. He stepped to the edge of the cliff and looked down.

The beautiful white mare, the moonlit mare of King Arthur, plunged with its legs still beating in a gallop toward a blanket of darkness. Then she disappeared into the gloom. Christopher winced as he heard her make impact with what was probably a rocky ravine beyond the shadows. He strained to hear more over the insect hum, but was accosted by another sound, a rush of air from behind him. He turned as scores and scores of bats came at him. The first few pairs knocked him onto his rump. The beating of their wings created a ghastly breath. He rolled to his side, tucked his legs into his chest and palmed his face for protection. They came and came, but didn't pause to attack him. In a handful of seconds they were gone.

Christopher loosened his muscles, sat up, then rose. He brushed pine needles and earth from his hair, elbows, and buttocks, then stared past the sheer rock to the last point he'd seen the horse, a dismal point that hung eternally in midair.

He heard Brenna come up from behind and slowly turned his head to regard her. "You all right?"

"I'm all right," she said, her rattled tone conveying she spoke only of her flesh, not her nerves. "Hallam's mount scratched herself on a tree back there. I guess you didn't —"

Christopher shook his head no. "Should we go down after my pack?"

"I don't want to go," she said, then sniffled and grimaced. "That poor mare. I don't want to see her."

Christopher flinched as his mind painted a picture of the mangled horse. "I guess it'll be too hard to get down there anyway. And it's dark. And we're running out of time."

Brenna wiped away an escaped tear, then raked fingers through her disheveled hair. She tried to get the mane out of her eyes once, twice, but on the third time she gave up with a snort; yet it was that snort which blew the strands up so that they stuck at her temples. "Out of time? We know everyone crossed the Parret River by way of that flatboat. They have to be here. I doubt anything happened to them in the foothills."

"You don't know that," Christopher said sharply, perhaps too sharply. She didn't deserve that. It wasn't her fault he'd lost the mare. "It's just," he began, then gauged his tone more carefully, "I won't rest easy until I'm sure they're all right."

He wasn't lying. He'd barely slept during their entire trek to Blytheheart. When he wasn't piked by nightmares, he tossed and turned and stared absently at the stars.

"All right," Brenna agreed. "First help me make a poultice for my rounsey." She leaned forward, examined the western cliffside. "It doesn't look like there's a way down from here. Let's try the east side."

As glum as Christopher felt, Brenna's take charge attitude lifted his spirits — maybe only to ankle height — but he was, for the first time, glad she had come along. "Thanks."

"For what?" she asked, fighting with her hair once again.

"For just . . . come on." He turned away from her, and moved into the trees.

After they'd made the crude poultice from vinegary cider and mud, and applied it to the long, rather deep scrape on the rounsey's right shoulder, Christopher told Brenna he wanted to sit a minute. His body had felt very heavy since they had ascended to the bluffs. He thought if he took the weight off his feet for a few moments he might feel better. He sat, nudged his back and head into the trunk of a pine tree, then let his arms fall onto his lap. It wasn't a four-poster bed, but for the time being, it was a piece of heaven.

The last thing he remembered seeing was the grainy image of Brenna. She gently stroked the forelock of the rounsey and shushed the ailing horse. The last thing he remembered thinking was that he had to get up.

6   Doyle and Montague spent two nights at the Bove Street Inn. Montague pawned two of his precious gemstone rings to pay for their room and board. The fat man threw his sacrifice into Doyle's face so many times that Doyle figured he was unrecognizable, for Montague's martyrdom surely masked his features as efficiently as, say, dung would.

An early evening fog rolled in off the eastern channel, and it soon became so thick that Doyle could barely see the peddlers' tents from his window across the street. He'd been waiting for Montague for about an hour now. The fat man was finally off to meet the secret friend who he'd said had just returned to the port from a trip to Gore.

Doyle rose from the hard wood of the window chair, crossed to one of the two trestle beds, and plopped onto his belly. He tore off the leather glove he'd been wearing since they had first come to the port and dropped it onto the floor. He'd bought the glove moons ago in Glastonbury and had stuffed the index finger and thumb with linen to hide the loss of his fingers. But the damned thing was uncomfortable, caused him to sweat, and, further, it was odd to be wearing a glove in the middle of the summer. People knew there was something wrong with his hand; they stared oddly at the glove — the same way Montague had when they'd first met. Still, an odd look was better than one of repulsion.

It was good to have the sweaty disguise off now. The fresh air cooled his hand. He rolled over onto his back, rested his palms on his shirt, and, staring at the ceiling braces, he wondered why Montague had not let him go along to meet his friend. They'd argued about it, but the brigand had explained something about the private aspect of his relationship with his friend, about protocol here in Blytheheart, about the tenuous nature of dealing with the abbot, about merchants being good diplomats. Doyle felt as if he'd been soaked in a washing trough by Montague, that there was much more going on here than came out of the fat man's mouth.

A knock came at the door. He looked toward the sound; it came again. Doyle sat up, then swung his legs over the side of the bed. "Coming." He stood, padded to the door, then gripped the latch firmly with his good hand. He wedged one foot at the base of the door to prevent someone from forcing it in the moment he slid the latch aside. "Who is it?"

"My name is Jennifer," she answered gently. "Montague sent me."

Doyle slid his foot back a little from the door's base, then threw the latch. Tensing, he opened the door enough to peer behind it. She was alone. He relaxed and widened the gap in the door.

Jennifer was his age, perhaps a year or two older, with long golden hair that was parted in the middle and fell just below her shoulders. Her brown shift had a plunging neckline and was tented by her ample bosom. Doyle had never seen breasts so proudly displayed between columns of hair, and found his gaze locked on them. In his youth he had been taught that nudity was ugly, but both he and Christopher had agreed that a naked woman was something to marvel at.

"Can I come in?" she asked, her voice a musical instrument he found very much to his liking.

Embarrassed, he lifted his gaze from her chest. He became suddenly aware of the heat in his cheeks as he moved aside and gestured with an arm for her to enter. She did so, and as he lowered his arm, he remembered his hand. Doyle quickly shut the door, then crossed to the bed. He fetched the glove from where he'd tossed it and, keeping his back to Jennifer, slid it over his three fingers. Then he turned around, lowered the gloved hand to his side, then changed his mind and hid it behind his back. He tossed his weight from one leg to the other. The heat in his cheeks rose and tingled his forehead.

She looked to the chair. "May I?"

"Uh, sure." Seventeen years alive in the realm, and it hit him like a crumbling curtain wall: he'd never, in all that time, been alone in a room with a woman this desirable.

He took a seat on the edge of his bed and tucked his gloved hand under his hip.

"I love foggy nights," she said. "They make me feel so cozy. How about you?"

Doyle was about to get down to business with her, ask why she was here, why Montague had sent her, but now her smile tangled his thoughts. "I guess I like foggy nights, too."

"How about the ocean?" she asked, shifting her position so that she fully faced him. A smooth, remarkably fine-haired calf appeared from beneath her shift. "Do you like the ocean?"

He grew a touch more comfortable with her, and knew he'd permitted a frown to pass over his face. "Yes, but —"

"I know, I know," she said. "You're wondering what this madwoman is doing in your room talking about the weather and the ocean."

Doyle's sigh was internal, but released his tension. He nodded.

"I think we should talk first. I love to talk. I love to get to know people. Morna says it's wrong, but I don't care."

"We should talk first?"

She nodded.

He stood. "Before what?"

"Montague sent me, like I said. He told me a little bit about you." She smoothed her hair with a palm, then rose to meet his gaze.

He stared at her a minute longer. He did not want to believe the conclusion he'd already reached. She appeared so pure, a golden dove. He tried to see some taint in her eyes, some line on her face that gave away what she really was; but all he saw was a beauty that at once enamored and disappointed him. He turned and rubbed a sore muscle on his neck. "You're a whore."

"Yes I am," she said plainly, taking no offense. He felt her hand come to rest on his and push it from the nape of his neck. Her fingers began to knead the muscle. "Do you hate whores?"

He made a crooked smile, then turned his head a little. Her massage felt good, very good. "No."

"The way you said that, I thought —"

"I'm not anyone to judge," he said, not meaning to cut her off.

"Neither am I."

"I don't know what Montague was thinking when he asked you to come here. Well, I do know, but I don't have any money."

"I've been paid," she said, and he felt her breath on the back of his ear.

"Did Montague pay you?"

"I work for Morna; he paid her."

Jennifer's hand was past his neck, massaging the back of his head. He leaned into her touch and a soft groan passed from his lips before he realized it had. He heard the lute players begin a tune that wafted from across the street and in through the open window. As he listened, he fell deeper into the trance her hand created. He pondered where Montague had acquired the money, and then something else she'd said woke another question. "What did Montague tell you about me?"

"He told me you were very handsome, but just as shy. He told me you were going to become a great merchant someday. He told me you were very lonely." A trace of sadness edged her voice.

He pulled away from her, turned around and held up his gloved hand. "He tell you about this?"

She stepped to him, close enough so that he no longer had to guess about the color of her eyes: gray-green. She gripped the wrist of his bad hand and began to remove his glove with her free one.

"No." He pulled back, but she held on.

She shushed him, moaned with exertion, then managed to rip the glove off before he could free his arm.

He reflexively drew the hand into his chest. Between gasps from the struggle, he asked, "Why did you do that?" Then his rage, a thousandscore of imprisoned devils, smashed free. "You want to see it? You want to? Here!" He thrust the three-fingered hand into her face.

She recoiled as her eyes grew wide. But then she recovered as quickly and came forward. She grabbed his hand in both of hers, flashed her gaze to him, then lowered it to his fingers.

She kissed his pinky.

She kissed his ring finger.

As she kissed his middle finger, Doyle's chest began to tremble. Tears spewed from his eyes. He yanked his hand from her grip and turned to collapse facedown onto the bed. He cried into the blanket.

"Doyle. It's all right." He felt her try to push him over, but he was too heavy for her.

He rolled onto his back and hid his face with his hands. He felt weak before her. It had been a long time since he'd openly cried. He'd been able to take pain and barely shed a tear. That, he knew, was what he had always done. What was it about Jennifer that made him release his emotions so freely? Was it the mere fact that she was a beautiful woman that made it so? Or was it something more? All he knew now was that he cried, cried over feeling so ugly before such beauty, cried over not feeling normal, feeling like half a man. But at the same time there was another feeling that seemed to lift, if only a little, the feeling that he was no longer alone in his pain.

"It's all right," Jennifer repeated.

"No, it's not all right," he said, his voice muffled by his hands. "You don't know what it's like having this. It'll never be all right."

She climbed on top of him, grabbed his wrists then wrenched his hands away from his face. He held his eyes shut. "Look at me," she ordered him. "Look at me."

He opened his eyes and felt fresh tears slide down his cheeks. He relaxed the tension in his arms after realizing he could not be more embarrassed than he already was. He surrendered to her will.

She sat up on his belly, slipped one arm up through the neckline of her dress and then followed with the other. She lowered the garment to expose her breasts, the small pink nipples hard as arrow tips. She leaned forward and wiped the tears from both his eyes.

Then Jennifer took his wounded hand, placed it gingerly on her left breast, rubbed the fingers over her nipple. She pursed her lips and moaned behind them.

Doyle's breath quickened. He sniffled as he reached out and touched Jennifer's other breast with his good hand. She fell forward, pressed her lips against his, and slid her tongue forward to touch his. He adjusted his lips, unleashed his own tongue in response, and made it dance with hers. He had never kissed a woman like this, but she made it seem like he had been doing it all of his life.

Soon she climbed off of him and slipped out of her dress. She twirled the garment into a rope that she snaked over her body. Her eyes bore a light that no living man could ignore. Doyle rose from the bed, fumbled with the drawstrings of his shirt and breeches, threw the clothes off, then hastened beneath the covers. She slipped into the bed, and his palms found a wondrous collection of warm, soft curves.

Jennifer did things to Doyle that caused him to make sounds he had never made before. She put her lips and tongue where he'd thought no woman would dare go. It was awkward when he was on top of her, but in that soft music that was her voice he listened, and learned, and experienced something too wonderful to be real.

Perhaps the only dent in the whole encounter was the creaky trestle bed.

Afterward, he lay on his side next to her. The candle on his nightstand tossed a gentle radiance over their naked bodies. He apologized for his outburst.

"What Montague said about you was right," she said, then sniffled and lowered her gaze. She closed her eyes and held them with her thumb and forefingers.

"What's wrong?"

She took a long while to collect herself. Finally, she broke the silence with a laugh that had no humor behind it. She turned to him, dropped her fingers, and opened her tear-filled eyes. "I guess it's my turn now." She sounded as embarrassed as he'd been about crying.

"Did Montague say something else about me?" Doyle asked. He knew the fat sack was capable of telling her just about anything that might account for her present tears.

"No. I told you all he said. But *I* didn't believe it. I guess I thought you really were some troubled archer with a butchered hand." She placed a finger on his cheek. "But you're not. I almost wish you were."

He grimaced. "Why?"

She snuggled up to him, placed her hand fully on his cheek, and brought her lips close to his. "Because of this . . ." She kissed him as she had the first time, long and hard and wet. A kiss he sensed she meant. And he kissed her back with equal force, feeling guilty about how desperately he needed it, about how he suddenly wanted to cling to her for the rest of his life. Now he thought no other woman but she would want him.

Jennifer pulled back and rolled over. "I have to go now."

They had turned the room into a great solar where the fantasies of kings and queens purged all fear and pain; now it was a room at an inn where a would-be merchant had just slept with a whore. The reality silenced his mouth, deafened his ears. He lay prone as he watched her dress. He dreaded her departure, and somehow felt betrayed. She said good-bye and quietly closed the door after her.

Doyle threw an arm over his eyes. He stayed that way for a long time. He thought only of her. He traced her face with a mental right hand that had five fingers, then let the hand fall down to her breasts, to her navel, then drift around her back and rest upon her small, tight buttocks. He shoved her close to him, dropped her head into the crook of his arm, and dived into her lips. Together they drifted on the breeze, high above Blytheheart. They soared and wheeled and loved.

Sometime later the door opened. He heard Montague's voice. "What's he got the door unlatched for, the fool."

Doyle pulled his arm off his face, sat up, and blinked to clear his eyes. The candle on his nightstand said he'd been lying in bed for longer than he'd realized.

Montague came over to him, and the fat man wore perhaps the widest smile Doyle had ever seen split his face. "And how are you this evening, laddie?"

Doyle shook his head and tried to hide his smile. "I guess I should say thank you. But where did you get the money?"

"It's all part of the deal I worked out with my friend."

Doyle had almost forgotten about Montague's meeting. "What happened? And now can you tell me who he is?"

Montague sat on his bed. The mattress buckled a whole lot under his mass. "*She* doesn't want you to know, but I'll tell you anyway. And you must never tell anyone about her relationship with the abbot."

Something clicked when Montague mentioned that his friend was female. "Her name's not Morna, is it?"

Montague looked surprised, then it hit him. "Jennifer told you?"

"She just told me she works for Morna. Let me guess, Morna and her trollops do certain favors for the abbot?"

"Shush! Lower your voice." Montague peered around

the room as if the abbot's spies had transformed themselves into flies that had found purchase on the walls. Then he made clear his action. "These walls are thin."

Doyle's lip rose in a sour grin. "I cannot wait to meet this abbot," he said quietly. "He makes deals with the Picts and Saxons — and sleeps with whores."

Montague winked. "And we should be glad he does. His, shall we say, appetite, will work to our benefit, laddie."

Montague's implication reeked of something. "Hold a moment. You're not thinking of doing what I think you're doing?"

"I first thought of threatening to expose him as a means for him to hire us," Montague said, rubbing a sore spot on one of his fingers, a spot that had only recently been covered by a gemstone ring, a spot that probably represented payment to Morna for Jennifer's services. "But that's very bad business, you understand. And would probably land us on a pyre. No, we're not more powerful than the abbot. Morna and I have come up with another plan that we think is even better."

"Before you tell me about it," Doyle said, "what can you tell me about Jennifer?"

"Stay away from that one, laddie," Montague said, his voice going stern. "She's trouble. And remember what she is."

"I didn't ask for advice; I asked about *her*."

Montague snickered. "I guess you'll learn the hard way, in more ways than one. Find out about her for yourself. But stay away. Now, listen to the plan."

Before Doyle could argue further, Montague spelled out the details of their meeting on the morrow with the abbot. He knew he should have been listening to Montague, but he couldn't direct his attention away from the remembrance of Jennifer on top of him and how he'd stroked her heavenly skin.

When he was finished, Montague asked for Doyle's opinion, to which Doyle replied, "I'm still not sure about it. Can you go over it one more time?"

7   Marigween's head throbbed. She was dimly aware of her body, of the pressure under her chest. As some saliva reached her tongue, she discovered a sour taste and remembered the ale. She heard the strain and groan of timbers, then felt her weight pitch involuntarily to the left. She tried to open her eyes, then remembered the blindfold. She tried to move her arms, found them still bound together at the wrists behind her back. Fragments of memory collected further. They had brought her here, blindfolded her, and forced the ale down her throat. She realized that while she had slept she had wet her shift.

The cog tipped again, a little more gently this time. She rolled onto her side, coughed, and then, before the nausea caused any real discomfort, she retched, retched again, then it all came up. There was no way of telling where the vomit had gone, onto the bed or over its side. A bed of bile and piss and darkness was her home now.

Her physical discomfort was, however, a paradise compared to the pain of losing little Baines. She coughed up more spew, and one cheek became wet with drool and something else. After the fit she tried to imagine what they had done with her baby. She'd seen him one minute, then the next he had been silent and gone. Was there any chance at all that Baines was still alive? She wanted to cling to that hope, but it might cause her even more pain if she discovered the worst. Yet that was what mothers did; they never lost hope; they never stopped praying; they never stopped loving.

The average mother was, however, not aboard a Saxon cog, bound and throwing up and awaiting the torture of foreigners. It was hard to maintain hope for her child when she had so little for herself. Torture would begin between her legs.

Timbers creaked again, but this time it wasn't the settling of the cog on the channel. She heard footsteps, loud ones, and they were spaced more apart than an average step, as if someone now descended a ladder.

"Who's there?" she asked, then wished she hadn't. They couldn't understand her anyway, and now they knew she was awake.

She heard someone draw near. Her blindfold was removed, and the skin it had covered seemed to leap from her face. She opened her eyes. The room was gratefully dark, illuminated by what was probably a single candle resting somewhere unseen. It only took a moment for her gaze to adjust.

A short man stood before her. His face was clean-shaven and very plain. There was nothing about it that she would remember. So, too, was his hair, not long, not short, just there, perhaps a bit gray. Admittedly, it was hard to see him while lying on her side, hard to note the rest of the shadowy room, which she decided was a small cabin interposed by the structural beams of the ship. In fact, her half-inverted view made her want to vomit again; she heaved, but there was no liquid reply.

"Easy there. I'm here to help — if you'll be nice about it," he suggested quietly.

She shivered. "I'm so ill. And I'm wet."

He rolled her down onto her chest.

"What are you doing?" She shivered again, this time from the raw thought that he might hurt her.

Then she realized he was untying the bindings on her wrist. "I'm going to clean you up," he said. "The hatch is locked from the outside — so forget about running."

Marigween had been so preoccupied by her grotesque condition that she only now noticed that the short man spoke her tongue.

"Are you a Celt?" she asked, feeling her hands come apart, the skin of her wrists bounding in freedom.

He moved to her legs. She'd barely felt the bindings that coiled over her boots. He made a noise that might have been a chuckle, but there was a trail of something else behind it, maybe sarcasm. "No, I'm no Celt," he answered as he struggled with a knot.

"But you know the language."

"I've been out of practice," the sailor confessed.

"It doesn't sound like it. Do you know what happened to my child?"

"No." His tone was flat; she couldn't tell if he'd lied or not.

As her legs came free, she fervently prayed their conversation had caused the man to lower his guard. Marigween pulled one knee toward her chest as she rolled onto her back. She thrust the leg forward and drove her foot into the short man's abdomen.

He flew backward to the opposite wall of the cabin, shrank toward the deck, then hit it with a low thud.

She sat up and looked for the leather cord that had bound her. She found it on the soaked blanket, snatched it, then hopped from the bed. She fell to her knees before the disoriented sailor, threw the cord over his head and wrapped it once, twice, around his neck; but, before she could pull it taut and squeeze him into hell, he slipped his fingers under the choker. He ripped the cord from his neck and out of her grip.

Marigween didn't see his hand coming from the right, only the shadow of it on the wall behind him, an image that reached her too late. His palm struck her cheek with a force that toppled her. She groaned as her face kissed the moist, splintery deck of the cabin, and she thought the fire in her skin might touch off a blaze in the small room.

He slammed her onto her back, sat upon her chest, and pinned her hands behind her head.

With her breath ragged and the taste of blood in her mouth, she stared at his gloomy face. His eyes were so narrow with anger that she could barely see them. A bead of sweat slid down his heavily pored nose, formed a drop which hung on the tip of his nose, then dropped to her neck. She thought he smelled terrible, then discovered that the odor came from herself.

"You don't have to hurt me."

"Maybe I do," he said.

At that moment, Marigween realized the mistake she'd made. She should have gone for the hatch and to hell with him. But he'd said the hatch was locked from the outside. Then again, he could have been lying. She stopped punishing herself; it didn't matter now — not much of anything did. He *was* going to hurt her. No amount of pleading would change that. She'd tried, failed, and would now pay.

He looked at her and tried to catch his breath. He squeezed her wrists tighter and tighter, but then, without warning, he released his grip and climbed quickly off of her. She sat up and looked at him as he moved a step back. His expression loosened from rage to something on the order of frustration. He rubbed the spot on his chest where she'd booted him.

She sprang up. Indeed, there was a short ladder of six rungs that led up to a hatch. She reached the ladder and, taking every other rung, climbed to the hatch. She slid the latch back and pushed up with a balled fist. The hatch would not give. She heard a voice from the other side of the wood, and then her captor shouted an unfamiliar reply from below.

Marigween went slack, and her will fled. She wanted to drop off the ladder, hit her head on the floor, and end the madness. She closed her eyes, let herself go, felt the hot, sticky air of the cabin rush up and lift her hair from her shoulders and neck.

But she felt the sailor there in an attempt to catch her, and the two of them crashed onto the deck. With her eyes still closed, and new sensations of pain birthing, Marigween curled herself into a ball and cried.

She heard him rise and say, "Were you not the captain's, I would've —" he broke off.

Marigween's imagination finished his sentence. She continued to cry as hard as anyone could. She tightened the fist that was her body, then ordered her heart to stop beating.

8

The insipid druid had been right. Orvin wouldn't kill himself over the fact that they had reached Blytheheart by sundown and had proven Merlin's calculations correct. He would, however, die if he didn't get something else to eat besides his words.

Repentance Row was barely visible through the fog, nor was there enough moon or torchlight to fully uncloak the cultivated fields of the tofts to their right. Even the lights from Saints Michael and George Cathedral on their left offered only a small token of illumination.

Merlin had been silent since descending the bluffs. That worried Orvin; when the druid kept to himself it meant he was thinking. And when Merlin thought too much, all of Britain was in jeopardy.

Perhaps Orvin had exaggerated just a little bit. But the druid had influence over Arthur, and that influence was not good. The king had to learn how to rule by himself. The way Orvin had trained the young saint to act independently, so should it be with Merlin and Arthur. He'd offered that advice to Merlin; the druid acknowledged the merit of the argument, then ignored it, supplying Orvin with another reason to detest the man.

"Do not fret, Sir Orvin," Merlin said as he shuffled over the cobblestoned street with effort, "there are no plans for the realm in my silence. Only plans of where I shall rest my head on this foggy eve."

Orvin stopped. He was hit by a jolt, a mental pillar from above that drove through his head and buried itself in his stomach. The pillar marked this spot, this moment, as some bizarre milestone in his relationship with the self-proclaimed wizard. "Get out of my mind," he ordered the druid.

Merlin's smile was a dull yellow thing in desperate need of polishing. "We've made progress, you and I," he said. "The longer we travel together, the closer our thoughts become. So it always is on a long journey."

A merchant's cart that was jam-packed with sacks of grain lumbered up the road toward them. Orvin held in his reply as they moved closer to the edge of the street. The two men driving the cart tipped their heads in a greeting as they passed. Once the cart was swallowed by the fog behind them, and the racket it made was nearly gone, Orvin resumed the conversation. "Our journey has been too long, and now you're amusing yourself by guessing at my thoughts — something which annoys me to the core! We've made no progress at all."

Merlin shook his head in disagreement. "I did not guess at your thoughts, Orvin. I've come to understand you, and your fear of me. And I see I've touched on a nerve."

Orvin turned away from the older one and resumed his trek down the row. He did not care if the druid followed, but knew he would. "The only thing I am afraid of is what you're doing to Pendragon's son," he called back.

The druid arrived at his side. He was out of breath and fought to keep up. "Won't your sky tell you what I'm going to do?"

Orvin stiffened his jaw and increased his pace, knowing it would cause the other pain. It had been too many days since he'd stared at the blue arch and drawn from it the feelings, the images, the sensations of what would be. Premonitions born in the clouds came and went; some he paid attention to and some he did not. But never, never had he been able to sense anything about the druid. It was as if Merlin had some power to block from the world feelings and imagery that concerned himself. Merlin was, after all, the man who had taught him the art; the druid probably knew many ways to hide himself from it.

"Trick cups and shells, disappearing cards, weighted dice, those are your games and the way you play them," Orvin said. His feet were just beyond excruciatingly tired, his back a notch beyond that. He almost felt like giving up the argument, but if his greatest pleasure — food — still eluded him, he would continue to indulge in his second-greatest pleasure as a means to forget about the misery.

Gazing ahead, Merlin replied, "One can only hold up a shield for so long before it is pounded into uselessness."

"Correct, druid. So why do you not admit you've been wrong? Leave Pendragon's son alone. He's capable."

"I was referring to the shield you are hiding behind, Orvin. You spent more time with me in your youth than you did with your father."

"That was not his fault. He was busy building a castle. If it weren't for him —"

"So I tried to teach you what he could not," Merlin said, cutting him off and keeping the conversation where he wanted it to go.

"And you failed, druid! You failed! You failed with me the same way you will fail with Arthur."

Merlin had not touched on a nerve; he'd touched on all of them. There were many reasons Orvin had for hating the druid, all of them seeming perfectly logical, all of them reasons any outsider would understand. But Orvin knew that his chief reason for loathing the wizard mixed reason and emotion, and that blend would not hold up to careful scrutiny. Yes, Orvin knew that, knew his reason was irrational, but he didn't care. It was Merlin's fault.

"I did not fail with you," Merlin said. "You believe you failed with your own son. And blame that failure on me. You think I could have made you a better father, a father who would've been able to talk Hasdale out of a vengeful quest. You believe if I had done the proper job, your son would be alive today."

Orvin thrust his foot out in front of Merlin. The druid tripped and fell forward onto the stone. It was a small miracle that the old man was able to break his fall — though only slightly — with the palms of his hands. Orvin walked past the man, not bothering to look back and see if the other was hurt. "A pox be on you for talking too much."

Orvin shuddered. His fragile ego had snapped like an overwindlassed bowstring. Tripping the druid was childish and improper to say the least, despicable to say the most.

"I loved you like a son, Orvin," Merlin said, his voice cracking as he tried to project it.

He did not want to admit it, but there was a smidgen

of guilt over hurting the old man; now Merlin's words ladled out a bellyful. Orvin stopped and turned around.

Merlin winced as he brushed dust from his hands and the knees of his robe. He set off toward Orvin with a noticeable limp, adding, "I loved Uther Pendragon no less, and Arthur, his son, with as much passion. I've never known three men such as you." He came within arm's length of Orvin and stopped. "I did everything I could for you, Orvin. Taught you all that I know. I could not convince you to leave the knighthood, and so I accepted that — just as you should accept that your father did everything he could for you, and you did everything you could for your son. But no man is more powerful than fate. I have tampered with it and have discovered there is no controlling it. It goes where it wants — even with a druid's intervention. Your father's fate, your fate, your son's fate, Arthur's fate, and even Britain's fate . . . none of them have ever been fully in my hands."

Orvin had, for many moons, rested on the comfortable pillow of blaming Merlin for everything. It was hard to pull that pillow away, to rest his head on the cold, hard rock of reason. Could it be that Merlin had admitted something was more powerful than himself? In all the years he'd known the druid, never once had he heard the man open up as much as he had on this eve. Was there an ulterior motive under his modest confession?

"Why are you telling me this?" Orvin asked, his gaze probing the other's.

"Because I believe that peace is not far from this realm, and not far from our hearts. You were a good father and good husband, Orvin. Much better than Uther. There was a time when I truly thought you had obtained that balance between mind and heart. And it was you I told the young Arthur to look to for an example. You were the embodiment back then. And in many ways, you still are. You took a saddlemaker's son and turned him into an excellent squire. Of course your young patron saint has made many errors, but he's done many great things, as you have. Now, if you'll permit me to walk with you, we should make haste for the monastery."

Merlin had offered a lot to ponder. Orvin had always assumed that the druid harbored a resentment toward him for not becoming a soothsayer. The druid had once said that he'd learned to tolerate Orvin. Had he now learned to love him again? So he said. Merlin was not wont to lie, but still, there was a nagging sensation that he wanted to make a reconciliation for some other reason than the fact that he felt Britain would be at peace and so should they. That analogy held no water. The druid could feel guilty, or was it something else?

Orvin thought of apologizing, but felt too awkward to do so. He simply turned from the druid as an indication that he agreed with the man: yes, they should be going. They had a duty and were wasting time.

Merlin's limp seemed to lessen as they walked. Orvin kept silent and the druid did likewise. They reached St. Christopher Street and Orvin smiled at the hand-painted signpost, a post that actually conveyed the name of the street in Latin, with more unfamiliar scribbling below it. He asked Merlin about the writing. The druid explained that it was probably put there for the benefit of the Saxons and Picts who traded here, and went on to give a brief summary of Blytheheart's political situation, a summary which left Orvin aghast. Marigween had made a grave error coming here. The port crawled with merchants and sailors. Did she really think the monks could protect her?

They reached Tintagel Street. Merlin said he would go off to a small inn behind the grain market to reserve them a room for the night while Orvin went to find Marigween's uncle at the monastery. Orvin suggested that Merlin come with him, but the druid reminded him that there was no love lost between himself and the Christian monks. Merlin would be more than unwelcome at the monastery, for the monks might even try to seize and imprison him for heresy. Orvin acknowledged the druid's reservations and went to the monastery alone.

Less than a quarter of an hour later, he waited in a corridor that led to the monastery's cloister court. The careful brother had gone off to fetch Marigween's uncle, who was having dinner in the frater. The brother had said that Orvin's timing was good, that High Mass had just ended.

Orvin considered himself a faithful Christian man, but one who could not relate to having to praise the Lord seven times a day, as was the calling of these monks. Prime, Terce, Nones, Matins, and Lauds, and a couple of others Orvin forgot, there was simply too much worshiping going on here and not enough good hard work. As a youth he'd often remarked that men who were too weak to be knights ought to become monks, but his opinion had been changed by a battle in which he'd had to enlist the aid of the monks at Queen's Camel. Those brothers had fought with more ferocity than any battle group Orvin had been able to muster at the time. Still, from the looks of the monastery, it appeared these brothers lived in comfort and certainly did not break their backs. Orvin was jealous of their comfort, but not of their duty to the Lord. He was most jealous of the fact that they had food right now, a meal he could smell all the way from the frater. It was stew. It had to be stew.

Robert stepped around a corner with the careful brother. He thanked the smaller man, who left in a pre-

occupied hurry. It was apt to describe the careful
brother as the smaller man, for any man would be the
smaller standing next to Robert. Indeed, the monk did
not break his back here, but rather, wore out his arm
lifting his fork to his mouth. He arrived before Orvin,
bowed his head slightly. "Sir Orvin of Shores. I am
Robert," he said with a polite smile, his voice the low,
thick baritone that seemed always to accompany a man
of his girth.

Orvin wasted no time. "I've come with urgent business. Your niece Marigween and her child left Shores to
come here. Has she arrived?"

The news sent Robert's brow up to touch his bangs.
"With her *child*? She never wrote about that."

The old knight thought a moment, realizing he'd
received his answer. If Robert didn't know about
Baines, then Marigween certainly hadn't arrived —
unless she was hiding the child from her uncle for some
reason. "She has a child, yes. Tell me, man, has she
arrived?"

Robert shook his head. "I thought she'd be here yesterday."

Orvin swore to himself. He had wished for everything
to be all right, for Marigween to have arrived here safely
so that he could rush back to the inn and gobble down all
the food his money could buy. It was a selfish thought,
but he'd traveled very far and was hungry beyond imagination. However, the more he thought about the young
woman, the more scared he became for her and the child
that he'd delivered. Now the feeling was stronger than
anything else. "I need your help, Robert."

"Anything," the monk said anxiously. "What can I
do?"

Orvin sat next to Merlin at a long, rectangular dining
table that was packed with men. He tore into some well-

done venison and washed the meat down with a tankard of ale. He explained to Merlin that the monks would help them search for Marigween and Baines. And while Orvin talked, he gradually became aware of an unsettling fact.

They were the only Celts at the table.

The dress of the sailors and loaders seated around them gave no indication of their homeland; it was their conversations that gave them away.

"Have you noticed that we're the only —"

"Quiet," Merlin interrupted. "They do not seem to mind — as we should not."

"All right, then, let's talk about what we do now. What if Marigween's not here? What if she was captured by that Saxon army? In fact, I don't think she is here. She would've gone directly to the monastery."

Merlin smoothed away his mustache, brought his tankard to his lips, sipped, then answered, "Marigween was not captured by the Saxons. My apple core proved that — though you still do not believe it. I tell you she is here in Blytheheart."

"Then why didn't she —" Orvin broke himself off, eyeing the sailors at the table, summoning up a picture of the fair Marigween in his mind. She was so beautiful; she had the power to awaken even a man of his age. Orvin looked at the way the sailors devoured their food like dogs, the semblance of Marigween frosted over the scene. Men like these could've gotten to her before she made it to the monastery. Merlin could be right. Marigween might still be here.

Some of the sailors noticed Orvin staring. They stopped eating and stared back at him.

It took only seconds for the whole table to drop off a cliff into silence. Every man's gaze was fixed and burned on Merlin and Orvin. Using Orvin's shoulder for support, the druid rose. "Time to go."

9 He looked young, like the boy she had once fallen in love with, not like the man she now knew. Even through the scars and hair on his face she could see the innocence, the charm, the kindness. All of it came through as he slept.

Brenna could watch him all morning, but she realized he would be angry with her if she did not wake him up soon. He had wanted to move out last night, yet she didn't have the heart to stir him. She had never seen him so exhausted.

The morning sun wrested away about half of Brenna's lingering chill; the rest of it would remain as long as she was in his presence. She had to stop thinking about him.

She turned away and walked back to her rounsey. He neighed as she scratched behind his ears. She checked his wound. The poultice seemed to bring down the swelling, but she'd still have to get him to a doctor.

"Oh, no. How long have I . . . it's morning!"

Moving around her rounsey, she found Christopher sitting up and rubbing the sand from his eyes. "I was just going to wake you."

"Why didn't you get me up last night?" He wasn't as angry as she'd expected he'd be, but he wasn't exactly happy about sleeping all night either.

"It wouldn't have mattered. You were too tired. I'm sorry, but you had to sleep." She stood over him, proffered a hand to help him up.

He ignored her hand and, with a groan, rocked himself into a standing position. "No, I didn't have to sleep. Didn't I tell you we were running out of time?"

She turned away from him. It was pointless to argue. His mind was set. If he wanted to blame his exhaustion on her, so be it. He kept saying they were running out of

time. She figured that if Marigween and the elders had
crossed the Parret River, the chances they'd made it to
Blytheheart were very good. His loved ones were probably at the monastery now. So how were she and
Christopher running out of time? It seemed more likely
he was running out of patience. He needed to know if
they were all right, and he needed to know days ago.

Brenna went to her sleeping blankets, lifted one, and
shook it out. She heard him cough behind her. She
folded the blanket and repeated the process on the next,
wishing she could shake Marigween and her baby out of
Christopher's life the way she shook the dirt from her
blanket. God would punish her for such a thought, but
He knew how much she cared for him. She wondered if
Marigween were in danger, would the former princess
be able to cope with it as bravely as Brenna had?
Perhaps she gave herself too much credit. She hadn't
exactly been brave when she'd journeyed all the way
from Gore to Shores; in fact, she'd been unnerved most
of the way. And when she'd been intercepted by that fat
Montague and his boys and nearly been raped, well, she
had been scared out of her wits. All right then, she
hadn't been brave. But she had been strong enough and
cunning enough to escape. And if danger came again,
this time she would be brave. Could Marigween do the
same if she was in trouble?

Life would be easy without Marigween and her baby.
Christopher's situation would be less complicated, and
Brenna could simply and stealthily slip back into his life.

But was he capable of hurting her still another time?
Would he go astray again? Was fantasizing about a relationship with him even worth the trouble?

She slung her quiver's strap over her shoulder, made
sure her riding bags weren't going anywhere but behind
her saddle, then mounted the rounsey. *Forget about loving him!* she ordered herself.

Christopher approached her, tucking his shirt into his breeches. "I'll lead you down," he said, indicating with a hand for her reins. "We'll fetch my riding bags from Llamrei later."

Brenna tossed him the reins. They started toward the east side of the bluffs. She asked him if he was hungry; he said he was not, but that was his pride talking and not his stomach. She'd forgotten the last time she'd seen him eat.

The air grew more humid as they traveled. Brenna repeatedly wiped sweat from her forehead. Christopher paid his perspiration no heed, and the hair at his temples was soon soaked.

They found a dirt path that took them down to an east-west cobblestoned lane, and turned left in direction of the monastery. It was noticeably cooler below the bluffs, a faint but near-steady breeze reaching them from the channel. Once they passed the great circular curtain wall of an extensive abbey, they encountered other people in the road, peasant farmers, craftsman, and the like. Brenna wanted to windlass her crossbow, ready a bolt in case of trouble, but Christopher told her no. She asked him for an explanation. He said if there was trouble he'd handle it, that this wasn't the open foothills, that there were laws here. Brenna wondered what law it was that denied a person the right to protect him or herself when threatened. Then she realized it was Christopher's ego that had probably concocted the law. He wanted to be her protector. He wanted to be the *man*. Reluctantly she appeased him and kept her bowstring unwindlassed. Her nerves, however, were pulled taut.

There was something about Blytheheart that didn't feel right. Brenna had never been here before so she didn't actually know how Blytheheart was supposed to feel. Perhaps she compared it to places like Glastonbury in her mind. Or maybe her suspicions came from the faces of the people. There was a look most Celts wore, a steady hard look of another day, another job to do, another denier to earn. It was true that some she'd passed wore that look, but others — they seemed different. It was probably nothing, just her fear of being in a strange, new place, a very vast city port.

They turned a corner, and were now on Repentance Row. Christopher pointed to the writing on the post marking the street; it had both Latin and some other scribble on it. "That's Saxon underneath the Latin," he said warily.

"There must be Saxons here," was all Brenna could add.

Was that it? Had she just seen Saxons and noted some kind of difference in them? Perhaps. Saxon writing on the sign clearly indicated the presence of the invaders. But weren't they being driven out of Britain? Apparently not so here. In fact, they were given deference by Blytheheart's sign makers. She grew more incredulous as she thought about it.

As they moved on, she noted a change in Christopher. He eyed the street even more suspiciously than he had before, and he kept closer to the rounsey.

Saints Michael and George Cathedral rose in a great architectural fanfare to their left, and Brenna eyed it with an awe that alerted Christopher. He told her to stop staring as if she'd never been here before. But as the street became more and more cluttered with people, and they neared the grain market, Brenna found herself once again gaping at the scene. So many people. So much activity. Where did all these people come from? How many of them were Saxons? They were packed together like the whole port was some kind of winter storage cellar. There were so many faces, so many eyes, she doubted they'd be given a second look now. People she looked at didn't seem to pay any attention to her.

She eyed an old woman who carried a bucket of water; a mounted old man who rubbed a hand over his bald, wet pate; two young girls dressed in torn shifts who chased each other. A pair of dogs barked and were kicked out of the way by a swearing man and his two companions. Brenna winced in sympathy for the poor beasts.

The monastery was on the east side at the end of the row, and the closer they got to its grounds, the faster Christopher led her rounsey. By the time they reached St. Christopher Street, and Brenna was about to make a joke about the signpost, Christopher dropped the reins and sprinted around the corner onto Tintagel Street.

Brenna clenched her teeth over being left alone. For a moment she tried to put herself in his position. Yes, she might have done the same, but she would have left a man alone in the street, not a vulnerable woman. Then again, maybe he didn't think of her as so vulnerable after all. Maybe his leaving her showed that he knew she could handle herself. And for a fleeting second she was glad he was gone. But in the bat of her eyelashes, she was suddenly engulfed in the strange tide of humanity that flooded the street. It was odd to feel so alone in such a large crowd. But it was a crowd of strangers. She gathered her reins and heeled the horse on.

She turned the corner and neared the front of the monastery. She spotted Christopher standing in front of one of two black, heavily ornamented wrought-iron doors that made up the monastery's main gate. The doors were similar to those on a prison cell, but much more decorative, containing patterns of ivy that were locked eternally in the metal. Christopher spoke to a monk who stood on the other side of the bars. Then the monk turned away and Christopher's face registered shock. He raked a hand through his hair, disheveling it even more than it was, then looked up to regard her. He seemed about to cry. "Orvin and Merlin made it here, all right. But Marigween didn't. They're searching the port for her and Baines."

Brenna gazed at the monastery, the grain market, and the cathedral. She looked over at the abbey, its surrounding tofts, the merchant stalls behind, and then at the outlying scores of tents which trailed off to the eastern horizon. All of this told of the immense task it would be to find Marigween. She felt a tingle of excitement over the thought of Marigween's demise, but constrained the evil thought. She would help him find Marigween no matter how long it took, and no matter how she really felt about it. She'd come here to help and nothing more. "Why don't we get some food so that we're strong and can join the search?"

Christopher just breathed, audibly trembling through each puff of air. She knew he couldn't think straight, that his thoughts were probably as jumbled and scattered as hers had been the day he'd said good-bye.

"That's what we're doing," Brenna said, answering herself. She stood in her saddle, pulled a boot from its stirrup, and swung down to the stone. She found the rounsey's reins. "Come on."

"All right," Christopher said, then rubbed his eyes.

They reached Lord Street, which was directly opposite the wharves. Pedestrian traffic here was nearly at a standstill. They had to shoulder their way through the crowd. Brenna almost wished they could stow the rounsey somewhere; the horse slowed them down and needed the attention of a doctor. It didn't look as if there would be a stable in this part of town. The storefronts were as jammed together as the people were here, and not a single shingle mentioned anything about horses. If they could find an inn, she knew there'd be a stable nearby. Someone along Merchant Row would probably steer them in the right direction.

Two men came into her narrow path, and one of them was exceedingly heavy. As she kept her gaze low, she brushed by the fat one. Then she heard a voice call, "Lassie?"

Brenna froze, turned slowly around.

"What are you stopping for?" she heard Christopher ask from the other side of the rounsey.

"You!" Brenna said. Then her breath was swept away as if the fat man had reached down into her throat and took it for himself.

There were very few people in the realm that Brenna never wanted to see again. There were even fewer people that Brenna wouldn't mind seeing dead. But there was only one person who topped both of those lists.

Before she had another second to contemplate his presence, his partner, a much leaner, familiar-looking man wearing a glove, moved around him.

"Doyle?" Christopher asked.

Brenna didn't have to see Christopher's face; his tone alone trumpeted the intense impact of seeing his banished friend. Christopher shifted past her and hurried toward Doyle. They stared at each other for a moment, and then she saw Doyle close his eyes, as if to hide some emotion. They embraced as Montague stood by, a smile growing on his odious face.

"Out of the way," a sun-weathered man grumbled. He moved by Brenna in the room she created for him, shouldering a thick coil of rope. She used his passage as a distraction to reach back into her quiver and snatch a bolt, then unconsciously tested the sharp point with her thumb.

Montague. A nose-picking conglomeration of contradictions. Like his boys, he was the lowest form of rabble in the realm. Montague. The brigand who had tried to rape her. What was Doyle doing with such a fiend?

Before Brenna knew what was happening she was lost in that eve:

*He dropped his flagon, marched up to her, and pawed
both her breasts with his greasy, dirty, thick hands. He
slid his thumbs and index fingers to her nipples and
tugged on them, moaning again as he had while kissing
her neck. She knew of no sound more repulsive. Then he
lowered his head to her left breast and wrapped his lips
around the nipple, sucked on it like a nursing newborn.*

Christopher and Doyle were asking and answering
questions about the gaps in their lives, and then she
heard Doyle introduce Montague to Christopher.
Hearing the brigand's name again was like the clash of a
sword on a shield to start a tournament, only this was
Brenna's tournament and the spoils went to the person
who killed Montague first. She'd have to get by
Christopher and Doyle to get at him, though.

With the sharp tip of the bolt sticking out of the bottom of her clenched fist, she stepped quickly toward the
brigand and drew her hand back above her head.

"No, lassie!" Montague yelled, his color fading fast.

Brenna screamed as she crashed into Doyle and
Christopher. As her arrow-armed fist came down to
within a finger's width of the fat man's blubbery breast,
Doyle's forearm was suddenly there to block and drive
her fist away.

"Brenna? What are you doing?" Christopher shouted
as he wrapped an arm around her waist and dragged her
away from Doyle and the fat man. She tried to twist out
of Christopher's hold, but he was too strong. She felt
him begin to pry the arrow from her grip.

Separated by a couple of yards, she glowered at the
fat man while trying to keep the arrow in her grasp.
"Him. He tried to — It was him! You fat pig! You fat,
oily, ugly terrible pig!"

Doyle looked at Montague, the former archer's face
burning with a question.

Christopher got the arrow away from her and dropped

it to the street. Then he held her wrist with a grip that felt unbreakable. "You know Montague?"

"On my way to Shores. He and his boys, they —"

"What did you do?" Doyle demanded, taking a step closer to the brigand.

Montague sighed and rolled his eyes as if the whole attempted rape had been just a slight misunderstanding. And then he voiced it as such. "The lassie. We bumped into each other unfortunately. But that was when I was a roadsman."

Brenna hissed. She gathered spit in her mouth and sent it aloft; it fell a foot short of the highwayman. Then she looked at Doyle. "You're not friends with him, are you Doyle? Tell me you're not! Please, tell me you're not!"

"What did he do to you, Brenna?" Christopher demanded, his tone remarkably similar to Doyle's. "*Exactly* what did he do?"

"He tried to . . ." She hated the tears that fell from her cheeks, but to stop them would be as hard as breaking Christopher's hold. Oh, if she could just get free.

Doyle and Christopher exchanged a look that she could not read. But the fact that Doyle then looked to Montague said something.

"Come now, my lads and lassie. We can talk this all out. But let's do it quickly." He tipped his head to Doyle. "My partner here and I are on our way to a meeting we cannot miss."

Christopher folded his arms over his chest. "Your meeting can wait."

10

The Saxon cog *Seajewel* had been a warship, and that was probably one of the reasons why

Jobark had been eager to take command of the vessel.
Equipped with fore-, after- and topcastles, the cog,
though running merchantman's duties, was ready for
any resistance it might encounter from the Celt war-
ships that patrolled the waters around Wales. But
there were no archers standing behind any of the castles' wooden parapets this morning, just a single short
man that paced in the aftercastle, debating an issue
that had bothered him all morning.

Seaver liked Jobark, admired the man, and had felt a
growing loyalty toward him — not just because the captain would get him home, but because he treated his
men fairly, even those impressed into service. Jobark
was a reasonable commander, perhaps the last man
alive who could be described as such. Kidnapping
sailors for the captain would be a pleasure.

But betraying Jobark might cost Seaver his life.

The captain disliked Kenric; he'd made that clear. But
in one way Jobark was exactly like Seaver's former
leader. The captain shared an affliction with Kenric that
made Seaver's allegiance to the sailor wane.

It was the eyes that bothered him the most. Female
eyes dull from pain. Women resigned to their fate. Once
proud, beautiful creatures now bitten and smacked into
submission.

Kenric and Jobark loved women. Loved them too
much. Violated them. Hurt them. Kept them as slaves of
pleasure. And killed them in a way Seaver thought the
worst form of torture. Kenric had once offered a young
nymph to him for a scouting job well-done. Seaver had
reasoned that her height, though average, somehow had
stripped away her beauty. But he dug into himself and
realized that it hadn't been her height at all; it'd been
her eyes that had left him feeling cold.

The Celt woman in the captain's cabin wore those same
eyes. Dull from pain. At once pleading and resigned.

After a lot of struggle he'd managed to clean and prepare her for Jobark. The captain had asked him to do it
as a special favor since Seaver spoke her tongue. He
understood her words and knew her pain, knew it in a
way the rest of the crew could not.

He'd murdered many men in his day, like that
armorer back in the castle's dungeon, and had walked
away from the blood without second thoughts. But it
was different with women. They affected Kenric and
Jobark in a lustful way; but with Seaver they were able
to inhabit his conscience and make him feel sorry for
them. They were able to clutch his heart. Women made
him feel vulnerable. He didn't see them in the same way
he knew other men did. When he looked at a woman, he
did not suddenly imagine himself plunging into her; he
imagined lying in bed with her, arms wrapped around
each other, a fire burning in a nearby hearth, snow
falling outside. He'd heard of a thing the Celts called
courtly love, that one had to win a woman's favor; it
was an idea that greatly appealed to him. Kenric and
Jobark should have had to win their women; they should
not have been allowed to grab, rape, and discard them
as quickly as they did. There was value in a woman's life
they could not see. Seaver had been raised by a wonderfully kind and giving woman, one he would soon see
again. She had devoted her life to his care and taught
him all he knew. There was no person alive he valued or
respected more than her.

Seaver hadn't been able to sleep last night. The Celt
woman's screams had kept him up. From his nearby
hammock he'd listened as Jobark fisted her into silence,
then groaned as he took his way with her. He knew the
pictures in his mind of what had happened were worse
than the truth, but that weak fact hadn't made him feel
any better about it.

All Seaver had to do was let her go. He couldn't listen

to those screams all the way to Ivory Point. But she was in his charge and the blame would be placed on him for her escape, just as it had been for Christopher's and his friends' escape from the castle. If Jobark found out that he had deliberately let her go . . . There was a curious legend about Saxon captains, that they reserved a special dagger for those who betrayed them, mutineers or otherwise; Jobark might dust his off for Seaver.

The boatswain, a young, lean, mean-looking fellow with rope-burned forearms, sauntered up the gangplank with six of his deck crew. He barked orders as the group fanned out and began to work with the rigging. They were due to shove off this morning, and soon the huge, square sail would unfurl and block out the sun. Blytheheart would become a distant speck on the horizon.

Seaver found it more difficult to make a decision. Should he free the Celt woman or not? Take the blame for the open latch or not? There was probably a way for him to plan her escape and not take the blame, but such a plan had not occurred to him; nor was there more time to figure one out. There was one other problem: where was the captain at this moment? Still in his quarters? Seaver had not seen him leave the cog but he could have gotten up early and done so. If he was still in his cabin with the Celt girl, the whole plan would fall apart. So be it then. If he was still with her, then she would ride to Ivory Point with them. He could live with himself if he at least tried to help her.

He passed through the hatch of the aftercastle, then descended the ladder into the shadows of the hold. This level of the cog was loaded as high as his shoulders with provisions bound for the ports between Blytheheart and Caledonia. The hold was so full that it was hard to locate the hatch which led to the cabins of the lower deck. Seaver rounded a corner of grain sacks and found the hatch he was looking for on the floor. He slid the latch and raised the wooden door. He moved down the ladder into the captain's cabin —

And found her on the floor, lying on her stomach. He scanned the room. The captain was not there. He quickly crossed to the Celt woman, fell to his knees, and brushed her thick, red mane away from her face. Was she dead? No. She stirred, then opened her eyes.

"I'm freeing you. Go," he told her, feeling a chill rush through him.

He heard footsteps on the ladder. He turned his head.

Jobark came off of the ladder, turned, and stood there. The captain was shirtless and wore a frown. "What's the matter with her?"

"Uh, I think she's sick," Seaver said. "I was going to fetch her something to eat, and when I came down to check on her, I found her like this." The words came out too fast. He looked to the beaten, red-haired woman and said softly, "If you can get up and run you'd better do it now."

"What are you telling her?" Jobark asked.

Seaver kneed himself a bit back from the Celt, hoping she'd bolt up; but she lay prone, breathing faintly. "I asked her if she was sick."

Jobark stepped forward. Seaver could see her watching his approach past a half-open eyelid. Her color was ashen, her body as limp as rags. No, she would not attempt an escape. But in her condition she would not scream all the way to Caledonia either. At least Seaver wouldn't have to bear that.

"She's not sick," Jobark said. His shadow drew fully over her. "She's just exhausted — from last night."

Perhaps it was Jobark's boast that did it; Seaver couldn't be sure. But something had obviously triggered the woman, for now she reached out and wrapped her arms around Jobark's legs, drew them together and yanked them toward her.

The captain fell backward, rump, shoulders, and head colliding with the timbers respectively. The new dark brown shift Seaver had given the Celt woman to wear flashed before his eyes as she rose and bounded over Jobark.

Seaver went to the captain, feigning his surprise. "Sir, are you —"

"Get her!" Jobark yelled as he raised a hand to the back of his head.

Seaver looked to the ladder. The Celt already had her hands on the top rung. *Good.* He complied with his orders and mounted the ladder as the Celt woman disappeared through the square doorway above him.

He crawled into the hold and stood. The Celt woman was fast. She must have already found the next hatch leading to the upper deck. Moving slowly, giving her time, he did the same.

Finally, he stepped out into the sunlight, even as the rigging crew was curiously eyeing the Celt woman as she raced barefoot down the gangplank. Seaver started after her. He heard Jobark burst from the hold behind him and shout to the deck crew for them to join in the pursuit.

11   Their own dispute on Pier Street had caused a small commotion, but it was nothing compared to the action centered around the wharf to their rear. The shouts of the sailors made Christopher turn away from Montague to see what all the excitement was about.

A woman came running down the gangplank of the cog, a woman with the same color hair as Marigween. As she hit the level surface of the wharf, the wind caught her thick locks and pulled them from her face.

Christopher's mouth did not fall open in surprise. He did not shout for her. He did not say anything. The image released a lightning bolt of battlefield reaction, and he burst off toward Marigween.

"It's Marigween!" he heard Doyle shout behind him.

Christopher battered through two men, then had a clean line of sight down the long wharf. She came straight for him. He'd never seen her run with such urgency, nor seen such a horrible expression twist her pretty face.

But then she spotted him. And shouted his name. And the grimace faded for a second into a smile; however, with a look over her shoulder, it returned.

He spotted the seamen pursuing her. The lead man was a very short fellow who looked —

Seaver! How? He should be back at the castle!

The shock of seeing the Saxon scout who had once been his teacher and then captor was enough to nearly halt Christopher in his tracks. If it weren't for Marigween's presence, he would have stopped dead right there. Nothing made sense at the moment. Doyle had shown up out of nowhere with a brigand on his arm who had tried to take his way with Brenna. And now Seaver was here, too. Christopher's past had been shoveled up and dumped here in Blytheheart.

Marigween was about twoscore yards away from him now. She dodged barrels and crates and repeatedly looked back at Seaver, who was heavy on her heels. Christopher did not have a plan once he and Marigween reached each other. Yes, they would turn and run. But what about the deck crew? He prayed Doyle and Montague could help.

Another few feet. Another few feet. He mentally crossed his fingers as he neared her, and then —

They connected.

She barely had the breath to utter his name. "Christopher."

"Go!" he ordered her. There wasn't even time to ask her about Baines. Was their son still aboard the cog? Was she leaving him behind? Christopher was about to turn and join Marigween, but he stopped.

"Kimball!" Seaver shouted, using the old Saxon name that Garrett, their former leader, had once given Christopher. Seaver used the name as a grim reminder. Yes, he and Seaver had both served in the same Saxon army, and for some reason the little man had to keep hammering home that reminder.

He braced himself for impact with the short man, while his gaze searched the Saxon's hands for a weapon and found none.

The short man's momentum now appeared greater than Christopher had anticipated. He leapt into the air, adding even more speed to his pursuit, and —

He howled.

Christopher reached out for the scout's neck.

They fell backward together onto the wharf, and as Christopher tried to roll away, he felt another set of hands on him. And then another, and another. There was a ring of faces above him: the deck crew of the cog. Fists came down and the sky turned to the color of flesh. He rolled into a ball, hearing Doyle scream from somewhere behind him. And then he heard Brenna shout something which was echoed by the *Fwit!* of her crossbow.

Seaver was not directly next to him anymore, and he listened to his voice originate from a position just a few yards away; the man was on his feet. He spoke in Saxon. "That's right! Bring her back here! Oh, she's not getting away! She's staying with us now! Yes she is!"

"Chris-to-pher," Doyle managed from somewhere nearby.

The fists kept coming down, but he didn't feel as many now. He chanced a look. Doyle was up there, wrestling with one of the deck crew. Two of the others were still on Christopher.

He rolled, and as he did so he roared and lashed out with one of his own fists, but connected with nothing but air. *Fwit!* Brenna had fired again. Someone collapsed to the timbers.

In the seconds of newfound freedom, Christopher pushed himself up and managed to stand. A wave of dizziness passed through him, and he was just now aware of the soreness from the blows to his body. The situation didn't look any better than he felt.

Two men dragged a kicking and screaming Marigween back toward the cog. They were already halfway there.

Doyle was locked in a hand-to-shoulder grip with a seaman about his size. They were too evenly matched and it seemed they'd stay that way forever.

Brenna had shot two of the crew, who lay on the wharf, moaning and gripping the bolts in their bodies. She'd caught one in the lower left torso, the other in the right bicep. But she would not fire again. Her bow lay on the wharf at her feet, apparently having been knocked away by another of the crew. The seaman laughed as he shoved her backward, then closed the gap and backhanded her cheek. She tried to get a bolt from her quiver, but the seaman used one of his beefy paws to slap Brenna's hand away.

Seaver, who'd probably been gloating for a second, darted behind Brenna and snatched a bolt from her quiver.

Christopher looked to Marigween. She would not escape from the sailors who held her.

He looked to Seaver. Was the Saxon going to use the bolt in his hand on Brenna?

Seaver directed the tip of the bolt toward him. "Look over there, Kimball," he said in Celt, then gestured with the bolt.

Christopher jerked his head a few inches. He had already seen what Seaver wanted him to: Marigween being taken away. But he looked to the mother of his son anyway, and the horror was suddenly fresher, more intense, maddening.

"We've got her," the former scout went on, "and I know she means something to you."

"What have you done with our child?" His sudden rage had let the question escape. He silently cursed himself for it.

"Go after her, Christopher!" Doyle shouted.

"Yes, Christopher, go!" Brenna yelled, adding her voice to Doyle's.

"Your child . . ." it took a second for the fact to register in the small man's mind, and when it did, he grinned darkly. "She is your *bride*." Seaver sang the word like it was part of some black religious song. "I almost let her go," he added, visibly amazed over current events. "I felt sorry for her." The short man actually began to foam a bit at the mouth, and he had to palm the bubbly spittle away. "Oh, to think about when you escaped. You stripped me of everything. And I was on my way to leave this cursed land, to leave my vengeance behind." His gaze lifted to the clouds. "But now — *I can't believe it!* — Woden has made justice possible." His attention returned to Christopher as he hemmed. "There's value in a woman's life, eh, Christopher?"

With that he launched off, back toward the cog. He'd moved so quickly that Christopher was delayed a second in his pursuit. But that second turned into a moment more. He hadn't realized it, but while Seaver had been talking, another of the deck crew must have slipped behind him. Now, as he turned, the man seized him by the shoulders and threw him forward toward the deck. He went down like a blind, helpless fool, listening to the shrieks of Marigween.

Christopher let out a groan as he scrambled back to his feet, and before the man that had thrown him could get another opportunity, he set his boots in motion to pursue Seaver.

All of the fighting had brought the loaders of the wharf over to the shore end of the pier for a better look. There were no human obstacles in his path to pursue Seaver. He looked beyond the short man and saw that Marigween was being forced up the gangplank.

He hated leaving his friends, but what else was there to do? The cog's sail was completely unfurled, its anchor lifted, its mooring ropes drawn in. Her bow was pointed toward the open channel. She was as ready as ever to set sail — with Marigween on board.

His boots clanked loudly over the timbers. Seaver was remarkably fast for a man with such short legs. And he did not waste an ounce of strength to turn around to see how close Christopher was. The short man hit the foot of the gangplank and screamed something about the plank to the deck crew. Christopher assumed they'd try to drop the plank before he reached it. He saw men armed with longbows gather in the aftercastle. Then an arrow arced in the air and stuck with a reverberating thud in the timbers only a yard ahead of him. He nearly tripped over the arrow as he veered around it. He heard the awful *twanging* of more bowstrings as each sent an arrow down toward him.

Christopher now knew it didn't matter if the Saxons dropped the gangplank or not. He would never make it that far. Reflexively, he raised his arms in the air as a futile shield, then altered his course to the immediate left. He reached the edge of the wharf and kept running— straight into the breeze.

The fall was over nearly before it had started, and the water rushed up, around, and then over him. The many sounds of his engagement with the cog's archers were cut off by a single drone of bubbles. He reached a point where his momentum and weight no longer propelled him downward, and he began to rise. He used the heel of one boot to wrench off the other; then he reached down and tore off the remaining one. He let his head come furtively above the surface. He drew in a long breath and blinked his eyes free of water.

He was about twenty yards from the rudder of the cog. The ship was pulling away from the wharf, and already, there was a twenty-foot gap between it and the mooring.

Clenching his teeth, he paddled like a dog toward the cog. Though the water provided better cover than the pier, it was still impossible to hide, and the archers unleashed more arrows in his direction. This was not unlike his escape from the castle of Shores, when he'd plunged into the moat and had swum to shore while under the fire of the Saxons. But back then he'd been swimming away from the bowmen, not *toward* them. And back then, once he'd reached the shore, he'd taken a hit. The memory made him shudder.

The aftercastle of the cog was crowded with archers, each jockeying for a better position, two actually fist-fighting over a chance to kill Christopher. And some-where behind them, somewhere within the bowels of that boat, was Marigween.

Arrows raked the water. Many arrows. So many that he quickly ran out of places to swim. He'd dart right to find an arrow, left to find its brother, and for-ward to find its sister falling straight for him. Every move seemed fruitless. The closer he got to the cog, the thicker the fire became. If he miraculously reached the rudder of the ship and was able to hang on to it and somehow climb up it, what would he do once on

board? It would be himself versus an entire merchantman's crew. The whole idea of going after the ship
suddenly made no sense. He'd be captured along with
Marigween and the both of them would be subjected
to Seaver's torture. He'd be no good to Marigween
then. He would just die with her. Free, there was still
a chance he could do something. He could catch up
with Seaver at their next port of call. Lay a trap.
Something.

But he had to stay alive to do any of that. He ducked
under the water and swam fiercely toward the pilings
that supported the wharf. He found the heavily barnacled surface of one of the poles and paddled around it,
putting the deck of the wharf above him. The pier's
wide expanse was a more-than-adequate shield from
the arrow fire. He listened as the shafts *thocked* and
skittered, studied the slots between the timbers some
ten feet above as waves lifted and dropped him. Then
he looked down and saw the stern of the cog float
away from the last trio of pilings. The ship was headed
northwest into the channel. The occasional metallic
pulley-work of its rigging reflected brief bursts of sunlight.

Christopher's arms and ribs were sore from being
pounded by the deck crew, and his stomach screamed
for food. His legs were exhausted from running and
swimming. He was emotionally drained by Marigween's
near-escape, recapture, and the uncertain fate of his son.
Framing this chaotic picture that was his life was the
hard, wooden fact that Lord Woodward had been murdered and Christopher, the most likely suspect, had disappeared from Shores.

He brushed aside a chunk of brown seaweed, then
swam from under the cover of the wharf. He felt guilty
as he looked up at the sky, about to ask: what will be? It
had been too long since he'd tried to employ Orvin's art.

He'd strayed from it because the sky had never revealed anything to him.

But this time the azure wash loomed down and scooped him up into its presence. And there, in the sky, he saw something, felt something he had never experienced before.

PART THREE

THE SAILORS OF SHORES

1

"How many did I lose back there? Three, four men?" Jobark asked, then huffed in disgust. "I want to know who that boy was — and I want to know now."

Seaver turned away from the captain's glower and set his palms on the rough wood of the parapet in the forecastle. He looked out across the sea.

The *Seajewel* was in the center of the Bristol channel, and to her east, the rocky coast was a line that meandered on the horizon. Several gulls took advantage of a southwest breeze and glided overhead, while others perched on the sea near dark, floating plains of seaweed. It was a superb day, perfect for sailing. The wind fully lifted the two thousand square feet of sail, and the sky was devoid of all but the thinnest, highest of clouds.

However, Jobark's attitude robbed the day of its beauty. Seaver thought about where to begin —

"You will not put your back to me. I lost my boatswain. Can you replace him?" Jobark grabbed Seaver's arm and yanked him around. The captain's eyes narrowed and a muscle in his cheek twitched.

"I'll get you a new boatswain at our next port of call," Seaver assured him steadily.

"You'd better, true enough."

Intimidation was something Seaver was used to, and it would take more than a ship's captain to quicken his pulse. His fate did, however, rest in this man's hands, and that meant that a bit of skillful diplomacy was in order — to keep him on the deck of the cog instead of floating along with the seaweed. "You wanted to know about the boy. His name is Christopher, though I like to call him Kimball. And one of the others back there, the tall archer, he is his friend. They, and one other, escaped from me."

A light came into Jobark's eyes. "So they are the reason you fled the castle. Your recompense to Kenric would have been your life. But what were the two boys doing here? Hunting you?"

"I'm not certain. But it seems your red-haired Celt girl is Christopher's bride. Perhaps all of them were tracking me and she accidentally got caught." Seaver frowned as he thought about that further. "Then again, no one would've been able to track me here."

"You're too good a scout, eh?" Jobark asked with a whisker of sarcasm.

Seaver was too intent on trying to account for the squire's presence in Blytheheart to bother with the barb. He thought aloud: "The archer was with him. Did they come after me for revenge? How would they have known I had escaped from the castle? They must've spotted me. But revenge. That's not their code. And even if they were on some quest to capture and bring me to justice, why would Kimball take along his bride?" Another fact surfaced. "He asked me about his child!" Excited, he gripped Jobark's shoulders. "I must speak with a member of the gang that took the Celt girl."

"Unhand me, Seaver," Jobark ordered quietly, a threat rather sloppily disguised in the request.

Seaver released the captain and was about to continue when Jobark waved a hand in front of his face. "You are wasting your time. Why not obtain answers from the girl?"

"Yes," Seaver agreed, warming with the embarrassment that he hadn't thought of that in the first place. "I'll go to your cabin now."

He turned to leave, but found the captain's outstretched arm in his way. "And I'll go with you," the man amended.

Seaver flipped the skipper a wounded look. "Have I lost your trust?"

Jobark sniggered. "She was the bride of your enemy. You want her dead, of course. But she's not yours to dispose of. She belongs to me — and I will decide what's to be done with her." He took a step closer to Seaver, let the hand of his blocking arm fall upon the shorter man's throat. Jobark tightened his grip until it hurt Seaver, if only a little. "If she dies, shall we say *unexplainably*, then you will be keelhauled, true enough."

"Oh, no," Seaver assured the man, "I don't want her dead. Dead she means nothing. I'll catch those young Celts and reel them in with her."

"Only after your work for me is done," Jobark corrected.

Seaver nodded. "Of course."

They questioned the Celt girl, but she glared at them in muted defiance — even when Seaver promised to tell her what had happened to her child. Unfortunately, she read easily through his lie. Seaver clenched his fists and suggested torturing the information out of her, but Jobark wanted her body smooth and unbludgeoned for his nightly pleasure.

The Celt girl's eyes were now even more troublesome to Seaver. The dull from pain look had waxed into a narrow, red rage that was carefully contained. He reached the resigned conclusion that if they did torture her, she would continue to remain silent — and still fix him with those eyes. Perhaps they'd be able to draw tears from

her, but nothing more. As in the past, it was the ones
who took their pain in silence that fully unnerved Seaver.
Disgusted, he left the cabin, leaving Jobark alone with
the young woman.

On deck, he questioned a few of the crew, and was
directed to Gar, the deckman working the bowline. Fighting
the dipping and rising of the ship, Seaver staggered from
stern to bow, leaned back on the snatch for the anchor
cable to brace himself, then accosted the rail-thin man.
"You were one of the fellows who got the Celt girl, yes?"

"Aye," Gar said, the muscles in his arms taut as he
adjusted the tension on a line. He regarded Seaver for a
half second, then turned his gaze upward to the point
where his rope divided into two ropes, one of which was
fastened to the topmast, the other snaking out of sight
behind the sail. "But let me say thanks, first."

Seaver frowned. "For what."

"For that little slap and throw back there. Helped us
plank off the chief. Hated that dog. We can do our jobs
without his barking."

So Seaver was a hero to the remaining members of
the deck crew for getting rid of their boss, the
boatswain. "You're welcome," he said, lapping up the
credit. "Now tell me about a baby."

"Not much to tell. We left it behind."

"Was it still alive?"

"It was; but I bundled it so tight it couldn't breathe."
Gar reported this fact with stoicism, keeping any
remorse he might have had to himself.

Seaver pushed up from the anchor snatch and took a
step toward the man. "Where did you leave it?"

Still focused on his rigging, Gar raised a hand and
cautioned him back. "Behind the Customs House." He
thought about that, then reaffirmed, "Aye, we left it
back there."

Seaver toyed with the facts, then considered the ques-

tions that spun up out of them. What if the child had survived and someone had found it? If he could get his hands
on that baby, he'd have a prize even more valuable than the
squire's bride, who, according to Jobark, didn't belong to
him anyway. If he tried to use the Celt girl, there would
always be Jobark in his way. If he had the child,
Christopher's child, then, indeed, he would have the squire.

With the situation as it stood, that thought would, for
now, have to be tucked away. The odds of the child's
surviving were pretty slim anyway. He placed himself in
the squire's position. If he were Christopher, he'd come
after the *Seajewel*, try to catch up to and or beat the
ship to the next port. The latter was highly unlikely, but
Seaver had learned not to underestimate the boy. He
wished he could use the squire's bride to lay a trap. He
thought of killing the captain. No, then he'd never get
home. Abruptly, he was hit with an icy breath of realiza-
tion. He was becoming the man he'd sworn he'd never
be. He'd promised himself that he wouldn't let his thirst
for vengeance keep him in Shores and turn him into a
fool. He knew that quest could blind a man. He was too
smart to let that happen. He had to slow down. He had
to remember his own life. He had to think about what
would happen after, say, he got his revenge. What then?
There would still be nowhere to go but home. Why not
abandon the whole idea of killing Christopher and just
go to Ivory Point? The problem with that was a certain
feeling that struck him when he'd first seen Christopher
back on the wharf. As improbable as the squire's
appearance had been, it had, all at once, felt natural and
inspired by Woden. Yes; he would return to Ivory Point.
But if Woden had gifted him with the opportunity for
justice and he did not take it, then he might suffer his
God's wrath. Woden did not act on chance; he willed
what would happen. And Seaver should not deny the
deity his wish. It was true that Seaver wanted revenge,

that it would taste like sweet meat. But he could turn
away from it — turn away from a chance to destroy the
boy who had destroyed his command. He knew he was
not obsessed; he simply respected and feared his God.

If he let Woden guide his step, he would never lose
sight of his true course. Faith in the Master's wishes was
everything. And what the Master wanted now was the
young squire killed.

2   Christopher sat with the others in a private dining room of the Bove Street Inn. The breeches and
shirt Doyle had given him to wear were warm and dry,
but still not enough to smother the cold. Brenna, who
was seated to his left, asked him time and again if he
was all right, and she kept putting more and more food
on his plate. He was glad she cared, even though her
concern was excessive.

Doyle sat at his right, and Montague was opposite
Doyle. Orvin was at one end of the table, Merlin at the
other. Christopher eyed the group a moment, wondering
where their grave faces were, where their concern was,
where their urgent desires to help him were hidden.
Why did they have to stop now? His frustration found
his throat. "She's out there with *him* and we're sitting
here eating lunch."

"You have to eat," Brenna insisted, her voice sounding
like it had come through teeth as clenched as his were.

She was, of course, right. He felt hungry and miserable, and was in no condition to sprint off after
Marigween. Besides that, they had to figure out how to
catch up to the cog. He'd run off half-cocked, and all
that had gotten him was wet.

"Who's paying for all this?" Doyle asked no one in particular, just before forking a steamed chunk of carrot into his mouth.

"I am," Merlin said.

"Hold a moment," Orvin shot back from across the table. "I thought you lost your purse when those boys stole our mules."

"What boys?" Brenna asked.

"Forget about all of this!" Christopher shouted, then rose. He beat a fist on the table. "We have to catch up to that ship!"

Brenna's hand found his wrist, and she began to tug him down toward his chair. "Easy," she said, quieting him. "We'll leave as soon as we can."

"That's right," Doyle said, chewing loudly.

Christopher shrank to his seat, feeling asinine for the outburst. He had to regain control of his emotions, untie the knots and replace them with a fresh new streak of determination. That was, of course, what he told himself. Accomplishing the task was another matter altogether.

Montague reached across the table with his fork and poked Doyle on the top of his good hand.

"Ouch! What was that —"

"We've a lot to talk about," Montague said. "Don't make any plans until we do."

Doyle glared at the fat man a moment, then shook his head in apparent disbelief.

"You don't have to come if you don't want to, Doyle. Besides, if someone who knows you've been banished spots you, word'll go back to the king. Then you won't only be banished. You'll be hunted," Brenna said, sounding a bit too assuming to Christopher. "We'll manage all right."

"I wasn't aware my banishment extended past Shores," Doyle said. "Or did I misinterpret the king?"

"I thought you were —"

"Here we go again," Christopher interrupted Brenna. "We're discussing trivial points when the mother of my son is on a ship full of Saxons."

Montague lowered his tankard from his lips. "They won't kill her, laddie. Not just yet. The way I read what I saw back on the wharf, that little Saxon's going to use her as bait. And you'll play right into his trap."

"No he won't," Doyle said curtly. "Not with us helping him."

"Like I said, laddie. We'll talk about that later." There was no mistaking the displeasure in the fat man's voice. It seemed he wasn't thrilled about Doyle's instantaneous decision to help rescue Marigween.

Christopher stared glumly at his food. He'd already eaten the potatoes, corn, and carrots that Brenna had piled there, and all that was left was the lamb. But he was full, and the meat looked too raw for his taste. He took a sip of cider from his tankard, set it down on the table, then sighed. "All right. How do we get Marigween back?" He looked to Orvin.

"Our ride is already docked at the wharf," Orvin informed them in one of the few precious moments when his mouth wasn't stuffed with food.

"Are you referring to the Pict cog?" Merlin asked.

"Exactly," Orvin confirmed.

"Yes," Doyle said, investing in the idea. "We make a deal with the captain of that ship. I'm sure we can find someone who speaks both Pict and Celt."

"I know someone who does," a portly, large-breasted woman said, arriving in the doorway like a gale.

She was, to Christopher's accounting, a female Montague, dressed in a rather vulgar multicolored fabric, the likes of which he had never seen before. Every one of her fingers was weighted down by a gaudy, gemstone ring. She flaunted an equally showy headband that had a blue jewel in its center. This third eye made

Christopher feel uncomfortable with her arrival, if only for the reason that it woke memories of Mallory, that crazed knight whom he had slain. Mallory had worn a headband similar to this woman's.

Montague rose and circled around the table, moving as if drawn by some powerful force to the woman. He took her hand and kissed it. "Morna. You look delicious this afternoon." As she blushed, he turned to the table. "This is a friend of mine. Morna. Meet Christopher, Doyle, and Brenna. And over there, Sir Orvin. And over here is —"

"Merlin the magician," Morna finished. "An honor."

"More advisor than sorcerer," Merlin said with a mild smile. "It's not my magic — but the land's."

Christopher looked to Orvin, knowing there'd be some reaction on his mentor's face. Surprisingly, Orvin just sat and stared.

"Morna, you were saying you know someone who could interpret for us?" Doyle asked.

"Come, sit down," Montague said, leading his friend by the hand to an empty chair beside his.

Once seated, Morna took up Doyle's question. "Ah, yes, I know someone who speaks the Pict language. In fact, she works for me." And then with an odd smile, she added, "Her name is Jennifer."

Doyle adjusted himself in his seat and averted his gaze. "That's good. We'll . . . need her." He suddenly did not sound very enthusiastic about the news.

Christopher leaned over to his friend. "What's wrong?"

"I'll tell you another time," he answered softly.

"It seems you'll be doing a lot of talking later," Christopher noted.

Merlin cleared his throat. "Orvin. After we're finished here, I suggest you, Christopher, and Jennifer go down to the cog and speak to the captain. We've no time to waste." The druid brushed a few crumbs out of his beard, then raised his brow in wait for a reply.

Orvin nodded his assent.

Something was definitely wrong. Orvin ought to be fighting with Merlin over the druid's idea, even if it was a good one. Did Orvin's compliance have something to do with what Christopher had felt and seen in the sky above the wharf? He was going to talk to Orvin about that anyway, but the old knight's new attitude regarding the druid intrigued him all the more.

With the food and drink filling his stomach, and now a new hope lifting his spirits, Christopher stood. "I'm ready to leave now," he said, looking at his mentor.

"All right," Orvin said.

"I'll meet you down there," Doyle chipped in behind him. Christopher had no objection to Doyle's volunteering to come along, though it seemed Montague would have a lot to say about it.

"One more grave matter," Merlin began, his tone sounding as if he wanted to slow everyone down, "there's a child we have to find."

"Baines might be on the cog," Christopher guessed.

Merlin shook his head negatively. "Marigween was captured by an impressment gang. They would not have taken your son with them."

"That's right," Doyle said. "Unless it was all somehow planned. But Seaver looked surprised to see us."

"Yes," Christopher agreed. "He didn't know about my son until I — until I told him."

"It is my belief that when Marigween was taken, your son was abandoned. It is of course my fervent hope that he is still alive. And if he is, he may very well be here in Blytheheart."

"So what do we do?" Christopher said with sudden urgency. "Merlin, will you help the monks search for him?"

Merlin shook his head, no. "They will not want my

help. But I'll search myself. I think it wise, however, that I first pay a visit to the Marshal's prison and question the two men whom Brenna shot."

"They wouldn't tell us anything back on the wharf," Brenna reminded. "What makes you think they'll talk now?"

"Perhaps they know nothing about Christopher's son. But I believe they will know the Saxon cog's next port of call."

Murmurs of agreement floated around the table.

"I'll inform Robert and the other monks of what has happened, and tell them to continue searching for the child," Orvin said, then glanced to Merlin. "And it would be helpful to get word of this back to Arthur. Your absence has surely been noted by now."

Christopher thought about that. Yes, if Arthur could be informed of what was happening here, it might make his former squire appear a notch less like a murderer on the run. The fact that he was in the company of Merlin and Orvin helped matters in more ways than one.

Merlin looked directly at Christopher, as if reading his fear. "I believe that by now the king is as upset with me as he is with you," the druid said. "But in my note I will defend your desertion as best I can. I will, however, have to tell him what you told me about Woodward."

How did the druid know? How could he possibly know that Christopher had yet to tell Arthur about Woodward's murder? Both he and Orvin had left the night Christopher was supposed to have confessed. Then he'd waited until morning, and then he still hadn't been able to do it because of the presence of Arthur's battle lords.

"I guessed right," Merlin said with a smile partially hidden by his beard. "Your voice revealed you that eve, Christopher. I knew you would delay in telling the king. And now your face informs me you've yet to do so."

Christopher wished his guesses were as accurate as the druid's. His future would look immeasurably brighter. "All right, Merlin. Tell the king. I should have done so myself. What little honor I had left, I lost back there. I should not have delayed."

Merlin lowered his brow, then stroked his beard. Then he said, "Honor, young man, is within the heart. And if it is truly there, it can never be lost, only hidden, only forgotten."

And with that, everyone rose. The serving wenches began to clear the table. Brenna said she was going to the stable to check on her rounsey. Doyle and Montague were going to their room for a private discussion, after which Doyle would meet them at the Pict cog. Morna told Christopher she'd have Jennifer meet them, then she took Merlin by the arm and told the druid she had a friend who could get him a carrier pigeon for the note to Arthur. It seemed she had a lot of friends in Blytheheart. And that probably meant she had some power. For a moment, he wondered what her connection was with Montague, then shrugged off the thought as he left the table with Orvin. They strode out of the inn into the late afternoon sunlight.

"I guess we can wait out here for Jennifer," Christopher said as he leaned against the side panel of the merchant's cart.

Orvin looked around, then pouted. "Nowhere to sit, young saint. And I'm not going to plop on this dirt."

As depressing as the circumstances were, Christopher knew he would feel far worse if not surrounded by his friends. He imagined what it would be like to stand here alone, waiting for someone named Jennifer to come down and meet him. His fate would rest in a stranger's hands. That might be the case now, but at least he wasn't alone. Though Orvin grimaced and complained, the old one's presence comforted him.

And Orvin's misery loved company as much as Christopher's.

"I want to go back inside," the old knight pleaded.

"Stay out here a while longer."

"But it's too hot."

"She'll be down. And since we have a moment, I want to talk to you." Christopher lifted his gaze to the sky. After a long, thoughtful moment, he said, "I saw something."

Orvin was suddenly next to him, and he grabbed him sharply by the shoulders. "You did? You did?"

Christopher's gaze was shaken down to the smiling old man. It was always hard to look at Orvin's teeth; they appeared to be made of some yellow-colored wood that had been eaten away by insects. "When I was in the water, I looked up to the sky and I . . ."

He closed his eyes as he continued, slipping easily into the memory. But then it wasn't a memory; it was happening to him once again. He was back, floating in the waves, and he felt exactly as he had earlier in the day. No recollection had ever been this real. His mind had somehow driven the sun back to the east.

The azure wash loomed down and scooped him up into its presence.

He floated in blue waves, waves made of air. There were no clouds, no birds, just him and all of the blue. He wondered what was happening and at once decided he was so hungry and tired that he was probably about to slip into a black sleep. This wasn't what would be; it was just a prank of his mind.

But then it was as if someone had read that thought, and the airscape abruptly changed, bursting into white-hot flames. He screamed and looked down at his body, which was engulfed in fire — but he felt no heat, no pain. Strangely, he was a part of this new place, this place made of red and yellow and orange, and if he chose to leave, he could, but it somehow felt reassuring to be here.

What's happening to me?

What am I supposed to see?

In a blink the flames were sucked away into a black abyss. Now he floated through a starless night.

Show me! he ordered the black. Show me what will be!

A single star appeared, and then its white light blossomed and its rays began to rotate. Soon the star took up half of all the black, and as it spun, it fired off rainbow-colored lightning bolts of energy. One came directly for Christopher. He had no time to react.

It struck his eyes.

He was in a small room that reeked of mildew and something dead, and his gaze was locked on a bed. Someone lay under the woolen covers. He could not lift his head to see who was in the bed or view any other part of the room. He heard someone crying. A woman. And then a baby added its tiny voice to her lamenting. Outside, beyond the room, he could hear people shouting. And then all sound was replaced by the beating of his own heart.

A heartbeat. Another.

The image of the bed was devoured by the front yard of the inn.

"Young saint! Are you all right?"

Christopher turned his head, saw Orvin staring at him intently. "I wanted"— he realized he was out of breath — "I wanted to tell you what I had seen back there, but I just saw something now." He swallowed, then put a hand to his chest, feeling like his ribs weren't enough to contain his pounding heart.

Once he grew calm, he told Orvin all that he had seen, then asked, "Was it really the sky?"

Orvin pressed his lips firmly together, staring at nothing in particular. "I have never experienced any-

thing like that. It might have been the sky. But I — I'm
not . . . I cannot be sure."

If Orvin didn't know what had happened to him,
then it probably wasn't the sky and was simply his
imagination lording over his weakened senses. But how
would that account for the feeling? "Orvin, when I was
in that room and heard that crying, I somehow *knew*
that the person lying in the bed was dead. Even if I
hadn't heard the crying or seen the body. Even if I
closed my eyes and hadn't seen anything. I *know* that
person was dead."

"Who do you think it was," Orvin asked.

Christopher paused. How could he —

"You do not think . . . Ha! I don't believe God's that
merciful, young saint," Orvin said, apparently no longer
taking him seriously. "I fear he'll keep me in this plague
we call Britain for a few more moons."

"I'm not jesting, Sir Orvin."

"Nor am I, squire," Orvin said, his tone dropping to
suggest that he controlled the conversation.

"I know no one likes to discuss their own death —"

"What makes you so sure it was me in that bed?" Orvin
said, cutting off Christopher's intended reassurance.

He thought about the question, and then wasn't sure
how to put his answer into words. He simply said, "I felt
it."

Orvin chuckled.

"No, it's true!" Christopher cried over the old man's
cackling.

Orvin collected himself. "Oh, young saint. We're all
going to die. The real question is when. What did your
vision show you about that?"

Christopher searched his memory. Nowhere had there
been an indication of time.

"And," Orvin continued, "how do you know you
were glimpsing the future and not the past?"

Christopher had been asking what would be; that was the only reason he believed what he'd seen was the future. Orvin was right. He could have been seeing the past. But was it his past? He had no recollection of ever standing over someone's deathbed. Why would the sky show him someone else's past? It seemed more likely the sky would show him *his* future.

"Does the sky play by any set of laws or rules?" he asked Orvin.

The old knight tucked a long lock of stray hair behind his ear. "Laws of nature, laws of men. But then —"

"What I mean is, does it have to be *my* past or *my* future I see?" Christopher interrupted.

The old man let the notion sink in, and as it did, his eyelids edged open a bit, and his gaze flinted with something. "I've always seen things from my perspective. Must it always be that way? Do you believe you saw the past or future from someone else's point of view?"

"Maybe."

"Now *that* is interesting," Orvin said. The idea ignited his banquet table expression, the one he always wore when he was about to eat. But then his hand went to the small of his back, as if someone had just thrust an anlace into his spine. "Where is this Jennifer?" he asked angrily. "Indeed, I will die out here — and before my time."

"Not out here," Christopher corrected, thinking of his vision. Yes; he still felt Orvin's death. But perhaps the image was not connected to the feeling.

At least he was sure about one thing: the uncertainty and confusion were simply his luck. He'd sought the future in the sky, and he'd finally received a reply, but one so perplexing that the blue heavens might as well have remained silent.

If, in fact, they had spoken to him at all.

3   Doyle tugged off his glove and let it drop onto the riding bag at the foot of his bed. "What do you want me to say? You want me to tell my friend I've more important business to attend to, is that it?" He swung around to face Montague.

The fat man sat at the window chair and stared down at the pedestrians milling about Bove Street. "We have to strike now while the abbot is ripe."

Doyle's incredulity led him a step closer to the man. "You don't think he knows about our incident on the wharf? You don't think he learned names? He'll probably want us out of Blytheheart anyway."

"He knows about it, laddie. But he has not learned names. At least not yet." Montague slipped a thumb into one of his nostrils, then used his forefinger to clamp the bridge of his nose.

"Quit that," Doyle said. "And how do you know what the abbot knows?"

"You're forgetting about Morna. She also deals with the abbot's chancellor." Montague removed his thumb from his nose, studied the findings on the finger then flicked them out through the open window.

"That still doesn't matter," Doyle said. He took a seat on the corner of his bed nearest Montague, settled his forearms on his hips, and gazed absently at the planks of the floor. "Christopher saved my life. He's my blood brother. There's no question about me helping him. But even if he was just an acquaintance I'd help him."

"Why?" Montague asked quietly.

Doyle rose from the bed, came up behind Montague, and thrust his three-fingered hand over the fat man's shoulder and let it hover inches from the brigand's face. Startled, Montague drew back as Doyle said, "You wanted to know about this. Now I'll tell you." He pulled his arm away and turned from Montague, walked toward the door and then spun on his heel to face the man once again.

He lapsed into the story of how he had killed Leslie and Innis, how afterward he'd felt so guilty that he had thrown himself to the Saxons in the hope that they would kill him. He told Montague how Seaver had butchered off his fingers so that he'd never be able to fire a longbow again. He spoke faster as he went on to describe how Christopher had rescued him from the castle, and was probably partly responsible for him not being hanged from a gallows tree for murder. Doyle owed his life to Christopher, but he also owed it to himself to prevent Seaver from maiming anyone else.

In short, it was a convincing and emotional story, one which left Montague remarkably speechless for many moments afterward. Finally, the plump man hoisted himself up from the window chair, and, scratching at his sweaty temple, he turned and said, "I'm not happy about delaying our meeting with the abbot, laddie. But I see your point. I'll tell Morna we're going to be busy for a while."

Doyle was hit head-on by the fat man's last comment. "You're coming?"

"I owe a little to your squire friend myself," he said, then lumbered past Doyle toward the door.

"What do you mean?"

Montague slid the door latch aside and opened the door. He paused, looked over his shoulder, and the frustration was all but gone from his face. "You think about it, laddie."

As he turned to go, Jennifer moved suddenly into the doorway. She and Montague exchanged a brief look as he skirted around her and left. After closing the door, she stepped almost silently into the room, light and lithe and graceful.

Doyle rose. He flashed back to their lovemaking, his hands clasped around the backs of her thighs, her ankles high in the air, her toes pointed. Gooseflesh began at the center of his spine and worked its way to the backs of his arms, sending the tiny hairs there reaching outward, as if they, too, wanted more.

"I can't stay long," she said. "I have to go down to meet your friend."

"I'm coming with you," he told her, repressing the strong desire to run a finger across her delicate cheek. She smelled too good, and her eyes were too bright.

"Oh," she said, caught just a hair off guard. "Then I didn't even have to come up here. But then I wanted to —"

"How come you —"

"— talk to you alone."

Doyle grinned. "You talk," he said. I'll listen."

"I just —" She swallowed. "I just wanted to say I'm sorry."

He nodded, not knowing why she had apologized. He wanted to ask her why, but maintained his silence.

"Last night. I led you to think — you and I, we can never —"

There were many ways he could have calmed her. His lips did the job most effectively. She didn't respond to him at first, attempting a feeble withdrawal from his advance, but he was an excellent marksman, and after a dozen rapid heartbeats, her tongue soon played hide-and-seek with his.

If Jennifer smelled too good and her eyes were too bright, then she tasted even better. As their arms found each other, Doyle marveled at the speed in which he'd fallen in love with her. Christopher had tried more than once to describe the feeling to him, but Doyle had never been able to wholly understand it until now. All at once everything his blood brother had been trying to tell him about Brenna and Marigween made perfect, crystalline sense. The love Doyle had for Jennifer made him feel proud and full and strong. It made him want to thrust his chest out and beat on it with his fists. He wanted to burst through the roof of the inn and shout to all of Blytheheart that he adored Jennifer and no one would ever take her away from him. When it came to this feeling, this love, he was like a varlet-in-training, naive and dreaming of glory. Doyle lifted her off her feet as he kissed her, then he pulled back and spun her around. She kept laughing and he kept on spinning until they were both so dizzy that they fell onto his bed.

But after catching her breath, her smile faded. "Why do I want this so badly?" She balled a hand into a fist and squeezed, her small knuckles turning pink and white.

"Because it's right." Doyle sighed. "You don't have to be a whore all of your life. I see far past that."

She lowered her gaze to the blanket. "No, Doyle. It has nothing to do with being a whore. It's what you want to do with your life. I don't want to interfere with any of your plans."

Doyle grabbed her hand with his good one. "I won't make plans without you."

She whimpered through a sigh, as if gripped in an icy agony, her gaze still averted.

"What is it?"

She looked him straight in the eye. "You don't understand. You can never understand."

"Yes I can!" He squeezed her hand. "If I knew what you were talking about!"

"One day you may work for the abbot. If he ever found out about us, it would destroy everything." She sniffled, then closed her eyes.

Doyle shook his head in disagreement, then smiled

weakly. "You of all people should know that the abbot won't hold my courting you against me — since he uses Morna's services himself." Doyle pondered her reservations further. Then a stray fact leapt home. "Wait. You're not, well, not the abbot's favored girl or something, are you?"

"Not exactly," she said softly, then opened her glossy eyes. "I'm his daughter."

Doyle drew back from her — only a few inches — but she noticed it. "His daughter?"

"Yes, not that he'd ever admit I am. No one else knows. No one but me and Morna, and now you. And maybe Montague. Let me say he's been a wonderful father." Her humor was as black as it came, her voice as sad as it had been the night before.

"Then I presume your mother was also in the same line of —"

"Morna is my mother," she finished for him, her tone dark, cynical. "She has been an even better parent than Father — teaching me her trade with an amazing amount of skill."

Lines formed on Jennifer's small face and drew toward her nose. She closed her eyes and began to sob. Doyle wrapped his arms around her and pulled her head into his chest. He stroked the back of her head with a gentle, even hand, feeling even more in love with her. He was truly not alone in his pain. She would understand his situation with his own parents. She would understand everything. In a sense they had both been banished from normal lives; both had parents with a warped view on how their children should be raised — if they could be called parents in the first place. She would understand his loneliness, relate to the condition of his soul. She could share in the idea of never being content, and knew the lost feeling of never having a true and complete family. They were both scarred.

And then there was God. Doyle still held a candle of contempt for Him. Surely, Jennifer had mixed feelings about the Lord. What kind of God would permit her to have a father who could never recognize her as a daughter. What kind of a God would curse her that way?

He knew he would one day reconcile with the Lord; but that day was many moons off. Perhaps they could help each other come to terms with Him. They needed each other. That fact was so obvious that it warmed him. What ever it would take, Doyle knew he had to be with her. He would only let her go if she denied him. Circumstances would not get in their way. He would fight to preserve their union.

Doyle reached down and wiped the tears from one of Jennifer's cheeks. He gently lifted her head away from his chest and looked down into her sore eyes. "It's you and I, Jennifer. You and I against the realm. We can do it together. It's hard. I know."

"It's never going to —"

He shushed her. "Our lives are going to change. Have faith in that and it will come to pass. I can't tell you how many times I have wanted to die. But being with you makes me want to *live*."

Though her face was still wet, her tears ceased. He felt as if he had made progress with her, but it was too risky to go deeper. He'd said enough for now.

He kissed her softly, drew back as she closed her eyes, then rubbed them with her fingertips. "Come on."

She sighed and sniffled again. "Your friends are probably wondering where I am."

He touched her cheek — as he'd wanted to before. "I can tell them to wait a while longer if —"

"No, I'm all right," she said, drawing up her shoulders. "Let's go."

4 The stable behind the Bove Street Inn was extensive and housed over one hundred steeds, Brenna guessed. As she led her rounsey past the south side of the weatherworn building, she observed that three of the stable's six rectangular doors were pushed fully open, and presently several horses and their owners entered and exited the stable. The stalls within were cast mostly in shadow, but Brenna could detect a lot of movement from inside.

She had thought the abbot of Glastonbury's stable was elaborate; it was a peasant's lean-to compared to the one before her. She moved behind the main stalls to come into full view of three other thatch-roofed barns. Judging from the hammering going on within one of them, she assumed it was the blacksmith's shop. She stopped a page and asked the young boy where she could find a doctor for her mount. He pointed to the smallest barn closest to St. Thomas Lane, and said, "Better make haste. The line is growing."

Brenna didn't understand the boy until she was directed behind the building by a farmer goading his slow-moving, rather sick-looking sow. There she found a long line of people who stood alongside their animals. One angry, middle-aged woman wrestled with the rope around her goat's neck, while another man had trouble getting his ox to move as the line stepped forward a bit. All shifted restlessly as they waited to pass through a large square doorway.

With a grimace, she found the end of the line and tapped on the shoulder of a thin, gray, slightly hunch-backed farmer in front of her. "Is everyone waiting to see the doctor?"

"It's our stock that need to see the doctor, love. But

we got to do the waitin' for them," he said in a dry tone that robbed the effect of his wit.

Brenna loosened up and settled in. She patted the rounsey's shoulder. The horse's wound, though not as swollen, looked worse. The skin beneath his hair was a blue-red and small bumps had erupted around the scrape. It was true that if the mount died, she would owe Hallam the money to buy a new one. But it was more out of concern for the horse's well-being than out of selfishness that had brought her here. It was in her power to save this rounsey, and the horse's eyes pleaded for her to do so.

She let her mind drift over recent events, landing here and there to survey the damage.

But her thoughts kept alighting on him.

No. Stop it. Stop it now. Or you're going to be hurt. You know that.

She forced herself away from his mental picture and thought about how she'd shot the two Saxon sailors. At the time it had been mechanically simple. Windlass, load, and fire. Windlass, load, and fire. Down number one. Down number two. Screams of agony. Now as she stared at the fuzzy picture of the men gripping their wounds, it dawned on her that she could have killed them. She hadn't thought about it then. She'd had to stop them. And it was her poor aim that had spared them. They probably shared that thought, probably believed that a young woman could never accurately fire a crossbow. But that wasn't true. Less than a moon ago she wouldn't have been able to hit the sailors, but her aim, though still wild, was improving. She felt good about that, yet the idea that she had almost taken two lives left an eerie impression on her. She had received the tiniest taste of what Christopher had once tried to define for her. He had said that every time he'd taken a life a little part of him had died with that person. A little part of what it was to be a man escaped from him. And though Brenna had not killed the sailors, the fact that she nearly had left the little parts of what it was to be a woman hanging on by spider-webs. She couldn't put her finger on the feeling, and would probably have as hard a time explaining it as Christopher had had, but she was aware of its effect on her, how it made her want to put the crossbow down for good. It wasn't that she knew killing was wrong and that God would punish her for it; it was something else that made her actions feel ugly and horrible. Whatever the case, she did not want to shoot anyone ever again. She hoped the Lord was listening to her thoughts.

Brenna had forced her mind away from Christopher, but had inadvertently allowed him to find a place in her introspection about shooting the sailors. At least think-ing of him indirectly did not tug as hard on her heart. She wondered if she loved him more than she felt sorry for him. His situation was bleak. She decided that both feelings were backed with iron, yet she could sympa-thize with him only to a point. The line was drawn at the feet of Marigween and his son. She would shed no tears over their loss. But to show joy over it when Christopher would be lamenting would be cruel and gain her nothing. It would make him resent her. To understate, it was a difficult situation. How would she tell him she was sorry about their loss without her joy seeping through? How would she tell him and make it sound sincere? She couldn't lie to him that way. Maybe she would not console him. Maybe it would be best to stay away and let him come to her when the time was right. And then she should tell him the truth, tell him of the struggle within her. Tell him she was not very sad about the deaths of Marigween and his son, that their lives only represented chains on her heart. With them gone, both she and Christopher were free to resume their love. Yes, she would tell him that. She knew how much he valued the truth. He could not hold her heart against her. She would only be speaking how she felt. He would have to thank her for that.

And he probably knew all about her feelings anyway.

Brenna felt the weight of a hand on her shoulder. Startled, she turned around.

It was Montague, his expression tentative.

"What do you want?" she demanded quickly, ripping his hand from her shoulder.

He closed his eyes, then lifted his palms to chest height in an act of surrender. "I can get you to the head of the line, if you'll permit me, lassie."

"No, thank you," she said curtly. She barely noticed that her stomach had become a cauldron. That is, she barely noticed until the heat flushed her face. "And if you're wise, you'll stay away from me."

Montague opened his eyes and lowered his palms. He leaned past the man in front of Brenna to view the length of the line. "You're going to be here a long time."

"That's all right," Brenna said darkly, her gaze turning and fixing on anything that wasn't him.

"I thought saving your life would be stronger than just an apology. I guess I thought wrong," he said from behind her.

She whirled to regard him. "I said thank you. I appreciate what you did for me. But don't expect it to wipe away the past." She blew air, then looked to her boots.

"I saved your life, lassie. That sailor was getting the best of you until I intervened. I don't think there's anything more I could ever do for you than that. And all I want in return is for you to tolerate me. I don't want an apology. I don't think that's possible. I'll give you as many sorrys as you want. So long as you don't cringe every time I walk into a room. What do you say?"

Brenna wanted to look up at Montague to see if he was being honest, or at least looked so, but memories of his attempted rape still gnawed at her already-frayed mental edges. She sensed the flicker of his tongue on her nipple, and quaked with the horror of being tied and taunted by his boys as if it were happening once again. Even Montague admitted that his actions had been inexcusable, and there was no way she could forgive him for them. She kept her gaze lowered and said, "If you want me to tolerate you, you have to stop something first."

"Anything. Montague can stop anything," he assured her, his tone tinged with the pent-up energy to leap at her command.

"My name is Brenna," she said slowly. "*Not* lassie."

"Aye, a simple matter, lass — Brenna," he said, already slipping. "I should tell you I talked to Christopher and Doyle about what happened before we ate. They don't exactly forgive me either, but rest assured, I've changed a lot since then. Doyle knows that. I chance to say that you and Christopher will discover the same if you give me time."

An evil thought occurred to Brenna. It seemed Montague was now at her disposal. It was obvious he wanted to preserve his friendship with Doyle, and in order to do so he had to reestablish relations with her. He'd seized the opportunity to save her, probably thinking it would gain him leverage in her forgiveness of him. He was trying very hard, what with talking with Doyle and Christopher, and now coming to her for a private apology. He wanted to get along with her so badly that he could probably taste it.

She could exploit his hunger for her acceptance.

Montague might go after the Saxon cog with them. Doyle certainly was, and the fat man would probably follow his friend. She could persuade the brigand to make sure that Marigween wasn't saved. In fact, he was the type of fellow who could make sure that Marigween would never be seen again.

Brenna shuddered. This was the most evil notion she
had had thus far. And base though it was, the fact
remained that she could probably get the fat man to do
it in return for full forgiveness.

Another, perhaps more clever thought came to her.
Even if she didn't go through with this plan, it would be a
unique way to test whether the fat man had really changed
or not. If he was now the angel he purported to be, he
might wholeheartedly refuse to take part in her little con-
spiracy. If he was still the highwayman she felt he was,
then he'd take the job and she would know the truth.

"What's wrong?" he asked. "Am I that repulsive to
look on? Do you think I'm lying about all of this?"

The line moved a few steps forward, and Brenna kept
pace with it. Montague assumed a place behind her. She
stopped and turned back to regard him. "Are you coming with us after Marigween?"

"I think I can lend a helpful hand, lass." His mouth
dropped as he realized his second slip. "Brenna," he corrected quickly.

"Do you want me to truly forgive you? That's possible," she teased.

"You don't have to. Like I said. But I hear a deal coming on. Explain."

She lowered her tone to the interrogative level of a
watchman. "Are you really sorry for what you did, or do
you just want to make sure you don't lose Doyle as a
partner?"

He frowned, looked away from her for a heartbeat to
consider that, then glanced solemnly back to her. "Do
you think what I did to you is the only thing I regret in
my life, Brenna? I could spend the rest of this day telling
you stories that would make you swoon with horror."
His gaze burned into hers. "If there is a God, I'll be
cleaning his garderobe after I die. Cleaning it for eternity. That will be my penance for all I've done, you see.

Running into you that foggy day is the least of things I have done to be sorry for. But yes, I regret what I did — what I did to *you*. Doyle has nothing to do with that. It's just unfortunate for me that you and he are friends. Believe that if you will, or not."

He'd uttered a word she could twist against him. "Why don't you start your penance now? Penance for what happened with me."

His expression clearly conveyed his confusion. "What more can I do than save your life?"

If Montague had lied about being sorry, he had done an excellent job. It was hard not to believe that he regretted the past. She didn't have to trick him. She could take what he'd said on faith, for it seemed to be more than enough. And yes, he had saved her, questionable motivations or not. He would probably not harm her again. But there was too much she didn't know about him to ladle out that kind of trust.

And there was also the still-lingering, ever-dark notion of actually employing the brigand to make Marigween vanish.

But what if Montague wouldn't do it? Yes, she'd be assured he was a changed man — but what if he went to Christopher and mentioned the plan to him? Then Christopher would distort her own sincere intentions to help. He would see her presence as merely an assurance of Marigween's death. He would think of her as a cruel, conniving, selfish, devilish woman. Everything would be ruined.

No, she couldn't go through with it. She shouldn't tell Montague about the plan. She fretted over what to tell him now. She'd set him up and now she'd have to deliver. What more could he do for her that would make her forgive him?

"Still thinking of things I can do?" he asked, his tone slightly higher and a trace playful.

"I had something in mind," she admitted, "but it won't work."

Once again, the line edged forward, and its movement must have reminded the fat man of his first offer. "I can still get us to the head of this line."

Brenna thought it over. It was a very thin olive branch, but one nonetheless. By taking the offer she was opening herself to him, only a little to be sure, yet it would be a first tiny step toward granting him absolution. It was hard to realize she was actually thinking about forgiving him when only a moment ago she had thought that that would be impossible, a fact driven home by the brigand's own words. To harbor resentment was wrong. She wasn't going to absolve him by the next moon, but there was no reason why she shouldn't let him do little things for her — at least for the time being.

She nodded her assent, and they shuffled out of line and headed toward the west side of the building, where Montague said there was another door.

"If you want my forgiveness," Brenna said, "you'll have to earn it. And that might take more than your lifetime."

"All I can do is try," he replied in earnest.

Brenna paused. "I still hate you," she told him, but knew her tone and expression spoke only weakly of the fact.

5   Marigween sat numb and bare on the cabin floor, surrounded by three damp, ale-breathed members of the deck crew. A three-foot plank with holes drilled in each end was forced between her ankles. Ropes were

threaded through the holes and coiled around her legs
to hold the wood in place. Another rope was fastened to
the plank's center, pulled taut, looped into a slipknot,
and dropped over her head. Her wrists were tied
together and a long length of rope snaked away from the
bindings. One man slung that rope over a ceiling beam.
The others gathered around, and Marigween felt her
arms lift suddenly over her head as they heaved her into
the air until she was three feet above the deck. They fastened the rope to another beam and then left under the
barking of the captain.

It was excruciatingly hard to keep her legs up —
but she had to — for if she were to let them fall
toward the deck the rope fastened to the plank
between her legs would choke her. She guessed she
had only several moments worth of strength to maintain this position. The captain knew that and hurried
out of his clothes, even as the last sailor sealed the
hatch above him. He hastened to the bed and dragged
it under her. He slid onto the mattress and began to
massage himself, resting only inches below her groin.
Marigween turned slowly. Her body was a single
tensed muscle that trembled with a failing exertion.
Her ankles edged down a bit, and the rope tightened
its grip around her neck. She gasped, then swore to
herself over her failure to keep the vow she'd taken to
stay detached. To connect with the black moment
would put her into it.

The captain let out a loud moan as he entered her,
then, after thrusting in and out a few times, he left himself deep inside her. He reached up to Marigween's
thigh and pushed her. As she rotated around his shaft,
she closed her eyes.

It was worse this time, far worse than the first occasion he'd raped her. That night she had tried to stop
him, but he had hit her and then screamed, and then he

had pulled out his dagger and put it to her throat. She'd never felt that alone, that hurt, that violated, that helpless. She'd blamed herself for what had happened, and now kept telling herself over and over that she could have stopped him, that she *should have* stopped him, that there was no reason for it to have happened. She was a princess. She was strong. He should not have had his way with her.

But these were just ineffectual thoughts.

She imagined what Christopher would think if he saw her now. He would not love her the way he had. He would look upon her as he would a whore — with disdain. It was all her fault. *She* had wanted to leave the cave; no one had forced her. She'd risked her own life and the life of their child. Now Baines was gone, and she spun above a grunting, smelly creature.

All she had to do was drop her legs, let the rope have its way with her. She would stop breathing and go to the castle of heaven, where she would join her father and mother. She imagined white, white edged in silver, and shadows made of wool that glided and floated and spread their wings and carried her toward the sun. It was beautiful, and there was no rise and fall of the ship, no sounds of the waves pounding against the hull, no moaning from the poison-breathed Saxon.

There was singing. Joyous singing. And it came from a chorus of little girls dressed in white robes. She felt their voices direct her to be with them in a place that was everywhere and nowhere, a perfect expanse of blue.

Then a bloodcurdling cry cut off the image, and Marigween opened her eyes.

Seaver stood over Jobark. The short man gripped the hilt of a dagger that was buried in the coughing captain's heart. Marigween's legs collided with Seaver, and he ceased her rotation. Then he yanked the dagger from the captain's chest and used it to saw at the rope fastened to the plank and her neck. It took several cuts before the rope finally snapped.

"What are you doing?" she asked weakly, thinking that he probably wanted her body now.

"You want to die, don't you?" he asked affirmatively.

"Yes." She wanted to add something, but thoughts wouldn't collect into words. The pain was terrific in her wrists, and the muscles under her arms felt as if they had been torn to shreds. She just wanted to make it stop, all of it, all of the hurt inside and out.

"I need you alive," he said, then he stepped around the bed, hopped up onto it, and began to cut into the rope that suspended her.

Marigween's gaze found the bleeding captain. His wound was small, a simple slot in his hairy chest outlined in blood. There was not a lot of blood, but enough to catch the eye. More grotesque was the blood spattered about his mouth and neck, the blood he'd coughed up just before he'd died. He looked as if he'd sat down to a meal of raw meat with his hands tied behind his back.

As Seaver continued to saw into the rope, Marigween felt the captain's shaft slip out of her groin. She shuddered with the idea that a dead man had been inside her. She felt a gag come on which she swallowed back. She felt the rope give way, then fell onto the captain's legs, the plank between her legs smashing into the dead sailor's throat. She was no longer suspended, but her legs and wrists were still bound. She tensed with the hope that Seaver would free her. She might be able to steal his dagger.

"I'm going to explain something to you," Seaver began, shifting around the bed to regard her with a stern expression that reminded her of her father. "Now that Jobark is dead, the crew's going to run free. Houge, the first mate, will assume command — but these sailors won't listen to him." He leaned toward her. "Do not forget you're the only woman on board."

He didn't have to clarify his last statement. She hadn't had the chance to count, but she presumed there were at least a dozen hands on board. "Let me die. Please. Don't keep me like this," she begged, then blinked back tears.

"We're getting off this ship at the next port," he said. "But to make it there you're going to be the captain and he" — he looked to the corpse of Jobark — "is going to be you." She didn't understand. He read that and added, "This eve you're going to don the garb of the captain, and you and I are going to dump his body overboard. I'll tell the crew the body is you. I'm sure it won't be the first time a woman was disposed of this way."

"And then what?" Marigween asked. "How long do you think I can pose as the captain?" She snickered. "We'll be lucky if any of this works. And why should I go along with it? How do I know you're not lying?" Then, without realizing that her frustration had increased the volume of her words, she shouted, "What is all of this?"

He slapped a palm on her mouth and said, "You've got no one left but me. I don't want you to die. And your being Christopher's bride doesn't change that. Now, you're going to go along with my plan because you don't have a choice. I could turn you over to the crew. Jobark's little amusement here is nothing compared to what they'd do to you."

Slowly, he lifted his hand from her mouth. She breathed deeply, then said, "Don't you think the crew will recognize me even with the captain's clothes on?"

"You'll don a cap to hide all that hair," he explained. "Once we've gotten rid of his body, you'll be sick in your quarters for the rest of the ride. I'll guard the door myself."

Marigween wondered if sometime during the whole intended affair she might be able to break free. She'd wondered that many times before. But now she came to a conclusion she should have come to much earlier:

Once free, where would she run?

She could jump ship, but she'd never be able to swim home. The cog had no dinghy, so that wasn't even an option. The only path toward true freedom would be to kill every man on board and pilot the ship herself. Marigween had been stripped of a lot, but she still possessed the wisdom to differentiate the possible from the impossible. She'd closed many mental doors in the recent hours, and had strayed toward the remaining open door of death. Seaver had come along and unlatched a new passage of opportunity, one which would at least get her off of the cog. The prison of water would be gone, and she would only have to contend with him.

But she still couldn't shake off the desire to die and the oppressive idea that she was tainted and would be unwanted by Christopher. Even in freedom she would still wear the wounds of her rape, wounds that ran deep and would probably never heal.

And what if she grew with child? What then? Would she carry around the baby of a dead Saxon sailor for nine moons? Could she cope with that burden?

Marigween felt her hands come free. She hadn't been aware that Seaver had been untying her. He moved to the bindings on her legs, saying, "Were I you, Marigween, I'd follow orders. That is, if you want to stay alive."

Indeed, that was the question that consumed her thoughts. She felt her stomach lurch as the bow of the cog was lifted by a wave.

Seaver hadn't planned on killing Jobark. As he untied the Celt girl's legs, he thought about how he might

have done things differently, but he kept reaching the
same conclusion: the murder of the captain. When
they had been up on the forecastle, the captain's tone
had angered Seaver, but he'd kept his emotions in
check. No rage had festered, and no quest for revenge
had tunneled his sight. It was a new plan for the
future which had made the stabbing come together.
First, he'd decided that it was Woden's will that he
kill Christopher. Then he had realized that without
either the Celt girl or the squire's child, Woden's
wishes would remain unfulfilled. Woden's wishes
were much more important than the petty desires of
Jobark. And at once Seaver had viewed the captain as
a mere obstacle.

He looked down to Jobark's body. *She's mine now,
old friend.* He finished untying the girl and handed her
his dagger, which she took almost apprehensively from
him. "There's my trust in you — right in your hand.
We're both prisoners, and I'll get us off of this ship."

She turned the point of the dagger toward her heart.
He was about to lurch forward to stop her, but the knife
fell from her trembling hand. She closed her eyes and
bowed her head.

For a moment, Seaver sympathized with her. He'd
thought of taking his own life after Christopher and his
friends had escaped from the castle. The feeling had
been a hunger never satisfied, a large hole in his being
in which everything had passed through. He'd been
turned into a man of nothingness. And he'd thought that
if he was nothing, what did it matter to go on?

That was how Marigween felt. And she should. She
was caught in the middle of a private war, a pawn — as
the Celts would say — in the higher orchestration of
Woden. Seaver looked upon her, and truly, he felt her
pain. It had once been his own, and still, even now, it
lurked in the shallow water of his heart, threatening to

surface at any time. Yes; he was a great leader of men. What was he now? If he asked himself that again, perhaps he'd use the dagger on himself.

Someone pounded on the ceiling hatch. Seaver slipped the remaining rope from the Celt girl's ankles. "I'll see to that," he said, turning away toward the ladder. "Be silent."

6 Orvin wanted to throttle the cocky captain of the Pict cog. He thought of how he had nearly strangled Merlin, and figured this time he'd see the act through to its life-taking finale. Yes, it would be no problem at all to kill the man right where he stood on the wharf, right before his boat and his crew.

"Can you repeat that?" Doyle asked the young, blond, woman named Jennifer.

"He says," she answered slowly, "that he has no desire to take on any passengers."

Christopher frowned. "You told him we'll pay him, right?"

Jennifer nodded. "He doesn't seem to care how much we're willing to pay. He says he has a schedule to keep and every bit of weight aboard his ship has to be accounted for. Our extra weight will slow him down."

The old knight ground his remaining molars. "Nonsense," he said. "If there's one true law in this realm it's that every man, king or beggar, has his price."

"But he's not from our land," Christopher pointed out.

Orvin flipped the young saint a hard look, then proceeded toward the skipper. The Pict was a head shorter than Orvin — but he didn't seem to mind that fact as

Orvin arrived before him and drew himself erect. He stared into the captain's gray, unflinching eyes. "Jennifer, tell him we'll pay equal the value of his entire cargo for passage." Orvin was in awe of his voice; the words had come out with more force than he'd anticipated.

Even Doyle looked awed. "Are you mad, Sir Orvin? No disrespect, but how do you propose to raise such a large sum?"

"We'll borrow it," Orvin said, thinking quickly, the muscularity of his tone softening. The idea was to get the captain to agree to take them and worry about payment later. The logic was faulty to be sure, but Orvin thought it best to cross this stream one stone at a time.

Jennifer let her tongue twist and turn and flit about the Pict vocabulary, and all of it sounded like the midnight talk of drunken knights. When she was done, the Pict captain flashed his canine teeth which were slightly larger than they should be and lent to him a houndlike appearance.

But whether he looked like a dog or not, he'd clearly read straight through Orvin's bluff. Now he shook his head negatively to confirm that fact.

Orvin spun around. "Blast!" He felt the air escape too quickly from his lungs. He coughed, coughed again, then saw the young saint approach. The boy beat a palm on Orvin's back in a feeble but well-intended attempt at aid.

"Don't get yourself so upset," Christopher told him. "It's not worth it. There has to be another way to catch up with that cog."

A small group of sailors had gathered on the starboard side of the cog to watch their captain negotiate with the Celts. Orvin could hear them laughing at him now, the captain chuckling the hardest and loudest of all as he strode back toward the gangplank.

"How dare they mock us!" Orvin growled as he tore himself away from his young apprentice to leer at the hooting Picts. He waved a fist in the air. "Your day will come! Arthur and his army will take care of you!"

Both Doyle and Christopher moved in front of him as if they suspected he was about to charge the ship and take on the crew. He felt the desire to do so, but his reason overpowered his temper. "It's all right, boys," he told them, feeling himself shrink a little. "I'm not going to do something rash."

"You already have," Doyle noted sourly. "Not that I mean any —"

"Disrespect?" Orvin asked, clipping the boy off with a tone of equal tartness, one he hoped hinted of his challenge.

"Let's go," Christopher suggested. "There's nothing more we can do here."

Orvin recognized the wisdom in the young saint's words. The longer he remained on the wharf, the greater the chance his temper would get the best of him again. And the next time his reason might not be able to save him. He sighed and turned toward the shoreline. Christopher, Doyle, and Jennifer joined him. With the breeze at their backs, they headed for firm ground.

"When do you think the next Celt ship will arrive here?" Doyle posed to the group.

"Someone at the Customs House might know. They must keep records of arrivals and departures," Christopher said. The young saint's voice conveyed his enthusiasm for the new idea.

What these boys failed to realize was that even if a ship, Celt or otherwise, did drop anchor as early as the morrow, it would still be some time before it finished its business in Blytheheart and was ready to leave. Add to that the uncertainty of whether the captain would take them on as passengers, and the fact that the Saxon cog would, by that time, have reached its next port, and the idea of waiting for another ship became an exercise in stupidity and futility.

But Orvin wouldn't douse the young saint's hopes. Not yet. Not until he at least checked on ship arrivals with the customs master.

Less than half an hour later, they all left the Customs House. Their ears rang with the news that the next Celt cog would not arrive for at least another quarter moon. There was no telling when the next Pict or Saxon cog would arrive, as the foreign captains were under no obligation to surrender their logs. The customs master further explained that in his opinion it would be at least several days before any ship arrived, and he based that opinion on the similar schedule of the past moon.

"We can't wait several days, let alone a week," Christopher said, pausing to absently scan the seafront shops along Pier Street. The squire's frustration flowed from the boy and infected Orvin, who thought harder and paced a little faster.

"What about mounts?" Doyle asked Christopher. "Maybe we can track their progress from land. They probably aren't too far off the coast."

Jennifer shook her head negatively even before Doyle finished his suggestion. "As you head north, the hills are rocky and steep, and if you decide to take the beach, you can only pass during low tide. There are points when the passage vanishes into the rough water and the cliffs. I've heard of a few who've drowned. But the inland path will slow you down." She looked to Christopher, her eyes full of sympathy. "I'm sorry."

During Jennifer's argument, an idea had come to Orvin. He'd rejected it at first but now it seemed like their only alternative. "I'm going to speak to Robert," he announced. "I want him to take me to see the abbot."

Doyle and Jennifer exchanged a look that Orvin found

hard to read. Doyle turned from her and said, "You think the abbot can help us?"

"I know one thing," Orvin began, aware of a faint smile passing over his lips. "Whatever the abbot wants, he gets. And if the abbot wants us on that Pict cog, we *will* be on it."

"You think he can order that captain to take us?" Christopher asked.

"Very good." The boy was bright. "Yes. Now, were I the abbot, a quiet threat would accomplish the task — as in bar the cog from trading in Blytheheart if the captain does not comply."

"Why would the abbot do that? What would he have to gain?" Doyle's attack made sense.

But Orvin was ready for it. "Robert is well respected at the monastery. The abbot would be doing a favor for one of his own. And it's *his* nest he protects better than anyone else's."

Orvin could tell from the boys' expressions that they agreed with his reasoning.

Jennifer's face conveyed the contrary. "That favor you speak of might cost the abbot."

"In what way, dear?" Orvin asked.

She twirled a finger through her blond hair, not absently but anxiously, Orvin thought. "The captain would surely be insulted by the abbot's threat and hence, he might choose to exclude Blytheheart from his trading. He could very well do that."

"Which would cost the abbot a lot more than a few deniers," Doyle said, stepping into the false light Jennifer had just shed on the conversation.

"Only an assumption," Orvin fired back at the young woman. "I don't think the abbot would choose money over the niece of one of his monks."

"I wish you were right," Jennifer said bitterly.

"Orvin, if you would, go to the abbey and see what

you can do," Christopher said. "We'll meet you back at the inn."

The old knight said his good-byes to the young folk, then watched them press their way up Pier Street and tangle into the crowd. He started for the intersection of Lord Street, and had only traveled twenty yards when he spotted a pair of sailors from the Pict cog walking toward him. Their gazes lit and their brows rose as they recognized him. Without the aid of the boys or a weapon at his side, Orvin's pulse was spurred. Trying to be discreet, he turned around and pretended that the shop he'd just passed had caught his eye. He stepped back to the shop's window, cupped hands around his eyes to shield the glare, and peered inside: a rope-maker's workshop. He turned and resumed his retreat.

Orvin passed the door of the Customs House and considered ducking inside, but then thought better of it. He would feel awkward explaining his return to the customs master. He kept moving and came upon the alley between the Customs House and Chancellor's House. He slipped down the passage, felt his heart stagger, then reasoned it was an exaggeration of his mind.

He shot a look over his shoulder and saw that the sailors were not in the alley. He hustled to the far corner of the passage, then darted left to utilize the Chancellor's House as a shield. He peered furtively around the corner. The sailors were paused at the mouth of the alley. He drew his head back, then whispered fervently to himself, "They did not see me. They did not."

After waiting another moment, he peered again and saw that the alley was clear. The incessant cry of a baby came from beyond the picket fence that was opposite the alley. The sound irritated him and he wished the child's mother would pacify it. He paused a last moment to catch his breath.

Orvin knew he was too old for such excitement. He'd been repeating that trite statement to himself since the first day he had met Christopher and had stitched the boy's wounds. That day had marked a radical change in his life, and it was situations like the present that were breathtaking reminders of the change.

Before he had met Christopher, life had been relatively peaceful. He had retired from knighthood and had been doing a bit of training here and there, helping his son Hasdale when he could. Then Donella had died. The illness had spent far too long inside her. That last bloodletting had been too much. He knew the doctor had been wrong. No one had believed him. It had been the bloodletting that had killed her, not the illness. With his love gone, he had partially retreated from Hasdale's court. His son's death had completed his withdrawal. He had no use for most of the realm.

It was the loss that had made him turn inward. The loss had been just shy of too much to bear. And now what he feared most was that the young patron saint might experience the very same loss — only his would occur all at once. Here was life acting as a mirror into the past, with Christopher playing his role, Marigween playing Donella, and the tiny child Baines serving as the lost Hasdale.

But there was still sand in the glass for Christopher's bride-to-be and son. And if Orvin had anything to do with it, the past would not repeat itself. This time woman and child would be saved.

7   From the window in Doyle's quarters, Christopher looked down on Bove Street, then up to

Blytheheart's sky, which was rippled with the orange-veined clouds of sunset.

"Do you see him yet?" Jennifer asked.

Christopher returned his gaze to the street. The majority of the pedestrians were donned in drab browns and grays, and Orvin's equally drab shirt and breeches would make him hard to find in the crowd. Christopher looked for one of Orvin's more notable features: his shock of white hair. And there, ambling from St. Thomas Lane onto Bove Street, was the old knight. He looked a bit disheveled and wholly out of breath. Christopher answered Jennifer, "Yes, I see him. He's coming now."

Just then the door opened, and Montague stepped into the room, followed by Brenna. Was Christopher's vision failing, or was Brenna actually in the fat man's presence and *not* trying to kill him? Indeed, Montague's actions back on the wharf must have somewhat softened the raven maid. She had behaved rather civilly at their meal, but there had been a heavy wooden table between her and the brigand.

"Well, this room's suddenly gotten a lot smaller," the fat man observed, eyeing the four people before him.

"Did you see Morna and Merlin down there?" Doyle asked Montague.

The fat man shook his head, his jowls trailing the movement. "No telling what's keeping them."

Christopher's gaze connected with Brenna's, and he gestured with his head for her to come over to the window. She did, and he whispered to her, "Is everything all right?"

She nodded. "For now." She looked to Montague, who was moving toward his bed to take the great burden of his belly off of his feet. "But watch him, if you would."

Christopher nodded, then he saw Doyle and Jennifer

come together for their own whispery conversation, leaving Montague to murmur over his tired legs.

"How are you feeling?" Brenna asked, gaining back his attention.

"I'm still sore," he said, then reached for and rubbed a rib, "but I think —"

"I meant here," she said, cutting him off and then placing an index finger on his left breast.

He drew in a deep breath, then let it out slowly. "Orvin will be up soon. Say a prayer he convinced the abbot."

Brenna withdrew her finger, clearly resigned that she wasn't going to draw true feelings from him. "What are you talking about? What happened?"

Christopher gave her a brief summary of what had happened, after which she closed her eyes.

"What are you doing?" he asked, eyeing her strangely.

She *tsk*ed, opened one eyelid. "Saying a prayer for you."

He waited a moment. Her eyes remained closed. "Are you done?"

Then, after another moment, she opened her eyes. "Now I am."

"Did you find a doctor for Hallam's rounsey?" he asked, then winced a bit as mention of her horse lit the memory of Arthur's prized — and now dead — mare.

She nodded. "He said the poultice we had made helped a lot, but it will take a long time for the wound to heal. The doctor said he had a stall available and offered to board the rounsey. Montague paid for it."

Christopher raised his brow in slight surprise. She wasn't exactly speaking highly of the brigand, merely stating the fact of his generosity. Still, it was ironic to hear her utter the words. The paint on the picture of her lunging at Montague with the bolt in her hand was still wet, and here she was already accepting small tokens of forgiveness. It was a characteristic of hers that he hadn't

witnessed too often, but times such as this reminded
him of it: she was not one to hold a grudge. In fact,
Brenna was not one to hold in any kind of hostilities for
very long. Christopher had completely shunned her, had
broken her heart, and she had come back to him wanting to be friends. And then she had insisted on coming
along to Blytheheart to help. He suspected she was here
out of something more than friendship but wasn't going
to venture into hazardous emotional territory to confirm
the fact. If she somehow still loved him, it was a love
that might be doomed to misery.

Christopher wished he could return to a fateful day,
the day Arthur had made him squire of the body, the
day that Marigween had stood behind that first trestle
table in the great hall, gracing the scene with her radiant
image, an image that had brought heat to his face. He
wanted to go back to that day —

And not see Marigween, the mother of his child.

It was a dark thought, brought on by his rekindled
feelings for Brenna. But what was done was done, and
at least for the moment he could stay focused on Brenna
in order to make sure nothing happened to her.

He regarded her gravely. "Brenna, no matter what
Orvin has to say, it's going to be Doyle and I that go
after Marigween. No one else."

She rolled her eyes. "We've been through this before,
Christopher. I came along to help you. I'm not stopping
here."

"You fought well down on the wharf, but you still
could have . . . it's just that if you die, I'll never forgive
myself. Never. I don't want the responsibility of your
life. It's just too much for me right now." He turned
from her and looked out through the window to the
peddlers' tents across the street. His gaze was caught by
a puff of smoke that rose above one of the tents. The
smoke was part of a magic show, he supposed.

"You're being selfish," she retorted. "You only care about how you feel." He heard her take a step toward him. "What about how I feel?" She still stood a few feet away, but her words felt as if they'd been shouted at point-blank range into his ears.

He craned his neck to regard her, his expression icing up. "How do you feel?"

"I-I want to help."

"You've been saying that, and *that* doesn't answer the question, does it?"

He knew he wasn't being fair, and he had just made the resolution not to wander into the land of her feelings. He was supposed to be telling her that there was no way she would be going after Marigween with them, supposed to be ordering her to stay here with Orvin and Merlin and the rest. Why was he prying into her feelings for him? What was it that made him suddenly need to know? Had her coy behavior finally become so irritating that he had had to put an end to it? No. Then what? Was it a simple desire to know that someone loved and cared about him? He could daresay that everyone in the room felt that way about him; certainly all were very concerned and, like her, wanting to help. What was it?

The answer to his pondering was so simple that he'd overlooked it. His love was responsible; it wanted to draw out Brenna's feelings so that they could mingle with his own. He was a victim of his heart, the moment simply another occasion of looking too deeply into Brenna's eyes. He had not forgotten Orvin's old admonition; he just repeatedly failed to observe it. The present course of his life was paved on that recurrent mistake.

"Why did you ask me to marry you that night?" she asked.

Brenna wasn't the conversational master of say an Orvin or a Merlin, but she was fairly skilled at the craft. Before Christopher realized it, he squirmed to find his own answer. And then he remembered. "That was just mad dreams — you didn't answer my question."

"Mad dreams? You didn't sound mad."

He frowned. "Forget about that."

"No. I want to know."

Orvin saved the day — simply by entering the room.

"Excuse me," Christopher told Brenna, then strode past her to accost the old knight at the door. "Orvin. "What happened? Tell us. Speak!"

But the old man was too winded to say anything, and he motioned with a hand toward a spot on the bed next to Montague. Christopher closed the door behind Orvin, then led him to the bed where he sat down with a wince, a crack of bones, and a moan. He took several more breaths before finally speaking. "Robert went in to see him. They wanted me to wait outside the door. But I heard the conversation."

Christopher noticed a flash of yellow on his periphery and craned his head to see Jennifer step to his side, her gaze intent on Orvin. He turned back to his mentor. "What did they say? Come on," he urged.

Orvin shook his head negatively, then let his gaze lift to find Jennifer's. "You were right about the abbot, young lady. You knew exactly what he'd say."

Jennifer straightened and turned away from Orvin, her face lacking the self-satisfaction Christopher presumed would be there. She exchanged a mysterious look with Doyle, then strode toward the window.

"I could've told you what he'd say," Montague threw in. "And we would've saved a lot of precious time. But no. You lads had to go running off with your own plans before you consulted me. Don't do that again."

Montague's authoritative tone went unmissed. Christopher smirked. Doyle shook his head as he was wont to do every time the brigand opened his mouth.

Orvin, on the other hand, wasn't going to react to the

remark with a simple display of countenance; oh, no.
Christopher watched the old knight slowly turn his gaze
toward Montague and fix him with a look so fiery that it
appeared the big man would, in seconds, burst into
flames. "These lads are trying to save a young woman's
life — not sitting on their fat rumps and asserting that
they can read minds."

Christopher was taken aback by Orvin's rebuttal.
Unfortunately the fat man brushed it off as he would
sweat from his forehead. "Listen to me, one and all," the
brigand   began,   then   directed   his   attention   to
Christopher. "If we want to save that young lass, laddie,
we must catch up with that ship. And we must set out
after it no later than this eve."

"Tell us something new. Like how we're going to do
that," Doyle challenged Montague. "Do you propose we
take a little fishing boat and row up the coast? That's
about all we'll find down there."

Christopher noticed a smile forming on Montague's
lips, a smile that made the shiny hairs of the highwayman's chin stand on end. Something was hidden
beneath that grin, and it gave Christopher pause.

Montague was brigand at heart. A highwayman.
Plain and simple, a criminal. That life had been in his
blood far too long for him to give it up completely.
What he would propose now was a course based on
opportunity and necessity, one that would require
great courage, skill, and the abandoning of guilt, and
finally, one that was, to say the least, morally questionable.

"We're going to steal that Pict cog," he confirmed.

Orvin hemmed. "What?"

"Steal the cog?" Doyle repeated as a grin split his
thinly bearded face. "How?"

"What do you know about cogs?" Montague asked
the archer. Then he looked to Christopher before he got

his answer. "What about you? Do you know how many crew members it takes to sail one?"

Christopher shook his head, no, then looked to Doyle, who shrugged.

Montague smoothed out his mustache. "Most cogs are ninety-eight feet long, sixty five and one half feet at the waterline, with a beam of twenty-three and one half feet, and a draft of ten feet. Their sail area is usually two thousand square feet." He smiled. "I worked for a ship-builder in my youth — can you tell? Never mind. All in all, most crews range from twelve to twenty-four, but I've seen as many as forty men crammed on board. But forget that. Here's the important part — with six or seven of us, we can get that boat moving."

"He's right. We can do that," Brenna said, stepping into the conversation both figuratively and literally as she moved to Christopher's side.

"I don't want to argue with you now, Brenna. I told you that you're not going," Christopher said softly, try-ing to shield his temper from the others.

"We'll need her, laddie," Montague said. "We can recruit sailors, to be sure. But I wouldn't trust a one of them. Better we do it ourselves."

"There are probably as many as eight or ten sailors on board that cog at any one time. And we'll have Picts on the wharf. And I could be wrong about all of that and the whole crew could be on board when we attack," Doyle said, finding as many holes in the plan as would be in his body if they tried it.

"Who said anything about an attack?" Montague asked.

Orvin rose from the bed. "I've heard enough of this." He faced Christopher. "Has it occurred to you that this northerner might want the ship for himself?"

It hadn't occurred to him; but it seemed unlikely. He shook his head.

The old knight turned toward the door.

"Orvin, please, let him finish," Christopher said, stopping the old knight with a hand on the other's arm.

"Yes, I too would like to hear how he proposes we snatch that ship out from under all of those sailors," Doyle said.

Orvin regarded Montague. "If you're not taking the ship for yourself — and you really do want to help these boys, then what is your plan?"

"My plan is to get the sailors away from the ship," the fat man answered.

After considering that, Orvin shook his head. "How?"

Montague looked to Jennifer, and raised his brow.

8

Tania lay in bed, listening to Hayes as he chopped carrots and turnips on the table in the main room. She wished she could get up and prepare the evening meal for herself and her husband, but the illness's grip was too strong. She knew that sloth and idleness left her vulnerable to evil, but there was little choice when the pain came. She hoped Hayes had found the right kind of eel at the market, one that was sparkling and large, with a white belly. She'd reminded him that the reddish trout were better in summer, and had asked him to purchase a half dozen for salting. He'd bought goat's milk before; at least she hadn't had to worry about that. She wanted to ask him about his shopping trip, but he'd been silent all day, and the same upon returning from the market. She knew her breath would be wasted.

She reached over to a stool beside the bed and drew

from it a clay mug. She brought the mug to her lips and sipped a bit of the steaming, sweet barley water. Hayes had prepared it with just the right combination of barley, licorice, and figs. The liquid seemed to dull the knives that tore into her chest and arms. She returned the mug to the stool, then looked down to the child bundled and nestled between her arm and shoulder.

The tiny boy slept quietly now. He had cried a lot this afternoon; he must have worn himself out. That was good. Hayes had little tolerance for the child's weeping. Gently, she patted his head, then let a finger run over the fine hair on his small scalp. He was lovely. Pure and full of life.

She heard a banging sound and realized it was not her husband's chopping. There it was again. Someone was knocking on the front door of their tofthouse, and the raps were loud enough to drown out her husband's work on the vegetables. She heard Hayes stop his chopping, then cross to the door.

"Good day, sir."

"Yes, good day," Hayes answered in the depressed tone he'd developed since she'd first brought the child home, a tone that had fallen away into reticence.

"Sorry to bother you, but Brother Pater and I are looking for a lost infant. Have you found or heard of anyone who has found one?"

Tania trembled as she slid her blanket down, then brought it back up to cover the child. Somehow the monks had learned about the lost baby. Perhaps they had saved its mother.

It wasn't fair! It wasn't fair to take the child away from her now. She desperately needed this newborn.

She would not survive without him.

"No, I'm afraid I cannot help you, brothers," Hayes said.

Tania shuddered through her sigh.

"Please keep an eye and an ear out for us then, if you will. Apologies for the intrusion."

"Good day, gentlemen."

"Good day."

The door squeaked closed. Tania heard Hayes move from the adjoining room, then saw him arrive in the doorway of their sleeping quarters. "I regret that," he said, tipping his head back toward the door, "and I will henceforth put my boot down. The child is going to the monastery." His face, which had grown more sun-browned and wrinkled over the years, was set.

But she knew she'd win the fight. If she could finally make him understand. "Please," she began, not realizing how hoarse the illness had made her voice this time, "don't take him there."

Hayes stepped into the room, and with the wave of a callused hand said, "Look at you, Tania. How can you raise a child from a sickbed?"

She pressed farther back into her pillow, but there was no escaping him. "Don't you see —"

"All I see is my sick wife who is dreaming of something that can never — and shouldn't — be." His tone was cruel, unlike him.

"It's this little one, Hayes. Don't you see?" She pushed the blanket down, revealing the child. "Without him I won't get better."

He made a crooked grin. "How is a child going to help you?"

"I need him — and he needs me. Without me he has no one. And because of that I have to live. Don't you see? I have to get better."

Hayes lowered his head, then pulled at his beard with his thumb and forefinger. She knew he did that only when he was nervous. "We're old, Tania," he began.

"I knew you would say that," she spat back, "I've been waiting for you to say that. It doesn't matter. We were good parents to our children and we can be the same for this little one."

"No." His tone was now almost too steady, too soft, his apparent resolve unnerving Tania. "We've done our work. Lived our lives. The Lord has blessed us."

"Blessed us with this child," she qualified, only now realizing she'd been hugging the infant tighter and tighter as they'd talked. She relaxed her arm around the boy.

He regarded her as he drew himself up to his full height. "I'll have no part in this — and neither will you." He started toward her and dropped his gaze to the boy. "Release the child."

She saw him now not as her husband, but as a creature bent on inflicting pain. She lifted and cradled the baby, then kicked out in order to drive herself toward the side of the bed.

But the tightness came too suddenly, a paralyzing flash of heat and locked muscles that was the illness rearing its ugly head. She could not leave the bed, but was able to fight through the seizure and keep her grip on the child.

Hayes hovered over her, searching with his hands for a way to wrest the child from her arms. "You'll kill me if you take him, do you know that? Do you know that you won't have a wife? Do you want me to rot away, is that it? Don't you love me anymore?"

"It's because I love you," he said, his voice weighted with the exertion of his prying hands, "that I'm doing this. What you want to do . . . it's not of God."

"How can it *not* be of God? I'm helping a poor child — and myself," she cried, feeling her tears stream across her cheeks.

The baby started to cry as Hayes tore it away from

her. He lifted the boy to his chest, then slid his forearm under the child's rump. For a moment lightning flashed in Tania's memory, and she was back to the days when Hayes would hold their own Stral under his arm the very same way. Her husband looked younger now, perfectly natural with the baby. It could be that way for a long time, she knew. If he wasn't so stubborn. They weren't stealing the child but blessing it with a good home.

"Come on, little one," Hayes said, turning away from her.

"Hayes . . . don't . . ."

He froze, then turned back to her. "It's God's will."

Sniffling, Tania backhanded the tears from an eye. "You're dooming him to the life of an orphan."

"How can you know that?" Hayes asked.

Tania bit her lower lip and felt the arm she'd used to hold the child tremble as the last threads that connected her to the boy began to fray. "I know," she started, closing her eyes, "that you cannot do this. Please. Oh, Lord above, give him the wisdom. Let him see that I am his wife, and have and will continue to honor him every day of his life. And that he is my husband, and has honored me every day of my life. I need the child. The child needs me. He needs us. What is wrong with that?"

When she opened her eyes, she found that the baby lay on the bed before her. Hayes was gone. She heard him exit through the front door and slam it shut after him.

The boy still whimpered, but grew calm as she lifted him into her arms — where he belonged. She studied the small, tear-stained face. The points of the illness's knives felt dull. There was a glow that Tania knew was in her eyes, a glow that likewise haloed her heart. The child was a barley water for her soul.

9   Alone in his quarters, Doyle set the quill Merlin
had loaned him down on the trunk, then studied the
map he'd been drawing on a ragged half yard of hemp.
Though crude, it did depict each and every storefront
along Pier Street, and it also included the Chancellor's
and Customs Houses, as well as a few neighboring
tofts.

Montague entered the room, turned back to make a
last cautionary glance into the hall, then stepped fully
inside. He closed the door and threw the latch.
"Finished yet, laddie?"

Doyle nodded, uncrossed his legs, and rose from the
floor. He picked up the map and handed it to Montague.

The fat man eyed the hemp, then nodded. "Good, this
is good. Fetch me the quill and I'll mark them off for
you."

He dipped the quill in the clay inkwell before handing
it to Montague. The brigand looked around, then
frowned at the trunk near Doyle's bed. "That won't do."
He looked at Doyle. "Lend me your back."

Doyle leaned over, and Montague spread the hemp
across the former archer's shoulders. The quill tickled a
bit as Montague scribbled, then he blew on his markings
to dry them.

Doyle wished Montague hadn't done that. The air was
suddenly foul with the fat man's bitter breath. "Can I
stand up yet?" he asked, breathing only through his
mouth now.

"Wait, let me just . . . all right then."

He straightened and turned to face Montague, who
held up the map for inspection. Several storefronts
which Doyle had chosen to identify as boxes with
anchors drawn inside them now had circles around

those anchors. "So those are the ones," Doyle remarked. "It's not going to be easy. They all share common walls, and those roofs —"

"Aye, the roofs will go, but the walls are made of stone. The damage should not be that extensive. Morna doesn't exactly approve of this part, but at least she sees the common benefit of it," Montague said, hinting at something Doyle didn't quite catch. The brigand crossed to the window, waving the map in the breeze of his momentum. He stared down into the street, which was now huddled in twilight. "I just wish we had more time."

Doyle thought what their plan would be like had they a quarter moon to prepare it. Surely it would be far more complex, at least a notch less dangerous, and he would not be as nervous.

But they had conceived the plan to render the Pict cog as vulnerable as possible only a few hours ago, and would now carry it out unrehearsed. They had one chance to make it all happen. The whole affair was akin to having a single arrow left in one's quiver to drop an advancing enemy soldier. The arrow comes out of its sheath; it locks into the bowstring and falls back into ninety pounds of draw. The enemy comes into sight and the time comes for the arrow to be fired.

And if the shot misses, his won't.

"Were you down at the back house just now?" Doyle asked, breaking himself free of his worries.

Montague winked as he nodded. "Morna and Jennifer have rounded up at least a score of lasses. She says she has fifteen of the crew in there so far. There is still no way to tell how many are left, unless . . ."

As Montague lapsed into a thought, Doyle's mind suddenly flooded with the image of a Pict sailor pounding into a wincing Jennifer. He shuddered the thought away, ground his teeth and balled his bad hand into a three-fingered fist. "Do you think —"

"Yes, I do," Montague answered before he could finish.

"How did you know what I was going —"

Montague turned away from the window. "Because I've come to know you, laddie. And I warned you about her." He took a few steps toward Doyle and locked gazes with him. "I reminded you of what she is. And now I wager you know *who* she is. Don't be a dolt and depend on her for anything — including love. She'll turn on you, trust me."

"Thanks for the advice," Doyle said grimly, "but I won't be needing it."

The fat man took a moment to yawn, then said, "I'm not telling you this because your relationship with her might damage the one we want to have with the abbot. If you think about it, laddie, if we get that cog, the abbot's going to hold Robert and the old man responsible. *They* went to him and asked him to order the Pict captain to take us. And the abbot might very well link them to us. So, as you now see, our future here in Blytheheart doesn't look all that bright anymore."

"I'm sorry," Doyle said, "but I have to help my friend."

"I know that, laddie, and we are. And who knows, it might all work out for the better." Montague's smile was small, but there.

"I hope so. But I keep getting the feeling that something is going to go wrong."

Montague crossed to the trunk and set the map down on it. He moved between the two trestle beds, sat on his own, then fell onto his back with another yawn. "What I need now is a brief nap, and then a heaping of mashed potatoes to warm my belly before we set sail." The old whimsy was back in his voice.

But this was the wrong time for it; or at least Doyle thought so. "I believe Caesar spoke as you do the day he died," Doyle said, trying to evoke a little fear in the brigand as he crossed to the window and sat on its ledge.

"I didn't know Caesar liked mashed potatoes," Montague remarked with feigned seriousness.

Doyle sighed, shook his head at the sprawled out, impromptu jester. "How much longer until the Vespers bell?"

"It should not be too long now. Everyone else had better be ready," Montague answered.

"I'm sure they are." Doyle thought of his blood brother. "I hope Christopher is still not arguing with Brenna."

"Uh-huh," Montague said, sounding as if he was already drifting off into the realm of dreams.

And the snores that followed only seconds after verified that fact.

Doyle absently picked at the warped wood of the sill. He rolled splinters between his fingers, then released them to the growing shadows that fettered the cobblestone below.

He thought it would be great if he could just get down to Pier Street and do his part. Now. This moment. Not later. Not at the toll of Vespers. Everything always had to happen in the future. Never now. Always then. He picked more furiously at the wood, tore off larger and larger splinters, and threw them down to the street. He thought about Jennifer again, of her sex with the Pict sailor. He had the faint hope that she had somehow managed to avoid having to go through with it, and though he didn't want to douse that feeling, he still knew in the deepest corner of his heart that she was, in fact, practicing her "craft," as she had called it, and helping their cause. He'd known what he was getting himself into; it was, however, too easy to shove reality aside. When he was with Jennifer he existed in a new and different world, one that had a lot less pain in it.

The present world, the world of the windowsill and the snoring brigand, was the reality in which Jennifer was a harlot and he was a maimed and banished archer.

"Ah, there it is. So simple. The dream brought it on," Montague said, interrupting his own snoring and then rocking himself abruptly to a sitting position. "And it may ease your mind a bit, laddie." He stood and swiped the backs of his hands across his eyes. "I'll meet you down there. I've a slight change to make and I won't be long." He started for the door.

"What are you talking about? What change? Are you changing your clothes or the plan?" Doyle asked, a nerve suddenly jumping in his shoulder.

"Behind the Customs House. After the last bell. Do not be tardy," Montague said as he opened the door, then promptly left.

Doyle swore aloud. He bit his lip as he tore himself away from the window and crossed the room for no particular reason. Then he spun around, went back to the window, stared off into the darkness, then spun away. The feeling was back. Something was going to go wrong. And that something had to do with Montague's sudden dream-induced idea. That fat man had said something about the idea easing his mind a bit. He considered that . . . and then he realized the idea must have something to do with Jennifer. But what? Would this idea take her away from the back house? More importantly, would it jeopardize her life? Doyle remembered something that Montague had said: *She says she has fifteen of the crew in there so far. There is still no way to tell how many are left, unless . . .*

He stepped to the trunk, dropped to his knees before it and threw aside the latch with a trembling hand. He lifted the lid.

Hidden within the chest was his crossbow with windlass attached, and along with it, his hard leather quiver, which now contained a dozen precious bolts tipped with phials of expensive quicklime. Where and how Montague had obtained the bolts was still a mystery; certainly Morna had something to do with it. Doyle lifted the quiver and slung its strap over his shoulder. He grabbed the bow with his good hand, placed it between his knees, and then locked the windlass's cranks into a downward position to streamline the weapon. He wished he had a leather breastplate reinforced with iron discs to protect him, or even a simple cervelière helmet to wear. The only thing Montague had made sure he'd be protecting was his identity, and that would be accomplished by an old cloak the fat man had given him. He took the cloak from the trunk and tied it clumsily under his chin. He pulled the hood up and tugged its edges as far forward as possible, hoping that his face was now cast in deep shadow. He crossed to the nightstand and blew out the candle. He turned to the light pooling at the base of the door and started forward. He tripped once before finding the latch.

Out in the hall, he held his crossbow under his cloak and moved as quickly and as silently as he could, though the occasional creak of a floorboard made him pause and flinch.

He reached the main kitchen of the inn. Two scullery boys were busy bringing in wood for the main hearth, chiding each other in the process. He slipped unnoticed past them and arrived at the back door. He stepped out into the slightly colder, damper air of the night.

The inn's main stable was approximately one hundred yards south, with its doors sealed for the night. Doyle froze as he spotted a lone hostler who walked along the wall of the building. The man rounded the corner of the stable and then was gone.

Keeping his own head low, Doyle stepped away from the inn and moved past a string of six or seven merchant's carts. He tracked over the low weeds and dewy grass until they broke off at St. Thomas Lane. A nightingale chirped somewhere nearby, but its enchantment was lost on Doyle. He listened for only one sound: the Vespers bell.

He walked briskly down St. Thomas Lane until he came to Guild Street. He noted a faint mist coming in from the south and cursed its appearance as he turned left, picking up his pace to a near-jog. A small knot of men loitered outside a tiny tavern to his left. Each man had a tankard of ale in his hand. Doyle felt their gazes turn toward him, though he paid them no heed. "What's your hurry?" one called out.

"Wife's waiting for me at the cathedral," he answered curtly from behind his hood.

That drew a chuckle from the men, who he decided were both bachelors and atheists.

Doyle passed several farmers and fishermen on the street, their tattered livery betraying their work. He slowed his pace down a bit so that he wasn't as obtrusive, but as he neared the wharves, he felt his stride return to its near-jog. He rounded the corner and stepped onto the third wharf. The deck of the Pict cog came into full view.

Four sailors were gathered on the deck, along with Montague and Jennifer. Montague spoke to the Picts while Jennifer translated.

So that was it. Montague was here to draw out the remaining members of the crew, who were obviously guarding the craft. The fat man was taking a big chance, putting Jennifer in a position where she could be kidnapped — just as Marigween had been. If the four sailors decided to do that, there would only be Montague in their way.

Correction. There would be nothing in their way.

Doyle shot toward one of the pilings that rose a yard

or so above the deck of the wharf, and there, hunkered next to it, hoping the Pict sailors on the deck had been too preoccupied with their conversation to have noticed him. He still had a clear view of the deck and would now not be spotted by the sailors. After two more exchanges, Jennifer and Montague turned and left the men, crossed onto the gangplank, and exited the ship without incident. They spoke softly to each other as they reached the wharf, then turned and headed toward the shore. Doyle admired the cut of Jennifer's shift, noticing it only as she drew closer. Her large, full breasts seemed to burst out of the garment. He stood, moved away from the piling, then adjusted the crossbow under his arm.

"Oh, who are you?" Jennifer gasped.

"It's me," he said, pulling back his hood enough to reveal himself.

"Laddie, what are you doing here?" Montague asked, clearly annoyed.

"I'd like to know the same of you," he answered in a similarly heated tone.

Montague resumed his walk, urging Jennifer with a hand to do the same. "Come on, now. They're watching us."

Doyle joined the two, asking, "You were trying to draw the rest of them out, weren't you?"

"Yes," Jennifer answered, "and I told him we'd already tried. Those last four will not leave the ship."

"That was pretty foolish, Monte," Doyle said. "Did you really think it would work?"

"I've worked greater miracles than that," the fat man said, sounding as smug as he was wounded.

"Then you'd better start laboring," Doyle suggested dryly. "We've a mist coming in from the south that's not going to aid us. And where's our night wind you predicted?"

"Wind or not it won't matter. We'll row her out if we have to. And the rest will take care of itself."

"You had better be right," Doyle said, then he regarded Jennifer. "You're coming with me."

"No, she's going back to the inn," Montague corrected.

"She's not leaving my sight," Doyle recorrected.

Jennifer hemmed.

"What?" Doyle asked.

"I'll go with you," she said.

"You know that's not what your mother wants," Montague reminded her, assuming — to Doyle's amazement — a parental tone.

"I'm getting on that cog with all of you. And no one is going to stop me."

Doyle smiled to himself; she sounded a lot like Brenna. She wanted to help and refused to be turned away.

A knell came from the great bell tower of Saints Michael and George Cathedral, the first of what Doyle knew would be seven.

"It's time," he said, then lunged forward into a sprint as he waved for Jennifer to follow.

"Don't stray from the plan," Montague called after them.

Doyle shook a fist in the air as his answer, and it took a moment longer for him to fully appreciate the irony in the fat man's words.

10

Christopher swam with Brenna between the barnacled pilings supporting the wharf. The water chilled him but was calm and appeared near-black in the shadow cast over it by the pier above. The Pict cog was a half dozen pilings ahead on their left. Unencum-

bered, they would bridge the distance before the last
Vespers bell resounded, but with Brenna weighted
down with her crossbow and quiver, and he with a
dagger sheathed and strapped to his calf as well as a
shortbow and quiver provided by Montague slung over
his own shoulders, he guessed it would take them a
few moments longer, a few moments they didn't have.

They should have been closer to the cog in the first
place, but there had been some movement on the wharf.
They had heard the footsteps of two persons, and later,
a third, that had made them back away from the ship.
Brenna had wanted to stay close, and though he didn't
want to admit it now, he'd been the one to suggest they
move away and wait to see what was happening. He
should have listened to Brenna instead of his apprehension. He hated being wet, but he hated being wrong
even more.

He cocked his head to Brenna and saw that a slight
grimace of exertion tightened her features. She caught
his eye and flashed him a brief smile. He still could not
believe that he had let her come with him. He'd reached
the decision on spite. She'd fought her war of attrition,
had worn down his defenses while simultaneously feeding his frustration until he'd given in to her will. And
then all at once he'd told her that not only would she
come along, but she would be with him, and the two of
them would be the first ones aboard the cog, the first
ones to face the remaining sailors. He'd told her to
make sure her soul was prepared. She'd smirked and
thrown the same words back to him.

What Christopher was taught about women and
what he saw in Brenna were kingdoms apart. Women
bore children, controlled the household, loved, honored,
and respected their husbands. They spoke discreetly and
kept silent as much as possible, dressed respectably, and
lived chastely. Women were a score of other enviable

things, and most of them had nothing to do at all with Brenna, or rather, she'd have nothing to do with them. The submissive way of the wench was clearly not her way. But Brenna had not been courageous and bold when he'd first met her. She had traveled from Gore to Shores, and along the way had avoided a rape to become a woman stronger than any other he had ever encountered. And his rejection of her had somehow added to her mental strength. She had a little trouble keeping up with him as they paddled together, but he sensed that her bravery was equal to his own. Though some would not tolerate such behavior from a woman, he could not help but admire her for it. He felt now as he had on the bluffs of Blytheheart, when her take-charge attitude had lifted his spirits. He had thanked her then and wanted to thank her now, but he kept silent. She hadn't understood his gratitude the first time; it was just as well.

"Are you all right?" she asked, looking back at him.

He hadn't noticed he had fallen behind her. He nodded, then swam hard to arrive at her side. "All the way, now," he said, out of breath. "All the way. And I'll go first."

"All right," she answered, then accidentally swallowed a bit of seawater. She grimaced and spat several times, then joined him.

Soon, they neared the weathered stern of the cog. The gulping noises here and there along the ship's keel were loud enough to cover their approach. Christopher placed his hand on the ship's rudder and felt how dangerously slimy it was. He threw his head back to survey the climb.

The rudder was actually two long separate pieces of timber bound together by four evenly spaced rusted iron couplers. Just below each coupler was an iron hinge that attached the rudder to the stern, affording thumb's-length gaps between the two. He kicked up, reached for the second hinge, and managed to lock three fingers onto it. He found the first submerged hinge with his foot and squashed a few toes into the gap. By the time he reached the third hinge, he was out of the water. His soaked clothes drizzled onto a blinking Brenna. Christopher's quiver had become a tankard, and he felt its sling tugging much too heavily on his shoulder. He didn't want to conspicuously dump the water out of it all at once so he paused, dumped a little, then a little more, then finally tipped the sack as far as he could without losing his arrows. Brenna picked up on his mistake, and as she reached the second hinge, she quietly emptied her own quiver.

There was a rectangular hole in the stern, just below the aftercastle, and extending from the hole was a large post that impaled and was bolted to the rudder. Christopher knew that behind this hole lay the tiller room. They had the option of climbing past the rudder post and squeezing into the small cabin, or going higher and slipping into the aftercastle itself, utilizing the wooden parapets for cover. The latter was the original plan and still seemed valid. He climbed past the rudder hole and let both of his hands fall onto the lower portion of a parapet. He pulled himself up and peered over the wood, saying a silent prayer that no one was in the aftercastle.

It was empty. In fact, no one was on the entire deck. But he knew the remaining Picts would soon be drawn out. He climbed over the parapet and fell gently to his knees in the aftercastle. He stripped off his quiver and shortbow, then crawled back to the rear parapet, where Brenna's hands had just appeared. He reached over, grabbed her wrists, and drew her up and over the wooden bulwark. Sniffling, she sloughed off her bow and quiver and crawled to the forward parapet, turned and let her back fall gently on it, then released a slightly repressed sigh.

Christopher stared through the mist that clung to the briny air. The moon was nearly full, resting on a black, pinpricked blanket. Silver light shimmered through the moisture and found Brenna. She'd pulled her hair back from her forehead and braided it in a single ponytail. Still glazed in seawater, long eyelashes flashing, she looked younger, something to marvel at — even while wearing a pair of Doyle's breeches and drawstring shirt. She had not balked when he'd told her she couldn't wear a shift for the swim; the fact was already obvious to her. And she was perfectly comfortable in his blood brother's clothing, too comfortable, some would argue — but not him. For a moment he wished that it had been she instead of Neil that had accompanied him to rescue Doyle; she wouldn't have been as nervous or complained as much as the short archer had. In that respect she was like Doyle, just as pensive and calm while in danger.

He made a quick survey of Pier Street. A long cart pulled by a team of four rounseys rattled its way east. Two cloaked figures sat in the cart, one gripping the team's reins. *They're as late as we are,* he thought with a half grin.

The cart was piled high with straw rushes, rushes Christopher knew had been moistened with lard. As the cart came directly opposite the first wharf to Christopher's left, he shot Brenna a look, and the both of them gathered their weapons. Brenna slipped a foot into the thin, iron-looped head of her bow while her hands found the cranks of the attached windlass. She cranked her bowstring into place. Christopher pulled back and released his bowstring several times to free it of water, then nocked an arrow into place. He huddled against the parapet and aimed at the hatch just past the single vertical spar that was the mainmast with its attached rigging and furled sail. Once again, he looked to the wharf.

With wooden wheels wobbling slightly, the approaching cart created a minor cacophony that competed with the hoofing of the team that pulled it. Then it veered off of the cobblestoned street and crossed onto the pier.

Christopher turned to Brenna. Her gaze shifted from the cart to him for a brief second, then fell on the main hatch. She shelved her crossbow on the top of a parapet and let her hand fall gingerly around the weapon's long trigger. She closed one eye and drew in a deep breath. She no longer had that heavens-lit youthful appearance; he saw her now as a grim fighter, one resigned to the bloodshed of combat. And as his gaze went to the hatch, to the cart, and then returned to her, he thought for a second that she could have been the one. Looking at her now, poised, the bow as natural and comfortable in her hands as the washboard he'd seen her use moons ago in Shores, he thought that she could have killed Woodward. He imagined her in the brambles of the eastern wood, where Woodward had taken the bolt.

Had she been watching Christopher? Following him?

Had she been the one to help?

Christopher averted his gaze, as if that would do the same to his thoughts. He did not want to believe his rekindled suspicions. She was a chambermaid from Shores, a young and innocent woman who could fire a crossbow. She was not a murderer.

But she looked more than capable of killing now.

He heard the cart come to a halt, and turned to see the two figures climb down and move to the tailgate. Their hooded cloaks might have disguised their features, but Christopher easily recognized the gait of his mentor Orvin, and had witnessed enough of Merlin's slow and

measured steps to be able to tell which was the druid —
even if the wizard had been accompanied by a stranger.
The two old men began unloading the greased rushes
onto the wharf.

A half-muted sound came from beneath the main
hatch: its bolt being slid aside. The door yawned open,
guided by a hand whose owner was obscured in
shadow.

"Wait," Christopher whispered to Brenna, then stared
down the end of his arrow, his right hand trembling
slightly as he fought to keep tension in the bowstring
and the arrow squarely nocked.

The man who came from the hatch was a short sailor,
probably Neil's height, with a similar stocky build that
made him an easier target. He stepped over the framework
of the hatch and moved toward the starboard railing. The
Pict brought something up to his mouth and then chewed
on it. His dinner had probably been interrupted by the
cart's arrival. He reached the railing and leaned over it,
then swallowed and squinted into the distance.

"Wait," Christopher whispered again.

"I *will*," Brenna gritted out softly.

Christopher turned his head slightly and saw what the
sailor saw: two cloaked figures unloading rushes near
the shoreline end of the wharf. It was, admittedly, an
odd sight.

The sailor shouted something in Pict, his voice split-
ting the night and Christopher's nerves. Christopher's
fingertips were moist with perspiration, and he felt his
grip on the arrow begin to falter. He relaxed the tension
in his bow, held the arrow between the middle finger
and forefinger of his left hand, and then wiped his right
hand on his shirt, which he'd forgotten was still wet.
His face, which should have been a little more dry by
now, was still wet with a mixture of new sweat and lingering seawater.

"What are you doing?" Brenna asked, shooting him a perplexed look.

"Nothing," he whispered curtly, then caught something in the air and sniffed again.

Over Brenna's shoulder, Christopher saw a faint glow arise from at least three thatched roofs of the peasant tofthouses that encompassed the abbey. Were he closer, he would have seen that the glow actually came from quicklimed arrows that had been ignited and shot into the mud and straw, but from his vantage point he still saw enough to know that Doyle was an accurate and busy marksman.

A new light came from one of the windmills. And then he spotted another shooting star arc over and then vanish behind the abbey's curtain wall. Sudden flames arose from within a few select guild shops along Pier Street. Shop windows soon clouded with smoke. These targets had been carefully chosen by Montague, for there were certain individuals that he wanted to see put temporarily out of business for some reason, and Doyle's bolts were summarily doing the trick.

Christopher wasn't the only one that noticed the scattered flames. The Pict sailor let out another cry directed at Merlin and Orvin, but cut himself short as he, too, took in the fires. He turned and shouted in the direction of the hatch.

"Now," Christopher ordered Brenna, wanting to wait for another Pict to come up on deck but hearing the word slip prematurely from his mouth.

It seemed she fired even before he'd finished the word and *Fwit!* her bolt split the air, homed in on the Pict at the railing and caught him in the neck as he was turning around. The sailor was carried by the wave of the bolt and thrown back into the railing. The sound of his collapse was remarkably small, as if he'd fallen on hay.

Christopher listened to Brenna grunt, then caught her

on his periphery struggling with her windlass as he trained his bow on the hatch.

"Hurry."

"I am. Wet bowstrings aren't exactly easy to work with."

Letting his gaze shift slightly to where the sailor lay, Christopher could see the shadow of the bolt sticking familiarly from the Pict's neck. Brenna knew just where to hit him and had severed his jugular vein.

He heard the footsteps of the second sailor as the man ascended the unseen ladder below the hatch, then saw the back of a shaven head as it rose into view.

Fwit!

Christopher lowered his bow to view his shot: the arrow headed for the back of the bald sailor's head, but the grainy darkness created an illusion. The shot was actually too high and grazed the top of the Pict's pate, coming to rest with a sharp thump in the wood of the raised hatch.

The sailor reacted perfectly to Christopher's poor marksmanship. He reached up, used the arrow impaled in the hatch as a handle and brought the wooden door down on top of himself. Christopher stood and ground his teeth as he heard the sailor lock the hatch.

Now the rest of the Picts below would gather whatever weapons they might have. Christopher remembered the archers from the Saxon cog. If this ship was armed anything like that vessel, then they were in for a fight, for the Picts would draw on a substantial arsenal. And they would either come back out to fight, or wait below for Christopher and Brenna to come in like invading rats. The foreigners would make a game out of their deaths.

The plan had been to draw them out and drop as many as possible. *Many* was the crucial word. Not *one*.

"Damn my shot to hell!" he cried.

"Swear all you want," Brenna said anxiously, slipping a bolt into her windlassed bow, "but let's get down there and finish them."

Christopher shook his head as he turned to watch Merlin and Orvin finish unloading the last of the rushes. The two moved away from the short wall of straw and headed up the wharf toward the cog.

"What are we waiting for?" Brenna asked. "Let's go."

He regarded her with a frown. "We're outnumbered. We'll wait for the others and then go below."

"We can't wait for the others. We don't know how long Morna can keep those sailors locked up — or how busy Doyle's fires are going to keep the marshal's guards."

"We're not going down there," Christopher shot back. She'd been pushing all the way from Shores, and he'd let her come a very long way, but his wall was now up.

"If we don't get rid of them now, all of this will be for nothing. Everyone will get on board and we won't be able to go anywhere. There's no wind. Or hadn't you noticed that? We have to get down there and use those oars."

Brenna was so consumed in her argument that she hadn't noticed she was pointing her bow directly at Christopher's heart. He flashed her a wide-eyed, annoyed look as he pushed the business end of the bow away from his chest. "Do you want to shoot me now and take care of those sailors yourself?"

It was a faint sound, nearly lost under the distant shouts and the incessant barking of a mongrel dog from the shoreline; it sounded like metal grinding on metal and was the tiniest of squeaks. Christopher looked over the edge of the parapet.

And there, directly below, they'd failed to notice a second hatch, a hatch that was presently dropping inward.

"Oh no." Christopher jerked his head back even as something blurred before his eyes and was gone.

"Now we'll see —" Brenna began and cut off, shoving into Christopher and aiming her bow downward.

Fwit!

On the heels of the bowstring's release was the distinctive thud of the projectile as it penetrated wood. She'd missed.

Having guessed what had blurred past him, Christopher grabbed Brenna and drove her toward the starboard side of the aftercastle. He looked up and saw the silhouette of the arrow as it fell beyond the port side of the cog.

"It's all right now," he said, then realized he'd inadvertently gotten a little too close to her. He was aware of the scent of her body. Her own sweat did something to the salty smell of the seawater, creating an odor that could become intoxicating, were he to inhale it for much longer.

With warming cheeks he removed his hands from her shoulders, then took a step back.

"Reload," Brenna said tersely.

Christopher nodded. She wanted to forget about their sudden closeness, and so would he. He reached back and drew a fresh arrow from his quiver, then nocked it into his shortbow.

Brenna crossed to the ladder on the port side of the aftercastle. Before he realized what she was doing, she slung one leg over the parapets, then the other, braced herself with a free hand, and began her descent. "Aim at the hatch down here for me," she said.

"Wait. What're you —"

"Please," she cried, "do it."

He hastened to the bulwark and pointed his bow down at the hatch from which the Pict arrow had come. He listened for sounds of the men below, but found his

ears filled with the footsteps of Orvin and Merlin as they
trudged their way up the cog's gangplank. He looked to
them and shouted, "Orvin. Merlin. They're still below."

The old men heeded his words, and once setting foot
on the deck, they moved as quickly as they could to the
ladder that led up to the forecastle. As they did so,
Christopher saw the main hatch lift a finger's length as
one of the sailors chanced a peek. *Fwit!* Christopher's
shot was enough to persuade the sailor to shut the hatch
and stay below, but it strayed a yard from its target, hit
the deck, and then skittered out of sight.

Orvin was just over the top of the ladder leading to
the forecastle when Christopher heard the crash from
directly below.

Mad girl!

Brenna had leapt onto the small hatch, broken
through it, and now plunged toward the lower deck.
Christopher heard the muffled shouting of the Picts as
he drew an arrow from his quiver, climbed on top of the
aftercastle's parapet, and jumped. He hit the deck
beside the hatch but slipped and fell sideways onto his
bow, nearly snapping the weapon in two. From the
lower deck, he heard the shuffle of feet followed by the
snap *Fwit!* of Brenna's crossbow. He thumbed off his
quiver and let his bow remain where it was on the deck.
He leaned forward, unsheathed the dagger strapped to
his calf, slid over the hatch, then let himself drop into
the darkness.

Orvin had once told him that bravery and insanity
walk the same path, begging, borrowing, and stealing
from each other. He had said that a great fighter can
detach himself from everything, and does not reason
with himself during combat. A great fighter does not
second-guess his actions. Therefore, a great fighter does
not consider that dropping into the hold of a ship full of
Picts is suicide.

I guess I am not a great fighter.

The small alcove that led to the hold reeked of something stale, but was mainly tinged with the not exactly pleasant odor of burlap. Christopher caught the smell even before his bare feet made contact with the deck. The impact sent a sharp, tingling pain up both of his ankles, a pain that reverberated through his knees and found his groin. He fought to maintain balance, but lost it and fell forward. He broke his fall with his free hand. He looked up and saw shadows playing over the ceiling and beams of the alcove. The shadows were drawn by the meager light of a single candle in its holder atop a ceiling beam at the far end of the hold. He heard something. He pushed back and up to his feet, and then listened. A shout came from the other end of the hold, and after it, a shuffling noise. He saw more shadows on the ceiling ahead. He crept forward and moved past a small hallway that opened up into the hold proper. The place was divided into rows and rows of crated and barreled cargo, a maze of provisions cast in an ominous gloom. There were scores and scores of hiding places for the Pict sailors. He'd known of the danger of entering the hold. But coming down hadn't been his decision, and moaning about it now was futile. He had to find Brenna, and they had to get out of here.

"Brenna?"

"Over here," she answered.

He looked to his right, and mentally leapt over crate, barrel, and grain sack to find her. Then he thought about the foolishness of his call. Now the Picts knew both of their locations. His new vulnerability made his skin crawl. He spun and eyed the dark corners of the hall behind him. Nothing. He moved to a pair of crates at the end of a line, ducked behind them and —

— ran into a Pict sailor hiding there. The Pict was down on his haunches, and Christopher's impact with him knocked both of them onto their rumps. Christopher rocked forward and tightened his grip on the dagger, while the Pict shook off the collision. Christopher saw the Pict clearly now, a gaunt, shadow-cheeked man who presently lifted and leveled his cross-bow.

In a heartbeat he dived forward, simultaneously swiping the crossbow away with his dagger hand while wrapping the fingers of his other hand around the sailor's throat.

The Pict said something to Christopher just before the dagger slid between his ribs and kissed his heart, something Christopher was glad he did not understand. Christopher closed his eyes and pulled the dagger from the sailor's chest. He opened his eyes, rose, and then moved away without looking back. He shadow-hugged the starboard hull and made his way closer to the bow end of the hold.

How does it feel to have killed another man, Christopher?

His gaze probed the cargo and ventured into corners and recesses for Brenna. He felt the blood on his dagger leak onto his forefinger.

How does it feel to have killed another man, Christopher?

He could answer the question in a word, but instead let it hang in his mind. He forged on.

A double row of barrels stacked two high trailed off to his left. A yard up from the row was a line of grain sacks piled about six high, four or so wide. Christopher moved into the open avenue between the barrel and grain sack rows. At the far end of both lines, a silhouette appeared. Christopher heard the release of a bow-string and dropped to the deck.

An arrow whistled overhead and he turned — just as it appeared in the hull behind him, at neck height. It would have been somehow fitting if he and Woodward had both died the same way. By now, everyone back at Shores probably thought that he had murdered the knight, and they would have attributed his ironic death to God's justice.

"Christopher," Brenna called out, her voice coming from a spot much closer to him. "Are you all right? What happened?"

"Quiet. I'll find you," he answered with feigned confidence, having only her faint voice to guide him.

He crossed to the grain sacks and hunkered next to them. He wished he could will his pulse to slow down. In fact, his heart felt like it was on the outside of his chest and slamming strangely downward on his ribs. He swallowed and tried to steady his breath.

Another arrow flew overhead and hit the hull behind him. This one caught one of the support beams at a bad angle and was deflected away. As he looked for where the arrow would drop, he rested his elbow on the edge of a grain sack, then felt something nudge it. Startled, he pulled back and plunged his dagger into the sack. He felt the blade penetrate the burlap and pierce something within, something that let out a tiny squeal. Christopher shuddered and grimaced as he ripped his dagger out of the sack, wiped both sides of the blade on it, then darted off.

It was difficult to move swiftly while keeping his head low. Intermittent arrows still fought for a piece of his flesh, but fell either behind or too far in front of him. The closer he drew to the bow of the hold, the easier it was to see. But in this better light, the Picts would also have the same advantage. And besides that, the hold had become much more narrow, and he could see the far corner where the port and starboard hulls joined, along with the spare rigging that was coiled in loops hanging in rows along both walls. On the port side below the rope was a rectangular pile of bundled wool, and Christopher spotted a shadow that rose slightly over the pile. Thankful for the near-silence of his bare feet, he slid between two stacks of oak bath vats and found Brenna seated and lying back on the bundles of wool.

"Oh, no, not you . . ."

Feeling as if one of the Picts had finally put an arrow in his chest, Christopher dropped to his knees before her. The dagger fell out of his hand.

There was an arrow in Brenna's right arm, near her bicep. The point of the arrow protruded from the back of her arm, and it was remarkably clean-looking, as if it had passed so quickly through her flesh that it hadn't had time to pick up any blood. In fact, the wound itself looked clean, with only a tiny ring of blood on the front of Brenna's damp shirt.

"Doyle's going to be upset," she said weakly. "He told me to take good care of his shirt. And now I've gone and ripped it." She smiled, an act Christopher found amazing.

He'd been shot in the calf while fleeing the castle and knew all too well the agony of an arrow wound. Brenna smiled through it. "What do you — what should I, we —" He broke himself off, barely able to speak, let alone help.

Brenna, her eyelids heavy, her mouth still curled in a wan smile, raised her good arm and pointed toward something behind him. "Get your dagger and cut the tip of this arrow off. Then you are going to tie your shirt around my arm and slide the shaft free."

Somewhere behind them, he heard a creak of wood. She noticed it, too. He got to his feet but kept himself hunched over, then looked to her crossbow and quiver that lay beside her. The bowstring was already windlassed into place. He moved to the quiver, withdrew a bolt, loaded the bow, then stood poised.

Fwit!

Christopher looked down, thinking he'd fired. No, an unseen Pict had, one also armed with a crossbow. He looked around for the bolt, assuming it had stuck in the hull behind him, but found nothing.

"Christopher!"

Brenna saw the Pict sailor leap down from the top of the stacked bath vats a half second before Christopher did, but her cry still came too late. Though Christopher was already turning in the direction of the man's assault, he still lacked the time to fire. The sailor came down on Christopher's bow and knocked it out of his hands. The Pict brought the bow to the deck and smashed it under him, then he lost his balance and fell forward onto Christopher. Both of them were driven back toward Brenna, who screamed as they collapsed on her.

Christopher looked up, seized the linen collar of the sailor with both hands, then forced him upward. He recognized this Pict as the bald one he'd nearly shot up on the deck, and saw that the man's pate had a slight cut across it. What was more unnerving was the large silver ring that dangled from between the man's nostrils. He appeared a living vision of black sleep, the worst kind of barbarian. Orvin had said that the barbarians with nose rings were cannibals. The Pict's snarl and crazed eyes were no argument against Orvin's report.

They rolled off of Brenna. Christopher released his grip on the man's shirt, found the sailor's neck, then pinned the Pict's head to the deck. But his triumph did not last more than a moment, for the sailor tore Christopher's hands away, then jolted him up and away with his powerful hips.

The sailor vocalized something that might have been a grunt or an actual word in his language. Christopher speculated it might be something about how he was about to breathe his last breath. He rolled to right himself, but was caught midway by the sailor, who leapt on him and used his chest to press Christopher's right side to the hard and splintery planks. He reached up, but his arm was forced down. The Pict now had him in a one-handed choke hold, and the sailor drew back his other hand, which was now balled into a fist.

The image of the dark brown ceiling and its interlocking beams and planks that framed the cut-by-a-hatchet face of the sailor suddenly vanished. There was only one thing that existed in the world now: the sailor's fleshy, white-knuckled fist; it filled Christopher's gaze just before he closed his eyes.

Christopher heard himself scream, and his voice sounded warped, too low, and unfamiliar to him.

Then he felt the Pict collapse onto him. Confused, he opened his eyes and struggled from beneath the now-limp, inert man. He managed to move the sailor far enough aside to view Brenna. She was on her knees and hunched over the Pict. She released her quivering hand from the dagger in the sailor's back, leaving the blade where she had rooted it: just below his left shoulder blade. Had Christopher been forced to act as she had, he would have chosen the same spot, catching the man's heart from the rear. Brenna was shocking in her savagery . . . and her bravery.

She blew out air, then sat back on her haunches, the horror over what she'd just done slowly tightening her brow and twisting her lip. He stared at her a moment, then opened his mouth to say something, but nothing would connect. Nothing made sense. He pursed his lips and listened to his own breathing, then shoved the body away and sat up.

"That's two," she said softly, after what would never be enough silence. "Now help me get this arrow out of my arm."

"That's three," he corrected. "I got another one on my way here."

"I thought I heard the sounds. How many do you think are left?"

"I don't know," he said, eyeing the cargo and the shadows of the cargo. He stood.

Before attending to Brenna's wound, he picked up and examined her bow. The left side of the T-bar had snapped off, rendering the bowstring limp. Were the bow an arbalest made of steel, it might have survived the sailor's weight. He discarded the weapon and crossed to the sailor. Christopher turned his head away and pulled the blade from the Pict's back.

Wincing, Brenna settled herself on the deck, trying in vain not to move her wounded arm. Christopher removed his shirt, then sat facing her. He reached up and tied the garment around her arm above the arrow, tightening the knot as best as he could. He picked up the dagger, gripped the arrow's iron tip, and then set the dagger down on the arrow shaft. Brenna steadied the shaft with her free hand. He picked a spot about a thumb's length down from the tip and began sawing. Brenna closed her eyes, and her face was never more creased with pain. He heard her breath turn short and shivery.

He stopped cutting, then released the arrow and rose. He crawled to her quiver, withdrew a bolt, and then proffered it to her. "Brenna." She opened her eyes. "Bite on this."

"I'm sorry. I know I'm making noise," she said.

It was as if the Picts had heard her. From directly below came the faint but discernible sound of movement. In unison, their gazes fell to the floor planks.

"You'd better hurry," Brenna warned, then took the bolt from him and placed it between her teeth.

He complied and resumed his sawing. Brenna fought valiantly against the pain, but she could not prevent the small, extremely high-pitched cries that escaped past the bolt, nor the tears that fell in an unrelenting current down her cheeks. Every vibration of the shaft woke new tremors of suffering in her.

Once the arrow was cut halfway down, Christopher considered snapping it off to speed up the process, but he realized that the end would then be rough and splintery, and bits of wood might get caught inside Brenna's arm. The cleaner the cut he made, the safer it would be to pull the shaft from her. So he sawed on, and he regretted each and every thrust of his blade. Sweat formed on his upper lip, and he licked and then blew it off. The cog rose, rocked gently to the left, and he almost lost his grip on the arrow. After several more swipes of the blade, the tip came away in his hand.

Brenna took the bolt out of her mouth. "Is it off?" she asked through a gasp.

He showed her the dark, gray point attached to a stubby portion of the shaft. He was ready to move in front of her and begin the truly cruel part of his doctoring: the removal of the arrow.

But before he could do anything, Brenna stuffed the bolt back in her mouth, clenched the arrow with her free hand, and, with a stifled groan, tore the shaft from her arm.

Christopher felt a surge of sympathetic pain in his own arm as he gaped at the blood stained arrow in Brenna's hand. "Why didn't you wait for —"

She looked to her arm. Blood surged beneath her beige shirt and stained it from the inside out. In a matter of seconds her sleeve was purpled and damp. As Christopher dropped the arrowhead in his hand and began a frantic search for something he could use to swathe the wound, from the corner of his eye he saw Brenna's eyes roll up in her head. She fainted and fell back into the tied bundles of wool.

11

"I've one bolt left," Doyle announced. "It's time to move."

Jennifer nodded while anxiously spying two tofts behind the Customs House. The roof of one farmhouse supported and fed a hungry column of red-and-orange flames. "This way?" she asked, turning back toward the alley between the Chancellor's and Customs Houses.

He seized her by the shoulder. "Around the back. This way," he said, indicating the direction with his head.

Though the alley was a shortcut, they could easily be trapped in it. He assumed that they had already been spotted, thus they jogged off eastward, paralleling the Customs House, bound for a four-foot picket fence that connected with and ran straight down off the circular curtain wall of the abbey.

"Oh, this hurts," Jennifer said, then slid an arm under her breasts.

"What?"

"They're bouncing all over. This dress doesn't hold them very well." Her grimace was met by his half grin, and she added, "but I'm sure you don't mind."

"I didn't say anything," Doyle said coyly, then turned from her, hiding his complete smile as they neared the fence.

The night mist had thinned, and Doyle was able to see beyond the glowing windows of the peasant homes on the east side of the abbey and all the way down to the backs of the tarp-covered stalls along Merchant Row. With the cleaner visibility came a deeper sense of urgency, and he knew he wasn't the only one with a better view of Blytheheart. If they were working under a glass, then he and Jennifer were just a few grains shy of being out of sand.

Arriving before the fence, he saw that the horizontal beams of the enclosure that could be used to scale it were not on their side. He leaned his bow against a picket, clenched the three fingers of his bad hand with the fingers of his good one, dropped to one knee, and offered Jennifer a boost.

"What if I slip?" she asked, looking slightly unnerved as she put a sandaled foot into his palms, then gripped a pair of pickets.

"Swing your leg and get your foot on that top beam. Then I'll push you over," he said calmly. "You won't slip."

As light as she was, the force of her body pressing on his hands was still altogether unpleasant. He brought her up higher, his vision obscured as her shift was caught by a gust of wind and whipped into his face. Another gust, and his head was completely under her dress, her bare hip brushing against his nose.

"What are you doing?" she asked, her voice strained with the effort of trying to get her free foot perched steadily on the fence beam.

"I'm trying to —" and abruptly she shifted her weight. His knee slipped sideways, and the rest of his weight followed the knee. His hands fell away from her sandal, and he crashed forward onto his shoulder. He hit the earth with an involuntary thud that was answered by a very deliberate moan.

He heard a giggle. And then another. He rolled over onto his rump, and as he brushed his shoulder free of dirt and bits of grass, he saw that Jennifer now stood on the other side of the fence and rested her arms on the pickets. "You were right," she began, her eyes burnished by moonlight. "I didn't slip."

Doyle couldn't help but smile weakly over her wit, then he grimaced as he rose to his feet, feeling a bit of dissipating fire on his knee. He passed her the bow then boosted himself onto the pickets, and, favoring his good hand, swung himself over the fence. As he hit the ground on the other side he nearly slipped again. "No, I won't fall," he told himself aloud, and his body seemed to believe the prediction. They resumed their run down Lord Street, and Jennifer once again cupped her breasts with a forearm.

Doyle shot her a sideways glance that fell to her chest. "If you need any help with those . . ." he let himself trail off.

"If you could be a woman for only one day, Doyle, you wouldn't be amused," she said, growing steadily out of breath.

They approached the intersection of Pier Street. To their right was the string of shops that looked out onto the wharves. He had set two of the six ablaze with his bolts. But the fire had spread to all of the shops, and not just by way of their roofs; the common walls between them were not constructed of stone, as Montague had informed him. He had tried to keep the damage minimal, but the whole east side of the street was now a great pyre, and the wall of the shop that abutted Lord Street was now collapsing toward the cobblestone.

"I thought you said we were only going to set a few small fires," Jennifer said, her face bathed in a yellow glow that swept over her as the shop's wall fell and sent a million tiny embers into the newly rising mushrooms of smoke.

Though Montague was not present, Doyle shook his head and sighed disgustedly. *Liar.* "Come on."

Once they had swerved around the debris of the fallen wall, Doyle paused to tap the tip of his quicklimed bolt onto the stone, shattering the phial. He brought the exposed white-powdered end of the shaft close to a burning piece of timber, and the lime ignited. Trailing behind Jennifer, he hurried across the street and turned onto the wharf where the Pict cog was moored. He heard shouting from behind him, and he imagined that it came from a group of alarmed guildsmen who would employ their wives, children, and probably a few guards in a bucket line to try to save the shops — even though they were already too late.

The row of rushes lay on the wharf — exactly as planned. Doyle breathed a sigh of relief. Jennifer slowed as she neared the small blockade, then stopped.

"Run over them!" he ordered her.

Tentatively, she stepped onto the wet-looking straw. The row was merely two feet high and about a yard wide. He wondered why she had stopped, but then realized that she hadn't been present when they'd conceived this part of the plan — not that she had missed much. Doyle judged this element of the scheme as rather weak, even though it would probably work. If they had had more time, he knew he would have conceived something much more elaborate. But it was just as well they did it Montague's way. Doyle would save his planning energy for the next time he decided to steal a Pict cog . . .

Jennifer moved from the rushes onto the wharf. Bits of the lard-covered straw clung to her sandals, and she slipped once but did not fall. With the blazing tip of his bow pointed skyward, Doyle leapt over the rushes. He joined Jennifer and the two of them hustled toward the cog.

Just ahead, a crossbow bolt struck the wharf, impaling itself with a tiny reverberation. Doyle stopped short, held Jennifer back, then squinted at the ship. He spotted three fuzzy lights dotting the keel, an illumination from within that escaped from the starboard rowing holes. The light slipping through the rear hole was suddenly eclipsed.

"Get down!" Doyle shoved Jennifer back toward the nearest piling. The arrow hit the wharf where she'd been standing, striking only her ghost. She turned toward the piling and dropped down next to it, then tried to get as far behind it as she could, nudging closer and closer to the edge of the wharf and the slick, sharp spines of the rocks that lay below.

Doyle assumed a position on the other side of the same piling. He lifted his bow and looked down his fiery line of sight. Then he shot a look to the ship. He saw no sign of Christopher and Brenna there, but then again, they might be busy with those Picts in the hold.

Or they might be dead.

No, I won't allow that, he commanded himself.

The rushes were in place, and that probably meant that Orvin and Merlin were aboard. Now it was up to Montague to haul home his fat hide. By now — making the wild assumption that all had gone well — a load of timber had been deliberately dropped in front of Saints Michael and George Cathedral, blocking its main doors. Those who had attended Vespers — probably more than half the inhabitants of Blytheheart — would, unbeknownst to them, be staying all the way until Matins and Lauds, for Montague had jammed the three rear service doors used by the abbot and monks. Doyle turned his gaze to the shore and let it sweep up Lord Street, where he spotted a horseman charging toward the wharf. Two more horsemen trailed not far behind the first.

Doyle turned, just as another arrow flew a mere arm's length past him. The slots in the cog's keel made suitable loopholes for the Picts, and they were getting a little too used to shooting through them. He and Jennifer had to move. A new arrow came toward him — joined by still another fired from the forward row hole.

He looked to the horseman and saw the grainy but distinguishable outline of Montague.

"Doyle . . ." Jennifer sang his name, a dark, fearful tune that said she wanted out and wanted out now.

He stole a look down the wharf. "Come on, Monte!"

The arrows fired at Doyle fell short — but by only a pair of planks.

Gritting his teeth, he removed his hand from his bow to scratch sweat from his beard. He realized his throat was unbearably dry; he swallowed. And it hurt. He took another look down the wharf.

Montague crossed Pier Street and then slammed his heels into the ribs of the brown rounsey under him. The horse responded weakly to the fat man's goading. He could hear the brigand shouting at the animal now as horse and rider closed in on the rushes. Montague looked over his shoulder at the riders fiercely pursuing him, and one of them, a guard wearing light armor and a helmet equipped with a nasal bar, screamed, "Halt!" He waved his quirt in the air, as if about to throw the whip.

The fat man directed his attention forward and let out a roar that must have startled his rounsey, for the horse launched into the air at the foot of the rushes.

Doyle turned his bow toward Montague, then closed one eye. He waited as the brigand's rounsey hit the wharf in a hollow clatter of hooves and then galloped out of his flaming line of sight.

He squeezed the trigger.

The fiery bolt streaked toward the rushes, and the planks of the wharf beneath it grew alive with light and then fell back into the death of darkness. The bolt struck the center of the short wall of straw.

The two guards leaned forward in their saddles and prepared to jump over the rushes, but the straw before them burst into a giant face of fire that exhaled clouds and clouds of smoke so heavy-looking that it was a miracle they rose at all.

Doyle couldn't see the guards anymore, but heard their mounts neighing and bucking. Then he did spot one guard falling over the east side of the wharf, apparently thrown from his horse; the man howled toward a future of broken bones.

It had been Merlin's idea to add the lard to the straw, and the flash fire and additional smoke it created had helped save Montague's life.

"All hands aboard!" the fat man yelled as he galloped past Doyle, unaware of the arrow fire coming from the cog.

"Keep your head low!" Doyle shouted back, but wasn't sure if the brigand had heard him. He rose and crossed to Jennifer, and she rose to meet him. They charged after Montague, moving as a tight pair, and Doyle kept himself on the cog side of the wharf to somewhat shield her from the incoming arrows. Three more missiles were fired at them in the time it took for them to reach the foot of the gangplank, and though Doyle felt the whispery passage of one near the back of his neck, both he and Jennifer arrived unscathed.

Montague's abandoned rounsey whinnied and bucked about the wharf near the gangplank. They hurried around the mount and made their ascent to the ship.

At the top, Doyle hopped down from the railing and saw Montague, whose gaze was focused on the deck to his left. Jennifer looked there too, and she cringed as Doyle turned and saw a Pict sailor lying dead from a bolt that had struck him in the neck. A bit of chewed food leaked from one corner of the sailor's open mouth.

"Brenna," was all Montague said.

"Jennifer? Over here," a voice called.

Doyle turned his head and saw Orvin waving to Jennifer from behind the waist-high parapets of the forecastle. Doyle looked to her. She caught his gaze. "Go." She nodded, then ran past him toward the ladder that would take her up to the small fortification.

"Here," Montague said, handing Doyle a dagger that

the fat man had pulled from a hip sheath. "Probably
tight quarters down there." Montague withdrew a similar blade from a sheath on his opposite hip. "Let's see
how many are left for us." Montague turned away and
walked to the main hatch, threw a latch, frowned, then
tested it with his boot. The wooden door was sealed
from below.

"Let's break it in," Doyle suggested.

Montague looked to the shoreline end of wharf. "That
fire is not going to help us much longer." Then, as if
he'd drawn an idea from the landscape, he turned away
from the hatch and strode past the thick pole of the
mast toward the stern of the cog. He stopped before
another hatch. From his angle, Doyle could not tell if
the hatch was sealed. Montague waved him over, and
Doyle hurried across the deck.

"Look at the wood over here, laddie. She's been broken in," he said, pointing to the splintery inner rim of
the hatch where a latch had once been. "Come on."

There was a ladder to the right that dropped into the
shadows. Doyle considered using it, but decided he was
not feeling particularly brave at the moment. The Picts
were waiting for them down there. And not for tea.

"Youth before age," Montague said with a slight bow
and a hand wave that pointed the way.

Denying himself more time to justify why he
shouldn't go down because it was soggy and dark and
dangerous and he'd met a beautiful woman and had
something to live for now, Doyle clenched the dagger in
his teeth, brought both arms close to his chest, and then
jumped into the hole.

He anticipated the impact perfectly, bending his knees
to avoid most of the pain. As expected, he heard the
snap of a crossbow trigger, but he was already rolling to
dodge the bolt while simultaneously removing the dagger from his mouth. He slammed into a wall, then

scrambled blindly toward a corner, hit it, and kept moving. He discovered he was in a narrow alcove of sorts, with deeply shadowed corners. The moonlight falling in through the broken hatch picked out a hall that led into the hold. He guessed that his adversary waited just around one corner of the hall. Guessing that the man was windlassing his weapon, Doyle got to his feet and, sounding not unlike Montague as the fat man had taken his horse over the rushes, he let out a roar as he charged through the hall.

He reached the end of the passage, turned a corner, swiped with his dagger, then whirled and swiped with it again into the opposite corner. He stood alone, panting.

"Laddie?"

"Monte, stay back there!" he yelled to the fat man as he hunkered down and slammed his back against a rear wall of the hold. "There's one right here."

His warning to Montague was followed by the immediate reply of the unseen Pict's crossbow, a sound which came from back in the alcove below the hatch.

"Laddie," Montague said in an odd tone, "he got me."

Doyle felt his face crease with shock, and then felt something drop inside him as he rose and spun back toward the hall. He'd thought the sailor had not been in the alcove but beyond it. The man had been in the room with him all the time. The Pict had hidden in the shadows or had known some other place to conceal himself. Doyle cursed himself for making the error, and if Montague was dead, he would blame himself.

He ran through the hall and approached the brigand, who sat at the foot of ladder in the alcove. The moonlight made the blood on him appear black. Montague had put his hand out to block the incoming bolt, and the shaft had passed through his palm, had made a deep gash in his shoulder, tearing open silk shirt and skin with equal disregard, and then had stuck in a rung of the ladder behind him. Doyle was nearly at the end of the hall when the fat man looked up and his eyes became very round. "He's right here, all right, laddie."

Doyle froze. "Where?" he demanded, feeling his panic slither up his back like a needle-covered snake. "Where? Where?" He took a step toward Montague — putting himself a foot inside the alcove — then spun around, expecting to find the sailor hiding behind either the port or stern side of the hall entrance. Nothing. But out of the corner of his eye he caught the flicker of a shadow in the far right corner, about three yards away from him. He ran two, three steps forward and dived. He stiffened his stomach muscles as he hit the floor, then was carried another few feet by his momentum. And out of the gloom came a pair of boots. He reached out with his free arm and wrapped it around the legs of the sailor while simultaneously punching his dagger into the side of one of the Pict's legs, catching what he presumed was the man's calf. The sailor made a sort of coughing, panting noise which was followed by a string of words. Doyle drew the man's legs together and brought him down to the deck. He fought through the sailor's wildly grasping hands and ripped his dagger from the Pict's leg. Still trying to wrestle himself free, the Pict managed a blind swipe — right into Doyle's blade. The noise that came from him now was unmistakably a scream.

The dagger entered and exited the sailor's body three times, and then there was no other sound in the alcove, save for the gentle rise and fall of the cog, and Doyle's labored breathing. He pulled himself away from the sailor and gritted his teeth as he looked down at his terrible handiwork. The feeling of power that surged through him was alluring, but it also reminded him of past mistakes. His rage, a beast usually at his command, ran wild at moments such as this, and when all was said and done, someone always lost his life.

There was a strange paradox at work. The more he killed, the easier the act was to perform. He knew what to expect when he killed a man, knew most of the sounds men made before they died. He knew what they looked like. There were few surprises. But the more he killed, the harder it was to live with himself.

He turned away from the dead Pict to find a shirtless Montague hovering over him. "What're you doing?" he said, then hauled himself up.

"I'm all right, laddie," the brigand lied, his silk shirt coiled around his bloody palm. He indicated with his good hand toward the sailor. "Just get me his shirt to wrap around my shoulder."

Doyle flipped the Pict onto his back and peeled off the sailor's thin, sweat-stained shirt. He set the garment on the crimson crease in the fat man's hairy shoulder, then tied it under his arm. "It doesn't look that bad," he told Montague — just to cheer the man, for the cut was deep, painful-looking, and certainly in need of stitching.

"Two more to go," Montague said. "Fetch your dagger and let's finish them."

An indistinct shuffle came from the hall. Doyle looked to Montague, who looked to the sound. Doyle walked quietly to his blade, picked it up, and crossed to the wall. He pressed his back against the wood, waiting just inside the doorway. He ventured a peek around the corner and saw the silhouette of a man approaching. There was something slightly familiar about the gait of the intruder. He took a chance.

"Christopher?"

"Doyle? Montague?"

His blood brother appeared in the alcove. Christopher's hair was damp, and his clothes clung to his body. Doyle moved from the wall and startled his friend, who flourished a blade.

"It's just me," Doyle said, coming into the moonlight.

Christopher's gaze swept from him to Montague to the dead Pict. "What happened?"

In the minute that followed, Montague delivered a brief, exaggerated version of his bout with the Pict sailor. Calling it a bout was an exaggeration in and of itself, but Doyle let the brigand have his moment in the limelight. Christopher filled them in on what had happened to him and Brenna in the hold. He'd managed to bandage her wound and it had ceased bleeding for now, but she was still not awake.

They counted the dead Picts and arrived at four, one on deck, one in the alcove and two others in the hold, after which Montague concluded, "The ship is ours, lads. Now, Doyle, you summon the two old men and Jennifer. Have Merlin see to Brenna. Then go down to the lower deck to help Christopher. All right then?" Montague winced, then gently touched his wounded shoulder.

After they nodded, Christopher slipped out of the hall, and Doyle crossed to the ladder, but then hesitated. "I thought you'd be crying and complaining about your wounds, Monte, not forging on with the plan like a relentless battle lord. What's happened to you?"

"Just go now, laddie," he said gravely. "I'll keep my complaints to myself until we're at sea."

Doyle turned toward the ladder, then hesitated once again as an odd thought struck him. "Why is it you always call me 'laddie'?" he asked.

"Just a habit," Montague said — but not before a pause that left Doyle wondering.

12

Christopher found a hatch that led to the lower deck and opened it. The room below him was well lit, as expected. He descended the ladder and emerged into a chamber about half as wide as the hold. Three rows of rowing benches stood on both port and starboard sides. Four of six torches burned brilliantly from their scones just above the row holes, and the ceiling about a yard or so above them was scorched black. On the floor, lying parallel to the benches, were the wooden oars, and each was nearly three times Christopher's size. He noted with satisfaction that near the handle of each oar was a hole, then looked to the row holes and did not see the horseshoe-shaped oarlocks Montague had described. He moved to the first hole, where he found the oarlock lying on the deck next to a pair of quivers just out of sight below a bench. The Picts had obviously removed the locks so that they could shoot through the apertures. Christopher fetched the lock and slid the round iron bar mounted to its base into a steel-lined opening on the sill of the rectangular row hole. He repeated the process on the remaining five holes, and by the time he was finished, he heard Doyle's descent into the chamber.

They exchanged no words as they went about the task of slipping each oar through its hole and securing it to its lock. They groaned under the weight of the oars, and when they were finished, Christopher rubbed his palms on his breeches. "I wager that when the Picts do row this cog, they have two men on each oar."

"I heard once that the old Greek ships had as many as tenscore oarsmen, but they had no sails," Doyle said. Then, studying the oars, he added, "This ship wasn't built to be rowed."

It certainly looked that way to Christopher. And with no wind to avail them, they had no other choice but to defy the design of the cog and row her at least partway out to sea.

But as he followed Doyle up the ladder, Christopher wondered who would actually be doing the rowing. Montague's hand and shoulder were injured. Brenna's arm would prevent her from helping. Merlin and Orvin lacked the strength. That left Doyle, Jennifer, and himself. He should have realized the fact earlier and only set three of the oars into place.

Once in the hold, Doyle reported, "I'm going up top to help Monte weigh the anchor and break our moorings."

Christopher nodded. "I want to check on Brenna."

He found Merlin and Orvin huddled over Brenna. The druid dabbed Brenna's wound with a damp rag. Her eyes were still closed and she looked pale. Christopher realized this was probably an accurate picture of what she would look like in death, and he was suddenly frightened for her life. "How is she? The arm is bad, I know, but has the bleeding stopped? Why is she not awake yet?"

"The blood she lost has made her weak," Merlin said, not looking back. "She may still bleed from within, but as you can see, no more blood comes from the wound."

"Should you stitch her?" he asked.

"If we can find what we need to do so, we will," Orvin said. He gestured for Christopher to help him up. Christopher complied, and the old man straightened and added, "Perhaps there will be something in the captain's cabin."

Christopher sensed the silent approach of someone from behind him. He shuddered, then spun around and came face to face with Jennifer. She must have been with them all the time, but he hadn't noticed her.

"I'm sorry," she said, startled herself by his surprise, and then, growing calm, she turned to look at Brenna. "I've seen that kind of wound before. She'll be all right."

"I hope so," Christopher said weakly.

"When she's awake we should give her Flemish broth to build her strength. I'm sure we can find some eggs down here to make it with."

"We'll do that," Christopher said, "but first I need you to help row. Do you think —"

"Recover, catch, drive, and release. I've done it before, but certainly not aboard a ship of this size," she confessed.

Christopher held back his surprise. "Fine. Go below and get ready. Doyle and I will meet you there."

Jennifer strode off, her shift billowing in her wake. Christopher knew that she had her own reason for wanting to come along, but so long as it didn't interfere with her aiding them, he was not interested in what it was. He did, however, hope that it had something to do with his blood brother. Jennifer was a strong and beautiful woman who seemed to put a new light in Doyle's eyes. He wished they'd had time to talk about her. Perhaps a moment would come.

Before he fully ascended the ladder leading to the upper deck of the cog, he smelled smoke and was able to glimpse over the rail to the wharf. The once-high flames of the burning rushes were now at only knee height, and on the other side of the fire he saw a knot of guards using their swords to drive the burning straw over the side of the wharf. Christopher skipped the last two rungs of the ladder and bounded onto the deck.

"Get your bow, Christopher!" Montague called from the port rail.

Regarding the brigand, Christopher immediately assumed the fat man wanted him to be ready for the guards about to breech their wall of fire on the wharf.

But from over Montague's shoulder he could see a pair of flickering lights on the calm channel. The lights were about a thousand yards west and approaching. He crossed to the rail, squinted, then saw that the lights were actually torches mounted on the bows of two rowboats. Each boat carried an oarsman and two armored shortbowmen. "What are they —"

"It's the harbor guard," Montague explained impatiently. "I thought the abbot had done away with them after his new deal with the Picts and Saxons."

"You thought wrong," Christopher noted sourly.

A loud splash came from the starboard side of the cog. Christopher looked to the sound and saw that Doyle had shoved the gangplank away from the rail, letting it fall into the channel. "Let's row!" he shouted.

"You'll have to hold them off," Christopher said, turning for the hatch.

Montague shook his head negatively. "Not alone. Get one of the old men up here."

"They're helping Brenna," Christopher argued, feeling betrayed as he looked at Montague, who had once brimmed with answers but who now stared at the dark world around him with troubled, glossy eyes.

"Let the druid help her, lad. Get me Orvin. I heard the codger boast twice of his fighting skills. We'll see what he's got." Montague took another look back at the rowboats, then leveled his gaze on Christopher. "We've struck the barrel's bottom, lad."

"Christopher, come on!" Doyle urged him as he began to climb down into the hold.

Christopher ran to the hatch, climbed down, and, in the flurry of moments that followed, he realized that he'd forgotten to retrieve his shortbow from where he'd left it on the deck near the aftercastle. Instead of going back for it, he opted to fetch the crossbow of the first Pict he had killed in the hold. After that, he alerted

Orvin that the old knight was needed up on deck and
gave him the bow. Then Christopher joined Doyle and
Jennifer at the oars. Doyle sat on the port side, while he
and Jennifer took the starboard. He felt the cog rock a
bit, then heard a beam or two hem under the force of
the channel.

"No, Christopher," Jennifer said from behind him.
"On the recovery, keep your oar out of the water and
feathered so that the back of the blade is parallel to the
surface of the water."

Doyle began to laugh. "I'm sorry, but are you not glad
she came along?"

Grimacing under the force the oar put on his chest
and arms, he answered, "I am. And I never thought rowing was this hard."

"I've a silly question," Jennifer said. "This ship has a
rudder. Who is at the tiller?"

Doyle looked at Christopher, who looked at his blood
brother. "I hope Monte has figured that one out," Doyle
said grimly.

As he rowed, Christopher stole glances through the
hole and watched their gradual departure from the
wharf. He saw the guards blocked at the fire wall finally
make it to the end of the dock. Armed only with
spathas, they could do nothing but wave their blades at
the ship. One dived into the dark channel and began
swimming after the cog, but Christopher lost sight of
the man. He doubted the guard would catch them.

Doyle announced the progress of the rowboats, and
Christopher thought he could hear an exchange of arrows
between Orvin and the guards. He itched with the desire
to rush up to the forecastle and relieve Orvin and
Montague. Occasionally he heard the fat man and the old
knight shouting orders to each other, but generally they
remained hushed. It was the guards in the rowboats that
created a cacophony by shouting threats and epithets.

He could tell he was still not rowing correctly, and tried to hide the shortcoming from Jennifer. As long as he created some momentum with his oar, he knew she and Doyle could take care of the rest. By any standard, they were creeping along, perhaps only a few hundred yards north of the wharf by now. He knew the rowboats were much faster.

Christopher brought his oar down and felt it stop in midair. He released it, then looked out through the row hole —

— just as a low thud resounded from the other side of the hull. A rowboat had reached them and come alongside.

"Doyle —"

"I know," he said, piecing it all together from the sounds. "Fetch one of those quivers. We're going topside." Doyle released his oar, letting the handle slam into the top rim of the row hole. He grabbed one of the arrow-filled quivers lying beneath his bench.

Christopher did likewise, and as he slid blindly from the bench into the center of the chamber, he collided with Jennifer. "You're not coming," he told her firmly.

"Well I-I can't stay here!" she stammered. "Even if I had the strength, all I would do is row us in circles."

"Then don't row. Just stay here."

"Jennifer?" Doyle called from the base of the ladder. "Do what he says."

She threw him a hard, disappointed look.

Doyle raised his brow. "Please?" he asked in a much softer tone.

She huffed, then her shoulders fell. They left her and her pout behind.

Once in the hold, Doyle's gaze darted everywhere. "Hurry, look around. They must have a bow lying somewhere around here. Did that other Pict you killed have one?"

"Yes, but I don't know what happened to it."

"Forget it then. I'll take over for Orvin," he said, and then he was at the ladder that would take them on deck in three quick steps.

While climbing, Christopher looked up. The sky was framed evenly by the wooden hatch, and now every star was evident. He recognized a pattern that Orvin called the Great Bear, a pattern that followed a circular motion in the sky, like many other groups of stars. He wished they were far out at sea, and he could lie back and study the stars all night.

A rumbling noise came from the deck. Two men screamed then collapsed, just beyond the hatch. Christopher rushed up the last two rungs of the ladder to find a guard pinning Montague's shoulders to the deck, but Doyle had already drawn an arrow from his quiver and was bringing it down toward the guard's back.

Christopher closed his eyes and listened to the sound of death. When he opened his eyes, he saw the guard lying prone beside the fat man. The guard's limbs flinched and his head trembled in the weird dance a body sometimes does after death. The wound on Montague's shoulder had reopened in the struggle, and as the fat man rolled himself up, Christopher saw that his hairy back was half-covered with blood.

"We got one, lads, and you got the other — but there's one more down there," Montague warned.

Doyle rushed to the port rail and looked down. A few seconds later, Christopher arrived at his side. Indeed, there was another man attempting to climb onto an oar and use it to reach one of the anchors for the rigging that extended about a yard down from the rail. The guard had removed his coat of mail and helmet in an attempt to lighten himself for the climb.

Turning his gaze to the forecastle, Doyle cried, "Sir Orvin. We need you."

"Here, boy," Orvin said, appearing above the parapets.

Doyle waved him over and the old knight descended the ladder. Christopher ran to the hatch below the aftercastle, fetched his shortbow, and returned to the rail — only to look down and see the guard sprawled out in the rowboat, an arrow jutting from his right breast.

"What did you do, throw one at him?" Christopher asked Doyle, feeling his mouth lift in a lopsided grin.

His blood brother smiled and began to chuckle under his breath.

"I do not believe it," Christopher said.

"No, no, no," Doyle said. "Jennifer got him. She must have found a bow down there. She shot him straight through the row hole. I think Brenna and Jennifer share a bit of blood."

"In that case you're both lucky," Brenna said, appearing from behind a door below the aftercastle that led to the tiller room. Shadowing her was Merlin, whose hand held open the door. There was not enough light to tell if her color had returned, but her smile told him enough. Her arm was freshly bandaged and hung in a makeshift burlap sling. She'd made it, and there were very warm feelings that swelled inside Christopher now, and he almost wished there was only the single feeling of relief. But he knew his life was far from that simple.

"Here comes the other boat!" Doyle said.

"Give me room," Orvin said, jockeying for a position at the rail. He lifted his bow. *Fwit!*

And lo and behold the old knight proved his aim was still true. He shot the oarsman of the second rowboat squarely in the back, and the two remaining guards made the instantaneous and wise decision to abandon their pursuit. One guard pushed the oarsman overboard while the other took up the oars and turned the boat back toward the shore.

Soon the port of Blytheheart was a rocky, glowing line to their south. Rooftop flames waved a tiny good-bye to them. They had escaped into the harbor with the cog — a minor miracle. But an even greater miracle had already occurred, one that Christopher had not even noticed until now.

Wind.

Montague ordered them to draw in the oars, and he and Doyle did so, laughing and joking and recounting their parts in the escape.

The night wore on, and Christopher soon discovered that there were few things more complicated in the realm than hoisting the sail on a cog. Montague shouted things like, "Get that topping lift higher, that's it, right, no it is supposed to support the yard!" and then he'd say, "No, tie the bowlines over here, and yes, fasten that knot on that sheet, and no they're called ratlines, lad, you use them to climb — not trip over."

It was an exercise in humility. Doyle knew a few more things about sailing than Christopher, but he, too, was worn into irritability by Montague's incessant corrections. Finally, the fat man, weakened by his yelling and loss of blood, asked to go below and join Orvin, who was preparing a meal with what he could find in the hold.

With Brenna and Merlin at the tiller, Doyle, Jennifer, and Christopher watching the lines from the bow, none of them exactly sure what they were doing, the cog sailed on over black waves whose size seemed determined by the wind. Behind them, the port narrowed into an insignificant speck on the dipping and rising horizon.

Christopher looked to Doyle, who seemed lost in thought as he stared up through the red sail. He turned his gaze to Jennifer. Her blond hair appeared as liquid rippling in the wind. She regarded him with a closed-lipped smile, then returned her gaze to the brace lines. A wave broke below the bow, kicking up a misty trailer into their faces. As Christopher palmed away the salty spray, he let his thoughts turn toward Marigween. All of this was for her, yet it had been a long time since he had been with her, both physically and mentally. Once again he sensed a feeling coming on, a tearing, as if he were on a torture rack. He looked to the door on the tiller room, then back up at the taut sail. He turned leeward, getting the wind out of his eyes, but they still felt sore.

The changes in his life had always seemed clear. He'd gone from saddlemaker's son to squire. Then from there to squire of the body, squire to King Arthur. He'd lost that title, but had, however, come to terms with the birth of his son. He'd accepted the responsibility of fatherhood. And so his life should have gone on from there. He should have served Lord Woodward and shown King Arthur that he was ready to reassume his rank as squire of the body. He should have been able to spend time with his child, to be the father he had promised he would be. He and Marigween should have been married, and though explaining their child would have been difficult and drawn a lot of criticism, with the king behind them, their acceptance would have been assured.

But what was all of this? Woodward's murder? Marigween's fleeing the cave and getting captured by Seaver? His child lost? Doyle appearing in Blytheheart with a man who had tried to rape Brenna? And Brenna. How in the world had she becomed mixed up in all of this? And now he was involved in the theft of a Pict cog, had killed men to obtain the craft, and was sailing toward who knew what. His life had been a fairly straight line. How had he strayed off course? What was the purpose of all of this — if there was one? Was God testing him? Was it God who had put that vision of someone's death in his mind? Was he supposed to learn or gain something from all of this? He dared not ask the sky what would be, for the answer might prove more disconcerting than the past.

He closed his eyes and listened to the voices of the wind and the sea.

PART
FOUR

THE SEARCH,
THE COUNCIL, AND ONE
TOO MANY FAREWELLS

1   Christopher lay in his hammock and was rocked gently back and forth by the cog's passage. He wondered how long he had slept. He guessed he had dozed off at least twice while watching the lines the night before. He remembered that Doyle had led him below and helped him into the hammock. But the rest of the night and early morning was lost in the mist of his exhaustion.

From the hammock came a slightly muffled straining of the ropes that was overpowered by the louder sounds of the waves breaking against the hull and the resulting reply of the beams around him. He scratched an itch on his arm. Then another. And then his legs began to itch. His body stiffened with the knowledge of why he was so itchy. He opened his eyes and squinted, but saw only a mottled brown. He sat up, forgetting he was in a hammock, and was pitched into the air. He fell forward onto the deck, and the wind blasted out of his lungs. His knees and elbows felt sore. But the itching felt worse.

"Christopher?" Brenna called. "What's wrong?"

He got to his feet and felt dizzy, felt as if the floor were dipping and rising. It was. He turned to face her. She was there for a moment, coming into focus in the dim, single candlelight of the crew's quarters, then lost as he pulled his shirt up and over his head. "Fleas!" he said from behind the shirt. His throat was dry and had made the word sound as horrible as what it implied. He threw the shirt to the deck, frantically rubbed his

arms and chest, then bent down to brush off his
exposed shins below his breeches. "This room is full of
fleas!"

She giggled under her breath, then he looked up. She
ran a thumb under her sling to adjust its place on her
neck, then came to him, inspecting him from his eyes to
his feet with a narrowed gaze. "You probably don't have
that many. And they're not going to kill you. I know six
ways to get rid of fleas."

"You're not going to dab me with birdlime, are you?"
he asked, having heard of a knight who'd undergone
that sticky form of flea exorcism.

Brenna frowned. "Birdlime? No. I think you can wash
them off with seawater. I don't think they like the salt."

He continued to scratch and swat away the tiny black
horrors that ran dizzying patterns across his flesh, and
he silently prayed that she was right. "How long have I
been down here?" he asked.

"The sun has been up a while now," she answered.
"The sky is more red than orange. It's pretty."

"I'd better get up there before I scratch myself raw,"
he said, glancing down a moment at the many
crosshatched red lines on his arms and chest.

"One question before you run off?" she asked, her
voice tentative.

"Quickly, please."

"I wanted to ask you again about that night at the
three rivers."

He drew in a deep breath, then let it out in a huff.
"You know that's not a brief question, Brenna. Let me
bathe, and then — *perhaps* — we'll talk about that."

Christopher left her behind, and after he splashed several buckets of seawater over himself, dried, changed,
and finger-combed his hair, he decided to heed his
groaning belly's cries and get a bite to eat. He had
planned to meet Doyle in the captain's quarters, where

Orvin had set up a makeshift dining table, but found
Brenna waiting there instead.

"Doyle said he was sorry he couldn't join us, but
Montague is teaching him something about the sail
now," Brenna said evenly.

He guessed she was glad they had been left alone, but
there was no hint of satisfaction in her tone. He wondered if she had orchestrated the moment. He smiled
crookedly, then slid onto a barrel chair before a barrel-
legged table that had a top made of several wide, loose
pieces of timber. On the table was a tray of smoked fish
and assorted raw vegetables, along with several ornate
tankards filled with ale. He looked at the food, then up
at Brenna. "Have you tried any?"

"I've been waiting for you."

It might have been his imagination, but her tone
seemed to imply something more. He took a long piece
of fish and broke it apart with his fingers. He felt her
gaze on him as he ate, then finally looked up to confirm
the fact. "What?" he asked.

Brenna looked down, embarrassed. "I apologize. It's
just good to see you," she said.

Odd girl. "Me? Christopher of Shores? With these
scars on my face? This flea trap?"

"When that sailor jumped down and knocked the bow
from your hands, and then when you fought with him, I
thought, well, you know what I thought."

He looked into her eyes, eyes so big that he fancied he
could see the reflection of his entire face in them. "All I
can say is thank you. It's not enough, I know."

She reached out to the tray, chose a spinach leaf, tore
a piece from it, then paused before placing it in her
mouth. "I thought by now I'd be able to forget about
killing him. He had to die to save you — but I killed
him. I didn't know anything about him. What right did I
have to end his life?"

"I . . . I understand. I know what it is you feel." He lifted his brow. "Let it go. Just let it go."

Christopher assumed they would reflect on that night at the three rivers, where he had inadvertently asked her to marry him. An unintentional marriage proposal seemed ludicrous. But it had happened. He wished the conversation centered around that night instead of her guilt over the killing. Though awkward, words about their relationship would not upset his stomach.

After a long moment of silent eating, Brenna asked, "How far off is the Port of Magdalene? Did Merlin say?"

"Last night he told me we might reach it before midday. But this morning he says before sundown. The two Saxons he questioned from Seaver's cog gave him only the name of the port; they never said how long it would take to reach it."

"I hope we arrive soon. I hate to think of Marigween with those Saxons. If I were she . . ." Brenna stared at another spinach leaf between her fingers.

It was the second time that Brenna's words had trailed off into thought. He could sense she wanted to say more. Her love was there. The conclusion was not a wild conceit. She had always been somber when speaking of Marigween, and that tone had revealed her jealousy. Her affection for him, though beaten back into a rear guard, was, to his eyes, in the fore. Yet he needed to hear it from her. He had to be sure. Why, he did not know. "Earlier, you wanted to talk about that night we camped at the three rivers. I'll tell you about it if you answer a simple question for me."

Her eyes widened. "All right."

He leveled his gaze on her, a deep, penetrating gaze that might have hinted to her that his question was serious and more than a little difficult to answer. "Do you still love me?"

She blushed, then looked away from him. "Why do you want to know?"

He would not let her throw back a question. He simply shrugged.

Brenna did something under the table with her hand, either scratched at the wood or rubbed her nails across her palm. "Let's talk about something else," she finally said.

"You do not want to know why I asked you to marry me?" he asked in his most convincing and enticing tone.

"No," she said curtly, then turned her head a little farther away from him.

He slid off of his barrel. "Then I'm going on deck."

As he made his way up to the hold, Christopher tried to think of ways to settle what was going on between himself and Brenna.

What exactly is going on between us?

Once he climbed up and over the frame of the main hatch, he stood on the sea-soaked deck. He found Montague standing next to the ladder that led up to forecastle. The bare-chested man's wounded hand and shoulder were freshly bandaged, and his good hand was cupped over his brow. He looked toward the east, toward shore. Christopher took a look for himself. He saw only a faint line of land on the horizon. "Have you spotted the port?" he asked, then stepped toward the brigand.

"No, lad. But know this: we're aboard a Pict cog in Celt waters. Understand?"

"You're looking for other ships?" Christopher asked, turning away from the man and crossing to the rail.

"Aye. Trading might be peaceful at the ports, but out here our cargo and ourselves are fair game. And that blasted red sail doesn't help."

Christopher turned from his second inspection of the horizon. He saw Doyle coming up through the small hatch below the aftercastle. "Are we there yet?" his blood brother asked to no one in particular. "I've been sick twice so far. My stomach cannot stand much more of this."

Jennifer arrived on deck behind Doyle, and her hair was instantly whipped into a frenzy by the breeze. "You cry like a child, Doyle. And I thought you a warrior," she teased.

"Warrior, yes," Doyle assured her, "seaman, no."

Montague chuckled briefly. "You sound as I did, laddie, back on the Quantock hills."

Behind Jennifer, the door to the tiller room opened and Merlin stepped out. The druid held a foot-long piece of twine, and tied to its bottom was a long, gray stone about half the length of a dagger. The wizard called the hanging rock his "lodestone," and said he could pinpoint directions with it. Christopher was a bit skeptical, as was everyone else, but the druid paid their doubt no heed. He swore by the stone, and now followed its movement with wide, intent eyes.

Then, suddenly, his wizened free hand went to his brow to screen out his periphery. He scanned the horizon a moment then stopped. He pointed. "There. Everyone, there! See the reflected light. That is the Port of Magdalene."

The druid, with his strange rock and ancient eyes, had been able to locate something that both Christopher and Montague had not. Christopher looked to where Merlin indicated and, indeed, saw reflected light flash from the shore.

"Magdalene," Jennifer said darkly. "A wonderful name for a port."

He cocked his head to where Jennifer and Doyle stood leaning on the rail. "What do you mean?" he asked her.

"Have a monk explain it to you sometime, Christopher," she answered, then turned into the wind so that her hair would blow out of her face.

Christopher looked at Doyle, who lifted his shoulder in a slight half shrug.

"All right, lads and lasses, enough tavern talk. Time to practice your seamanship once again," Montague barked. "Merlin? Back in the tiller room with you. Listen for my calls to steer us in. Now, you two lads, follow my instructions and you won't get hurt." He smiled over that, then looked around. "Where are Brenna and Orvin? Jennifer, go below and summon them. We'll need their help."

Before long, Christopher was able to identify the light from the shoreline; it came from two polished crosses atop the spires of one of Magdalene's churches. He mused for a moment that God had called them to shore, He in all of his divine, and in this case, reflected light.

And then, moments later, a second smaller but still meaningful miracle came into view. Magdalene had two wharves, and docked at one of them was the Saxon cog. Flooding with an anxiety that set him pacing along the rail, Christopher stared at the stern of the ship. He wished he could see through the hull to a cabin where Marigween might be imprisoned. "It's here!" he cried to the others. "The cog's there!"

Longshoremen gathered into a throng on the unoccupied wharf. Apparently a ship's arrival was of great import, signifying monetary gain to many of its inhabitants. The shoremen waved and paced about. One even jumped into the air with joy. All of them, it seemed, could not wait to load or unload cargo, as if they'd been waiting days for the opportunity. They were not the passive, weather-weary loaders of Blytheheart, who probably saw twice the number of ships arrive at their port. A ship's arrival was an event here.

Christopher looked above the wharves to the bluffs behind the small port; they rose much higher than the ones that cast shadows over Blytheheart. Magdalene's marshal probably had many hidden lookout points strung along the peaks. Their approach to the port had probably been carefully monitored.

Two small rowboats were launched from the shore to pull in and help navigate the cog. Soon it came time for the sail to be furled, and if getting it up had been a difficult task, drawing it in seemed nearly impossible; the wind, once a welcome friend, was now a foe. By the time the task was complete, Montague had no voice, which Doyle described with a broad grin as a blessing. Christopher did not miss the brigand's shouting, but he did miss the singsong cadences of the fat man's northern accent.

After a few moments, Doyle tossed down the mooring lines to the three men in each of the rowboats. The cog was guided deftly toward the wharf, and, in what seemed like a very long, nerve-racking time to Christopher, they finally were secured to the pier.

Montague explained to one of the longshoremen that they did not have a gangplank of their own, that it had been lost. The shoreman frowned and sent two others off to fetch one.

Doyle ambled over to Christopher. "How do you feel? Are you ready?"

"We're going to do it Merlin's way first. If that doesn't work, then I'll consider what you said last night," Christopher said, referring to Doyle's idea that they employ a few guards and storm the Saxon cog. The idea was ill conceived and reckless, but knowing Doyle, he'd find a way to make it work.

"They already know we're here," Doyle said, "and they've done one of two things: kept Marigween on board and even more guarded than she was before, or moved her off of the ship."

"In which case we are in trouble," Christopher said sadly.

"No, in which case we find her."

"I'm glad you're with me," Christopher said, feeling that ever-present pang of wanting to thank everyone around him for all that they were doing but knowing they would brush him off for it.

Doyle did just that by turning to look to Montague. "Monte, what's keeping us? I don't want to spend another second on this flea boat," he informed his partner, then cocked his head back to Christopher, "and yes, I got them too."

Once they were off the ship, Christopher and Doyle were directed by one of the longshoremen to the Customs House, where they were told they would find the marshal. As he and his friend moved into the busy street traffic, Christopher sensed they were being watched. The notion made his shoulders draw together and made him cock his head once, twice, then an obvious third time to the somberly clad loaders and merchants that shuffled in the path behind them.

"Yes, Christopher, they're watching us. Pretend you do not notice. They're all asking themselves what a small, motley group of Celts is doing with a Pict cog." Doyle did not turn his head as he spoke; his gaze was fixed on the knots of people that lay in front of them. "We should have let Jennifer do all of the talking from the start. We might have been able to fool them. But Monte had to go and open his mouth."

"I would've been surprised if he hadn't," Christopher added. He would have allowed himself a smile if he hadn't been under the scrutiny of the citizens of Magdalene. "It's too late now. We'll just have to see what the marshal says."

"He's not going to help us," Doyle said.

"We have to at least try," Christopher countered.

They entered the marshal's office and found the man seated behind his warped desk. There was a tray that contained a piece of blackened meat and a half-eaten loaf of dark grain bread on top of the desk, along with an inkwell, quill, and a small pile of scrolls.

The marshal looked up and regarded them with tired-looking eyes. "And what problem have you to dump in my lap?" he asked, then cocked his brow and resumed chewing his food with what was left of his teeth.

Christopher opened his mouth, but Doyle was already answering, "We're from the cog that just docked, sir. And we have some questions."

The marshal swallowed first, then decided to react. "From the cog, eh? Well, I've some questions for you first."

"We'll answer your questions," a familiar voice came from the doorway opposite the marshal's desk. Christopher turned. Montague was supposed to be taking care of business with the customs master back on the wharf, namely the business of explanations, which in truth was really the business of lies. Why he was here was anybody's guess.

Doyle did not feel like guessing. "Monte . . . what are you —"

The fat man waved his partner's question off with a hand, then paraded into the room, trailed by a worried-looking Orvin. "It's all taken care of, laddie." He turned his head toward the marshal. "What is it you want to know" — he hemmed — "kind sir?"

"That is a Pict cog you're sailing," the smaller man began, narrowing his eyes. "Just how did you come by it?"

"Why sir, that is a cog out there. Not a Pict cog. And she's a fine vessel. Been in my family for a long time. She was stolen by the Picts and only recently recovered. Forgive our foreign sail and lack of banner. We shall take care of those discrepancies immediately."

Orvin moved to Christopher, seized his arm, and led

him to a far corner of the room while Doyle and
Montague tightened their half circle on the marshal.

"Young saint, we must act swiftly. That lout is going
to mean the death of us all. Word of the ship's theft will
reach here soon." Orvin's voice was as creased with tension as his face. "We went to the customs master, and
Montague lied to him as well."

"What about the Saxon cog?" Christopher asked.
"Has anyone seen Marigween?"

"Better you should hear it from me," Orvin said
softly. "The captain of the cog was lost. There was a
mutiny. The first mate has assumed command."

"Did you speak to him?" he asked, feeling his hands
begin to tremble.

Orvin shrugged. "How?"

Christopher had forgotten that he was the only one of
the group that spoke Saxon. He turned toward the half-
open door. "I have to talk to him." He darted toward the
daylight.

"No, wait, young saint!" he heard Orvin cry behind
him.

"Where's he off to?" Montague asked, interrupting
himself from his conversation with the marshal.

"Doyle, go after him!" Orvin ordered.

Running through the streets of a port as busy as
Magdalene was no small feat. But if Christopher
attempted to do the same in Blytheheart, he would not
get very far, for that port's streets were twice as con-
gested as Magdalene's. Rounding shoulder after shoulder, startling farmer and merchant alike, Christopher
steered himself into the wind, in the direction of the
wharves. He did not look back to see if Doyle followed;
surely he did.

By the time he set foot on the wharf, he was wholly
out of breath and felt beads of sweat march in lances
down his spine. The sandals he had found in the crew's

quarters flapped noisily and hollowly against the pier. Then he felt a hand slap on his shoulder and drag him to a stop. The hand wrenched him around.

Doyle eyed him with disappointment, but said nothing.

"Let," Christopher panted, "me go. I have to talk to them."

"Not alone."

One of the marshal's guards stepped up, his armor looking hot and heavy, his face reflecting that sentiment. "Trouble here?" He looked to Doyle. "Caught a thief have you?"

"No, sir. Just a friend," Doyle said. "No trouble here at all. Sorry to have bothered you." Doyle made a rather unceremonious bow that was perhaps a little too much tribute to pay to a lowly guard.

A guard. One of the marshal's guards. A show of arms. A threat. The idea congealed, and Christopher took the man by the elbow. "I need to borrow you, sir, only for a moment. You will say nothing, not that they'd understand you anyway. I am just going to have a chat with the first mate of that Saxon cog, there, and your presence will, shall I say, reinforce my words."

Doyle looked confused. "What now, Christopher?"

"Have a pinch of faith in me. And watch my back."

"I'll play none of your games," the guard protested, his teeth coming together like a dog that had just snapped.

"Oh, come on now, sir. A single moment of your time. You may help to save a woman's life," Christopher urged.

"You're not lying?" he asked in a warning tone.

"No," Christopher said, then he dropped his voice to sound as grave as he felt. "Not about this."

The guard thought it over, then rolled his eyes and finally shrugged his resigned agreement. They walked to the gangplank and stopped at its foot. They were spotted by two of the deck crew from the rail, and one of them, a lanky, dark-skinned man, appeared to recognize

Christopher. He turned and muttered something to the other crewman.

"I want Seaver," Christopher called up to the Saxons, "and the girl he has." He burned with the desire to rush up the gangplank, choke life out of these fools, and then rush down into the hold. He ground his teeth and tried to think logically, tried to make the trembling go away.

"Ha! Only Woden knows where that rat is now," the man called back. "And I thought you were a Celt."

"What did he say?" Doyle asked.

Christopher shushed his friend while keeping his gaze on the Saxon. He cocked a thumb toward the guard. "This man is prepared to call the garrison. On the marshal's order we'll board this ship."

"Have you no ears? Seaver is gone. And he took the girl with him. Houge thinks Seaver killed the captain and dumped him overboard — and I think so, too." The Saxon's gaze lifted to the port behind them. "Houge's out there right now searching for the rat."

"What's he saying?" Doyle asked impatiently. "Come on, Christopher."

The guard's patience had also worn thin. "I've a job to do, young fools. I do not know what this is about, but I am not aiding foreigners." With that, he spun and marched away, his armor jingling a testy little tune.

Christopher watched him go a moment, then he regarded the Saxons. "Tell Houge Christopher of Shores will have a word with him when he returns."

The sweaty Saxon smiled at his shipmate. "Christopher of Shores," he repeated mockingly.

Christopher bit back a reply, deciding not to waste any more of his breath on these swabs. "Well," he said, looking somberly at Doyle, "maybe Seaver *has* taken Marigween off of the cog."

"Yes, he has, and we've no time to waste," Doyle said, indicating with his head toward the shore.

2   Brenna stood in the forecastle and leaned back
against the post. She looked up past the rooftops of
Magdalene to the tree-shrouded bluffs, where some of
the leaves had changed from a pale green to a light
shade of yellow. She felt a twitch in her wound. Her
arm had remained swollen and still throbbed. She had
hoped that by now at least one or both of the ills
would have ceased. The sling helped ease the pain, but
consequently, it made her feel defenseless. She'd come
so far, proved so much to herself, only to be shot down
into the world of invalids. Perhaps that was an exaggeration, but it felt real enough. Christopher had told
her of the news concerning Seaver and Marigween,
and now he and Doyle were out scouring the port. She
decided she would not stand around and do nothing.
She would help search herself — despite Christopher's
orders to the contrary. Merlin and Jennifer were the
only ones left on board the cog, for Montague and
Orvin were still off discussing the cog's cargo with the
customs master. She turned away from the skyline of
the port to the starboard rail, where Merlin stood
stroking his beard pensively and mumbling something
to himself. She remembered a question that had
occurred to her earlier. "Merlin?"

The druid did not look up.

"Merlin?"

The old man's head jolted back. He opened his eyes
very wide, and at that moment Brenna assumed he had
spotted her, but he stood, looking through her, then he
whirled around, muttered something, and headed for
the main hatch.

She had been warned about the magician, but thus far
he had proven to be a kind, gentle old man — and a

very good doctor. This bizarre behavior seemed uncharacteristic of the druid. But she had been warned. Orvin said that Merlin was in a good-hearted phase now, but he might easily slip back into evil. Brenna was not sure what that meant, but she hoped his current behavior was not a sign of bad things to come. All she had wanted to do was ask the old man for advice. Brenna assumed there was no better man to go to for advice than Merlin, he who advises the king of Britain. But her question involved love — and what did the druid really know about it? Maybe he knew a lot. She'd shelve the question for now and start off on her search. She wondered if she should tell them she was leaving, then decided it would be wise to let one of them know.

Brenna found Jennifer in the captain's quarters. The blond woman pulled on a shift that might have come from one of the cargo crates. Brenna felt her stomach tighten with jealousy over the other's clean garment, and she wanted one for herself. But before she could voice that notion, Jennifer was already lifting another shift from the captain's small trestle bed. "I found one for you too, Brenna. There's a whole box of them down there, clean and neatly folded. I wager they fetch a few deniers."

She had, at first, been slightly intimidated by Jennifer's presence, though the blond woman's attention rarely strayed from Doyle. She clearly had no eyes for Christopher, but she was an exceedingly buxom and beautiful woman. Brenna could only imagine having breasts such as Jennifer's. During the past two days, Jennifer had been soft-spoken and polite, and Brenna had not really had the opportunity to get to know her. The young woman was clearly offering more than a shift, and it seemed they had been thrown together for a purpose. Doyle had compared them to each other. Yes, they were both strong, and, she thought cockily, a bit beautiful. Were it not for their strikingly different hair,

they could almost be called twins — certainly in temper-
ament. But while Jennifer had clearly won Doyle's favor,
Brenna and Christopher's relationship was still a fact of
the past. Perhaps Jennifer could provide her with a
course of action. There was always something to be
learned, and Jennifer had, after all, encountered many
men. But those were not relationships in the conven-
tional sense. She had vowed not to judge the woman,
though when she had first learned of Jennifer's harlot-
ing, she had immediately condemned her. But then she
had met the young woman, had seen how she wanted to
help Christopher and how Doyle regarded her. Brenna
could not envision herself as a whore, but for some it
was obviously a comfortable and profitable lifestyle. She
wondered how sinful it really was. Would every whore
burn in hell? Even someone as selfless as Jennifer?

Brenna crossed to the bed and took the garment.
"Will you help me put it on? It's hard with this sling."

Jennifer nodded and helped her take off the shirt and
breeches Doyle had let her borrow.

"I'm going ashore to help search for Marigween," she
told Jennifer.

"So am I," Doyle's girl friend said.

They exchanged a smile. It was an odd moment of
shared thought, shared action and reaction. "You just
cannot sit here, can you?" Brenna asked rhetorically.

"No," she said, fastening the drawstring at Brenna's
nape, "and if we do not help, those two will never find
Marigween." Jennifer moved in front of Brenna, then
helped her back into her sling. "There. You're much
prettier now. And we're off."

"What about Merlin?" Brenna asked, hesitating.

Jennifer drew back. "Have you seen him of late? He
acts mad."

"Yes, he does. But we should at least try to tell him
we're leaving," Brenna suggested.

"I'll go to him, then I'll join you on deck."

Jennifer left the quarters, and in a few moments Brenna was on the now windswept deck, trying to find the right angle so that she wasn't smothered in black curls. Jennifer appeared after a few moments, shaking her head. "Forget Merlin. He's in a world of his own. My words were to the walls."

"Is that mumbling he does part of his religion?" Brenna asked. "Does he even have a religion?"

Jennifer shrugged. "I've heard only rumors about the druids, so I'll only chance to say that he'll be all right. Let's make haste."

They climbed down from the cog and began a brisk, steady walk over the wharf. Jennifer kept close to Brenna, and at one point said softly, "I've a dagger strapped on my calf — in case of trouble."

"Where's mine?" Brenna asked in mock seriousness.

Jennifer grinned. "I should have thought about that. You still have a free hand — and I know you can use it."

Once past the street that paralleled the bay, Brenna stopped and looked around. They were at an intersection of side streets. The gable-roofed storefronts were so numerous and packed so tightly together that they made Brenna feel a bit too closed-in. The entire scene reflected the immensity of their task. "Where do we start?" she asked.

"Seaver would not stay here — especially if he assumed we'd find him. So what would he do?" Jennifer posed.

"Leave," Brenna said, knowing Jennifer was going somewhere with the conversation but uncertain of its final destination.

"On foot?" she asked.

"No, they would need mounts — ah, yes, the stables."

Jennifer turned to peer down the east side of the street, then looked to the west. "We just have to find them."

After walking several blocks, and growing more and more frustrated, they stopped a large-bellied hawker who stood in the street and handed out samples of the day's ale. He gave them the directions and a long, exaggerated wink that sent a chill through Brenna.

At the stables they accosted the chief hostler, who had a mouth so tiny it looked as if he had never smiled once in his life.

"He's a short man," Jennifer explained again to the man. "And she is very fair and has long, red hair. She's rather beautiful, I'm told. Are you sure you have not seen them?"

The hostler shook his head negatively as he had before. "Have you not chores to attend to? Why must you bother me so? I've enough trouble as it is without the likes of you wenches to raise my temper further."

Jennifer bristled. "We'll leave you then. And we apologize that our simple questions have annoyed you. Come on, Brenna." She spun around, dug her right foot into the sandy earth, and kicked back, sending a small cloud of dust and dirt onto the hostler's boots. And then she stomped off.

"Go on, leave! And don't return!" the hostler shouted.

Brenna hurried to catch up with her heated friend. "You didn't have to do that," she said loudly, still aghast over the other's defiance. "He was just in an ill mood."

"You two? Wait!" a voice cried from behind them.

They turned in unison. A hostler apprentice, his clothes dusty and trapping stray horsehair, ran up to them and stopped. "I heard what you asked Terry," he said, out of breath. "He should have told you that last night two mounts were stolen."

Brenna seized the boy's shoulders. "What else do you know?"

His complexion lightened a shade, and the boy visibly

shivered. "Th-th-th-that's all. But the two you seek may be the culprits. I was just thinking that."

She released the hostler and smoothed out his shirt. "And you thought well to tell us."

"I must be off. Terry will punish me if he discovers I'm gone." He spun around and jogged off, back toward the stable.

Brenna regarded Jennifer, opening her eyes as wide as she could. "Do you believe —" she began, then cut herself off.

Jennifer was already nodding. "Seaver and Marigween are not here. Let's go back to the cog. Christopher and Doyle will probably return soon. We can tell them this. In the meantime, let's think about where that little Saxon would go from here."

They turned down several streets until they were on the main east–west road that would take them to the shoreline. Brenna thought hard about where Seaver would go, but she kept abandoning that question and focusing on what seemed the more important matter of winning back Christopher's love. And then she would curse herself for thinking such a thing, then reward herself for her rekindled hope. She loved him, hated his situation, wanted to help him — but, in truth, did not want him to find Marigween. Yet she would not prevent him from finding her. In fact, what she and Jennifer had just learned would certainly help him.

Brenna had been very ill once, and the pain had been a hot knife in her stomach. Her mother had told her she'd eaten some sour food. She remembered the feeling distinctly, for when she thought of her life now, that same unsettled and nauseating experience returned. She could not reach a moment of clarity, a moment where she would know — without question — what course she should take for her life. She wanted that badly, wanted

him badly. Why was she helping him to get farther out
of her life? She wished she could fully and truthfully
answer that question for herself. She had once said she
wanted to be his friend. Yes, she did want to be his
friend — but that would be only part of a much deeper
experience she wanted to share with him, something
that was greater and more heart-encompassing than
their first relationship.

"North," Jennifer said out of nowhere.

"What?"

"North." Jennifer stopped. "North to Caledonia. It's
simple. That's where he's taking her. Why did I keep
going south in my head?"

"Caledonia?" Brenna asked. "I've never heard of it."

"It's a land occupied by the Saxons. Many of their
ships are built in the port towns along its coast. More
than half of the customers at the back house come from
there," Jennifer noted with an edge. "Seaver is a Saxon.
He's going home."

After beginning to walk, Brenna's stomach was punc-
tured by a familiar and dreaded blade. Jennifer hurried
up beside her. "I think I'm right. What do you think?"

Brenna felt as if she bled from within. "Yes, you're
probably right. Christopher will find Marigween and
defeat Seaver. The happy couple will be married and
live in bliss until they are dead." She increased her pace
and dug her nails into her palms.

Jennifer quickened her own step. "So now we learn
why Brenna wants to help Christopher."

She came to a jarring halt, and all of it, all of the
frustration and locked away love and pain rushed to
Brenna's eyes. She bit her lip and lowered her gaze
at the rutted street. The tears came. She closed her
eyes. "I cannot help it. Oh, dear Lord, I love him,"
she said in a voice so faint that she scarcely had
heard it herself.

"I've seen it, Brenna," Jennifer said. "You can see it in my eyes when they find Doyle."

She sniffed. "He has a son. He will never leave her for me. She was once a princess. I have been nothing but a maid and a nurse."

Jennifer crossed in front of Brenna, then cradled Brenna's chin in her thumb and forefinger, forcing Brenna to look into her eyes. "It's obvious that he regards you as very special," Jennifer said. "And perhaps there is something more there. But if you expected more from him, you shouldn't have come along. He needs only friends now."

"I thought we could be friends. I truly did. I didn't want to lose him and I thought I would be all right around him. But I'm not. And now he's going to find her. And I'll be cast aside again." Brenna shifted her head, pulling herself out of Jennifer's grasp. She closed her eyes and wiped her cheeks.

"If it makes you feel better," Jennifer said in a soft, consoling tone, "we might be wrong. The theft of those two horses could simply be a coincidence. Perhaps Seaver and Marigween are long gone by now. But all of that aside, you should not tempt Christopher. If he returns to your side, let it be his decision, not your luring that brings him."

Brenna opened her eyes. "I'm not luring him, am I?"

"Your mere presence does that, I'm afraid."

"Then I should leave. And if he loves me, he'll come back to me."

"At least then there will be no disputing the truth," Jennifer answered.

"And if he doesn't return?" Brenna stared at Jennifer, waiting for a reply. Jennifer stood there, looking at her, a frown slowly coming over her face. Then Brenna realized the blond woman was not looking at her at all, but past her. Brenna craned her neck and saw two ragged-looking, sun-darkened longshoremen standing about a score of yards away. Both men gawked at them.

"Let's get to the other side of the street," Jennifer suggested nervously.

They moved slowly, crossing the street at an angle that would put them farther away from the young fools. But the fools did the same.

Jennifer stopped, putting her back to the longshoremen. Brenna did likewise. "We're not playing a game with this filth." And then she was at her leg, and the blade was suddenly in her hand. She whirled, brandished the dagger, and then charged toward the longshoremen, shouting, "Brenna! Come on!"

The two loaders were taken completely by surprise and fell sideways against a storefront wall. Brenna sprinted past the men and began to close the gap between herself and Jennifer. After a moment, she cocked her head back to see if the shoremen followed. She shivered as she noted they were no longer on the street. She ran a little farther and then stopped. The bouncing of her arm was now too painful to bear. She called to Jennifer. The other ceased her sprint, then bent down and tucked her blade back into its calf sheath.

"This is no castle courtyard," Brenna said, reaching her companion. "We're simply not safe."

"There is no port that is safe for a woman," she answered, and then smiled. "At least one who's unarmed."

"They probably wouldn't have bothered us if others were about."

"Don't put that kind of boldness past them," Jennifer corrected. "I could tell you a story or two of the shoremen in Blytheheart."

"Tell me then," Brenna said. "And help me stop thinking about *him*."

3   "Not a soul saw them," Doyle said as he stepped
onto the gangplank, then let out a huff. "We either asked
all the wrong people, or every one of them lied to us."

"They have no reason to lie," Christopher said, following his friend up the steep board. He paused a
moment to look back at the port. "He's gone with her,
all right. He's not here."

"But where would he go?" Doyle asked.

"North. To Caledonia, I suspect," Jennifer called from
above.

Christopher hurried up the plank and crossed onto
the deck. He moved around the main hatch to where
Jennifer and Brenna stood near the starboard rail.
"What makes you say that?"

Brenna leapt into the conversation with an excited
summary of a trip she and Jennifer had made to the stables. The story's impact was partially lost on
Christopher, for he tensed over hearing that Brenna
had — once again — failed to heed his words. No, she
hadn't kept herself safe, but had ventured into a dangerous port. Brenna finished her story and garnished it
with a self-satisfied grin.

Christopher leered her smile into a frown, then asked,
"Brenna? Do you want to die?"

She pushed herself off of the rail. "Sometimes."

He took a step toward her. "I let you come with me
all the way from Shores." He circled behind her, then
leaned into her ear. "I couldn't stop you. I should have
known then that you wouldn't listen to a single word of
mine." He stepped back in front of her, staring her
down as if she were a squire in training. "I was not
being overprotective in telling you to stay here at the
cog. I was being wise."

Jennifer nudged herself between him and Brenna. "Let me ask you a question, Christopher. You and Doyle searched all day. What did you find?"

"Nothing," Doyle said from behind him.

Christopher craned his neck to shoot a look at his blood brother, who leaned on the mast. "Thanks," he said darkly.

"Then you see," Jennifer continued in a tone more urgent than before, "were it not for us you would not know about the two stolen horses."

"Two stolen horses may mean nothing," Christopher argued.

Brenna seized his shirt by the collar. "It's not a coincidence, Christopher."

"How do you know that?"

"We do not know for sure, but do as we have and place yourself in Seaver's boots. You would not stay in Magdalene and you would need mounts to travel."

Christopher turned, and by doing so he tore Brenna's hand off of his shirt. "To travel where? To Caledonia?" He walked toward the forecastle for no particular reason, trying to paint a mental picture of Seaver and Marigween cantering north. "And how can you be certain — if he did, indeed, steal the horses — that he's headed north? Why not south? Why not even back to Blytheheart? Why not east? Or northeast to the Savernake forest? Or to the Cotswold hills, or up the Severn to Gloucester? What makes you certain that he is headed to Caledonia?"

Jennifer let out a small, but audible puff of air. "He is going home. Think about it, Christopher. What was he doing on the cog in the first place? You said yourself that you could not figure out why he was not back in Shores. Perhaps he's running away from the war. Perhaps he's running home." She had placed exaggerated emphasis on the word *home*, and it seemed to ring out like a Vespers' bell and get carried on a wind that circled the ship.

Home. How would he discover the truth? Were it only as simple as willing it into his mind. . . .

Christopher moved abruptly to the main hatch. He descended the ladder into the hold. To his astonishment, the vast cargo area was empty, and even the now-lonely deck beams had been swept and mopped. He descended another ladder into the crew's quarters, where he found Orvin seated on the floor and in the process of tying his long white hair into a ponytail with a short piece of leather cord.

"I wanted to see you, but I assumed you were still out with Montague. And here you are," Christopher said.

"I am always to be found when I'm needed, young saint," Orvin said, his voice edged with the effort of tying his hair. He fiddled with the knot on the cord once, twice, then huffed and slammed the cord into his lap.

"Here," Christopher said, crossing past the man and dropping to his knees behind him. "Let me do it."

Orvin passed him the cord. "Donella used to do this for me. She always said my hair was too long, even after she would cut it for me."

As Christopher gathered Orvin's thin, coarse locks into a tail, he asked, "What happened to the cargo?"

"That bloated pig made some kind of reckless and lawless deal with the customs master, and I believe he bribed the marshal as well. If he comes back at all, it will be with a sack full of shillings — a sack which might cost us our heads."

Christopher thought that if Doyle was in the room, the former archer would, at the moment, be shaking his head over the impudence of the brigand. Since Doyle was not present, Christopher did the headshaking for his blood brother. "I had a feeling he'd find some way to profit from this whole affair."

"Our cause was noble, young saint. But our methods were not. I fear to show my face in Blytheheart now. Marigween's Uncle Robert and I will be blamed for taking the cog. And if I'm caught, the abbot might even turn me over to the Picts. But the more I think about it, the more I do not care." He laughed. "What would they do with an old man? I'm on the wall-walk between life and death already. They will simply give me a push. That is all."

Christopher finished tying Orvin's hair and adjusted the cord. He rose and moved to face his mentor. "I'm sorry, Orvin. I did not mean for any of this to happen. When I think of all we've done to come after Marigween, I become ill. And it may have all been for nothing."

Orvin tapped his palm on the floor. "These decks are fairly solid and thick. But the hatches were open, and I heard what Jennifer said. Listen to her."

He squatted to level his gaze with Orvin's. "Do you know something, Orvin? Have you seen something? Is she correct? Has Seaver gone north to Caledonia? Are you sure?"

"The scrolls of the sky are rolled and sealed for now. Why, I cannot tell you. I only know that were I you, I would go north, for every time that I did not heed a woman's words I plunged into trouble. They *know*, Christopher." He offered his leathery hand. "Now, help me up. I've a cold, but delicious stew to prepare."

Christopher almost considered leaving his mentor on the floor, for he knew all too well the horror of one of Orvin's stews, but perhaps a cold one would somehow taste better. As he lifted Orvin to his feet, he said a small but fervent prayer for God to guide the old man in his cooking, for he knew all aboard were surely very hungry.

And, as it turned out later, the stew was thick and

meaty and sweet. Montague returned to the ship in the middle of the meal. The brigand sat himself down on the floor opposite Christopher and was handed a bowl of stew by Jennifer before he even asked for it.

Prior to the fat man's appearance, the conversation had been dominated by Christopher, who had announced that he and he alone would go north to look for Marigween. Doyle had had a full quiver of reasons why he should go along, and it had taken the archer many shots before Christopher finally succumbed to his friend's fiery persuasion. What had been odd was that Brenna had not spoken. She had appeared as if about to say something, but had exchanged a look with Jennifer and then had kept strangely silent.

"All right, lads and lasses," Montague said, as he was wont to do when beginning one of his speeches about what their next plan of action would be — as decided by him, of course, "I've been paid for our cargo, and have already employed a few good craftsmen to make us a new sail so that we're not mistaken for Picts anymore. They assure me the sail will be ready by morning — and for what we're paying for it, it had better be. All we need to know now is where we're going."

Doyle regarded his partner. "Christopher and I are headed north to Caledonia, Monte. We believe Seaver and Marigween are up there. We'll need provisions and mounts."

"I'll purchase three horses for us immediately, laddie. We've easily enough for them *and* the provisions." The fat man turned to Merlin. "We'll need you to sail —"

"Thank you, Montague," Christopher said, cutting off the brigand before his thoughts went any further, "but we need you to get everyone back to Blytheheart. And then, if you would, sir, escort Orvin, Merlin, and Brenna back to Shores. I'll pay you for it . . . somehow. If we've shares of the money from the cargo, then you can have mine."

"And you can have mine," Brenna said.

"And mine," Jennifer added. "Though I think we'll be protecting you more than you us. You've a wounded hand and shoulder to nurse."

"You can hold on to my share for me, Monte," Doyle said. "Borrow from it if need be. But I want it." Jennifer scowled at Doyle, who flashed her a wounded look. "I was going to spend it on you," Doyle told her, then, under the heat of her continued stare, he corrected, "strike that, Monte. Keep my share as well."

Christopher set his stew bowl down, then unfolded his legs and rubbed the stiffness out of them. "It's settled then. We leave on the morrow."

At sunrise, Christopher thanked and said his good-byes to Orvin and Merlin. Orvin gave him a long, tight hug, and told him he'd await his return back in Shores. Christopher left the cog with Montague, Doyle, Jennifer, and Brenna. While Montague and the ladies went off to purchase the supplies, Doyle and Christopher headed for the stable, where they found two strong, young rounseys, and fought over the black one, which Doyle said looked "nobler."

Christopher looked into the eyes of the brown rounsey, who stared back dumbly. "You'll not throw me, will you?" he asked the mount. "No, I guess not." He let Doyle take the black mount. The hostler tending to them explained that bits, bridles and reins would not be a problem, as he had many to sell. Saddles, on the other hand, were hard to come by in the port and had to be ordered. Christopher knew the hostler's dilemma well, being the son of a saddlemaker. Riding bareback would be uncomfortable and not exactly safe, but certainly easier than stealing a Pict cog. Putting it into that perspective made the lack of a saddle seem a minor inconvenience.

"We'll have to steal a couple of saddles," Doyle whispered in his ear.

Christopher shook his head slowly. "There'll be no more stealing."

Doyle shrugged. "We could try to ride sidesaddle — without a saddle. But we're going to fall off a lot."

They led the rounseys to the edge of the property encompassing the stable house, and while they were double-checking the shoes on their mounts, the others returned with two riding bags filled with provisions.

"It won't get you that far, lads, but at least it's a start. You'll find a purse in each to buy a trifle more food, but after that you'll be on your own," Montague said, then he noticed the mounts. "Where are your saddles?"

"They have to be ordered," Doyle said.

"And we cannot wait for them," Christopher finished.

"We'll see about that," Montague said, then dropped the riding bags he'd been holding and marched past them.

The fat man was a wonder to see. He managed to talk the chief hostler out of two saddles for what Christopher considered to be a rather meager sum. If Montague had offered the man a ridiculous amount of money and had obtained the saddles, that would have been one thing, but the fact that he managed to strike a deal as lean as he did was, in short, a feat of bartering.

While Doyle took Jennifer's hand and led her behind the stable house to say a private good-bye, Christopher stood with Montague and Brenna, feeling like he should be taking Brenna off for an intimate farewell. But he knew that if he were alone with her, knowing he might not see her again for many moons, he might be tempted to touch her, to kiss her, for no one would know but them. But that betrayal of Marigween would sit too heavily on his heart. And it was not fair to Brenna either.

He could barely make eye contact with the raven maid now, and she appeared to have the same trouble.

"I'll leave you now," Montague said. "And wait across the street."

As the brigand left, Christopher gazed longingly at him, for his intimacy with Brenna was suddenly awkward. Christopher felt that if he opened his mouth to say something, Brenna would do exactly the same, and their words would clash against each other like shields. He wondered if she thought the same, for as he finally managed to look upon her, he saw that her lips were pursed and her gaze could still not find his. Then she did something that sent him back a few years. She began to twirl her index finger through her long, black curls. It was one of Brenna's habits, and he had seen her do it many times, but the morning light that played over her now made her look much younger, as if she had stepped out of their first moon together and into quite possibly their last.

"We've done this a few times, haven't we?" she asked, turning a bit away from him.

He smiled weakly. "I don't like to think about the last time I bade you farewell," he admitted. "But I remember the first time very clearly. Do you?"

She lifted her head, stared solemnly at him a moment, then nodded. "You were off to your first battle with Lord Hasdale."

He closed his eyes. "I remember thinking that I had to come back, if only to stop your tears." He drew in a deep breath, opening his eyes as he let it out. "I'm a fool, Brenna. I ruined both of our lives."

She bit her lower lip, as if trying desperately to keep something in. Her blinking became forced and excessive, and finally she closed her eyes. "You did not ruin our lives, Christopher. What has happened has happened. I wish there were a way to undo things, but there isn't."

"I've wished that many times," he said. "If there was a way back, I would not have betrayed our love, for I know now that it is something that will never die in me." It must have been the notion that he might never see her again that had made him utter his last; he was suddenly angry at himself for pouring his heart out to her, yet somehow relieved at finally admitting aloud that his love was still there. He would remember the moment as a time of weakness, a time of great release.

"I don't need to tell you how I feel about you," she said. "I want —"

"— your actions speak loudest," Christopher interrupted her. "I don't want to hurt you, Brenna. I've done enough of that already. I wish I knew where to go from here."

"I'm going home," she said. "That's all I can do. And I was wrong."

"About what?"

"I love you, Christopher." She stepped quickly up to him, kissed his cheek, then drew back and bowed her head. "I had to tell you that." She turned swiftly away and started off.

He remembered their past agreement: he would tell her why he had asked her to marry him if she would tell him if she still loved him. "I asked you to marry me," he shouted after her, "because in some other life you are my bride — and will always be."

He knew she had heard him, but she kept moving.

First moon:
For a half score of days Doyle and Christopher followed a natural path through the bluffs that rose over the coastline. The days were hot and humid, the nights windy but still humid. It seemed that the farther north they traveled, the farther inland their course took them. They tried to keep the ocean in sight, but soon the cliffs

became too steep and rocky for the rounseys. They reasoned that Seaver would have encountered the same
problems and he, too, was surely following the easier
course through the sparsely wooded foothills that shied
behind the mighty bluffs. In the valleys, there were pines
and live oaks and several other trees that Christopher
did not recognize, along with gorse and ivy. At first he
began to keep an eye out for fauna, catching a glimpse
of a hare here, a small fox there, but soon his vision
blurred into the masses of sky, tree trunks, and ground.

They came upon a narrow stream that trickled down
from the foothills into a small valley. They watered their
horses, and Doyle was able to catch a fish with his bare
hands. Unfortunately, Montague had forgotten to purchase a flint stone for them, and while Doyle was able to
eat the strong-smelling meat raw, Christopher declined,
calling his blood brother "a true barbarian." Rested, and
now preparing to leave, they spotted a man descending
a slope to their north. He approached them unsteadily,
and soon Christopher saw that his off-centered gait was
due to his age. He was a broad-shouldered man with a
barrel for a waistline, and dressed in torn, sun-bleached
breeches and drawstring shirt. He had a sack slung over
his back. When he saw Christopher and Doyle, he froze
for a moment, then waved and came forward.

"Hello," Doyle said as he stepped up to the old fellow.

"Been coming here for over fivescore moons," the
man began in a voice that sounded like he had food in
his mouth yet it appeared he did not, "and in all that
time less than a half score of travelers have visited me
and my runnel. And less than half that number have
been Celts."

"We did not mean to intrude," Christopher tossed in.
"We just meant to water our mounts. We're leaving
now."

"Stay a while if you choose," the man said. "It's been

a rare moon, this one, for twice have I had the pleasure of company, and it's not my runnel, really, but any of the leeches you may find in it *are* mine."

"Is there a town nearby? A doctor you work for?" Christopher asked the leech gatherer.

"A good morning's walk back there," he said, cocking a thumb over his shoulder, then lowering it. "She's not much, and her name has changed so many times that I cannot remember what it is this day, but if you need a place to pass the night, she'll do. And if it's Saxons you're worried about — don't. They come and go peacefully. They stopped their raids . . ." he trailed off, frowning over what was apparently a lost thought. "Oh, it's no matter," he said. "If you've time, I'll take you. Was only a short time ago that I led a man and his sick wife there."

"I trust we can find it ourselves," Doyle said.

A lever fell in Christopher's mind, and a gear ground to a halt. "Tell me about this man and his sick wife," he urged the gatherer.

"I offered him a few of my leeches to help bleed her, but I don't believe he really understood me. He spoke Celt, but not very much."

"His wife," Doyle said, picking up on Christopher's suspicion, "did she have long, red locks? Was she rather pale? And he — was he short?"

The gatherer squinted into his memory a moment, then looked up, his brow rising. "You know them? Are you, are you following them?"

Christopher rushed up to the man, and fortunately repressed the desire to seize the drawstring on the gatherer's shirt and choke the full story out of him. Instead, he clenched his fist, stiffened his entire frame, then demanded, "Exactly how long ago did you help them?"

"I don't know — two, three, four days past. I don't account for things like that," the man said defensively.

"Did they stay at the town long?" Doyle asked, taking up a position to Christopher's right.

"I don't know."

"All right then, friend. Thank you," Doyle replied, gesturing with his head to Christopher that they leave.

As they swung up onto their mounts, the gatherer dropped his sack, opened it, and began to rifle through it for something. Christopher kicked his rounsey into a leap over the stream, hearing Doyle do likewise behind him. The gatherer beckoned that they need not rush off, that the man and his wife were surely many days ahead and another half day would not matter.

Christopher fell into the rhythm of his lathering horse, his body pumping as if it were another muscle on the beast's back. They arrived at the town, scoured it for Seaver and Marigween, then learned that the two had left possibly three days prior to their arrival. They purchased more food and a flint stone with the money Montague had provided them, spent the night at a tiny inn with only two guest rooms, and left the inn before sunrise.

Second Moon:

The humidity of the previous moon was gone, and the air was now crisp and tinged with the scent of brine. The foothills slowly donned the many-hued cloak of fall, and it was not until noon that the night's frost would completely melt away. Christopher and Doyle pulled their woolen sleeping blankets over their shoulders as they forged on. Now some seven weeks into their search, Christopher's hope was still very strong, but not quite as powerful as it had been the day they had left the leech gatherer. This was due, in part, to the fact that three days before they had lost the tracks left by Seaver's and Marigween's mounts. They had come upon an extensive tract of open land that had been due east of the foothills. The earth had been sandy and had been swept clean by a powerful wind that had risen with the nights and had died with the days. And now, the farther they traveled across the heath, the darker and stranger it became.

"Have you ever seen a field such as this?" Doyle said, looking ahead at the thorny, wine-colored brambles.

Christopher shook his head, no, as he rode alongside his blood brother. Occasionally, they encountered patches of ground that had been blackened. It was not until later in the day, when the clouds joined into a single gray mantle, that Christopher realized the origin of the black patches. Thunder resounded in the distance, and to Christopher, it was the drunken applause of some giant spectator who mocked their search. He felt his rounsey shiver. Lightning rippled through the gray wash above, but did not strike the ground.

"Did you see that?" Doyle asked, his gaze on the heavens.

"It stays up there," Christopher said, then pointed ahead at a particularly wide expanse of blackened foliage. "But not all of the time."

"We'll be next," Doyle said.

There was no immediate shelter to be found. All they could do was forge on. He whispered a prayer to his namesake. "St. Christopher, guide us through."

As night fell, the sky remained gray, and the thunder and lightning slipped off with the day. The expected rain never came. They stretched out on their blankets and stared up into the gloom.

"It's been nearly two full moons," Doyle said in a tired tone. "How much farther north do you think he's pushing?"

Christopher closed his eyes. He let the darkness wipe across his head, and then imagined that it engulfed the rest of his body. He wished he could peer through that darkness into a place that would illuminate him, provide him with an answer to Doyle's question. With his eyes still closed, he prayed for a light in all of the darkness.

Then he snapped his eyelids open, and the gray sky pervaded. "I don't know," he said, recognizing the sadness in his voice, feeling his hope slip back another notch. "But we'll keep after him."

Third moon:

Days away from the heath, and thankful for leaving that Devil's domain behind, they returned to the foothills, hoping to rediscover Seaver and Marigween's trail. Doyle remarked that the air smelled like All Saints' Day. It certainly felt like the eleventh moon of the year to Christopher. At night, he would shiver and shiver, and barely be able to fall asleep. He would manage only a few hours of rest. Their small cookfires never seemed to keep him warm enough.

They preferred to walk their horses now, to keep closer to the ground, where it was warmer. Their hair and beards had grown a thumbnail's length longer, but Christopher knew it would take a lot more hair than that to cut the cold. He longed for a pair of gloves, for a hood, for long stockings, and, most of all, for the time to come to eat, a small pleasure that had become the most meaningful and monotony-breaking part of each day. Days would blur into each other, but meals would not. He could remember exactly what he had eaten the day before, and three days before that. He wished now that something would leap out of the landscape and shock them with the fact that it was not another tree, another rock, another brook, or another slope.

Then Doyle picked up a set of hoofprints. The indentation left by the shoes matched the prints they'd previously followed. But there was only a single set of prints. Could Seaver have abandoned the other horse? Were he and Marigween riding on one mount? There was no way for them to know for sure. What was more disturbing was the fact that the prints led off to the northeast, away from the coast. If Christopher and Doyle were to follow the prints, the chances of their encountering the villages they occasionally relied on would grow very slim. They would have to live completely off the land. What would happen when they ran out of bolts for their crossbows? Could they capture their prey bare-handed?

"I believe we should ignore these tracks and go on. Probably a hunter, nothing more," Doyle said, his warm breath turning to white vapors that were carried on the breeze.

Christopher rubbed his palms for heat. "It's easier to stay on our present course, but what if —"

"What if we follow the tracks and I'm right? Then we're far off course, we'll run out of bolts, we'll have nothing to eat, and Seaver and Marigween will be long gone. We've been through this already." Doyle pointed an index finger at him. "You have to make a decision, Christopher. I'm not going to make it for you. I'm just offering my opinion."

Christopher closed his eyes and rubbed the cold lids. "You don't want me to blame you if you're wrong, eh?"

"I'll go where you go, and there'll be no hard feelings," his blood brother said.

What would you do, Orvin?

But the old man wasn't there to give Christopher advice. There was only land, sky, and the decision. He opened his eyes, ran a finger across his upper lip, for his nose was running, then looked to the path ahead: tree-covered slopes that slowly ascended to the horizon. He looked to the northeast path that followed the tracks: more slopes, more trees, nothing to indicate right or wrong, no sign, no mystery revealed, nothing. He looked up to the sky and saw a line of clouds that seemed to parallel the path ahead. Perhaps it was a sign, perhaps not. But he made the decision. He'd hold the clouds responsible if the course was wrong.

They abandoned the tracks and walked on. Both were silent for nearly the rest of the day.

At sunset, they spotted the silhouette of a structure that stood atop the summit of a slope.

"Mount your horse," Doyle said.

They kicked their rounseys into trots and ascended the slopes before them. The silhouette grew slowly lighter, black fading into a dark gray into the light gray of stone. The building was no bigger than a small barn, and judging from the pale green vines laying siege to its walls, it had been deserted long ago. They dismounted some twenty yards away from the ruins, then weaved through patches of yellow grass and leafless shrubbery to look for an entrance on the structure's opposite side. They came upon an arched doorway, where a good portion of its right wall had caved in. The mound of debris that blocked the entrance was not very tall, but it was fused together with ice that had formed in its cracks, making for a dangerous ascent. Gingerly, Christopher mounted the rubble, keeping a hand on the opposite wall for balance. Doyle followed him, and with only a few slips, they crossed the rocks and made the small leap inside.

Christopher turned to see the building's door leaning against the wall to the right of the doorway. The wood was warped and had been ravaged by insects.

"What do you think this place was?" Doyle asked, bending down to examine something on the dirt floor that had caught his eye. He rose with a small object in his good hand.

After shrugging at Doyle's question, Christopher asked, "What have you there?"

Doyle huffed in surprise. "It's a shoe nail. It looks

fairly new." He turned and let his gaze sweep over the floor. Then something else caught his eye: a view through an arched hole in the wall that was once a window. He moved quickly to the stone sill and rested a hand on it. "Better come over here."

Christopher crossed to the window and stared down into a wide, sparsely wooded valley that was split in two nearly equal parts by a long rectangular shadow. A haze rose above the shadow, and on first glance the distorted air seemed an illusion created by the setting sun. He blinked, stared again, and then knew.

"That's an army down there," Doyle said in grim confirmation. "Care to place a bet on whose?"

"Blast," Christopher said, under his breath.

"This place was probably an old looking post," Doyle said. "If we go east, we'll probably find the remains of an old motte-and-bailey castle." He lifted his hand, stared at the nail between his fingers, then rolled it around. "This must've fallen out of someone's pack."

"Forget about that nail. What are we going to do about that army?" Christopher asked, tipping his head toward the great shadow below.

"Besides avoid them? Nothing." Doyle left the window and headed for the doorway.

"Where are you going?"

"Wait here."

Christopher took another look at the valley, then turned from the window. His gaze fell upon the corner of a small ditch that sneaked out from the side of a fallen wall stone. He stepped to the stone, moved around it, and then stopped.

"Doyle? Doyle, come here!"

His blood brother raced over the mound, slipped and collapsed at its bottom, then came to a tumbling and grunting halt. Christopher rushed to him and offered a hand.

"I hope this is important," Doyle said, wincing as he waved off Christopher's hand, rose, then brushed himself off.

Christopher pointed at the stone. "There was a cookfire behind that stone. I touched the ground. It's still warm."

Doyle held up the nail. "This one matches our own. The smithy was the same."

"Which is to say —"

"Yes, they might have been here."

Fourth Moon:

On the day they guessed was the eve of Christmas, Christopher and Doyle traveled well into the evening. Since leaving the ruins of the looking post, they had not found a single clue that would indicate they were headed in the right direction. Ironically, Christopher had employed the old scouting skills Seaver had taught him to avoid the army, which, it had turned out, was from Pictland. Doyle had looked up to the sky and had asked God not to throw another army in his path; he had stumbled upon too many thus far, and enough was enough.

The moon was nearly full and it seemed brighter than normal, as if polished to a sheen by the clouds that wandered past it. Christopher looked for the Great Bear in the sky, but the pattern was lost in the moonlight. He abandoned the sky and looked ahead.

They had returned to the foothills, having turned west some days back, and the beech and pine trunks that were by day a cold brown and an even colder gray by night, were now like pillars of silver, and Christopher's imagination ran away with the idea that these pillars supported a fine, glossy canopy over a grand walkway that led up to a castle of gold, a castle where Marigween sat on the throne. He walked just ahead of his horse, kept his lead on the reins short, and smoothed out his shirt with his free hand. Now he was prepared to greet the queen of the castle of gold.

"That's enough for today," Doyle called from behind him.

Christopher began to answer, but his lips, which had dried together, stung as he pulled them apart. "We're almost there." His voice was barely audible, his throat so dry that it hurt to talk.

"Where? It doesn't matter if we stop here or there. Wherever there is, I'm sure it's in the forest."

"We're not stopping now," Christopher said, then hemmed, tried to gather some moisture in his mouth.

"It's Christmas Eve," Doyle said.

"Perhaps."

"Let's assume it is and stop."

"For what purpose? So we can have a great banquet of roots and what's left of that hare you shot?"

"It's food. At least we're alive."

Christopher did not look back. "We're going on."

"You want to go on because I want to stop," Doyle said, raising his voice.

It had not happened all at once; it had come on gradually, much as the moon had grown full. When they ate, he noticed that Doyle took a little more food for himself. When they built a fire, it was Christopher who always gathered the wood while Doyle would work the stone, the other having argued that he knew how to get a fire started swifter than anyone. It was always Christopher who assumed the point on their trek, since, Doyle had once again argued, that it was Christopher's bride-to-be they were after. Were they to encounter danger, Christopher would obviously be the first one to fall. Doyle could lead the way once in a while, but no, he refused. And then he was always preoccupied with his missing fingers. He incessantly scratched the scars until they were raw and bled, then had to be bandaged.

Those were the glaring and major irritants, and they were largely the source of Christopher's growing resentment. But soon, the smallest things that his blood brother did set him off, such as his whistling; his pointing out of a particular bird that struck him as odd or colorful; his recalling the glory days of his first battle; and even his occasional snoring at night. In his mind's eye, Christopher saw a pair of horns growing from his friend's head, and he wanted to ram those horns into a tree and continue on alone with his journey. Then he would no longer have to listen to Doyle's I-am-older-and-wiser-than-you tone of voice. He would be able to end a day's travel when he wanted to, not when Doyle said so.

"I'm stopping here," Doyle said.

Christopher neither turned around nor stopped. He heard Doyle mutter something to his rounsey, then noticed the sudden silence behind him. Somewhere deep inside, he had expected Doyle to resignedly follow him, not take up such a defiant position. After all, Christopher had resignedly heeded a lot of Doyle's wishes, and now, for the first time, he wanted Doyle to listen to him.

Whether it was the cold that snarled up his back and bit his nose and cheeks, the anger that was the only thing that completely filled his stomach, the frustration that made his teeth grind every time he thought of Seaver and Marigween out there, out of reach, or the plain and simple fact that Doyle had insulted him, Christopher did not care. The only thing he knew now was the desire to let his friend know how he felt. Truly know.

He stopped, dropped his reins, then ran back toward Doyle, whose gaze was trained on the blanket he was in the process of unfolding. Christopher seized his friend's shirt in his hands, just as the former archer looked up and realized what was happening. Christopher threw

Doyle backward toward the hard, winter earth, and as he released his grip on Doyle's shirt, Doyle seized his wrists and dragged him down. What little wind was in Christopher's chest escaped with choking abruptness as he rolled off of Doyle and landed on his back.

"What madness is this?" Doyle screamed.

Christopher rolled onto his stomach, rose to his hands and knees, and crawled toward Doyle. "You're going to listen to me from now on!"

Doyle sat up, and, with surprising ease, he thrust himself to his feet — even before Christopher had time to react. "It doesn't matter if I listen to you or not!" Doyle replied, the whites of his enraged eyes igniting the darkness of the forest. "Nothing matters anymore. Nothing. Do you hear me? Nothing!"

Christopher stared at Doyle. He panted and felt his anger slip from him like sweat. He closed his eyes as the reality of what he had just done hit home. Doyle was right. Nothing mattered. Nothing. And nothing made sense. Doyle was helping him, yet he had struck out at his friend. Why? Why had he grown to despise the very person who had helped him for these past moons?

He shivered. The boughs of the surrounding trees rustled with a breeze, and he heard leaves swirl at his feet. Slowly, with his eyes still closed, he stood, drew in a deep breath, then opened his eyes. He looked at Doyle, whose countenance was masked in shadow. "I'm sorry."

Abruptly, Doyle turned, fetched his blanket then crossed to his rounsey. He took his reins in his hand, then began to trudge off in the direction of Christopher's mount.

"Where are you going?"

"There," Doyle said angrily.

"Where?"

"I don't know, Christopher. You tell me."

*   *   *

Fifth Moon:

It was a small inlet shared by three tofts. At the shore
was a single quay with two small rowboats moored to it.
The main houses were set well back from the beach,
with the bluffs at their shoulders and their snow-
covered fallow fields sweeping out like long, wintry
doormats in front of them. Smoke rose from the vent
holes in the thatched roofs of the houses. There was a
windmill between the first and second house, but two of
its blades were wrecked, probably having been blown
off in a storm or having been so heavily weighted down
by snow that they had snapped off.

The midday sky was of a color better forgotten. Had
it been sunny, Christopher's spirits might have lifted a
little. After all, they were approaching a bit of civiliza-
tion, could hopefully get something warm to eat, then
perhaps find a warm place to spend the night. But the
past score of days forging along the coastline had
stripped him of nearly all of his happiness. Doyle's
words rang repeatedly in his head. *Nothing matters.*
Nothing matters. He wondered why he even looked for
Marigween and Seaver anymore. It seemed a fool's
quest now. Every part of his body seemed to hang too
heavily from him. With each footstep he had to repress
the desire to collapse. All he wanted now was to sleep.
To sleep away everything.

They reached the first house, and Doyle knocked on
the door. An old, rotund woman appeared from behind
the door, and, after taking one look at them, her mole-
dappled jaw fell slack.

Christopher spoke to her in Saxon, but she frowned,
drew her shoulders together and shook her head negatively. He tried a greeting in Celt. She smiled and
returned the greeting. Doyle pressed their last two
deniers into her palm, and she pulled them inside the
house. In the moments that followed, they met the old

woman's husband, a man whose face had so many wrinkles there seemed scarcely room left over for a mouth, nose and eyes. Soon, the four of them sat down to the warm meal Christopher had been hoping for. As they ate, Christopher answered the couple's questions, filling them in on his quest to find Marigween.

"What's north of this inlet?" Doyle asked the old farmer.

"Not much," the man admitted, "'less you go all the way on up to Ivory Point. That's a Saxon port, to be sure though."

Christopher and Doyle exchanged a look. Christopher asked, "How long would it take to get there from here?"

"Better part of a moon. Providing it doesn't snow." The man let his gaze lift to the ceiling. "And it will."

They spent the night at the old couple's farm, and left early in the morning before the two rose from their slumber. Halfway through the day, the old man's words came to pass, but he had only mentioned snow.

Not a blizzard.

Sixth Moon:

If Christopher never saw the color white again in his life, he would not miss it. And if never the felt the cold or the wind again, he would not miss them either. If he never saw another snowflake for the rest of his life, he would still get along quite nicely. The storm had lasted nearly seven days, and at night they had dug themselves burrows in which they had slept. On the fourth night, Doyle's rounsey had died, and on the fifth, Christopher's had also fallen for good. By the time the sky turned blue, and the sun threw a blinding glare off the snowy landscape, it was already too late. Though the weather was with them now, their hearts rebelled. Christopher knew Doyle was ready to give up — even though his blood brother might never admit to the fact.

They would not be able to reach Ivory Point. They
would be lucky to make it back to the inlet. He offered
the facts to Doyle, who looked at him for a long time, then,
as expected, turned his gaze away and remained quiet.

"Do you believe I'm wrong?" he asked his friend.

Doyle kept his head lowered, staring at the snow,
which rose up just past Christopher's ankles. He cleared
his throat. "Do you want to go back?"

"Do you?"

Turning his head, Doyle surveyed the towering drifts
of snow that blocked their path, and Christopher could
not be sure, but his friend looked to be as humbled by
the snowscape as he was. "I'll go on if you want to."

"But you want to give up," Christopher pried.

"I'll go on — if you want to," Doyle repeated, a
noticeable edge in his voice.

Christopher grimaced, for his skin was cold and tight,
and it felt like it might crack and drop off of his face. He
closed his eyes down to slits.

How can I give up?

*You have to live. If you die, there will never be any
hope for her. Hope lives with you.*

*What hope will there be for her now — if I abandon
the search?*

She's strong. She'll live. You'll find her.

One day.

Forgive me, Marigween.

Christopher blinked away his emerging tears, then
turned back to the trail of deep prints they had left in
the snow. "Come on," he muttered to Doyle.

There was little sun around Tania now. Scarcely any
light at all. The edges of the home she knew as
Blytheheart had darkened and closed in to a point. She
heard the baby she had found behind her toft cry one
last time before there were no more sounds, no more

point, only a sea of darkness where the only thing she felt was peace. The knives of the sickness were gone.

She floated toward a distant, shimmering island. From the shimmer, a glittering hand reached toward her.

4 Doyle and Christopher entered the Bove Street Inn. They stepped into the foyer that led to the main dining room, then set their sacks down. Doyle glanced at Christopher. There was a tiny light in the other's eyes, and his cheeks bloomed a very pale red.

Twice during their journey home Doyle had tried to lift Christopher's spirits by telling him that he had made the right decision. Doyle had assured his friend that another time would come, but Christopher had barely paid attention to Doyle's words. His mood had gone from sour to nothing. He had worn a blank, emotionless stare and had spoken in a steady, almost whispery voice that had conveyed little feeling.

But now there seemed to be life in Christopher's face. And Doyle felt a heat enter his own cheeks. He had waited eleven moons to see Jennifer. He needed her to be here, needed for nothing to have happened to her.

"Boy?" he called to a passing scullery lad who struggled with a stack of dirty plates. "Is Morna here?"

"She's in the kitchen," he cried, then hurried around a corner. "I'll fetch her." A second later they heard a crash of plates, then —

"You clumsy oaf!"

"It was an accident!"

Doyle flipped Christopher a small smile. Christopher's return smile was wan, but there.

They stood there like guests waiting to be greeted, though Doyle knew they were not. The time away had brought back the formality of entering the place, as if for the first time.

Morna bustled into the foyer. She was as large and gaudy as Doyle remembered, though her hair seemed a tad grayer at the temples. When her gaze fell upon them she stopped, gaped, and then her gaze lifted to the rafters. "Jennifer? Monte?" she called loudly. "They're back!"

She rushed to Christopher and hugged him as if he were a lost son. As Doyle watched, knowing the same was in store for him, he began to feel even more uncomfortable than he already was. Before he knew it, Morna's too-ample bosom was squashed against his chest and her thick arms had his own arms pinned at his sides.

A shirtless Montague entered the foyer first. The wound on his shoulder had healed but had left a deep scar where hair refused to grow. He pulled his breeches a little higher over his sagging belly, then stopped, beaming.

Doyle politely pried his way out of Morna's embrace, took a step toward the brigand, and returned the other's grin. "I thought you wouldn't be here, Monte. I thought you'd be chancellor of Blytheheart by now and living in the big house."

The fat man embraced him as roughly as Morna had, slapping him on the back several times. He pulled back and answered, "I thought so too, laddie."

Before they could speak further, Doyle spotted Jennifer over Montague's shoulder. An imaginary hand rose up through the wooden floor of the inn, seized Doyle's heart, and shook it violently. Noticing Doyle's gaze, Montague cocked his head toward Jennifer, then took several steps backward. The fat man had cleared the path. Nothing stood between Doyle and Jennifer, not distance, not time.

But Doyle's boots felt bolted to the floor. He watched her glide toward him. She brought a hand up and pulled on his beard, then ran a finger along the length of his hair, from center part on down. "You need a haircut," she said softly.

Jennifer's hair looked different as well. Her blond locks were longer, and maybe lighter than he remembered them — or had his memory failed? He was not sure. The discrepancy hardly mattered. "Will you cut it for me?" he asked.

She leaned in close. "If you kiss me," she whispered.

He looked at Christopher, who was trying to find something to look at other than them, then to Morna, and finally to Montague.

Morna hemmed, threw Montague a look that might have said, "Let's leave them alone," then considered Christopher. "Young man? It's to the bath with you first. And then a feast. Sound good?" she asked.

Christopher nodded, then followed Morna and Montague through the foyer and into the main dining room.

"How come no one's asked —" Doyle began.

"Because she's not here," Jennifer interrupted. "It's obvious. If you had found Marigween, you would have brought her in here with you."

"You are all wise," Doyle admitted. "I think he appreciates that."

"It must hurt Christopher enough already. He does not need us to remind him."

Doyle nodded. He let his gaze fall quickly to her body and imagined her shift gone. Then he found her gaze. "About that kiss."

She closed her eyes as she wrapped her arms around him.

And the many moons of waiting were truly over.

*   *   *

Montague talked himself hoarse during their meal. He
told Doyle and Christopher that he had sold the Pict
cog at the Port of Magdalene and taken the others back
to Blytheheart on horseback, since sailing the stolen
ship back to Blytheheart would have been — to say the
least — bold and unwise. The journey from there to
Shores had been swift and happily uneventful. Orvin,
Merlin, and Brenna were safe and sound, and what was
more, word had it that Arthur was winning back the
castle from the Saxons. It was, however, a rumor since
there had been no way for the brigand to get close to
the fortress to have a look for himself with all of
Arthur's men cordoning the area.

The news from Blytheheart was not as uplifting.
There was still no sign of Christopher's son, and the
search had long been called off, though the monks all
kept a watchful eye when they were out. Marigween's
uncle Robert had been implicated in the theft of the
Pict cog by the abbot, had been imprisoned for a
short while, but was released because of the persever-
ing arguments of his brother monks. The Picts had
sent one of their battle lords to meet with the abbot
to demand reimbursement for the cog. The abbot,
under the threat of an attack, had been forced to
make the payment, and was now passing on that
expense to the citizens of the port, levying higher
taxes. Thankfully, the merchant trade was busier than
ever, and the number of ships docking at the port had
nearly doubled. The higher taxes seemed to be
defrayed by the sheer volume of business passing
through Blytheheart, and, Montague explained, a
noticeable increase in the port's population. The fat
man was bold enough to add that their theft of the
Pict cog had not really mattered, since the abbot
would have raised the taxes anyway, according to the

volume of trade. Doyle suspected he had said that for
Christopher's benefit, hoping to alleviate some of the
squire's guilt over having affected the lives of everyone who lived at the port.

After the meal, Doyle and Jennifer retired to a room.
She dragged a window chair away from the sill and gestured that he sit in it. She wrapped a linen towel over
him, left the room for a moment, and then returned
with a small pair of scissors.

"Do not make it too short," Doyle warned her, his
voice lifted by the fear that she might give him a pudding-
basin cut, a style he loathed. "And no bangs. Please."

She giggled. "I won't ruin you. I'm the one who has to
look at you, remember?"

He sighed. "Go ahead."

She clipped. He winced. This went on for a while,
until she said, "I was beginning to believe you were not
going to return."

"For a time I believed the same," he answered. A bit
of hair fell onto his nose and made him itch. He swatted
it away, then closed his eyes.

"I prayed you would come back."

"Did you really pray?" he asked. "Do you get down
on your hands and knees and ask God to bring me
back?"

She withdrew her scissors and circled to face him.
"What is that supposed to mean? You don't believe me?"

"No, I — I mean yes, I believe you prayed. But what
about God?"

"What about Him?"

"Obviously you believe in Him," he noted.

Her frown deepened. "Yes."

"You've had a rough life thus far."

"What does that have to do with —"

"Don't you get angry sometimes? Angry at Him?"

Jennifer's frown slipped into a look that might have

been pensive. She stared past him and out through the open window. "It's not His fault. It's simply what happened. Or happens."

"I resent Him sometimes," Doyle admitted. "For my hand. For my parents. All of it. He's supposed to be gentle and kind and forgiving. Why has He done this to us?"

She turned from the window, stared him directly in the eye, and then touched his cheek. "To bring us together."

The next morning, in the yard outside the stables, Doyle checked Christopher's saddle straps to make sure all were secure. "You're ready," he reported, then stood back to rejoin Morna, Jennifer, and Montague.

"Thanks, Doyle," Christopher said, from atop his mount. "I wish you could come back with me."

"No fear," Montague said. "We'll keep him safe and busy" — he eyed Jennifer, winked — "and loved."

"Safe home," Doyle told his friend. "And give Arthur my regards. Tell him there is no bitterness in my heart." Doyle meant that, and he wished he could tell it to the king himself.

"I will." Christopher regarded Morna. "And thank you," he said with a shrug. "The words are plain but all I have." Christopher pursed his lips. He heeled his mount, reined the horse around, then trotted away toward the bluffs.

"I wish he had found her," Morna said as all of them watched Christopher leave.

"She may be dead," Montague noted soberly.

"She's alive," Doyle said, "and we're not done looking for her."

"What do you mean?" Jennifer asked, then grabbed his arm.

"Yes, tell me, laddie," Montague joined in. "*This* I want to hear."

5   The practice field below the castle of Shores
was cast in twilight. Christopher trotted into the field,
and soon he gained a clearer view of the castle's western wall.

Or at least what was left of it.

Nearly half of the heavy stone rampart had been
smashed away, exposing the outer bailey. The wall that
made up the inner bailey had also been mangoneled
apart, and he could now see the outer wall of the first
story of the keep. It was as if a giant had come along
and taken several vicious bites out of the fortress.

That giant was, of course, King Arthur.

Christopher rode on toward the castle, and he was
struck by more and more of the devastation. He was so
transfixed by the ruined structure, he barely saw anything else. Then he heard the charge of a horse and
looked down.

A mounted figure drove hard from the east, toward
him. He glanced curiously at the rider a moment, then
took up his crossbow, which was already windlassed.
He nocked a bolt, then leveled and aimed the weapon.

"Christopher!" the rider called.

After another moment, Christopher recognized the
rider's squat frame. "Neil? What are you — how did you
know I'd be —"

"We've watchmen all around here now. One of them
spotted your approach," Neil answered before
Christopher could finish. "And he happens to be a
friend of mine. All of which is to say that luck brings me
here to welcome you!" He reined his courser to a halt. It
was a magnificent mount, reminding Christopher that
he had been away from such excellent steeds for far too
long.

"We've much to talk about," Neil added.

Christopher eyed the castle. "That we do."

Neil took the hint. "They're gone, Christopher. It's been a glorious day. The battle is won. The castle is ours. Arthur stands in it now."

"Stands in what? A pile of rubble?" Christopher asked dryly.

"Always a price to pay, eh?" Neil said, taking the fact a bit too lightly for Christopher's liking. "Now. Let's ride back," he said, steering his mount around. "Brenna told me all about Blytheheart and that Pict cog. You tell me about the trip north. You didn't find her?"

Christopher goaded his rounsey to join the other horse, and as he came alongside Neil, he answered, "No."

"I'm sorry," Neil said, his voice low and sympathetic.

"Not as sorry as me. Now. Take me to King Arthur."

The great hall of the castle of Shores — the one Christopher remembered from his youth, the one where he had been proclaimed squire of the body of all of Britain — was a smoldering, acrid storehouse for debris. In the light of two torches burning from wall sconces, he saw a jagged, gaping hole six yards wide in the east wall of the room where a mangonel stone had broken through. The stone lay on the opposite side of the hall amid piles of charred rafters and wooden floorboards that in some places rose well over Christopher's head. He lifted his gaze and was able to see all the way up to the stone roof of the keep. It dawned on him that every floor between here and the rooftop wall-walks had gone up in flames and then had collapsed into the great hall. The main fires had probably been extinguished days before, but it would take some time before the smell and faint wisps of smoke finally diminished.

He probed deeper into the wreckage and spotted a crushed shield, then a crossbow bolt sticking from a beam, and then a mangled pike. He expected to find a body or two, but thus far there were none; they must have been cleared away. He was glad for that. The place reminded him of the burned-out chapel where he had found his parents murdered. He remembered coughing hard and feeling his guts attempt to turn inside out. The smoke had taken its toll on him. The smoke, and the Saxons.

The nausea returned, but then diminished as he purged the past from his mind.

"Quite a mess, wouldn't you agree?" someone asked from the other end of the room.

Christopher stepped forward, and, after rounding another pile of rubble, he found Arthur. The king wore a simple pair of breeches and drawstring shirt, and he sat cross-legged in a corner, resting his chin in a palm. The pose was uncharacteristic of a king, childish and odd, Christopher thought as he nodded.

Arthur thrust himself up and groaned a bit over his apparently stiff muscles. "That Kenric was a stubborn one. In order to save the castle we had to destroy it." He eyed the rubble with contempt, and now it was clear to Christopher that the king was troubled. His odd pose had been a result of something boiling within him.

"Thank you for seeing me, my lord," Christopher said. "I know that Merlin and Orvin have informed you of what has happened to me —"

"From the time you left them at Magdalene," Arthur interjected. Watching his step, he moved into the center of the room. "Come closer. I can't see you very well in these shadows."

Christopher complied and brought himself to within a yard of his liege. Arthur had changed very little; his eyes were still as green as the slopes of the Mendips in spring, his hair and beard still as dark as the Savernake forest. "Can you see me now, my lord?"

"I can. And what I see before me is —"

"I beg your pardon, my lord," Christopher broke in quickly, sensing that Arthur was ready to pass judgment on him, "but if I may tell you exactly what happened in the eastern wood —"

"I already know what happened," Arthur pointed out, silencing Christopher with a wave of his hand, "and I believe your story as you told it to Orvin and Merlin."

Christopher sighed.

"But you were wrong to lie to me," Arthur continued, his tone dropping to uncomfortable depths. "You lied to me and to the battle lords. You knew that Woodward was dead — and yet you lied."

He swallowed back his premature sigh, then felt a shudder wipe across his shoulder. "I wanted to speak to you in private, my lord. I feared the battle lords would not believe me. I did not want them to know."

Arthur pursed his lips and shook his head negatively. Then he said, "I must tell you that Lancelot has had several meetings with the battle lords. They believe it was you who murdered Woodward." Arthur ran a hand through his hair, tugged through a tangle, then scratched the back of his neck.

Christopher clenched his fists, not in anger, but in a battle to remain stiff, standing, fighting off the urge to throw himself at the king's feet. "But you believe me, my lord. You said so. And you are the king. Is that not all that matters?"

Arthur puffed air in disgust, turned away for a moment, as if brooding over something, then finally regarded Christopher. "When one of their own was struck down, the battle lords warned me that justice must prevail. They told me that someone must pay for the murder. If there is no justice, there is nothing."

"Then the true murderer must be found," Christopher concluded.

"If I overrule the battle lords, I will lose their loyalty. I have worked very hard for this union. I need their skill and their respect. I must build a new realm. And justice must come to pass."

Christopher's eyes burned with these facts. He shuddered again, then a second and third time. "If they believe I am guilty, then . . ."

"On the morrow you will stand before a council. You will be heard along with them. Afterward, I will make my judgment."

"Will I be shackled now?"

Arthur nodded. "And you'll stay in my tent. Woodward was a friend to many. Their bitterness runs deep." The king gestured toward the archway exit behind them.

"One more item, my lord?"

"What is it?"

He paused, ordering and reordering the words in his head until finally he could hesitate no more. "Your horse. I —"

"That junior squire you have been training — Clive, I believe his name is? — he came to me one morning and told me what he had done. Merlin informed me of the animal's accidental death."

"I will do whatever I must to repay you," Christopher said emphatically.

"I'd worry more about your life now than the repayment of a horse," Arthur said, putting it all into perspective. "I've had time to get over that loss, time to get over my anger." His gaze went out of focus as he looked up past Christopher. "There once was a face that launched a thousand ships. Men would do anything for her. So it was with you."

6   Brenna found Christopher lying faceup on the trestle bed. His wrists were bound in heavy iron manacles and resting on his belly, and his ankles were shackled as well. His eyes were closed, and in the shade of Arthur's tent, his hair and beard looked longer than they actually were, drawn out by the shadows. He resembled a shaggy highwayman, and his manacles were the result of a criminal's life. Gazing at him now, it was hard to remember that he had once been squire of the body.

She stood at his bedside, wondering how she would wake him. She thought her argument with the guards outside the tent would have stirred him, but his slumber was deep. She thought of kissing him awake. She thought of peeling off her shift, sliding into the bed next to him, and running her fingers through the soft hairs on his chest. She thought of all the nights she had spent thinking about him before closing her own eyes to rest. She had played over all that had happened to them, the journey to Blytheheart, the stealing of the Pict cog, their good-bye at Magdalene. She thought of the night he had asked her to marry him. She hung on to that moment, hung eternally it seemed. But the wishes and memories and everything else that crashed and foamed like midnight waves inside her meant little now.

He might be sentenced to hang. This might be the last night she would talk to him alive. If Neil's plan did not work, this would be their final good-bye. The more she thought about that, the more she wanted to cry. And the tears came as they often did, swiftly and uncontrollably. She leaned over him, and a tear ran off of her cheek and fell onto his.

His eyes opened, and he blinked the world into focus.

"Brenna?" he asked, rasping, his voice rusty from the disuse of sleep.

She wiped her eyes. "I'm sorry. I know you must be tired. It's a long ride here. Too long."

He sat up. "I was hoping Neil would tell you I returned."

She sniffled. "He did." She wiped her eyes again, drew in a deep breath, let it out, then realized she was trembling. "I'm sorry you didn't find them, Christopher. I know you may not believe me, but it's true."

He looked at the edge of the bed. "Sit down." As she did so, he covered a yawn with a palm, and his chains jingled. "I — I have to start getting used to the fact that they're gone. That's going to take a long time."

"I know."

"Do you really?" he asked, furrowing his brow.

"Yes I do," she replied. "And sometimes you never get used to the fact. Sometimes you hang on and can never let go."

He softened a bit. "It will never be the same for us, you know that, Brenna, don't you? I cannot simply forget about my son and Marigween and leap back into your arms."

"I wouldn't want you to do that," she said.

"Yes you would."

She shook her head slowly, no. No. "I lost you. You lost them. We're both wounded soldiers, as it were. And the wounds need time to heal."

He nodded. "How is your arm, by the way?"

"If I move it in certain ways, it hurts a little. And sometimes it keeps me up at night. But Merlin's poultices worked."

"Good." He stroked his thin beard. "Have you heard about the council on the morrow?"

Brenna nodded. "I'm worried." She bit her lower lip and wondered if she should tell Christopher about Neil's plan. Neil had insisted that Christopher not be told, for he would surely be against the plan.

"I don't think Arthur can help me this time," Christopher said. "They could sentence me to hang."

"They have yet to hear your account," she said, her voice rising. "You have to make them believe you."

He smirked. "Their ears are already deaf, I assure you. Woodward was shot. I fled and have been gone for nearly twelve moons."

"If you are guilty, then why would you return?" she asked.

"Perhaps out of remorse. They probably believe I've come to pay my debt."

She huffed over his resigned attitude. "Then you have to tell them why you fled. You have to explain everything to them. It all happened at once. It was not your fault."

His sigh was very long and very loud. "I'm sure they've already heard why I fled. And they all know about the child I had out of wedlock with Marigween. They see me as a fornicator — and a murderer."

Brenna's anxiety brought her to her feet. "But everyone knew Marigween would not have him. She would have taken her own life first."

He ripped the blanket off his lap. "That has nothing to do with it. The only way I will be found innocent is if the real murderer appears and confesses."

There it was again. She shook with it. If she could only tell him that they had a plan.

No. Neil is right.

He collapsed onto his back, sighed again, swore under his breath, then stared at the sloping ceiling of the tent. "What's happened to my life? Maybe Father was right. I should have been a saddlemaker — then none of this would have happened. Now please, leave me, Brenna."

Now was the time to be strong, not to feel sorry for himself. She wished he knew how much she cared for him, how much all of his friends cared for him. He had seen it in the past, but had forgotten too easily. He'd already condemned himself. If he only knew how desperately his friends wanted to save him.

7

Marigween finished packing the cauldron with the stew, boiled fish, and oatmeal pudding. She began to lift the pot, wanting to bring it to the hearth where Seaver had built a fire, but it was far too heavy for her.

"Let me do that," Seaver said. With tiny Devin slung in one arm, he stepped fully into the main room of their farmhouse.

"All right." She set down the cauldron's handle, went to him, and reached out to accept her baby.

Before Seaver handed her the child, he lifted the boy in the air and shook him a little. "Would you look at this strong boy? Would you look at him?"

She smiled. Oftentimes she wondered if Seaver loved the baby more than she did — despite the fact that the child was not his. Was it possible? His actions said it was. "There," she said, accepting Devin. "Mother's going to feed you now."

While Seaver went to the table and lifted the cauldron, she took Devin to the rocking chair in the far corner of the room, and settled down. She loosened the drawstring on her shift and exposed one of her breasts. Devin drank heartily.

Seaver groaned as he wiped his hands and stepped away from the hearth, then he went back to it to double-check that the cauldron hung securely from its chain above the fire. "I think you have this pot loaded up even more than mother used to — and that is difficult to believe."

Marigween felt a pang at the mention of Edris. She had only known the woman for five moons, but in that time she had learned enough Saxon to hold simple conversations with her. She was glad to have been able to thank her in Saxon for midwifing Devin. Nearly a moon had passed since Edris's passing. Her death had turned Seaver into a boy whose emotions were readily displayed. The strong shield he had held up for so long, the one that had helped them escape from the cog and drive all the way north to Ivory Point, had fallen. And Marigween couldn't be sure, but it was that pouring out of Seaver's heart that had probably brought her as close as ever to him.

How had hate gone to tolerance, then to friendship, and then to love?

She watched him go to the window and draw in a deep breath through his nose as he inspected the toft. "The summer will be cool. And the rains will come. I can smell them." He laughed. "My father had gone from warrior to farmer. And so it is I follow his path. But I don't think his first crop was as rich and abundant as ours will be."

Marigween looked at him, and though she heard his words she ignored them. She realized how difficult it was to pinpoint where in the past twelve moons she had come to love him. Was it along the journey here, when she had grown ill and he had nursed her back to health? Was it the kindness he extended to her once in Ivory Point, kindness combined with an unconditional acceptance of her pregnancy? The child was a product of rape, yet he loved it like Christopher never would have. Was it that fact that made her love him? Or perhaps it was the situation as a whole? She had a home, a man who could easily become her husband and would provide for her; he had already proven that.

And what was most important, she had a son back.

A son. A child to care for, a boy named after her father who would remind her of him and fill the void created by Baines's loss. Seaver had made sure the things that had been absent from her life were now present: a father, a mother, a child, a home.

But did she truly love him? Or did she love him because she thought no one else would accept her the way he did? That question she could not answer, but she couldn't deny that what she felt for Seaver was love. After all, she was free to leave Ivory Point. Seaver had made that clear. But she had stayed. And he had been honest in everything he had done for her. There were no secrets, no lies.

He turned his attention from the window, looked at her, then smiled. "There is a glow all around you. I wish you could see it."

She did not have to see the glow. It was more important that she felt it. Life was not all that bad now. She thought of how it would be to grow old here.

A tapping sound came from the ceiling. And then more tapping. And then the tapping became a steady drone.

"There's our rain," Seaver said.

"I've never known anyone with eyes for the weather like you," she told him.

"Not eyes, but a nose," he said, then took a step toward her. "Do you remember the morning after Mother's pyre, when we were down at the port? Do you remember those sailors we bumped into?"

"How could I not? They knocked that grain sack right off of your shoulder," she answered, seeing the incident replay in her mind. "And they spoke Celt."

"Ah, yes, they were impressed. But one of them, he pulled me aside —"

"Yes, I forgot to ask you what he had said," Marigween broke in. "He thought you were a Celt, didn't he?"

"Yes. And he apologized. And then he told me he had never seen a woman as fair as you, nor one with hair as shiny and red as yours. He told me I had a beautiful wife — that I should treasure her."

"Did you tell him I wasn't —" she cut herself off, realizing what he was getting at.

"It might be premature, but I have been thinking about it since then. A troth. You and I. It's what I want. And I want you to think about it."

Marigween looked down, stroked Devin's head. "I will, Seaver." She hoped he did not notice her trembling.

8

The guards who dragged Christopher out of a sound sleep and out of Arthur's tent smelled like spoiling fruit. As they shoved him along the trail that led to the castle's north curtain wall, he asked them, "While I was gone, the king did not forbid bathing, did he?"

"No," the dumber-looking guard answered.

"Then why have neither of you exercised your free right to clean yourselves?"

"Insults will only serve up pain — murderer!" one of them shouted in his ear, then tripped him to the damp, rutted earth.

Gripping the back of his shirt, the two began to hoist him to his feet. Then Christopher saw a shadow pass over the ground that was etched by the rising sun.

"That will be all, guards. The king has instructed me to bring him." The voice was wonderfully old, wonderfully familiar.

Christopher looked into Orvin's eyes and saw the anger in them directed at the guards. He turned to the guard who had shouted at him. "You'd better heed Sir Orvin."

The two oafs released him, nodded politely to Orvin, then marched off, holding back their murmurs until they felt they were out of earshot — but were not.

Orvin rolled his eyes. "Peasant levy. Dolts."

Christopher raised his arms to hug his mentor, but he remembered his shackles. Orvin noticed them too, and he frowned and shook his head, an act that made Christopher feel embarrassed. He had let his mentor down. He crawled into a mental hole, hunkered down, and shivered there.

"Young saint who has traveled the realm far and wide. You have returned. And you look as bad as I," the old one said with a grin that was ugly and marvelous at the same time, for it began to lure him out of his despair.

"Look at me, Orvin," Christopher said, extending his arms, gazing at his manacled ankles, "this is what my life has come to. What happened to the days of the tournament? The defeat of Mallory? What happened to my rank?"

Orvin turned around, waved for Christopher to follow, then began walking. "There is nothing more powerful in the realm than a woman. She has the power to build a man — or destroy him."

Christopher sighed resignedly. "And I have looked too deeply into her eyes."

"As you always have, first with the raven maid and then again with Marigween. Your vision, your wisdom, your honor has too often been blinded by love." He wrapped an arm around Christopher's shoulder. "It seems to me that many aspects of squiring can be taught; but ah, loving, loving cannot."

"Tell me Orvin, where is the council to be held? Are the battle lords already there?"

"Forget the council, forget all that has happened. What are you?" Orvin asked, stopping dead in the middle of the trail.

"What do you mean?"

Orvin widened his eyes and seized Christopher's shirt at the collar. "What are you?"

"Uh, uh, a man."

"A man, just any man? No. A dead man? Maybe." Orvin released his collar. "No. What you are is a true servant. A servant to your heart, to your mind, and to God. Those who will judge you, they are no better. They are all servants. Their honor is no greater than yours."

"Honor? I've none left," Christopher said weakly.

Orvin's hand came out of nowhere and connected with Christopher's cheek. "Wrong! You've a lot of honor — honor you must defend now. You know your word to be true. And God will see that the truth is heard."

There were few times in the past when Christopher had seen Orvin as furious or as unraveled. It was as if the old man wanted to assume his place, but since he could not, he became a bellows to heat the fire within Christopher, a fire which began on the outside, on his face.

"All right. I believe you," Christopher said, rubbing his cheek.

"Be passionate, young saint. You will be defending your life!" Orvin swung around, then resumed his pace. "And you'd better do a good job of it."

Christopher hesitated. "Did you see anything, Orvin? Do you already know? Is it God's will that I'm to die?"

"What I know . . . and what will be . . . there's only darkness. But if darkness says something, we've a lot to worry about. Now come on."

A horse-drawn cart and driver waited for them at the end of the trail.

"What's this?" Christopher asked.

"You don't expect me to walk all the way there, do you?" Orvin answered with a question of his own, and a rather pronounced grimace.

"How far away is the council?"

Orvin waved the driver over to the rear of the cart, then answered. "We're going to the eastern wood. To the place where Woodward's body was found. That's where the council is being held." He regarded the driver. "You think you can get me on this flatbed? — because I sure as the day cannot make it up on my own."

After several unsuccessful tries, the driver was finally able to boost Orvin onto the cart. Christopher put his back to the flatbed and jumped up. He landed on his rump and then crawled around. Orvin's expression said he envied Christopher's agility. During the ride, the old man spent most of his time complaining to the driver, directing him to steer around the ruts and rocks in the path. Once they hit the perimeter of the field that led to the eastern wood, the ground leveled out, and the ride became smooth.

There was a curious peace that pervaded Christopher; it had come on slowly, and now fully blanketed him. He considered it a calm before the great storm brewed in that clearing of the forest. Before he knew it, they were threading their way through those trees and headed for that storm — but the calm was still there.

"Hold nothing back, young saint," Orvin said softly, following behind him. "And when you speak to them, move around, look into each of their eyes. Show them that truth fears nothing."

It had been raining the last time Christopher had been in the eastern forest, and its scent had been fully alive. Now, so many moons later, it seemed little had changed.

The rain was replaced by morning dew, but the strong, mossy odor was still here. The stretch of time that lay between the day Woodward had been murdered and the present was shrinking fast. The details of what had happened were returning with remarkable clarity. It was wise of Arthur to hold the council in the wood.

A fallen beech tree lay ahead; its thin gnarled trunk marked the entrance to the clearing. He looked beyond the tree and saw that a few of the battle lords stood in the clearing. Once on the other side of the trunk, he took several more tentative steps, and then stopped.

Sirs Carney, Gauter, Ector, Nolan, Bryan, Richard, Bors, Cardew, Allan, Uryens, Leondegrance, and Lancelot were all present. They stood around in knots of three or four, murmuring amongst themselves. Sirs Nolan and Bryan were inspecting the brambles, from where Christopher suspected the crossbow bolt had come.

As Orvin came up next to Christopher, the battle lords noticed their appearance, and as Christopher expected them to, they fell silent as they regarded him for a moment, then turned back to their conversations.

"When the king arrives I'll ask him to unchain you," Orvin said.

He nodded. Then, after a moment, said, "I wish Montague were here."

Orvin snorted.

"No, I do," Christopher said, gazing at the battle lords, at the way the sun filtered down through the canopy of boughs and cast a few in shadow, a few in light. "He'd be able to get me out of this — what with that mouth of his."

"He would lie to get you out of this," Orvin pointed out. "You forget that freedom rests on the foundation of truth. Now," he said, looking around, "why is it that my presence is always required in places that do not have comfortable seats?"

Christopher ignored Orvin as the old man shuffled a few steps away to find a place to sit down. His attention was drawn to the opposite side of the clearing, where, among the trees, he spotted as many as half a score of junior and senior squires gathering to watch the council. He noted the tallest of them and made eye contact with the young, blond-haired man, then averted his gaze. He was Robert of Queen's Camel, the new squire of the body, and Neil's friend.

"Christopher?"

He looked askance and saw Clive stride across the clearing, toward him. "Hello, Clive."

"I said a prayer for you last night." The young boy gazed shyly at Christopher's feet. "I wanted you to know that."

"Thank you. I'm afraid I haven't been a very good example."

Clive looked at him. "Yes, you have. All of us have been talking about you for moons, about how you risked everything to save someone you loved. You're gallant, Christopher, you are."

"With gallantry comes responsibility. And I failed to assume responsibility for what happened here. You, on the other hand, accepted the responsibility of stealing the king's horse and confessed to your crime. That is something to be proud of. *That* is gallantry."

Once again, Clive's gaze found the forest floor. "I thought you would be angry with me. I just couldn't hold it in anymore. The king told me he would have punished me even more severely had I lied about it. I spent three days in the stocks — the longest three days of my life."

"I'm not angry with you, Clive. You did what a knight would have done. Despite my inadequacy as a trainer, you still managed to find the right path. Stay there now."

"I will. And God help you this day, Christopher."

With that he turned and walked back toward his friends.

Christopher sensed the approach of someone from behind. He half turned to spot Brenna and Neil stepping over the fallen beech. They came toward him. Brenna carried a small basket covered with a thin linen cloth. As she got closer, she pulled away the cloth to reveal some pears and a small loaf of bread.

"Is that for me?" he asked her, his mouth already watering.

Brenna nodded. "I knew they wouldn't feed you. Guards don't think about such things until their prisoners are falling down with hunger."

"The king could've told them to feed me, but he has a lot on his mind," he told her, snatching the loaf and diving into it with his teeth. He bit off a large piece and chewed it heartily. "He's a land to rebuild."

"Are you ready to address them?" Neil asked, then added, "I know you have some sort of plan simmering in that head of yours."

He shrugged. "All I can tell them is the truth."

"The king!" a voice cried from the other side of the clearing. "Here comes the king!"

Christopher returned the loaf to Brenna's basket. "Thank you for bringing this."

Something was building in Brenna's eyes, a powerful emotion she seemed to be warring with — and losing. She said nothing, then closed her eyes, stepped up to him, and gave him a long, hard hug. She released him and turned away without looking.

"The truth, Christopher," Neil said. "You are right. Tell them the truth." He nodded his agreement, then turned to find Brenna, who had walked quickly off in a path that took her around the edge of the clearing.

Arthur marched forward, wearing his surcoat and a particularly ornate tabard. Merlin trailed behind Arthur, and when the druid spotted Christopher, he gave him a slow, serious nod.

The king looked at the crowd that had gathered around the clearing, then he frowned. "I thought this was to be a private council," he said.

"We could spend most of the morning driving them away, but I think it is wise to get this council underway," Merlin said to him. "If they are silent, they will pose no problem."

"I hope you're right, Merlin," Arthur fired back. Then he stepped to the center of the clearing and raised a hand. "Silence." The murmuring tapered off, but a few of the junior squires were still chattering behind the king. He whirled around to face them. "Silence!" The word trailed off and fell away into the chirping of the birds and the rustle of the leaves by the breeze. "Battle lords, you will come forward and be seated in a circle around this clearing."

"My lord, I beg your pardon," Nolan said, scratching an itch on his temple, "but you want us to sit on the dirt here?"

"Yes — without protest."

And Nolan was the first and last man to argue.

Slowly, the battle lords were seated in the ordered circle. There was something about this formation that struck Christopher. He would be standing in the middle of them, telling his story, looking *down* at them. They were not up on a dais, appearing high and mighty and very intimidating. The king had obviously planned this arrangement, and Christopher would thank the man for it, no matter how the council decided.

"Now," Arthur began, "we will first hear from Lord Uryens, who will speak for the council majority." Arthur moved to the perimeter of the circle and found a seat of his own on the ground.

Uryens had some trouble getting up, and one of his

junior squires rushed to aid him as the other battle lords began to hoot and guffaw.

"Enough!" Arthur yelled.

The laughs died off as Uryens moved to the center of the clearing and faced Christopher. "We, the council of battle lords, based on what we have seen and heard, do hereby accuse Christopher of Shores of the murder of Lord Woodward of Shores. It is pointless to drag through every minor detail. What we know is this: Woodward set a meeting with Christopher the day before the latter was to return to service. Woodward was found dead on the very spot in which I now stand. The morrow after, when asked about Woodward, Christopher lied and said he had not seen him, when, in fact he had left Woodward dead. And then the boy disappeared for nearly a whole year. Everyone who knew Christopher and Woodward or anything about the murder has been questioned." He looked Christopher straight in the eye. "The guilty finger points to you, boy. We've had many moons to make up our minds."

"Are you finished?" Arthur asked the battle lord.

He cocked his head to regard the king. "Not yet." He turned and began to pace along the perimeter of battle lords, firing occasional glances at Christopher. "Not only do the events — Woodward's murder, your lying and sudden disappearance — point the finger at you, but you had a reason to kill Woodward, didn't you?"

Though Uryens's gaze was now fully upon him, Christopher was unsure if he was supposed to answer. He looked to the king.

"Do you want him to answer?" Arthur asked the battle lord.

"I'll answer it for him, and I beg of you, I don't mean to shock everyone present. But Christopher here had a son out of wedlock with the former princess Marigween, a woman who all knew was betrothed to Woodward."

Uryens had set the crowd up for a gasp, and it was no surprise to Christopher that it came.

"You see," the battle lord went on, resuming his circular pace, "Woodward was a problem for Christopher. He had betrayed the very master he was supposed to serve. And when Woodward called a meeting out here, perhaps a private one to discuss their relationship, Christopher saw it as a perfect opportunity to rid a problem from his life. But he's not a very good murderer. He left many of his ends untied. And so we stand — excuse me, *sit* — here this day, and are finally able to mete out justice." Uryens returned to his place and was helped to the ground by his squire.

Christopher looked to Arthur, whose gaze found his. "Christopher, you may speak now."

He began to step into the circle when a hand seized the back of his shirt and yanked him backward. He turned to find Orvin standing behind him. "Wait here," the old man said. He moved in front of Christopher and went to Arthur, then spoke softly to the king. Christopher could not hear their words, but after a moment Arthur produced a ring of keys from his pocket and handed them to Orvin, who returned to Christopher. "I almost forgot, young saint," Orvin said as he unlocked Christopher's shackles. "Accept my apology."

Once free, Christopher took a moment to rub his ankles and wrists. "It's good to get them off," he said.

"This is not unlike combat, Christopher. Do not think, just act. And the truth will come," Orvin advised. "Now go."

Christopher stepped toward the center of the clearing, and he felt as if his heart were beating in triplets. The path between his mouth and stomach was tight and dry. For a moment, the sun flashed in his eyes and blinded him. He found a spot that was slightly off-center and out of the glare.

He regarded the brambles, and simply began. "The bolt came from there. Woodward had tossed me a sword, but I didn't pick it up. He came at me with his own blade." He cleared his throat and tried to gather spit; there wasn't much to be had. "You see, it was he who wanted to rid his life of a problem. Yes, I had betrayed him, and he wanted me to pay for that. Had that bolt not struck him down, there is no doubt in my mind that I would be dead." He turned around to face the battle lords behind him, their incredulous looks setting off all of his nervous twitches, the eyelids, the shaking leg, and a new one, the incessant rubbing of his wrists where the manacles had been. "After Woodward was shot, I fell to the ground myself, thinking I, too, would be hit. I waited for a long while. Then finally I got up. I didn't know what to do. I ran. And as you already know, I went to Sir Orvin and Lord Merlin. I told them what had happened. And as you also already know, I was forced to leave because Marigween put herself in danger — and I had to help her. She's lost now. But I had to try. That is the only reason why I left Shores."

"My lord, may I question him?" Uryens asked Arthur.

"You may."

As he turned to face the battle lord, the knight asked, "Couldn't you have asked Marigween to go to Blytheheart, thus giving you a reason to run?"

"I could have, but I did not. And I have the word of Lord Merlin to rest on." Christopher looked to the druid.

"He speaks the truth," Merlin said.

Uryens folded his arms across his chest in frustration. "Then tell me, Christopher, if we're to believe your story, then who is going to pay for the crime of Lord Woodward's murder?"

"The real murderer," Christopher answered, and that

brought a volley of laughs from the crowd, as it was all too obvious to them. "I believe one of two things. I believe the person who murdered Lord Woodward wanted him dead — or simply was trying to save me from being murdered, and is now too scared to come forward."

"You're wrong!" The shout came from the direction of the group of squires.

Christopher turned his head and saw Robert of Queen's Camel, squire of the body, shoulder his way past his peers to step between Sirs Cardew and Bors, and then come to rest in the clearing.

What is this dolt up to? Does he want to see me hang? Was he the one? Had Neil been wrong?

"Robert, why have you interrupted us?" Arthur asked him annoyedly.

"Because Christopher is wrong, my lord. The murderer is not too scared to come forward. I am the murderer. I shot Woodward with my crossbow."

The gasp that had followed Uryens's announcement that Christopher had fathered a child out of wedlock with Marigween was nothing compared to the one that shot through the crowd at the moment.

Another shout resounded above the growing cacophony, "No, my lord! He's wrong!" Neil charged forward and brandished his loaded crossbow. He whirled around with the weapon and swept its business end past the heads of the council members, who ducked and raised their arms for cover. He went on, "This is the very bow I used to save my friend Christopher from being murdered by Lord Woodward."

"Don't listen to him!" a woman screamed. Just as it dawned on Christopher whose voice it was, Brenna ran into the clearing and tore the crossbow out of Neil's hands. "He only wants to save me from punishment! I shot Woodward to save Christopher!"

9

Doyle had spent the week after Christopher left Blytheheart questioning as many sailors from as many ships as he could. He had spread the rumor that he would pay handsomely for some information on a red-haired woman who might be living in Ivory Point, or even farther north. Most of the Saxons who dwelled in Caledonia were dark-haired and of a much rougher complexion than Marigween. It had seemed to Doyle that if she was alive, perhaps living as Seaver's servant and or prisoner, she should be easy to spot.

And then Doyle had met two sailors who had accurately described Marigween. But what had been more, they had also described Seaver. That night, Doyle had sent word by way of carrier pigeon to Merlin.

Now, three days later, he and Montague walked down St. Thomas Lane toward the inn. Doyle could no longer hold back his frustration. "Why haven't we heard from them yet?"

"Calm yourself, laddie. You heard what the man said. The carrier pigeon probably just got there — if it did at all."

"He promised us it would. He gave us his best bird. It made it — and I know Christopher will come, no matter what the cost."

"He'll come, all right. But how can we be sure those sailors are right? How can we really be sure that red-haired woman up in Ivory Point is Marigween?"

Doyle narrowed his brow in thought. Then it struck him. "We'll have to go up there — to be sure."

"Oh no, we're not. I'm not riding all the way —"

"We'll sail this time. The weather's agreeable."

Montague huffed incredulously. "And who's going to

take us? Or should I ask, whose cog are we going to
steal this time?"

Doyle pressed on. "We will catch a ride on the same
Celt cog that brought us the information. She's been
docked for a while and will probably be shoving off
soon. She's headed up there."

Montague shook his head, *tsk*ing a half dozen times.
"Laddie, laddie. You want us to go up there and rescue
her for him?"

"We could do that."

"What if he doesn't want us to? You saw the way he
was with us. He's not fond of help; it makes him feel
guilty. And what if I don't want to? Aye, it's not our
business is it? And speaking of business, what about
ours? I've a revised proposition to offer to the abbot . . ."

Doyle crossed in front of his partner, then placed a
palm on Montague's beefy chest to halt the man. "If
Christopher could get here before the cog shoves off, we
could all go together."

Montague shot a look to the northeast where the cog
was docked. "He'd have to leave soon to do that. And
that still will not guarantee —"

"If he got the message on time, I'm sure he's already
preparing to leave," Doyle said, breaking in, feeling his
anxiety build over the idea of finally getting Marigween
back at Christopher's side.

Montague pushed past Doyle's palm and forged on.
"You forgot about that murder. What about that?"

Doyle turned and rushed to catch up with the brig-
and. "If he's not here by the time the cog draws anchor,
then we'll go without him."

"You might be going alone," Montague said out of the
corner of his mouth.

"You'll say that as you're boarding the ship, Monte.
You just want to be appreciated."

"And what's wrong with that?"

"Nothing."

They reached the inn and found Jennifer in the doorway, waving them forward. "Come on! Hurry!"

Doyle ran ahead of Montague. "What is it?"

"Come see for yourself!" Jennifer cried.

10

Arthur bolted to his feet. "You three! Hold your tongues!" he screamed at Robert of Queen's Camel, Neil, and Brenna, whom he pointed to and then gestured that she set down the crossbow in her hands. She did. "And the rest of you," he said, calming down, "will hold your tongues as well."

Christopher was dumbfounded over the spectacle which had just taken place. Here he was accused of murdering Lord Woodward, and now the squire of the body, Neil, and Brenna were fighting over who really committed the crime. Never before had he heard about or witnessed for himself criminals who bickered over credit. The average sane person would not fight over the chance to swing from a gallows tree. What were they up to? Was Robert the true criminal and Neil was trying to save him? Or was Brenna the true criminal and Neil was trying to save her? Or was Neil the true criminal and Robert was trying to save him?

If he continued asking himself these questions, he would become as insane as they were.

Arthur waved the three disrupters forward. They stood in a line before the king, and Christopher circled behind Arthur so that he could look at their faces.

"Would you like me to question them, my lord?" Uryens asked.

"No," Arthur said, peering over Robert's shoulder to

the battle lord. "Just listen." He regarded Robert. "Robert of Queen's Camel, am I to understand correctly that you are admitting to the crime of murdering Woodward of Shores?"

The squire's features were hard, set. "You are, my lord."

"And what of their claims?" the king asked, turning his gaze upon Neil and Brenna.

"What they say is not true."

Neil shook his head negatively. Arthur noticed this. "You disagree?"

"I do, lord. I, Neil of Shores killed Woodward. But in defending my friend's life." Christopher could hear the tremor in Neil's voice.

"My lord, if I may?" Brenna asked, and the tremor in her voice was even more noticeable than Neil's.

Arthur nodded.

"I have not kept my feelings toward Christopher a secret during past moons. I have always watched him. The night he went to meet Lord Woodward, I knew he was in danger. I followed him to this place and hid in those brambles over there," she said, pointing toward the bushes. "When I saw Woodward about to strike Christopher down, I had to shoot him. I had no choice."

Uryens sprang to his feet, stepped toward the middle of the clearing just behind the three suspects, turned back to the battle lords who were watching him, and then shouted, "This is preposterous! And all it really is, is a clever diversion by these three to confuse us, to take our eyes off of the real criminal — Christopher there — and make us doubt that he did it, when, in fact, he did."

Merlin, who had been leaning against a tree trunk, intently watching the proceedings, came forward. "A word if I may, King Arthur."

Arthur cocked his head to look at the druid. "Merlin, your wisdom has guided us for many moons now. If you've something to say that will throw a bit of light on all of this confusion, go ahead! Do so!" While Arthur had been keeping his temper in check, now it clearly threatened to explode.

"Lord Woodward is dead. And —"

"We know that, wizard!" someone shouted, and Christopher eyed the council to see if it had been one of the battle lords who had interrupted Merlin. They all stared innocently at the druid.

"To the stocks with the next person besides Merlin who opens his mouth," Arthur barked.

Merlin's soft, almost musical voice was given ample room. "What we have seen and heard is most confusing — even without these three coming forward and admitting their guilt. It seems to me that Lord Woodward had as much reason to kill Christopher as Christopher had to kill him. Would all agree to that?"

A few of the battle lords nodded, a few voiced their "ayes," while a few sat motionless and silent.

"Whatever you are getting at, I suggest you *charge* toward it," Arthur said.

The druid raised his palm, as if to ask for more time. "Christopher told me that he thought that the person who killed Woodward wanted Woodward dead or simply wanted to save Christopher. So we have two reasons why the murder occurred. But the truth of the matter is this: if the person who pulled the trigger on the crossbow did so because he or she wanted Woodward dead, then we have a murder. If not, if it was to save Christopher, then I believe we have something else."

"My liege," Uryens said, "if I may speak?" But the battle lord did not wait for Arthur's nod and quickly added, "The only people who know what happened in this clearing on that night are Christopher and Woodward. We may never know what truly happened."

Merlin stepped past Arthur, past the three suspects,

and walked up to Uryens. The druid stared at the much
younger man, who appeared to feel the heat of his gaze.
Merlin began, "You speak the truth, Uryens. That is why
if the council does not choose to accept Christopher's
word, then it also cannot punish him."

"But what about these three?" Uryens asked, tossing a
look to Robert, Neil, and Brenna. "If one them is the murderer, then I am wrong. Then there *is* another witness."

"And how are we to decide which of the three speaks
the truth?" Merlin posed. "All of them seem equally
capable of the act, and all them have a reason to help
Christopher or each other."

Uryens wrung his hands, then stared at his boots.
Finally, he looked up at the other battle lords, then he
regarded Merlin. But the druid had already turned away
and was headed back to his tree.

Lancelot rose from his seat. "My lord. How can this
crime go unpunished?"

"Was it a crime?" someone cried from behind the
knight.

The king's champion swung around and searched for
the shouter. "A man is dead, shot in the neck."

"Lancelot," Arthur called to the knight, who turned
around, "philosophy aside. Be seated." The knight complied as Arthur turned to the council. "If we believe
Christopher's word, then he is only guilty of lying to us
about what had happened and there is a killer — whom
we may never find — among us." He moved in front of
the trio of admitted killers. "It could be one of these
three, or not. The question as I see it will remain unanswered for now. We came here this day to decide the
fate of this young man," Arthur said, pointing an index
finger at Christopher, "and this young man alone. It
started here for him. And it will end here for him. That
is the kind of justice I want in our new realm. If you
doubt whether Christopher killed Woodward, then you

must accept his account of what happened here as true.
If there is no doubt in your mind that he killed
Woodward, then likewise you know what to do. Those
council members who believe Christopher did not kill
Woodward please rise."

Christopher looked upon the scene as if it were a
dream. He had managed to detach himself so far from
this reality that he felt as if he were floating among the
boughs overhead and looking down on the whole affair.
Yet, there was, underlying all of the false detachment
and glazed-eyed viewing, the very real notion that his
fate was about to be decided.

Here and now.

One by one some of the battle lords rose, each mus-
tering a murmur from those watching. Lancelot,
Leondegrance, and — surprisingly — Uryens stood.
After a long moment, when it appeared no other knight
would rise, Christopher counted the men standing

Six. A tie.

Of the six men seated, Christopher knew that four
had been close personal friends of Woodward's.

"Gentlemen. Are you sure about your decisions?"
Arthur asked the council.

The battle lords exchanged glances, and some nodded.

"Will not one more man rise with us?" Lancelot
asked. "Are you *that* sure of his guilt?"

Lord Nolan huffed. "Lancelot. You were the one who
could not believe this crime would go unpunished."

"It will not go unpunished," the knight corrected.
"But we must punish the right person."

Arthur drew in a deep breath. "If no other man will
stand, then I cannot base my ruling on this council's
suggestion, but on my own judgment."

Here it comes.

Christopher looked at Brenna. She tried to smile, but

could not. He looked at Neil, who winked. He turned
his head and spotted Orvin, who nodded. He returned
his gaze to the king.

"I cannot find Christopher guilty of this crime with
three others standing here wanting to admit to it. Their
presence makes me doubt his guilt. But not only that, if
they are here only to save him and they had nothing to
do with the murder, then it makes me admire them and
Christopher all the more. They are willing to give their
lives for their friend. And any man who keeps such
friends is worthy of my admiration." Arthur crossed to
Christopher. "You will be punished, but not for this
crime. I will decide later what that will entail." He
looked to the group. "This council is adjourned until
the morrow. At that time, we will question these
three."

The battle lords who were seated rose, and the crowd
shuffled into the clearing, perhaps thirty people all told.
Christopher bowed politely to the king and began to
turn toward Orvin, but Arthur stopped him with his
hand. "What is it, my lord?"

"You'll be leaving Shores immediately," the king said.

"Do you believe one of the battle lords will try to kill
me?" he asked.

"That is still a possibility, but not the reason I want
you to leave. Merlin told me he received word from
Blytheheart. A message from your friend Doyle. They
request your presence. They believe they've found
Marigween."

For a moment, Christopher's breath vanished. And
that moment was followed by an immediate decision.
"With your permission, my lord."

"Once again, your timing is most inopportune, but
you may go. You must," the king said.

Christopher bowed again, and this time he was able
to leave the king. As he moved toward Neil and Brenna,

62

6 2PETER TELEP

who were on the opposite side or the clearing, Clive
came up to him. "You told the truth, Christopher. And
it worked."

"Never forget. We're true servants, you and I." He
smiled at the junior squire, then left him behind. As he
neared Neil and Brenna, he shouted, "They found her.
Doyle thinks he's found Marigween. I have to go to
Blytheheart right away."

"Not again, Christopher," Neil said skeptically.

"I have to," he argued.

"God be with you," Brenna said softly.

He looked at her, at the sudden pain in her eyes.
"There is no way I could ever thank you for this."

"Just pray they don't find any of us guilty," Neil said.

"Here for only two days and already going," Brenna
observed. "Do not forget where your home is."

"Never."

11 Christopher set foot onto the Bove Street
Inn's stoop. Then he looked up, for the distinct and
somehow familiar sound of a baby crying came from a
second story window. He lowered his gaze and
knocked on the door, mumbling under his breath for
the child to stop its annoying whining. He was tired,
had traveled all night, and wanted some rest and quiet.
But the sound also reminded him of the way Baines
used to cry, and it was too early in the morning to confront painful memories. The only thing he wanted to
confront now was the staircase that would lead him to
a trestle bed.

The door swung inward, and Morna, wearing a long
night robe, her hair covered by a dark scarf wound

around her head, appeared in the foyer. "Good morning," she said softly.

"Early, I know, forgive me," Christopher said. Morna stepped back and gestured for him to come inside. He did, and she closed the door behind him. "Did you receive my message?"

She nodded. "Two days ago. We thought you would at least be another day. Did you take care of your mount?"

"The hostlers weren't up, so I slipped her into a stall myself, if that's all right?"

"Of course," she said, then turned toward the hallway that led to the staircase. "I know the others are anxious to see you."

"No, Morna. Don't wake them. If you've got an open bed, I'd love to lie down for just a little while," he said, fighting back a yawn.

"I've got an open bed, but I doubt you'll get any rest, what with your son crying as he's been all night."

What did she say? My son? "What?"

Her hand went to her mouth. "Oh, they're going to be upset with me."

He grabbed her hand. "My son is here? Where is he? Take me to him! Was that him I heard outside?"

"Yes, yes. Come on. I'm sure Jennifer is up." She turned for the hallway, and he followed her toward the stairs.

During the climb, Christopher wanted to run over Morna and dart for the room where his son was, but he held back his anxiety, and by doing so, suddenly felt very much awake. They turned down another hallway, and Morna paused before the second door on the left and knocked. Jennifer answered and was about to say something, but when her gaze fell upon Christopher, she simply closed her mouth and fully opened the door.

He rushed into the room, and there, lying on a trestle bed in the far corner of the room, illuminated by the

glow of the candles burning on two nightstands, was his
son. He lifted the boy into his arms, marveled at how
heavy the child had become, how dark and long his hair
had grown. "Baines, Baines, you little knight. Where
have you been? Did you go sailing like your father?"

He regarded Jennifer and Morna, who looked at him
with the child in his arms, expressions of amazement
locked on their faces. And it was only then that
Christopher noticed that Baines was not crying, not
making a sound, just lying contentedly in his arms.

"Everything is set, lads. Our passage has been booked,
she'll draw anchor on the morrow, and in three or four
days we'll be docking at Ivory Point. And don't forget
to thank Morna. She loaned us the money for this
excursion." Montague leaned forward in his chair at the
dining table, shoveled another heaping spoonful of
steaming porridge into his mouth, then swallowed
loudly. Unfortunately the brigand's aim was off-center,
and a good part of his lower mustache was now covered with the gruel. The fat man was, of course,
unaware of this, and it made his smile look all the more
silly.

Doyle, who sat across from Montague, half grinned at
Christopher. No, they would not tell Montague to wipe
his mouth. Then his friend rose. "Are you ready?"

He nodded.

"Where are you going?" Montague asked.

"There's someone he wants to thank," Doyle
answered, tipping his head toward Christopher.

They left the inn, and Doyle led him to the toft, all the
while talking about how much Jennifer loved taking care
of Baines, how excellent a job she did in every area
except keeping the small boy quiet. It was a short and
refreshing walk and they arrived in short order. He
rapped on the door of the main house.

The old man answered and stepped outside. "Good day, young men."

"Good day — Hayes is it?" Christopher asked.

"That's right. Who are you?"

"My friend brought me here because I wanted to thank you," Christopher half explained.

The old man frowned. "For what? Who are you?" he asked again.

"I am Christopher of Shores. And that child you turned over to the monks? He's mine. I just wanted to —"

"Oh, now I see," Hayes said, his tone suddenly growing dark. "Forget it. Were it my son you found, I would hope you would've done the same. Is that all?"

Hayes' curt behavior left a sour taste in Christopher's mouth, but Christopher understood it. "Uh, yes. Thank you. Again."

Hayes nodded abruptly, then turned back toward the door.

"And I'm very sorry about your wife," he quickly added.

Hayes paused. He answered without turning around. "She's the one you should thank. She thought your son would save her life. Perhaps he did . . . for a while." With that, he pushed in his door and shuffled behind it.

"What did he mean by that?" Doyle asked.

Christopher shrugged.

Doyle pursed his lips and shook his head. "Ah, the old ones. Will we ever become as strange as them?"

Christopher started away from the main house. "If we do, we'll probably never know it."

12

Ivory Point's trade fell somewhere in between that of the ports of Blytheheart and Magdalene.

As for weather, its summers were cooler and more windy than those of the other ports, pleasant actually, but its summers were wholly misleading. Christopher had experienced a little of the region's winter, and though he had never made it all the way to the port, he'd seen enough to know that Ivory Point was a fitting name for what became a white wasteland for at least four moons out of every year.

The Pict-Saxon alliance was found everywhere, on the signposts, the merchants' shingles, and in the conversations that often contained both languages or a variation of each. The captain of the Celt cog had instructed Christopher to speak only in Saxon, and for Doyle and Montague to remain quiet, that way they would avoid unnecessary questions. Celts were merely tolerated at Ivory Point, treated very much the same way Saxons and Picts were at Blytheheart.

The sailors that Doyle had questioned said they had seen Seaver and Marigween at the coastline, but that did not necessarily mean they had taken up residence nearby. Instead of scouring the entire port as they had attempted to do back at Magdalene, Christopher opted to ask a few merchants that had probably already done business with Seaver and Marigween. While describing the short man and red-haired woman to a baker who was pulling loaves out of his brick oven, they were overheard by one of the patrons, a sun-wrinkled woman in a coarse woolen shift who told them she believed those two lived up on the northeast slopes, on a toft that had once belonged to the short man's mother.

As a token of his thanks for the information, Christopher paid for the woman's loaves. They left the shop and headed for the toft.

"I've sharpened my dagger for him," Doyle said quietly as they walked up a narrow street that led to the outskirts of the port. "And when I see him, I intend to use it."

"We're not here for revenge," Christopher fired back. "We're here for Marigween."

A group of three men, who appeared to be construction laborers, ambled down the street toward them.

"Shut your mouths, lads," Montague said in a hushed but firm tone.

The men moved by them, nodded, and were gone without incident.

By late afternoon they believed they had found the toft. Furtively, they circled around the unfenced farm and moved into the tall pine trees that stretched up the slopes to the rear. There was a main house, two small barns, a well, and a small, single-story mill. The land was divided into three separate fields, two of which bore the green gridwork of cultivation, the other lying fallow.

"I still think we're dolts for waiting up here," Doyle complained. "I say we should go down there, bust in the door, slice his throat, and take Marigween."

"Suppose we go down there, bust in the door and discover we're in the wrong toft? What then?" Christopher asked.

The answer was all too obvious to Doyle. "Then we apologize and ask where we may find the right one."

"So we can bust that door in." Christopher shook his head. "We're not doing that. We're not doing anything until we're sure."

"I think we're sure," Montague called back. The fat man stood behind a pine trunk a few yards below them. "Come see for yourselves."

Christopher hurried down to the tree and joined Montague. Covering his brow, he squinted at the toft and saw a figure moving from the main house toward the well. He could not see her face, but her hair told him all he needed to know.

He burst from behind the tree and sprinted down the slope. "Marigween!" The wind whipped through his hair, and his eyes burned, but he would not remove his gaze from her. He drew closer, and her features came into focus. She looked up, then dropped the wooden pail in her hand and, for a reason that he could not fathom, she ran back toward the main house. "Marigween! Stop! It's me! It's Christopher!"

But she ignored him, rounded a corner of the house, and was gone. He barely felt the yellowed grass and dirt below his boots, barely felt the muscles working in his legs as he came closer to the thatch-roofed structure. He rounded the same corner she had, looked to his right, and there, there was the main door. He froze before it, and, panting, pulled the latch: locked. He pounded on the door. "Marigween! Open up! It's me! It's Christopher!"

Her reply was muffled by the door. "Go away!"

He continued beating his fists upon the wood. "No! Open up! It's me!"

And then the desire, which was a hammer that beat inside his head and heart, was too much to take. He jogged back a few yards, then made a running start. He turned to one side and slammed shoulder first into the door. The latch gave —

— and he found himself crashing into a wide room with a stone hearth directly ahead of him. His momentum brought him toward the hearth, but his foot was caught by something and he was tripped to the wooden floor, collapsing just a finger's length shy of the hearth's hard stone.

"No! It cannot be! It is you!" Marigween cried.

He rolled onto his back and sat up. Then, ignoring the pain of the fall, he rose to his feet. "I came for you, Marigween! I've been looking for so long!" He stepped toward her with his arms outstretched.

She took a step back.

Then came the sound of the shuffle of feet, and Montague and Doyle arrived in the doorway, both gripping daggers. "Where's Seaver?" Doyle asked, in what had to be his most threatening tone.

From another room came the cry of a baby.

Marigween turned away and strode into a narrow hall. Christopher held an index finger up to his friends: wait here, then he followed her. They moved into a small room, where, in a tiny, hand-carved cradle, lay an infant. Marigween lifted the baby into her arms and put its head over her shoulder. Then she patted its back. "There now, Devin. Don't cry. Shush. I'm here."

Doyle stepped into the doorway, and once again repeated his question. "Where's Seaver?"

Christopher tossed him a hard look.

Marigween's gaze favored Doyle. "Why should I tell you? So you can kill him?"

At the moment, Christopher could care less where Seaver happened to be. The child sparked a serious question. "Is this child yours?"

"Yes, he is," she answered defensively. "His father was Jobark, the captain of that Saxon cog."

Christopher turned his gaze away from her. "Dear Lord," he uttered grimly.

"I knew you'd feel that way," she said bitterly. He looked at her, then felt somehow incriminated by her scowl. "Get out!" she suddenly screamed. "All of you! Get out of this house!"

Doyle snorted. "I do not believe this!"

Christopher crossed to the doorway. "Wait outside," he ordered his friend, in *his* most threatening tone. "He might be coming back."

As Doyle resignedly turned away, he mumbled, "We come all the way here to save her, and what does she do? Throw us out."

After watching his friend leave, Christopher moved back inside the room. He took a now-cautious step toward Marigween, whose cheeks were stained with tear lines.

Once again, she retreated from his advance.

"Marigween. What happened to you?"

She pulled her baby closer to her. "What do you think happened to me? I was kidnapped. I was raped. You haven't figured that out?"

He had never heard nor felt the ice that was in her now. "I mean you," he corrected himself emphatically.

"I've a new life now, Christopher. I've a new son," she said, widening her eyes.

He stepped toward her, and she backed off. He kept coming, and backed her into the wall. "What did he do to you? What lies did he tell you?"

"He did nothing!" she retorted, her voice already hoarse from yelling. "I grew ill on the way up here and he saved me. He saved me from that Saxon crew. His mother midwifed my child! He's taken care of me." She paused to sniffle. "And he loves me."

Christopher found himself taking a step away from her, as if she had contracted something evil. "How could he love you? He's a barbarian."

"No more than you," she shot back.

"And you love him?"

She turned toward a window, flashing a defiant cheek. "I told you to leave." She sighed. "I'm sorry you came all the way here. But this is my life now — and you are not welcome."

"No," Christopher replied, shaking his head. "No, no, it cannot be true."

"It is."

He looked away, and then he thought of their child. "What am I to tell Baines when he gets older?" he asked.

She huffed. "Don't try to lure me away with lies. I know you haven't found Baines. He's dead."

Christopher looked at her, but she would not return his gaze. "Marigween. Listen to me. An old farmer's wife found him the night you were taken by the Saxons. She kept him. But then she died. Her husband brought him to the monks. He's at the inn now. He's waiting for his mother."

Her free hand coiled into a fist which she shook as she spoke. "Don't lie! I — I was just beginning to let him go — to let both of you go — and you had to come here."

"I know it's been a long time. But you couldn't have changed that much," he said.

She whirled and glowered at him. "Yes I have!" If her red eyes could, they would've flamed him to ashes. "Look at me! I'm filthy! I'm dirty! I have the child of a dead man in my arms! It's too late for me. Now go."

"It's never too late. Never." He raked a hand through his hair, and for the briefest of moments stood back in his mind to reflect on what was happening. How could he have ever suspected that she would want to remain with Seaver? Where had her feelings for him gone? To the Saxon? "Are you telling me you stopped loving me? Is that it?"

"I *had* to stop loving you," she said.

"Why?"

"Because of what happened to me!"

"You shouldn't have."

"It's already done. Are you going to leave?"

He wiped a hand across his cheek and blew out air. "I'll go, I'll go," he said. "I — I just have to know why you want to stay here."

"I'm accepted here, Christopher," she replied quickly. "He knows everything that has happened to me. And nothing stops his feelings."

"You think I won't accept you? You think I won't accept your child?"

"I do not think," she replied slowly, "I know."

Christopher sat cross-legged on a bed of pine needles, and he looked up through the natural lattice of boughs. The bellies of the cloud clusters were stained the pale orange of sunset. He studied the sky a moment, then said, "Perhaps it is you who have lied to me. Not you, God, but your sky. That room, that woman and child crying. What do they mean? Was it Marigween and her new child? Can they help me now?"

He dropped his gaze to the toft in the valley. All was still, save for the blades of the mill, which spun slowly, and the bucket hanging above the well, which rocked to and fro. Then he saw him, atop a rounsey, cantering toward the main house. He guided the horse around the building and dismounted before the smaller barn. He led the animal inside, appeared a moment later, then walked toward the main house.

"There he is," Doyle said, standing behind Christopher. "I've been waiting far too long for this. Monte? Let's go down and exact a bit of revenge."

Looking up over his shoulder, Christopher gritted out, "You've no right to do anything."

Doyle held up his bad hand and shook it with each word. "This gives me the right."

Christopher rose and turned around, just as Montague came trudging up next to Doyle. The fat man chewed something, probably a bit of the dried pork from his pack. Christopher looked back to Doyle. "I don't know what he's done to her — maybe nothing. But she wants to stay. Perhaps when he's not around, I can talk her into leaving. If we go down there and kill him, then she'll never forgive us — forgive me — for that."

"What does that matter?" Doyle said. "If we kill him, then she'll have to come with us. And eventually she'll forget about him the way she forgot about you."

Montague swallowed, then sighed. "No, laddie, that logic is as faulty as a rotted firkin. Christopher is right. If we kill him and take her, that makes us no better than the rogues who snatched her in the first place."

Doyle snickered. "Then what are we supposed to do: sit around for days while we wait for him to leave so that Christopher can go down there and maybe talk her into leaving? And if he doesn't, then am I supposed to walk around for the rest of my life with this hand — while that rat devil lives up here in bliss with a former princess?"

"Did you come up here for me?" Christopher asked, probing Doyle's eyes with his gaze. "Or for yourself."

"I came here so that justice could be done in both of our lives," Doyle replied, his tone softer.

Christopher considered Doyle's words as he wiped sweat from his beard. Then he reached a conclusion. "If we kill Seaver, in a way, we kill her. Do you understand?"

"He tried to kill you. He stole your bride-to-be. How can you sit here?" Doyle asked, flipping him a sardonic half grin.

Christopher lowered his head and closed his eyes. "What has it been, twelve moons? In all that time I never thought they would come to know each other, to actually — I cannot believe it — love each other." He opened his eyes. "My God, maybe she is right. Maybe I will never accept her. But I'm a fool! I should have remembered what happened to Garrett and me. I hated the man. Then I came to respect him. And it tore me up when he died. It's no different between the two of them. Then again, it is; it's deeper." He looked up to the sky. "Why didn't I see it?"

"I take it back, Monte," Doyle said. "He's been calm because he's gone mad."

Christopher turned around and bent down to pick up a clump of pine needles; he threw them as hard as he could. "I'm not mad. I'm just a fool. A fool for dragging you up here." He started walking. "Let's go."

"Go where, laddie?" Montague asked. "Our ride home won't be shoving off for another day or two, and I'm not sleeping there with all that loading and unloading going on."

"What about the inn?" Christopher asked, pausing.

"What about money?" Montague countered.

Christopher shot him an accusing look. "I thought you were taking care of that."

"An easy job. I've none to care for."

Doyle wiped a bead of sweat from his lip. "We've no money at all?"

"I wasn't sure how long we'd be here," Montague confessed. "And I frowned on borrowing more from Morna. She's done enough already."

"All right, then. "We've got packs. We'll camp here this eve. We'll go down to the cog on the morrow and ask the boatswain when she's drawing anchor."

Montague and Doyle reflected on that, and the fat man was the first to nod. Doyle followed him with a shrug and then a sigh of disgust.

"And don't try anything this eve," Christopher warned his blood brother. "You know I sleep lightly."

"What's this?" Montague asked, taking a step forward and squinting over Christopher's shoulder. Doyle noticed it too.

Christopher spun around.

There he was, the short Saxon whom Marigween now had feelings for, running from the main house to the barn. He vanished behind the door.

"He must be fetching his mount," Doyle hazarded.

Montague huffed. "Where's he going in such a rush?"

"He knows we're here," Christopher heard himself say.

Seaver appeared atop his rounsey. He quirted the horse into a gallop away from the barn. He was not headed in the direction of the port proper, but north toward another toft.

"You're right, Christopher. She probably told him we're here," Doyle concluded darkly. "We should have stayed there, waited for him, and killed him — like I said."

As he was becoming wont to do, Christopher darted off and headed down the slope toward the main house.

He crossed the stretch of grassy ground between the base of the slope and the house in what seemed like only a handful of moments. Out of breath, he arrived at the front door. "Marigween? It's Christopher again. Open up."

The door yawned inward, and there she was. She had the baby in the crook of one arm, and she looked as tearful as he had left her. He moved into the doorway. "Where did he go?"

"He's . . . I've never seen him like . . ."

Christopher turned and beat a fist on the front door. "You told him we were here?"

She nodded. "He . . . he went mad. He said he never finished Woden's work. I think he wants to kill you."

And her words came back to him. "Don't think," he corrected her, "know."

"I couldn't," she gasped, "I'm sorry. I just had to tell him. He kept asking why I was crying."

Christopher drew in a long breath and gathered his thoughts. "I'm going back to Blytheheart. I want you to come with me. Let me prove to you that I accept you." He raised his fist and spoke slowly. "Give me the chance."

"It's too late, Christopher," she said between sobs. "It's too late."

"Christopher?" Doyle called from somewhere outside. "Look!"

Christopher hurried to the doorway and saw that Montague and Doyle now jogged toward the house. The fat man appeared flushed and pressed a palm to his heart. Doyle pointed to the north, where three horsemen rose over a slope. Sunlight reflected off what had to be spathas in their grips. Apparently, Seaver had friends who were not only loyal, but available at the drop of a denier. Which was, of course, Christopher's luck. He craned his head, and fixed Marigween with a wide-eyed gaze. "Do you have any other mounts."

"There are two more rounseys in the barn," she said.

He flipped a look back to the horsemen, then back to her. He proffered his hand. "Come with me now."

She closed her eyes tightly and shook her head.

He took another look at the horsemen, then glimpsed at Marigween, who now sobbed into a palm.

You will be with me. Someday.

Christopher shot out of the doorway. "To the barn!" he screamed to his friends.

He ran around the main house, and as he did so, he felt a twinge of pain run through his calf: the old arrow wound. The pain sparked a bad memory that at this moment was darkly fitting, for it was Seaver's forces that had been responsible for the injury.

Christopher reached the barn, pushed in one of the doors, then limped inside. In the hazy light filtering in from the doorway behind him, he probed the barn for the horses. There, one, two, in the rear stalls on the right. Panting, he hobbled to the back of the barn, opened one stall door, then the other. Good and bad luck were almost evenly balanced: the mounts, though not saddled, were bridled, and their saddles hung on the wall behind them.

Doyle ran into the barn. "Why don't we stay and take them on?" he asked, as he came to a halt.

"It's not worth it," Christopher argued. "She won't come with me. Let's leave." He fetched the first rounsey's reins. "I'll ride behind you. We'll give Montague the other horse."

"I'll put my dagger against his sword any day," Doyle said.

Christopher replied through gritted teeth. "I know Montague wants to leave. If you want to take on all three of them yourself, then I won't stop you."

Montague trudged into the barn. "Lads, if they do not kill me, all of this running will."

"Monte, get over here and saddle up this horse," Doyle ordered his partner, then turned to Christopher and yanked the reins out of his hand. "I don't know where you think we're going to ride to . . ." Doyle led the rounsey out of the stall. Christopher took his friend's cue and removed the saddle from the wall.

"We'll get back to the cog, lads," Montague said, reaching for his own saddle. "If they try anything there, at least we'll have an armed deck crew to back us up."

"Maybe," Doyle said in an ominous tone, "but were I one of them, I wouldn't risk my life to defend passengers."

"Even if they do not help us, they certainly won't permit Saxons on board. All we have to do is make it to the cog first," Montague said.

"I hate running away," Doyle said to anyone caring to listen.

Christopher's hands trembled as he made all of the usual preparations to ride, things he had done so many times he could do them in his sleep, but now they seemed impossibly hard. He struggled with the saddle's buckle.

"What's the matter?" Doyle asked urgently.

"It won't . . . there! Let's go."

Doyle helped him up, and he hung on to the rear of the saddle, his feet dangling in midair. They charged out of the barn.

But even before the harsh sunlight filled his gaze, Christopher heard the dangerously close thunder of hooves. He craned his head toward the sound, squinted, saw flashes of bouncing light, then a clouded view of the landscape, and finally the three riders, who made a wide turn in unison around the main house.

He'd figured they would have at least a ten-horse-length lead on the Saxons, but they'd spent too much time in the barn. As Doyle guided their rounsey over a long, lazy hogback that ran parallel to the slope they had hidden in, the Saxons came within two lengths.

Christopher stole a glance back at them. He saw Seaver furiously heeling his mount, his reins pulled up tight and clenched firmly in one hand, his spatha held steady and pointed forward in the other. The short man seemed to lack something, a sense of regality, a cocksure demeanor, a glow of what Christopher could only imagine and describe as power. Seaver was no longer the leader of men who had paraded around the wall-walk and had casually ordered Christopher's death. With no army to back him up, the Saxon should be less intimidating.

But if the regality and power were missing, they had been replaced by something else, a glow in the Saxon's eyes that now chilled Christopher. The Saxons called it the light of Woden. Christopher called it the light of obsession. And though he'd seen it drive men to their deaths, it also made them much more dangerous. It was an alluring light, one Christopher had stepped into far too many times. Yes, Seaver would fight for his new life with as much force as Christopher would summon to restore his old one.

He turned his gaze ahead, tightened his grip on the

saddle, and pressed his legs against the horse. "Remember that day you tried to outrace me over the tourney ground?" he asked Doyle.

"Yes," Doyle called back.

"Can you ride even faster than that?"

"As long as Monte keeps up his pace."

Christopher guessed that if Montague were to take a motto it would be: *First to eat, first to retreat*. And the brigand could engage in both of those acts faster than anyone. The fat man may not have been able to run, but he rode now like a man half his size. He found his way away around ruts in the ground and made it onto the trail that led east to the port as if he were atop a bird instead of a horse.

Christopher knew that riding at breakneck speeds in the slopes and foothills that meandered down to the port was difficult, but as they gradually proved, not impossible.

The impossible lay ahead. Montague directed his horse for the main east–west path that ran through the heart of the port. Granted, it was the most direct route to the Celt cog —

But it was also Ivory Point's Merchant Row, and it was clogged with seamen, serf farmers, and traders. The booths of craftsmen lined both sides of the narrow street, and many of them had set up tables in front of their booths to further display their wares. Some of these tables extended two to three yards into the road.

He craned his head to the Saxons: an arrowhead of horsemen coming on, locked onto their target. He looked ahead, and sensed what was about to happen.

Had it been up to Christopher, he would have reined to a halt and taken off on foot through the maze of people. But Montague led this escape, and the fat man was not about to inconvenience himself just because three- or fourscore merchants and shoppers were in his way.

"Hang on!" Doyle shouted, then slammed his heels twice into the mount's ribs.

Montague's horse hit the cobblestoned street, and amid the clatter of his rounsey's hooves, he shouted, "Out of the way! OUT OF THE WAY!"

Jarred as the rounsey crossed from dirt to stone, Christopher nearly lost his grip on the saddle. Preoccupied by trying to hang on, he failed to see what was happening ahead. But he heard the first cries.

And the first crash.

Christopher looked up and saw that Montague had plowed into a table of fresh produce and knocked it onto its side. Onions, potatoes, and several roots Christopher did not recognize lay in a heap beside the table, and on his knees before the heap was the gray-bearded proprietor, who shook a fist in the air. Then the whole scene of destruction fell back into their wake.

Faces flashed into view, most of them wearing the same expression. And the aftermath of Montague's riding blurred by with equal speed. Shoppers, in their effort to avoid Montague's horse, slammed themselves into each other and into the booths on either side of the street. One fat man's arm got caught on the awning pole of a tanner's booth, and the support snapped, bringing the whole awning down on top of him and the tanner. A few yards ahead, on the opposite side of the street, a woman lay on her back across a merchant's table, surrounded by several men. Had Montague hit her, or had she fainted?

Christopher peered over Doyle's shoulder and noted that Montague was swiftly approaching an intersection, and in the middle of the cross street, stopped dead and blocking their path, was a cart hitched to a mule. The driver of the cart repeatedly whipped the rump of the animal, but the beast refused to move.

The fat man attempted to steer right around the cart,

putting himself very close to the booths to his right, but he failed to notice the overhanging shingle of a baker. He looked up just as his face connected with the hard, wooden sign. The brigand fell backward, and his boots slipped from his stirrups. For a second, he hung in the air, a bloated pigeon whose wings had just failed, then he came down and made a perfect and complete landing on top of a table that was stacked four-high with freshly baked loaves. The legs of the table leaned so far to the right that they snapped off, and once again, the fat man fell.

Doyle pulled hard on the reins and came nearly as close to the shingle as Montague had — close enough for Christopher to reach up and grab it with both hands. He let himself be pulled off of the rounsey to hang from the sign a moment, then he dropped to the cobblestone and spun around. "Montague?"

The fat man groaned as he rubbed his nose with one hand, and reached back for a loaf with the other. "The world's a blur, but it smells so sweet," he said weakly.

Seaver and his comrades rode up and reined to a halt. The short man shot him a fierce look. "Kimball!" Then he began to swing himself out of his saddle.

"Monte! Get up!" Doyle shouted, then he dismounted in a flash and drew his dagger from his hip sheath. He locked his gaze on Seaver and the other two Saxons.

Christopher trembled and his breath was ragged. He heard a growing chorus of shouts from down the street, but they didn't matter now. His gaze left Doyle and went to the Saxons, then it fell upon Montague, who sat up with a deep sigh. There, belted at the fat man's ample waist, was his dagger. Christopher leaned over, snatched the blade from the brigand, then turned it on Seaver.

The short Saxon made a lopsided grin, then turned his head to glance at Doyle. "Quite an escape you made from the castle. Too bad you couldn't take your fingers with you."

Doyle exhaled — a sound that was more growl than breath. He narrowed his gaze. A nerve in his neck throbbed, and his face was flushed. Christopher was sure that in the next second his blood brother would charge the short man.

"Laddie, we'd better finish this later," Montague said from somewhere behind Christopher.

And then Christopher turned his head left, drawn by a sound he'd heard a moment ago, a sound that was now much louder. A wave of merchants and patrons, some of them armed with swords and shortbows, rolled wildly toward them. Even if they and the Saxons joined ranks — an absurd idea, to be sure — they were outnumbered by at least five to one. That fact alone was enough to convince Christopher that Montague was right; a glance down at the pathetic dagger in his hand carved the decision in stone.

Seaver and the other two Saxons turned to regard the mob, and that was the second Christopher needed. "Run!" he screamed. "Run!" And then he sprinted by Doyle.

Christopher arced past the cart that was stuck in the road, then continued on. Soon, the road dropped into a lazy grade all the way down to the wharves.

Abandoning the horses had been both a good and bad idea. It had been easier to weave through the crowd on foot, but now it seemed just as disruptive. He looked back over his shoulder. Doyle was a score of yards behind, Montague a yard or so farther back. He could not see Seaver, whose head was surely obscured by the taller shoppers, but he picked out the other two Saxons, who elbowed a clear path for themselves. He turned back to the road ahead —

And at the nearest intersection, two lances of

armored crossbowmen jogged into view and began to cordon off the street. Christopher had seen a few of these guards when they had first come ashore, and had been told by the cog's captain to steer well clear of them; the port was presently controlled by a Saxon warlord, and he'd placed his elite guard at the dockside. They were excellent men-at-arms, with short tempers and orders to kill troublemakers. The trick now would be to hide and let the guards finish off Seaver and his friends. A simple idea amid a not-so-simple situation.

Christopher shuffled right. He turned the dagger upside down in his hand and held it close to his hip. Here, at the end of the street, the buildings were two stories, and the place was devoid of merchant booths. He moved to the nearest door, found it open, then paused before entering to look for Doyle and Montague. He squinted but saw only the crowd. He decided to duck into the building and peer at the street from behind the cracked open door. If Montague and Doyle were to pass, he'd call to them. He opened the door and stepped into a room lined on both sides with barrels and firkins that were stacked nearly to the ceiling. At the rear of the room was a high counter, and behind it, a hallway that led off to a rear door. There was an intersecting hall that in one direction probably led to a staircase. The merchant who resided here was in the ale and cider business, a middleman exporter, and wherever he was, Christopher hoped he stayed there. He turned back toward the door, shut it to a crack, then moved to —

The door slammed inward and connected with Christopher's forehead, knocking him flat onto his back.

He heard the man's voice before he saw him. "Why do you keep running, Kimball? Why don't we finish this here and now?"

Christopher's gaze focused on the tip of Seaver's spatha, which was poised about a thumb's length away

from his nose. He pushed himself backward in a crab-
walk retreat, his dagger still concealed in his grip.

Seaver advanced, holding the gap with his spatha.

"What is this?" The voice belonged to a man, and it
came from behind them.

The short Saxon turned his head, and in that flash
Christopher lifted his right leg and slammed his boot
into Seaver's blade, knocking it away but not out of the
Saxon's grip. He sat up while simultaneously flipping
his wrist up and bringing his dagger to bear. He brought
it down toward Seaver's foot.

But the short man was faster, jumping out of the way
as the blade sank into the wooden floor of the shop.
Christopher heard the merchant stepping from around
the counter, and he saw that Seaver now moved away.
Christopher craned his neck in time to see Seaver thrust
his spatha into the merchant's heart and withdraw it as
quickly.

"You've killed me!" the man yelled, then collapsed to
his stomach.

Christopher wrenched his dagger out of the floor,
then hauled himself up. Through the open door of the
shop, he caught a glimpse of one of the elite guards
walking by; the young man's gaze swept the street from
side to side, and his crossbow was at the ready.

"They catch us," he began, turning his attention fully
to Seaver, who closed in with his spatha, "and we're
both dead."

Seaver narrowed his brow. "I failed Woden, Kimball.
That's why you came here. That's why you've ruined my
new life." He beat a fist once on his chest. "I'm already
dead because I gave up his work."

"I came for Marigween. But she won't leave. And so
I'm going. Just let me go," Christopher said, then gently
eased the door closed behind him. "Why try to kill me?
What does any of it matter? What does revenge matter?

We were once friends. Let me go and you'll have your life back. I didn't ruin anything."

"I lost my command because of you. And now I've lost her," he said.

"Are you listening? You haven't lost her. She will not leave."

"She will. She'll leave for you. But —" he trailed off into his thought, paused, then lunged with his blade.

Christopher parried with his dagger, but the blade slid off the much larger weapon, which kept coming at him. Were it not for a reflexive turn to the right, the point of the spatha would have struck him squarely in the heart. As it was, the blade caught his left shoulder at a tight angle, and the dreaded sting came. But he kept turning, pulling the blade out of his shoulder, freeing himself of the short man. He knew the wound was more slice than stab, but he couldn't sense how bad it was.

He bolted forward, rounded the counter and headed into the hall toward the rear door of the shop. As he reached the intersecting hall, he realized that someone on the other side of the door was pounding on it. Suddenly, the rear exit did not look promising. He turned around. Seaver came toward him. He stole a look to his right, saw a staircase, then started for it. Now he felt his shoulder begin to throb, and he detected the dampness of blood on his shirt.

Taking the stairs two at a time, in short order he reached a small landing, then turned and hustled up a dozen more steps. He reached a door, threw the latch, and shuffled into a sleeping quarters that looked generally dusty, unused, and reeked of mold. There was a large, open window on the opposite side of the room that looked down onto the market street, and a bed up against the right wall. To his immediate left was a small desk cluttered with scrolls, and behind it several traveling trunks. He turned, closed the door, then threw the

inside latch. He backed away from the door, expecting
Seaver to begin rapping on it. He waited, but heard
nothing, save for a few shouts, the bark of a dog from
down below in the street, and the very distant tapping of
someone on the rear door of the shop. The pungent
smell of the room was a curiosity, and he could not
understand its presence in light of the open window. He
moved to the bed, took a long whiff of the woolen blanket covering it, and realized the odor was created by the
blanket. It smelled as if someone had died in the bed.
He rose and stepped backward, and for a moment, his
gaze froze.

The bed, the blanket, the room. He'd seen them
before. They were from the vision he'd had in the channel. A strange shock rocked through him, made him feel
dizzy, made him feel as if he stood outside of his body.
Perhaps the vision he'd seen in the channel was of his
own future. But where was —

*He heard someone crying. A woman. And then a baby
added its tiny voice to the lamenting. Outside, he heard
people shouting. For a heartbeat, he felt as if he could
not lift his head, but the sensation vanished, and he
looked up.*

*Marigween stood behind the closed door, her child in
her arms. She stared at the bed, and her eyes brimmed
with tears. Christopher looked toward the object of her
sorrow.*

*Seaver was on his back, eyes closed, the hilt of a dag-
ger sticking from his chest. Christopher averted his gaze
and opened his palm, his empty palm, the palm where
his dagger had once been. Then he looked at Marigween
and thought of all that had happened to her, all he had
put her through. She had found a small corner of peace,
of love, and even that he had taken from her.*

The door to the room smashed inward and passed
through the image of Marigween and her child. They

dissolved into the form of Seaver, who came wildly forward and broke his fall on the bed. He pushed up on his forearms and stood. He steadied himself and lifted his spatha, then crossed slowly around the bed.

Christopher backed toward the window, then chanced a look down. No, he would not be doing much walking in this lifetime if he opted to jump. Not only that, it seemed that the number of guards combing the street had doubled. He already saw three. It would be hard to run from them with broken legs.

He turned his attention back to Seaver, then let the dagger fall from his palm and clatter softly onto the floor. "I cannot fight you, Seaver. Marigween needs you."

"What kind of noble folly is this?" Seaver asked, his bewilderment splayed across his face. "You would have me kill you now — and not defend yourself?"

Christopher shook his head, no, not to the question but to accompany his own thought. "We don't have to fight. All you have to do is walk away."

"He's not going anywhere," Doyle said, standing before the open door, rolling his dagger in his palm.

Seaver spun around, took one look at Doyle, then abruptly turned back and thrust his spatha toward Christopher's heart.

Grimacing, Christopher caught the blade with both hands before it pierced his chest. As Seaver applied more pressure to the weapon, it slid slowly forward, cutting into Christopher's palms. Groaning, Christopher was forced back into the window, then smashed into it. Shards of glass rained upon his head and shoulders. He felt the thin wood of the window frame give way, and knew if Seaver pushed just a little harder he'd be on a swift trip to the ground.

But Seaver whipped the blade out of Christopher's grip and shifted back, just as Doyle was about to bury his dagger in the nape of the short man's neck. Seaver made a horizontal swipe across Doyle's chest, and the archer jumped back, avoiding the spatha by a hair's width.

"I took your fingers, archer, now I take your life." Seaver stepped forward and made a back slash toward Doyle, who once again dodged the blade's path.

Christopher looked to his dagger.

Seaver kept coming at Doyle. The short Saxon made another slash left from high to low, then another back slash, then a stab, a feint, and a surprise slash at Doyle's legs.

You have to do it. Pick up the dagger. Use it.

What about Marigween?

What if Seaver kills Doyle?

The mind-set of combat fit like an old, worn-in gauntlet. Acting — not thinking — Christopher let his body do the work. He barely felt himself lean down, shards of glass falling from him, and fetch the blade. His legs carried him across the room in three running steps, and his blade hand drew back and came forward toward Seaver's back.

The short Saxon cocked his head over his shoulder.

But he was too late. Christopher gritted his teeth and closed his eyes as he punched the blade home, just below Seaver's left shoulder blade. He opened his eyes and pulled back from the man.

Seaver turned slowly toward him, and his cheeks sunk in. He looked about to vomit, and his eyes begged for something. The spatha slipped from his hand.

Doyle circled around the man and retrieved the spatha. He took Seaver's right forearm in his hand and held out the Saxon's hand.

"No more, Doyle. He's already going to . . ."

Doyle shook his head, then spoke softly in Seaver's ear. "Let this be the last thing you feel." He drew the spatha high over his head and brought it down on Seaver's wrist, hacking off the short man's hand.

As blood shot from Seaver's wrist in irregular pulses, Doyle released the man. Seaver stepped forward. He now wore a strange, vacant look on his face. He managed three more steps, and arrived at the window, leaving a bloody trail in his wake. A blood pool formed at his feet. He seemed to take a look down, and then let himself fall forward.

Christopher could not move. He stared at the red ribbon on the floor that ended at a small hunk of fingered flesh. Nothing completely registered in his mind. He was aware of the fact that Seaver was now dead, but the fact meant nothing. All he could see was the path of blood.

A woman's scream wafted up to the window, and it broke Christopher's shock.

Doyle went to the window and gazed down. "The guards will be everywhere now. We'd best make haste."

Christopher hazarded a look to the street. Seaver's body lay prone, its arms and legs twisted in unnatural directions. "It's so grim. All of this. Seaver and I, we fought with great armies, fought in castles, inspired many men. And it all comes to this. This room. This Godforsaken port. It makes me feel like our lives — his and mine — are really worth nothing."

Doyle grabbed him by his shirt collar. "Don't believe that. This was just an ugly matter. It's over." He released Christopher with a jolt. "Now we go. Monte's downstairs with a couple of guards' uniforms. We'll be escorting him back to the cog as our prisoner."

"What about Seaver's two friends?"

Doyle raised his brow. "The guards picked them up already." He started for the door.

"You and Monte go," Christopher said. "I have to see Marigween one more time."

Doyle stopped and blew out a sigh that must have

contained all the air in his chest. "Why do you always have to make things difficult?"

Christopher looked at his friend, and there was something immediately understood between them, something Christopher could not describe but felt was there.

Doyle closed his eyes, then nodded resignedly. "All right. But Monte's not going to like it." He opened his eyes, squinted into a thought, then brightened. "There's a wagon out back hitched to an old mare. We'll use that."

13

They approached Seaver's toft, and something odd caught Christopher's gaze. The front door on the main house swung open and creaked loudly in the breeze. Then he heard a sobbing from within the house, a sobbing that came from more than one person. Doyle and Montague, who were hidden among the barrels on the flatbed, began to stir. Christopher reined the mare to a halt, then jumped down from the cart and ran toward the door.

He sprang into the main room, and his gaze immediately fell to the floor ahead. What he saw there brought him to his knees, made his breath stagger, and his head shudder.

Two middle-aged women sat on the floor, and one of them had Marigween's head in her lap. Marigween's white shift was drenched with blood from the waist down, and Christopher spotted many long slashes snaking horribly from her wrists up her delicate forearms. The knife she'd used lay at her feet. He heard a baby's cry, and only then noticed that the other woman cradled Devin in her arms.

"Who are you?" the one holding Marigween managed to ask.

Christopher swallowed, then gasped several times before replying in Saxon. "I am Christopher of Shores."

"Did you know her?" the woman continued.

"Oh . . . dear Lord," Montague said, from behind him.

"Who are you?" the woman asked Montague, not waiting for Christopher's reply.

Montague's answer was probably a look, since he neither spoke nor understood Saxon.

A hand fell upon Christopher's shoulder, and Doyle crouched at his side. "I'm sorry."

Christopher began to tremble, and what little breath he had left threatened to vanish. "Oh, God, we shouldn't have come."

"It's my fault, Christopher," Doyle said. "I should have stopped searching."

Christopher shut his eyes, then bowed his head. "No one's to blame but me."

He traced her life over and over, and he imagined what it had been like for her to have lost her mother. He knew how hard it had been for her to accept her father's death, and worse, she had been present when the man had been murdered by Mallory. Furthermore, she had been betrothed to a man she did not love, and had a child with another man out of wedlock. She had been forced to live in seclusion and had rebelled against that life, an act which had left her so vulnerable that she had been raped. She had lost her dignity, her self-respect. She had fought to regain them, and had been on the brink of winning them back — when Christopher had come along and reminded her of their lost child, of their lost love, of their lost world. He knew now his presence in Ivory Point was the blade that had ended her life.

"Your friends are Celts," the woman said, cutting Christopher's dark reverie short. "Like her."

Christopher looked up at the woman. "I'm also a Celt. Marigween was the mother of my child."

"This child?" the other woman asked.

"No, but what will happen to this one?"

"I'm not sure. I'll raise him if Vorn will permit it."

"Will you burn her?"

The woman who held Marigween nodded.

Christopher shifted forward on his knees. He leaned over Marigween and ran his fingers along her cheek. There was a time when he had seen her as an angel, an angel in a pale linen shift that flowed like ivory honey over her lithe frame. Her eyes had lit on him, and a lance of adrenaline had impaled his being. Without thinking, only reacting, he had dismounted and ran toward her, calling, "Marigween," as he did now, "Marigween, Marigween, Marigween."

She had been a dream. A dream made real.

14 The journey back to Blytheheart could not have been more miserable. The cog ran head-on into a storm which threatened to sink the vessel. Christopher spent two days vomiting in the crew's cabin, and he felt the storm and the nausea were, in part, small punishments for what had happened to Marigween. He deserved to be ill. He deserved to be punished for a very long time. While Doyle and Montague feared for their lives, clinging nervously to their hammocks, Christopher was not at all concerned with dying. He could not stop thinking about her. He repeatedly unfurled the scrolls of the past, flipped from image to

image, but always came back to her pale, lifeless face.
With every fall of the ship he felt himself sink deeper
and deeper into despair. He argued with himself that he
should have fought to take Marigween's body back to
Shores where she could be given a proper funeral. He
said that he should have taken her child and found a
way to raise it as his own, instead of leaving it with the
women. But doing those things took time, and time
they did not have. They had been forced to leave Ivory
Point to avoid being captured by the elite guards.
Staying any longer would have further endangered his
friends. He reassured himself that another time would
come. One day he might go back for the child. But
then he told himself that was a lie. Then he told himself it was not. The guilt roared and he beat it back. He
clamped its snout in his hand, but then let it go.

He'd eaten very little during the trip, and by the time
they moored at Blytheheart on a cool, clear evening,
Doyle told him that he looked gaunt and pale, and had
better start eating. They went to the inn, and
Christopher asked to be left alone in his room with
Baines. The boy soon fell asleep in his arms, and then,
after several hours, a knock came at the door, and disgusted, Christopher rose from the trestle bed and
answered it.

Marigween's uncle Robert stood in the doorway,
looking tired and sullen. "Christopher. May I come in?"

Christopher nodded and made way as the heavy monk
ambled into the room. Robert crossed to the window
chair, turned it toward the bed, then sat down.
Christopher took the monk's cue and plopped himself
gently on his bed, careful not to wake Baines.
"Montague told you?" he asked quietly.

Robert nodded, and then a tear slipped from one of
his eyes. He wiped his cheek, then said, "There was so
much pain in her life. But she was strong. I thought —"

"She's gone to hell, hasn't she?" Christopher asked
darkly.

"I do not know," Robert said, but it sounded like a
lie, a denial, a fact he did not want to face.

"You should," Christopher countered.

"You're angry."

"At myself."

"It's not your fault."

Christopher looked away. "What do you know of my
innocence?"

"I know a lot. She wrote me."

"But she didn't tell you everything." Christopher
looked to his sleeping son.

"No."

He sighed, then tossed the monk a sour look. "Why
are you here?

"For brotherhood," he replied, leaning forward. "It's
not God's will that you suffer alone."

Christopher pushed himself off of the bed, walked
around the monk and went to the window. He stared
down at the street, a strip of ruts, sand, and shadows
that was devoid of people. "Was it God's will that I was
blamed for a murder? Was it God's will that Marigween
was raped and then took her own life because of me?"
He craned his head to glare at the monk, balling his
hands into fists. "I took everything I believe, the code of
knights and squires, and threw it all away to try to save
her. I stole, I killed, I used my friends — all for nothing."

"No, not for nothing," Robert said, raising his voice.
"You thought only of her. You wanted to help her, and
you did everything you could."

Christopher huffed. "How do you know?"

"Your friend Doyle told me everything." He stood,
fixing Christopher with a hard look. "All of us have suffered, Christopher. You, me, your friends. We all tried
to act rightly and justly. And God knows that. But it was

not God's will that Marigween live. We must believe that. He has a purpose for what He does. And we must not question His will."

"But we never had a chance," Christopher said, feeling the burn of tears in his eyes, "we never had a chance to become a real family. Why would God not want that for us?"

Robert closed his eyes and pursed his lips. "Perhaps for you, he still does."

15

"You must have resembled him when you were his age," Brenna said, smiling at Baines, whose gaze was fixed on the ceiling of her tent. The shifting shadows of the boughs of the trees that hung over the shelter seemed to pass through the fabric and create a pattern of dancing lines for the young one's entertainment.

Christopher unfolded his legs to stretch them. "I'm going to see King Arthur this evening. Would you mind watching him? I was going to leave him with Orvin, but I'm afraid of what he might feed him. Have you ever tasted Orvin's cooking?"

Brenna smiled. "I'll watch him," she said, then smiled more deeply over something else. "I'm surprised you haven't asked me about the council."

"I saw Neil. He told me the council's decision," Christopher informed her.

"And what do you think?"

"I'm not sure." He looked at her intently. "Brenna, you can tell me now. Did you do it?"

She bit her lower lip and sighed. "I wish I had; then all of this would truly be over."

"Do you know who did it? Did Neil or Robert of Queen's Camel?"

"No, of course not. But we've all been banished just the same."

"At least they believe that whoever killed Woodward did it to save me," Christopher added. "That kept you all from the gallows tree, though I doubt any of you would have made it there. Orvin would've figured out something."

"They decided to spare us by one voice."

"So you'll leave on the morrow?" he asked.

She nodded. "I've sent word to Doyle."

"I'll be going with you," Christopher said.

"No, you cannot. Arthur will want you here."

Christopher frowned. "For what? I'm not in his service. And what other knight would want me as a senior squire?"

"It would be best to talk to the king about that."

He sighed. "I will. I wish I could go to him immediately, but he insists on seeing me this evening."

She paused, then said, "There's something else. It's about Marigween —"

And that was as far as he let her go. "You've already said you're sorry. And so has everyone else. I don't want to talk about what happened."

"I know, but it's more about me than her." Still seated, she pushed herself closer to him, then lowered her voice. "I must tell you that I once wished she —"

"Don't say it. Don't."

"I have to."

"Forget it. It's over. We're on to another life."

"You told me that in some other life I am —"

"You are my bride. And will always be."

EPILOGUE

"Have you been watching the sky with Orvin, my lord?" Christopher asked Arthur as they strolled along the east side of the castle's moat.

"I have not, but that figure up there is well-known." Arthur paused to take another look at the stars. "Just as you were named after the patron saint of travelers, so was I after those stars. Arth, the great bear."

"A fitting name, my lord," Christopher said, gazing at the points of light scattered across the dark blue vault.

"They're part of the dream, as I wish you were a part of it. But there are things in this world more important than wishes." He lowered his head and turned his green eyes on Christopher.

"Then you'll honor my request, my lord?" he asked.

Arthur lowered his gaze slightly. "The day your friends were banished was the day I knew I had lost you."

Christopher tensed. "May I ask you something, my lord?"

Arthur nodded.

"When I was stripped of my rank as squire of the body, why did you place me in Woodward's service when you knew there would be hostility between us?"

The king drew in a long breath. "The truth is, I thought I could teach you a hard lesson, one you needed to learn. I never saw this future."

Christopher nodded slightly at the irony. "Nor I."

Arthur returned his attention to the night sky. "You'll leave, but you won't be far." He stroked his beard and squinted in thought. "I don't know what it is that makes me so fond of you, Christopher. Others have asked me, and I have no answer for them. I do see myself in you, but there is something else, something about you that makes me believe that my kingdom will sorely miss your heart and spirit." He sighed. "I hate to see you go." Then he looked down to Christopher. "If I ever call, will you come?"

Christopher did not hesitate. "I will, my lord."

"One land, one king under these stars. The day has come. A free land for all, even Saxons, Picts, Angles, and Jutes. I spared some of Kenric's battle lords and offered them their freedom in exchange for spreading the word of a truce. Already the trade is free, why not the land?"

He shrugged, for he had no answer. In fact, he had argued that very same point to Arthur moons ago; to hear his words echo from the king was nothing short of miraculous. "I share your dream, my lord. And even in Blytheheart, I will still be a part of it."

Arthur turned and resumed his pace. "What will you do there?"

Christopher joined the king. "I've a son to raise, and saddles to make." He smiled, though he knew the king could not see him. "I remember how much I had despised saddle making, and how much I had wanted to become a squire."

"Ah, yes, life sometimes takes you back to where you started. But you do not have to complete your circle, Christopher, you could join mine. Leondegrance is giving me a round table for my knights. You could be at that table."

Christopher pursed his lips. Yes, he could see himself very clearly, a knight, admired, loved, respected, and honored by all. But he saw only himself, not his friends, or his son. "It is not my time, my lord."

The king stopped again, then faced him. "Still a true servant?"

"Always."

The king withdrew his broadsword from his scabbard and raised it over Christopher's head. "You already possess a knight's heart. You simply need to be conferred."

Christopher was about to raise his hand and stop the blade, just as he had the first time Arthur had tried to make him a knight. But the king lowered the blade and turned the hilt toward him, offering him the weapon. And then he recognized it as the broadsword Baines had given him long ago, the one Christopher had lost in his escape from the castle.

"You found it," Christopher said excitedly, then took the sword into his grip and let his gaze run up and down its length.

"An archer stumbled upon it when storming the walls," Arthur answered. "Your friend Neil knew it was yours. It is a magnificent weapon. It is a knight's sword."

He looked at the king, and then felt a tingle rise up his back. "Thank you."

"Hold on to it. You may need it one day." Arthur's smile glistened.

Christopher straightened. "By your leave?"

"Good-bye, Christopher. May God bless and keep you."

"Farewell, my lord. And may God bless you and the kingdom."

Christopher slowly turned away, and it hurt to put his back to Arthur. He started off in the direction they had come, back toward the wandering chain of cookfire lights that led to the ramparts.

He had told Brenna he would never forget where his home was, and though he would be off to Blytheheart on the morrow with her, Robert, and Neil, he knew he would one day return to this place, this place called Shores, this place Arthur now called Camelot.

CALIBAN'S HOUR by Tad Williams

Can an eternity of love be contained in an hour? The answer lies in the enchanting tale of magic and mystery from the *New York Times* bestselling author of *To Green Angel Tower* and *Tailchaser's Song*. ($4.99 Paperback)

DEMON SWORD by Ken Hood

An exhilarating heroic fantasy, *Demon Sword* takes place in the Scottish lands of a fanciful Renaissance Europe where our hero, an aspiring prizefighter named Toby, finds himself possessed by a demon spirit. But soon it appears that the king is possessed by the demon spirit and Toby is possessed by the spirit of the king! ($4.99 Paperback)